FALLING

Also by Simona Ahrnstedt

All In

FALLING

SIMONA AHRNSTEDT

Translated from the Swedish
by Alice Menzies

KENSINGTON BOOKS
www.kensingtonbooks.com

KENSINGTON BOOKS are published by

Kensington Publishing Corp.
119 West 40th Street
New York, NY 10018

All Kensington titles, imprints, and distributed lines are available at special quantity discounts for bulk purchases for sales promotion, premiums, fundraising, educational, or institutional use.

Special book excerpts or customized printings can also be created to fit specific needs. For details, write or phone the office of the Kensington Sales Manager: Kensington Publishing Corp., 119 West 40th Street, New York, NY 10018. Attn. Sales Department. Phone: 1-800-221-2647.

Kensington and the K logo Reg. U.S. Pat. & TM Off.

eISBN-13: 978-1-4967-0622-5
eISBN-10: 1-4967-0622-6
First Kensington Electronic Edition: August 2017

ISBN-13: 978-1-4967-0621-8
ISBN-10: 1-4967-0621-8
First Kensington Trade Paperback Printing: August 2017

10 9 8 7 6 5 4 3 2 1

Printed in the United States of America

FALLING

The child hid behind a small bush. It was the rainy season, and the leaves, lush and green, were covered with insects. The child, his small frame shaking with fear, crouched on the red soil. The jeep and the men had come out of nowhere. Violent, brutal men, pouring out of the car, shouting, creating clouds of ruddy dust. The boy could only stare at the unfolding scene. The angry men had guns. They were waving them and yelling at the woman. And then they took her.

She fought, because she was a strong woman, but she had no chance against them. She screamed when they threw her into the car. It took off in a big cloud of dust and sand. Then there was silence. Not even the insects made a sound.

The boy stayed behind the bush for a long time.

He had nowhere to go. The woman had been the only one who cared for him.

Now there was no one.

Chapter 1

As Alexander De la Grip, Swedish count, international playboy, most eligible man under thirty (according to gossip rags), and no-good lazy-ass (according to his father), slowly came to life, he had absolutely no idea where he was.

He blinked, trying to assess his surroundings. It was early morning, at least judging by the light that came through a window at the other side of the room. He was naked and in a strange bed, which in itself was nothing out of the ordinary. But *where* he was—on which continent, in which country or city—well, that was all a blur.

Not that this was unusual either.

He made a quick assessment of his state of being.

He was hungover, obviously, but not brutally so. He seemed to have all his limbs and nothing ached. Splendid.

He reached for his cell on the unfamiliar nightstand. It was only eight in the morning; he usually slept much longer. But he felt okay despite the early hour. That was the plus side of regular drinking and partying—you built up a tolerance. Even though, as the previous night started to come back to him, he did remember a *lot* of drinking before winding up here.

Wherever *here* was.

Alexander racked his brain, vaguely recalling champagne, vodka, music, women—plenty of it all. He scratched his stubble. At some point there had also been a cab drive through Stockholm. Yes! Stockholm. Sweden. Home.

He turned his head. A young woman was sleeping soundly beside him. Her long hair was spread out on the pillow, her smooth skin lightly tanned. Alexander's gaze lingered on her bare back. Yes, her he remembered, he thought with a grin. She'd been pretty last night, when they'd started to flirt at the fourth or maybe fifth bar he visited. Sexy and energetic. Impressively determined, almost missile-like when she had spotted him. She had a lisp, too, and in his drunken state he'd found that sexy as hell. In all honesty, she was a bit too young for him, if he'd had those kinds of scruples, which he didn't. Twenty-ish, wide-eyed and giggly. The occasional flash of ruthlessness in her pretty eyes. He had been too drunk to care about that yesterday, when they were flirting, and later fucking, but he remembered it now. Not that ruthlessness bothered him too much.

Few things did.

He climbed out of bed.

Her name was something super Swedish. Linda, or Jenny maybe, and she was . . . Alexander frowned as he searched for his scattered clothes. A journalist? No. He pulled on his underwear and his pants, and started to look for his shirt, leather jacket, and shoes. Student? Model? Nope, that wasn't it either. Something that involved more than long legs and an eating disorder.

He shoved his cell into his pocket, pulled the blanket up over her back, and headed for the door. He opened it soundlessly and was soon out on the street, getting his bearings. Right, she lived in Södermalm, the hipster, boho part of Stockholm. He put on his sunglasses. Young men with beards and MacBooks crowded the streets. Parents with children in brightly colored clothes, and pale, young women with skinny dogs. He kind of liked Södermalm. He bought a coffee at a deli, then hailed a cab. As he hopped into it his cell phone rang.

Looking at the screen, he felt the familiar sense of unease when he saw the caller: his mother. He rejected the call. They would meet soon enough; no need to suffer more than necessary.

The next time his phone rang, Romeo Rozzi's name flashed on the display. Alexander answered the call from his best friend with a cheerful "Talk to me, baby," while the capitol passed outside the window. Spring had arrived in Stockholm, the morning traffic wasn't too bad, and Alexander could feel the last of the previous night's indulgences being driven out by the coffee.

"I just wanted to check if you were okay," said Romeo. If it was eight in the morning in Sweden, it was two a.m. in New York. But Romeo, hard-working, world-renowned chef, never went to bed before dawn.

"And why wouldn't I be okay?" Alexander asked, then finished the last of the strong black coffee. You couldn't get coffee like this in New York.

Deep sigh. Clattering in the background. "Don't you remember?" Romeo asked, his voice that of a man with the weight of the world on his shoulders.

"That's right. I called you, didn't I?" He didn't remember why, though. It was a double-edged sword, this drinking-to-forget business.

"You were pretty wasted," Romeo said, his voice filled with disapproval.

"But being drunk is one of my best states."

Romeo sighed loudly on the other end of the line. "I Googled the girl."

"Why on earth would you do that?" asked Alexander.

"She's a blogger and Instagrammer," Romeo said, ignoring his question. "I checked her out. She has a huge following, publishes gossip and vulgar pictures. You said you were going to give her something to write about. Did you? Did you sleep with her?"

Linda. That was her name. Lusty Linda. Alexander pieced together the remaining fragments of a rather uninhibited night, remembering Linda's probing questions, wincing a little when some of the things they had tried out flashed before his eyes.

"I guess I did," he replied, forcing cheer into his voice and at the same time trying to work out whether he really cared if he was hung out to dry by yet another fame-hungry Instagram account, or anywhere else for that matter. He was used to it. He was prey, no matter what he did.

Another deep sigh from Romeo. "Do you take anything seriously?"

"Don't be stupid. I'm dead serious about my partying."

"You know what I mean."

Alexander fell silent, because he *did* know what Romeo meant.

The past six months he'd partied harder than ever. Sometimes it actually felt like he was *trying* to gift the tabloids and social media with gossip. Not that he would ever admit to it.

"Alessandro. I worry about you," Romeo continued.

"I'm a grown man and you worry too much," he said lightly. Alexander considered that maybe this time he really was headed off the rails with the drinking and the partying and the women. But staying sober probably meant going crazy. He didn't care much for going crazy. He glanced outside the car. Taxicabs, people, bikes passed by. Street after street after street. Alexander caught sight of glittering water.

"I'm almost home. Can I give you a call later?" he said, not sure he could keep up his show of bravado too much longer. Romeo was a nag and a mother hen. But he was Alexander's best friend and he *cared*. Stupid thing that. Caring.

"Just tell me how it feels to be back in Sweden," said Romeo.

Alexander looked at his watch. Almost nine. "I think I'm still drunk, I need a shave, I have a meeting with my bankers today, and I'm jet-lagged as hell, so it *feels* like I need a drink." Not to mention he was going to have to meet his mom this weekend. He almost groaned.

"Yes, well, be careful with that. Being a drunk is not a good look on anyone."

"Fuck off."

"Yeah, yeah. By the way, that Swedish prince of yours, Carl Philip. Do you know him?"

"I've met him," Alexander said dispassionately.

"He's hot. I'd love to cook for him. Among other things."

Alexander snorted. "If I see His Royal Highness, I'll let him know," he said. He disconnected at the same time that the taxi pulled up outside Hotel Diplomat, where he always stayed when he was in town. He looked up at the pristine white façade. No matter how hard he tried, and he did try, he couldn't drink away the fact that he was back in Stockholm to do the one thing he hated most of all. To face his demons. Or, at least, to meet his family.

Fuck.

Chapter 2

Isobel Sørensen chained her bike, unclipped her helmet, pulled the heavy doors open, and hurried up the old marble stairs. Wiping sweat off her forehead she opened the door with the brass sign that read MEDPAX. In the reception area, with its dark mahogany furniture, framed prizes, and twenty-year-old magazine clippings on the walls, she was greeted by two oil paintings in golden frames: one of Isobel's mother, the other of her grandfather, the founders of Medpax.

A door at the back opened, and Leila Dibah, the general secretary of the foundation, stuck her head out.

"Sorry I'm late," Isobel said, lifting her hand in a greeting. "Work was chaos."

"You're not late," Leila said with that slight accent that betrayed her Persian origins. Fifty-two-year old Leila was a clinical psychologist, and Isobel had always thought that she had the perfect eyes for her profession. Focused, unreadable, unwavering. Leila opened the door to Medpax's only conference room. "Let's sit here," she said, and let Isobel in. They sat at the table, Leila in front of stacks of papers and binders. Isobel reached for a decanter with water and a glass. She hadn't drunk anything since lunch.

"How's work?" asked Leila as Isobel poured a second glass of water.

"At the clinic?" Isobel shrugged and downed the water. She'd seen twenty-two patients today. That was nothing. When she was out in the field she could treat over a hundred patients a day. Malnourished, wounded, dying patients. Nobody starved to death before her eyes at the clinic. No one died from simple treatable diseases or infections. Nothing unbearable happened. "It's hectic but okay," she said.

Leila searched her face. "You work too much," she stated.

"No, I don't." Isobel worked at the clinic, and here at Medpax when she had time, and she *was* a fully committed field doctor for Doctors Without Borders. But life wasn't supposed to be easy; she just did what she had to do to pull her weight.

Leila sighed. "I just got a phone call. Sven can't go to Chad."

"Shit."

"Yeah."

During its golden years, Medpax, a small but renowned humanitarian aid organization, had run three pediatric hospitals in Africa. One in Chad, one in the Congo, and one in Cameroon. As the years went by, two of the hospitals were taken over by the authorities in their respective countries, and now they had only the hospital in Chad left. Day to day, it was run by medical personnel from Chad, assorted volunteers, and field-workers from other aid organizations, but Medpax was the driving force behind it. Sven was a surgeon and had been scheduled to go there at the end of the month.

"But why?" Isobel asked. No one from Medpax had been in Chad since the previous fall; the plan was for Sven to head down there, assess what changes needed to be implemented in the future, and create a formal course of action. This was a huge setback. Someone from Medpax *had* to go there. Sven would have been perfect.

"His wife doesn't want him to," Leila said.

"You're kidding."

"She gave him an ultimatum. Sven says he has got to give his marriage priority."

"I see." The cynical side of Isobel wondered why Sven—infamous for having slept with virtually every female nurse he'd ever met—suddenly thought he needed to give his marriage priority, but she said nothing. Going out into the field had to be an individual's own choice.

Leila nodded. "But it was actually because of something else I asked you here." She took out one of the binders, opened it, and placed it in front of Isobel. "I wanted to show you this. We have a problem with one of our donors. A serious financial problem."

Isobel looked at the neat rows, trying to decipher them. "It seems to be a foundation of some kind," she said after a while.

Leila bowed her head affirmatively. "They've given loads of money in the past, but the donations suddenly stopped."

Medpax lived off its donors.

"But are we really so dependent on them? One single donor?" Isobel asked.

"We are now. We lost quite a few of our donors before I started, as you know."

Isobel nodded. It was an understatement. They had *bled*.

"And since then, several of our applications have been rejected, and we haven't managed to make up the shortfall yet."

Leila had joined Medpax a couple of years ago. Medpax finances had been in bad shape at that time. With the force of a Persian conqueror she had managed to salvage what she could when she joined the organization, but the fact was that her predecessor, Blanche Sørensen, had become increasingly less successful at maintaining the important relationships with the organization's donors.

Isobel knew, of course, that none of this was *her* fault, but she still squirmed at Leila's words. Blanche was, after all, her mother.

"We can't afford to lose them. I don't really know why the donations have stopped. No one at the foundation has bothered to return my calls, though I've left several messages."

Isobel studied the documents. The name of the foundation told her nothing, but the address was one of Stockholm's most exclusive streets, so maybe the trustees simply didn't think it was worth their while to return calls from anyone at a tiny humanitarian organization.

"When exactly did they stop?" Isobel asked, still trying to understand the figures.

"Just before Christmas."

Isobel had been in Liberia then. She'd gone there with Doctors Without Borders to fight an Ebola outbreak. Seen more dead bodies, ravaged communities, and traumatized medical staff than she could bear to think about. She had worked in refugee camps, war zones, and the aftermath of natural disasters since she was in her teens. Her first summer job had been as a volunteer. She had seen it all. But still. Liberia . . . It had been weeks before she managed to get past the worst of the nightmares.

"You should have said something. Maybe I could have helped."

"Asking for help really isn't my strong suit."

Isobel snorted at the understatement. "What's his or her name?"

"Who?"

Isobel nodded at the binder. "Whoever's behind the foundation?"

"Here," said Leila, pointing at a name. "A man. Alexander De la Grip."

The name went through her like a jolt. She sat up. "You're joking," she said.

Leila looked up. "You know him?"

Isobel had lost count of how many lists she'd seen Alexander De la Grip's name on.

Best-Dressed Bachelors in the World.

Richest Swedes under Thirty.

World's Most Handsome Men.

Or how many gossip rags he had appeared in. Not because she actively looked for his name, but because Alexander De la Grip and his escapades were like an ongoing, everlasting, *disgusting* serial in the media.

"We've met," she said calmly, but was shocked to her core.

She and Alexander De la Grip had met, by chance, last summer. He had flirted with her, and she had told him to go to hell.

Literally.

Several times.

She wanted to smack her forehead on the table. Every time Alexander De la Grip had ever spoken to her, in that deep aristocratic voice of his, she had been nothing but rude in return. She wasn't proud of it; she usually was much smoother than that. She was a field doctor, for Christ's sake—she could take annoying men in stride. But it was as though Alexander's entire *being* had irritated her back then. The drunken eyes, the diva-like existence, the way women fawned over him. Was he really that easily insulted, that petty? Stupid question; *of course* he was. Alexander De la Grip's ego was probably more fragile than a compromised immune system. She had snubbed him, and in revenge he had cut off the money to Medpax. It was the simplest and therefore most plausible explanation.

Leila studied her with piercing black eyes over the rim of her glasses. "Could we talk to him? Get him to change his mind? Maybe over a lunch?"

Isobel toyed with the papers. "I guess we could try," she reluctantly replied. There was nothing unusual about meeting potential donors over lunch, dinner, or sometimes even breakfast. She had done it many times before, knew she was good at it and that people were impressed by her and her heritage. That was one of her roles at Medpax. But the thought of sucking up to that spoiled, privileged jet-setter . . . Well, it was all her own fault. Pride goeth before a fall, and so on.

"Could you take care of it?" Leila asked.

Isobel regained her composure, gave Leila an unruffled look, and simply said, "Sure."

"Good. Because if we don't find more money soon, we're done. We'll have to close Medpax down before summer."

"You're exaggerating." Leila did have a tendency toward the melodramatic; surely things couldn't be that bad.

But Leila gestured at the papers before them. "Feel free to double-check, though I've already done it. Without money, there won't be any more aid work. It's simple math."

Isobel groaned.

They sat in silence.

"You look tired," Leila finally said. "How are you sleeping?"

Isobel gave her a dubious look. "I hope you're not doing a psychological assessment."

Leila didn't miss a beat. "Do you need one?"

Isobel looked out the windows. There were smells and images from Liberia she still couldn't shut out. But she had been back for three months now. It was getting better and life was, on the whole, back to normal.

"I stopped taking the sleeping pills. I bicycle a lot; I'm fine," she said evasively. It was basically the truth.

"We really need someone down at the pediatric hospital right now—you know that as well as I do," Leila eventually said.

"I'm not a pediatrician," she protested, but without too much conviction. It was a ludicrous objection, and they both knew it. With what Isobel could do, the experience she had, there wasn't a field hospital on earth that wouldn't benefit from having her on staff. And she had been there before. She knew the hospital, knew the staff. Even knew some of the young patients who turned up over and over. For a moment she pictured solemn, dark eyes in a small, hungry face. Was he still alive?

"I hate to ask. I know you have a lot on your plate, and I know you need to recharge, but could you at least think about it?"

"Okay."

"And while you're thinking about Chad, you may as well think about Skåne, too."

Crap. Isobel had managed to forget all about that spectacle. Medpax was involved in a big charity event somewhere in the southern Swedish countryside. Rich people, business representatives, politicians, and assorted members of the upper class would gather there in a beautiful castle. They would mingle, drink too much wine, eat stupidly expensive food, and with any luck, be convinced to donate lots of money.

"Isn't it enough that I butter up De la Grip?"

"But everyone likes you, Isobel. Third-generation Medpax, dazzling conscience of the world and all that. Plus, you're a young woman. That always sells. Just think how much money we can bring in if you go."

"Isn't this emotional blackmail?"

"Absolutely," Leila agreed. She tapped a column of figures with her index finger. "But if you don't sort things out with Alexander De la Grip, it'll just be like putting a Band-Aid on an open wound anyway. We need to build up a buffer, bring in regular amounts."

In other words, she was expected to fawn over one of the world's most immoral men before she traveled down to Skåne to suck up to even more rich people. Now she really did feel ill.

"Can you handle it, Isobel?"

"Yes."

She could, because, for the most part, she could manage almost anything. Though it did cross her mind that she might have preferred to stay in Liberia, battling Ebola, after all.

Chapter 3

Alexander hid a huge yawn behind his hand.

He was brain-numbingly hungover.

Well, technically, he might still be drunk.

He took a deep breath. The last days and nights of vodka, cocktails, and champagne combined with jet lag had, eventually, overcome him. Jesus. He hadn't felt like this since he was thirteen and an older friend had shown him the best way to empty his parents' liquor cabinet.

He shifted uneasily in his desk chair. He was dressed in a suit, but he hadn't managed to find a tie, never mind do up shirt buttons; he'd opted for a T-shirt beneath his jacket instead. The faces of the four middle-aged men watching him from the other side of the conference table were filled with distaste.

He laid a hand on the desktop, hoping the cool surface would help stabilize him.

"Should we start?" he asked, swallowing down a wave of nausea.

One of the men took out a folder and the others followed suit. Soon, the table in front of Alexander was covered in Important Papers. These were his bankers and lawyers, the men who took care of the Swedish side of his considerable fortune. They were important, highly respected members of the Old Guard, and judging by their expressions, they didn't appreciate Alexander's having demanded they come to his foundation's spacious offices. An hour earlier he had sent a text ordering them to gather here, rather than his visiting them individually as they had originally planned. In his current condition, Alexander wouldn't have made it. Christ, he had barely even made it this far, and the foundation was practically within crawling distance of his hotel.

Now they were here, looking as if they had swallowed anything from lemons to flies. But Alexander couldn't have cared less if he disrupted their schedules.

"Correct me if I'm wrong, but the fees I pay you are somewhere between scandalous and astronomical, right?" he said coolly.

"I beg your pardon?" said the one to the left. Alexander didn't remember his name.

"I just thought we might dial down the hostility a little. Maybe fake a smile or two even?"

The men shifted nervously in their seats, and he decided to fire them all if they didn't comply. After all, bankers were a dime a dozen.

The men exchanged uncertain glances. Then lips relaxed, brows smoothed out, teeth shone.

Alexander shook his head, couldn't bring himself to care when it really came down to it. "Let's just get this over with."

There was a knock at the door, and a woman brought a tray into the room. Coffee, thank God. She poured the contents of the silver pot into delicate cups and set down a plate of round mint chocolates in colorful foil wrappers—Alexander hated them. Did anyone actually ever eat them? He picked up a cup while the men took out their pens and started to arrange the piles of paper into some kind of order. Alexander drank his coffee and looked gloomily at the stacks of documents he was clearly expected to sign. The tallest of the piles was almost four inches.

"We need your signature on these," one of the men said, with a gesture toward the Important Papers. "I'm afraid I have to insist," he added, as though he knew that Alexander was on the verge of getting up, going out through the doorway, and never coming back.

He didn't really know why he hated this so much. Back in New York he was in complete control of his affairs. Maybe it was because these men, with their accusing looks, reminded him of his father. Maybe he just couldn't bear anything relating to Swedish finance. He'd needed to get some distance from Sweden after what had happened last summer—and he'd done it by burying his head in the sand and ignoring his duties. Now he was paying the price.

"Give them here, then," he muttered.

Grimly, he started to work his way through the piles. Sheet after sheet after sheet.

The words "Sign here, here and here" went on repeat.

Investments. Payments. Authorizations.

As the clock neared lunchtime, they were still barely halfway through the piles, and Alexander decided he needed something other than coffee to drink, needed to breathe something other than the stale air in the meeting room.

"Let's take ten," he said, quickly leaving the room. He closed his eyes and took a deep breath. He wished he could say that it felt good, dealing with all of this, that the coffee had helped with his hangover, but . . . He opened his eyes when he heard voices and caught sight of a tall, red-haired woman standing with her back to him. She was making gestures to the woman behind the reception counter.

"I can't just give out his number," he heard the receptionist say as he approached them. She sounded annoyed, as though she was repeating something she had already said a number of times.

"But is he in Stockholm? Can you at least tell me that? I sent him an e-mail, but he didn't reply. Is he coming to Sweden? If so, do you know how I can get in touch with him? There has to be some way I can get hold of Mr. De la Grip."

Alexander's eyes narrowed in recognition. He had heard that voice before.

The receptionist glanced up, caught sight of Alexander, and gave him a warning look. But the redhead must have noticed, because she turned around and he recognized her instantly.

Isobel Sørensen.

Well, well. A smile tilted his lips. This was much more fun than signing papers. He sauntered toward the reception desk. Even from a distance, Isobel was as pretty as Alexander remembered. Although pretty wasn't the right word. Isobel Sørensen was beautiful. Beautiful in the way that wildfires and explosions and catastrophes are beautiful. He flashed her a wide grin, and after a moment she smiled back—a polite smile that came nowhere close to reaching her eyes.

"I've been trying to contact you," she said, extending her hand to him. He received a firm handshake before she took a step back and pinned him with a searching look. He resisted the urge to run his hand over his stubble. He was almost regretting his decision not to shave.

"I e-mailed you. I just came by to try to get a phone number. You're impossible to get ahold of."

"And yet here we are."

It was no surprise that she hadn't managed to get through to him. Any e-mails from the foundation went straight from his in-box to a folder that he hadn't opened in . . . He didn't even know how long. There had to be hundreds of unopened messages in there by now.

"It's okay," he reassured the receptionist before turning back to Isobel. He turned up the charm, gave her a lazy smile. "I had no idea you were so eager to see me. What can I do for you?"

Something flashed in her eyes. Was it anger?

The door to the meeting room opened. "Alexander?"

Damn, he'd already forgotten about the gloomy bank people.

"Let's break for lunch," he called dismissively to the man who had looked out. "I need to take this."

He was genuinely curious about what Isobel Sørensen might want with him. He remembered her very clearly, not that he'd given her a single thought these past six months. If someone had asked him what he thought Isobel made of him, he would have replied, She's one of the few women who hasn't fallen for my charm; it's inconceivable. Whenever they'd met, Isobel had been dismissive, hostile, or downright rude. He found that, naturally, completely irresistible. He raised an eyebrow at the receptionist. "Is there a room we can use?" He turned to Isobel. "Coffee?"

"No, thanks."

The receptionist tottered past, and Alexander gestured for Isobel to precede him. It was his upbringing, in his very bones; he couldn't be impolite to a woman even if he tried. But the courtesy also gave him an excellent opportunity to study Isobel from behind. He took in her Windbreaker, her ponytail, and her long legs. There were flecks of dirt on her shapeless pants, and it took a moment before Alexander realized they must be from cycling. When was the last time he'd been on a bike? And such flat, practical shoes. They were among the least sexy things he had ever seen, and he wondered whether he hadn't just imagined how attractive she was. Isobel sat down. No, he hadn't imagined it at all. He couldn't remember when, if ever, he had seen a more beautiful woman. He would give anything to see her in a tight-fitting dress. Or, even better, naked. Under the layers of practical cotton and sensible colors, he suspected there were plenty of interesting curves and exciting secrets to explore. He sat down. The day that had started so abysmally had just taken a dramatic turn for the better.

Isobel crossed her legs, and he couldn't help but wonder what they looked like. They had to be strong, if she rode her bike everywhere. She gave him a demanding look. What on earth did she want? A thought struck him. He hadn't slept with her, had he? Christ, he surely wouldn't have forgotten if he had. He racked his memory and, as a result, didn't realize that she had already started talking.

"Sorry," he said. "Could you repeat that?"

She blinked. Her face remained calm, but he caught a flicker in her eyes. It vanished as quickly as it had appeared, as though a feeling had managed to come loose within her but had been resolutely pushed back. She started again, slowly and exaggeratedly this time around, as though she was talking to a child.

"You have every right to do as you please. It's your money, I get that. But I really want to apologize. And I'm still hoping you'll be able to see the bigger picture here, too, that your actions affect so many more people than just me. That this is about people, real flesh-and-blood people."

Alexander scratched his forehead. Isobel may as well have been speaking a dead language, he understood so little of what she was saying.

He opened his mouth to speak but closed it again as she continued.

"It's nothing short of a catastrophe for the people affected. What happened between us . . . like I said, I wish I could undo it. But this is serious, especially for the children. I'm not exaggerating when I say we're talking about life and death here." She picked up a folder and started to lay out pictures of undernourished children and what looked like hospital beds, as well as sheets of paper filled with columns.

"Isobel . . ." Alexander began. He had to stop to clear his throat. "You'll have to forgive me. I've had a tough morning, but I don't quite follow."

She placed her hands in her lap and gave him a long look. Two faint, pink patches had flared up on her cheeks. A furrow had appeared between her eyebrows, which were utterly fascinating in themselves. Fiery red against her pale forehead. She was such a beauty, he could just imagine it: arriving at one of the nightclubs in New York with her on his arm. Or, even more appealing, Isobel beneath him, in his bed, naked.

Damn it, she'd said something he hadn't heard again. He forced himself to focus.

"We're completely dependent on our donors."

"Okay," he said, without understanding what the hell that had to do with him. He really wished the caffeine he'd poured into himself would somehow disperse the fog in his head. "So if I've understood this correctly," he tried to summarize, "there's a lack of money somewhere?" But even as he uttered the words, he knew he had misunderstood something vital.

Isobel blinked several times. Her mouth was taut, causing the last of her professional composure to vanish. "Let me repeat the most important things," she replied tersely, launching into a new, quite forceful monologue about famine, children, and money.

This time Alexander made a serious attempt to keep up. Regardless of what Isobel thought of him, he wasn't actually an idiot. And finally he managed to decipher what she was saying.

"We gave your organization money. Then we stopped. And you're . . . uh . . . upset."

"I know you did it to get revenge, but I . . ."

"Revenge?" he interrupted. This really wasn't very easy to follow.

"Yeah, well, you know. Because I . . ."

She actually blushed a little at this point. Was it wrong that a blushing woman turned him on? Normally, she looked like a damned Amazon, and that small weakness just made her extra sexy.

"Because I was rude."

"Rude? Aha, you mean when you told me to go fuck myself?" he asked helpfully. "Or do you mean that time when you turned your back on me at Arlanda Airport? Or maybe it was when you pretended not to understand Swedish? Sorry, it's just there were so many times, I don't know which one you mean."

More red streaks had appeared on her throat. Her skin was almost translucent, white like silk or cream, dotted with golden freckles.

"So the reason you're here now, yelling at me—"

"I'm not yelling," she interrupted.

"The reason for this *conversation* is, you said something mean, I got offended, cut off the donations to your life-saving organization, and thus caused mass mortality among children in Africa?" he summarized.

"Not Africa. Chad."

"Is that where you were headed when we ran into each other at the airport?"

"Yes."

"You said Africa then," he pointed out.

"I didn't think you would know where Chad was," she replied sullenly.

"Hmm."

Most of what she was saying sounded completely unfamiliar, but what did he know? He'd been drunk pretty much 24/7 for a long time. Many things from the past six months were hazy.

"Medpax does such incredibly important work in Chad. But we're a small organization, and that means we're vulnerable. I'm really sorry if I offended you. I'd love to show you the work we do." She started pulling more files from her canvas bag, and Alexander held up his hand to stop her.

"Please," he groaned. "No more papers."

She stopped what she was doing and gave him a stiff smile.

"Will you at least think about what I said?"

"Absolutely."

She gave him a distrustful look. "It's really important."

"I said I would," he snapped.

Maybe it was because he had spent the morning being held in contempt by four men whose families he probably bankrolled.

Maybe it was just that he wasn't used to women like Isobel. But his head was spinning, and he was starting to get sick of all this hostility.

He hadn't come back to Stockholm to be insulted by people he hadn't mistreated. At least not intentionally, anyway.

"Medpax has started a number of vaccination programs. We're doing incredibly important work—with malaria, with undernourishment. We've—"

"Isobel, I will," he interrupted. If he had to listen to another word about dying children and heroic doctors, he was going to explode.

"Because this isn't just some little hobby project. Our doctors make a real difference. You have to realize that . . ."

Alexander straightened in his seat. He laid a hand on the table and looked at Isobel. "The thing is, I don't *have to* do anything."

He still wasn't quite sure what all this was about. He was still drunk, for Christ's sake, but he understood enough to know that this artificially polite doctor probably wanted a shitload of money from him. "I'll look into it, as I've already said several times." He wanted to add something about how fund-raisers generally didn't show such clear contempt for people they were trying to get money from, but he didn't have the energy.

"All the same, I think that—" she started.

"Enough," he said curtly, getting to his feet and blinking with dizziness. He probably should eat something. "I'll call you," he told her as firmly as he could.

She looked as if she wanted to say something else, but she started to gather her papers together instead. She put them into her faded bag and got up.

"Thanks for your time," she said, holding out her hand again.

Alexander took it and gave it a firm shake, but then had the most bizarre impulse to pull her hand to his mouth and kiss it. He made do just looking down at their joined hands. She had long fingers, trimmed nails, no jewelry. Competent doctor's hands.

"I'll call you," he repeated.

She withdrew and headed for the door with the threadbare bag slung over her shoulder. Her Windbreaker rustled faintly.

He hurried over to open the door for her.

She gave him a long look, and even though she said nothing, he could tell from her gray eyes, the same color as a sunless November day, that her already low impression of him had sunk even further after their meeting. For some reason, this bothered him.

"Bye, Isobel," he said softly.

She disappeared without a word, and his gaze lingered on the door for a long while.

Chapter 4

As Isobel met with patients and wrote up case histories the next day, she couldn't shake the feeling that she had completely mishandled the meeting with Alexander De la Grip. No matter how hard she worked, she couldn't escape the fact she had blown it with the foundation. Big time.

How was that even possible, she asked herself as she took blood pressures and wrote out prescriptions for stomach ulcers. She, who was known for her adaptability and her cool-headedness. She, the doctor whom the most hysterical and demanding patients were sent to. The one who calmed down agitated nurses and frantic field workers. Who gave lectures on the importance of social skills to medical students. She had marched up to Alexander De la Grip and acted like an overwrought teenager. In his office. In the exclusive headquarters of the foundation Medpax relied on for its survival.

What was the word she was looking for?

Right. Stupid.

But she had become unexpectedly nervous. Alexander was so striking it was virtually impossible to take in. No man had the right to look that good; it was verging on unnatural. Despite the messy blond hair, scruffy stubble, and crumpled clothes, he had been so attractive that she'd had trouble looking at him without blushing. In addition to that, Alexander De la Grip was both aristocratic and rich. And not just ordinary rich, but *rich* rich. Not that she had ever believed life was fair, but *come on*. How could it be *that* unfair? The final straw had been his bloodshot eyes and the fact that he reeked of alcohol. He'd had the nerve to stand there in his office, people swarming around him, and look as though he hadn't done anything but party this past week—all while she was fighting for Medpax's survival. It was just too much. And so she had allowed herself to be affected by things she shouldn't have cared about, let petty feelings shape her reaction, and it had been a disaster. Isobel closed the door, picked up the phone, and called Leila.

"Has Alexander De la Grip called you?" she asked when Leila answered.

"No. Should he have?"

Isobel leaned back and put her feet up on the desk. She had at least eight, maybe more, patients still to see, but she decided she had time for one quick call. "I had a go at him yesterday. I probably insulted him. Again. So no, I don't think so."

"I see. How are you today, then?"

"I'm a nutcase. What's wrong with me? Feel free to analyze me."

Leila snorted. "I don't need to analyze you, because it's not hard to figure you out. You were probably an overachiever while you were still in the womb. You're always worried about being a fake. Everyone you meet admires you, but you don't realize that yourself because you're constantly trying to work out how to get your self-centered mother and dead father to be proud of you. Did I forget anything?"

Isobel closed her eyes, unsure of whether it had been a really good or a really bad idea to call Leila. "Nope, that was pretty . . . exhaustive," she replied meekly.

"You're the one everyone wants on their team, Isobel." Leila's voice was kind.

"But I made a fool of myself."

"Yes. Welcome to the real world, where people sometimes make fools of themselves. Let it go."

"What kind of psychobabble is that? It's not that freaking easy to just let it go."

"No, but you don't want things to be easy. There you go, that one's on me."

Isobel brought in her next patient, a PR consultant she saw regularly for insomnia and a slipped disk. She refrained from telling him that he might sleep better if he stopped cheating on his wife, just gave him a prescription for painkillers and a follow-up appointment as far in the future as she could. After that, she listened to a stressed journalist who complained about a "kinda sore throat," but who also had a sky-high temperature. Isobel knew it was scarlet fever even before the lab results came back and confirmed it. When she finally looked up at the clock, it was already three, and she decided to skip the staff coffee break and shut herself in her room instead. She ate crackers with orange marmalade in front of her computer, Googling "Alexander De la Grip + images." He had seemed more muscular now than when she had last seen him, this past summer, and he had been big even then. Tall, much taller than she, and she was used to looking down at most men she met; during her youth, she always had to fight the urge to stoop.

"Stand up straight, Isobel."

"You're so tall. Do you play basketball?"

"Why are your pants always too short, Isobel?"

What did it matter if he was tall? But it mattered. Big, tall men were attractive. She was used to judging a person's measurements without asking any direct questions; with a glance she could determine what they weighed and how tall they were. Alexander had to be at least six foot five and weigh somewhere between two hundred thirty and two hundred forty pounds—wide shoulders, a muscular neck, tight abs. She scrolled through the pictures, spotted the famous one in which he was half-naked and covered in oil, with two naked women at his feet, and compared it with the most recent one she could find, as well as with her own memory. He must have done something. Joined a gym, maybe? She brushed the crumbs into the trash basket, closed the browser, and called her next patient in.

Once Isobel had dealt with the last of her patients, she put on her helmet and cycled home. A group of field workers were meeting for a beer in Södermalm that evening, but she had mixed feelings about going. She should probably join them. It wasn't good for her to isolate herself, she knew that. Tomorrow, she told herself. I'll deal with things tomorrow.

She ate a microwaved meal in front of the TV, read an article on malaria in a medical journal, and drank red tea.

Tomorrow, she thought again as she lay in bed, exhausted but still sleepless. Tomorrow I'll fix it all, become a better person. She closed her eyes, but it was no use. Sleep would not come, no matter how tired she felt. She stared into the darkness. That small, hungry face came to her again, as it so often did. Marius. She missed him. A street urchin who had no one. A starving, lonely child, trying to survive on his own in one of the poorest countries in the world. When he had arrived at the hospital last fall he had been lifeless. Hovering between life and death for a week. Weighing too little, coughing too much. Was he still alive? Well?

Ah, but this dithering was madness; she knew what she should do. What she wanted. She glanced at the clock, picked up her cell, and sent a message to Leila.

Made up my mind. Going to Chad.

The psychologist didn't reply.

Probably because she had a life.

Isobel lay on her side, looking out the window. Several hours passed before she fell into a restless sleep.

Chapter 5

Gina Adan tied a white apron around her waist as she silently counted the glasses on the silver tray—tall, crystal flutes filled with champagne on top of solid antique silver. It would be heavy. She was strong but knew she couldn't take too many at once.

She glanced out the window. Spring sunshine was beaming down on Gyllgarn Castle. The daffodils were in full bloom along its yellow walls, and the lawn was covered with small groups of guests here for the christening—men in suits and women in high heels and silky dresses. Inside the castle, vases and pots were filled with flowers, and every surface had been cleaned and polished. Gina smoothed the apron. She loved this castle and its ancient history, its furniture, knick-knacks, and not least its paintings of stern noblemen and velvet-clad women from the past three hundred years, peering down at her wherever she went. It was Swedish, exotic, and as far from where she had grown up as you could get. There were very few castles in Somalia.

Gina had worked jobs like this since she was sixteen. That meant that for the past six years, she had worked on the fringes of the Swedish upper class, serving them at christenings, graduations, and weddings, cleaning their enormous villas in posh Djursholm and their grand apartments in even posher Östermalm in the city. She didn't mind. For the most part, they paid well, and she liked the flexible hours. Sure, men sometimes accosted her, made slimy propositions or comments about her skin color, and some of the women could be really nasty, but that was her life, and it wasn't any worse among the elite than anywhere else.

Gina rubbed at a mark on the silver and then picked up the tray.

But she had seriously misjudged the weight, and when one of the filled glasses started to slide, her heart leaped into her throat. The crystal glasses were heirlooms and the champagne was very expensive.

She cursed, picturing the entire tray falling to the floor before her, but a pair of strong hands reached out and saved her at the last moment.

"Thanks," she said, relieved. A lazy smile met her gaze, and it was as though the sun had just started to shine straight into the kitchen.

"Hi there," said Alexander De la Grip. He held the heavy tray steady for her. "That was about to end badly. Lucky I turned up."

"Hi," Gina said, returning the smile because it was impossible to do anything else when Alexander beamed at you.

"It's been a while," she continued, taking the tray back from him. She hadn't seen Alexander since the summer before. He looked well. Though he always did.

"No, I haven't been in Sweden since last fall."

His words were distinct and his appearance immaculate, but she couldn't help noting that he already looked quite inebriated.

"Too busy partying?" She tried to remember how many newspapers she had seen him in over the past six months but gave up at ten.

"It's a hard job, but someone's gotta be the black sheep of the family," he said, holding the door open for her. When she looked closer, there was a haunted look on his beautiful face, a familiar sight at family gatherings, even if he mostly managed to hide it.

"And how is Sweden's most beautiful champagne waitress?" he asked, the haunted look gone and in its stead another million-dollar smile.

"I'm pretty good."

"Let me know if there's anything else I can help with," he said. "Hold open more doors, catch more trays." He winked. "I have endless suggestions."

"Mmm," she said with a suspicious look. Alexander always flirted with her. But he did the same with everyone, which was actually quite egalitarian.

She snuck past him and went out to work, leaving him to his own devices.

The thirsty guests quickly cleared the tray, and Gina began to pick up empty glasses while she took quick peeks at the glamorous party-goers before heading back to the kitchen to swap the used glasses for fresh ones, pour out more champagne, and restart the service.

When she stepped outside again, Alexander's older brother, Count Peter De la Grip, approached alone across the grass. Gina hesitated. She didn't like Peter and would have preferred to avoid him alto-gether, but since he was headed straight toward her, she forced her-self to hold out the tray and give him a polite smile.

"Hello," he said as he took a glass. He thanked her and then stood silently beside her. Gina didn't know what to do; it felt impolite to just leave. But to her, Peter De la Grip was the archetypal aristocrat: arrogant, convinced of his own superiority and others' inferiority. She glanced at him, standing next to her with a glass in his hand and his gaze fixed in the air. None of the other guests came over to him. He looked different, she realized. He had lost weight since she'd last seen him, which must have been that morning last year, the morning of the infamous shareholders' meeting where the De la Grips lost their controlling ownership of Investum, the family firm. That had been surreal, even for her, and she wasn't affected personally. Peter probably hadn't had an easy time of it this past year, she would give him that. And this castle, she suddenly realized, it had been his. Peter and his nasty wife had lived here at Gyllgarn like a king and queen. But then he had lost it in the same takeover, his wife had filed for a divorce, and now . . . Gina realized that she had no idea what Peter De la Grip did these days. He had completely disappeared from her radar. She stood silently next to him, her weight on one foot, and wondered whether he would notice if she snuck away.

Peter sighed loudly and turned to her. He looked tired. He put the glass back on the tray.

"Thanks," he said. "That was good." As he walked away across the grass, it seemed as though people averted their eyes and turned their backs. Gina glanced at the flute he had set back on the tray. It was still full.

Alexander studied Gina's progress from the corner of his eye as he talked to a countess with whom he had attended boarding school. The countess was pretty, but Gina was incredibly beautiful. Long, slim limbs. Cheekbones any model would kill for. If Gina didn't work for his family, then . . . Automatically he flashed the countess a bedroom smile and continued to let his thoughts wander. Gina had been talking to Peter, and that troubled him. It was one thing to flirt with Gina himself, because he would never actually cross the line with someone in a dependent position. But with Peter you never knew. Alexander exhaled only after Peter left Gina's side.

The countess looked puzzled, and Alexander gave her an apologetic look. He hadn't realized how ready he was to throw himself at his big brother if he set a foot even slightly wrong. They hadn't seen one another since the board meeting when Peter unexpectedly—no, *shockingly*—had voted against their father and sealed the deal on the De la Grip family finally losing control of Investum. They hadn't spoken since, which suited Alexander fine. There were a lot of people he disliked or despised, but Peter had his own special position in the People I Despise category. The countess moved on, and Alexander watched as Peter was swallowed up by the crowd. With a bit of luck, he could avoid his big brother today, and ideally for the rest of his life.

"Alexander!"

He turned toward the familiar, Russian-accented voice.

"Uncle Eugene," he said warmly. Eugene was one of the few members of his family, other than his sister, Natalia, whom he truly loved.

His uncle gave him one of his typical bear-like hugs, noisy Russian kisses on his cheeks and all. Eugene looked well. Dressed in bright colors, clean-shaven, smelling of aftershave.

"Now that you're in Sweden, you must come down to see me in Skåne," Eugene insisted. He waved his glass in the air. "I'm hosting a charity ball. People who want to raise money for something or other are coming. The environment, I think. You know how much I love the environment."

Alexander raised an eyebrow.

Eugene seemed to be thinking.

"Or was it world peace? Something like that. Either way, it'll be an entire weekend of performance and business and mingling. Lots of people like you."

"Like me?"

"Yes, you know. Beautiful people with too little sense and too much money. Jet set. Together we'll contribute to making the world a better place."

"I'll try to come," Alexander lied. He liked his uncle, and he really should visit the estate—he did own it, after all. But a charity ball in the countryside? It wasn't exactly his idea of a fun weekend.

Eugene shook his head as though he knew precisely what was going through Alexander's mind. "It would be good if you came down. It's been too long since we spent any time together," was all he said.

Alexander made a noncommittal sound and then was saved by his big sister, Natalia. She held the day's guest of honor in her arms. Alexander gave his sister a hug with one arm before noticing that his baby niece was enthusiastically blowing bubbles from her own spit. He studied the child. "She must've gotten that from David's side."

"Molly's unusually advanced, I have to say," Natalia replied loyally. She looked down at her daughter's sticky chin. "Even if it's not always obvious."

Alexander laughed. "So why aren't I godfather to this little miracle?"

He saw a flash of regret in Natalia's golden eyes, but her voice was steady when she answered: "I need someone reliable, Alexander."

He froze for a moment before he pulled himself together again. "You're right. I'm not exactly the right person to keep someone on the straight and narrow." He smiled to cover up the fact that he was unexpectedly hurt by the way his beloved sister had so obviously weighed him up and found him wanting.

Natalia squeezed his arm. "David and I are so happy you came to the christening," she said in a conciliatory tone.

Alexander raised a skeptical eyebrow. "Really? David is happy? Why do I find that hard to believe?" Natalia's husband and he weren't exactly loving brothers-in-law.

"Yes," said Natalia firmly. "At least he's not unhappy," she added, and Alexander gave her a wink. Sweet Natalia, she couldn't tell a lie if her life depended upon it.

"Well, he'd better not be unhappy since he has you." Natalia and David had married last fall, just weeks after David had crushed the De la Grip family empire. And weeks after he had impregnated Natalia. And caused her to lose pretty much everything that had made her who she was. As courtships went, it had been pretty lousy.

Yeah, it had been a crazy year, but not all of the craziness had been David Hammar's fault, Alexander admitted to himself. Not that he would ever disclose that to Natalia. He enjoyed despising David too much for that.

"So how's married life with the family's archenemy?" he asked instead.

Eugene gave him a disapproving look.

"He's not the archenemy," protested Natalia. She bit her lip and kissed Molly on the head, closing her eyes briefly as she inhaled the baby's scent. "Not anymore, at least. And certainly not mine. Oh, please, don't bring all that up when you meet him. It's all in the past."

"Of course, dear," Eugene said.

"If you say so," Alexander murmured.

But David Hammar's ruthless vendetta *had* rocked the entire foundation of the De la Grip family, and things had changed forever. Not that Alexander really cared that much for the family empire. To be honest he mostly disliked David on principle. The man was too full of himself, too damn capable. But since Natalia's eyes implored him to behave, and since he loved her too much to cause her pain on purpose, he decided to play nice. Well, as nice as he could. He gulped down the last of his champagne, ignoring Eugene's censorious frown.

"So, how does it feel to be back here?" he asked instead, waving toward the yellow castle.

"Honestly I'm just glad we could squeeze in the christening. Gyllgarn has a fully booked schedule the whole spring." She smiled at Molly and made a cooing sound. Molly blew a happy bubble of spit in return. "We're going to run activities for kids and teenagers in need here. Soccer tournaments. Riding."

Alexander couldn't help but pull a face at the enthusiasm in his big sister's voice. But in his family, Natalia had always been the one with the most heart. Not that there had ever been much competition. They were a rather fucked-up group.

"That seems to be in these days, saving the world," he said, looking meaningfully at Eugene. He took another glass of champagne from a passing tray. He had planned to stay relatively sober, but really, why bother? "I suppose your democratizing the castle like that isn't too popular?"

"There's nothing I care about less than what people say. I'm trying to do something good."

And then Alexander spotted a familiar figure out of the corner of his eye. He braced himself, swallowing down the champagne.

"And just when it looked like good would triumph, evil turned up to restore the balance," he mumbled as their mother, Ebba De la Grip, approached them.

"Mom's not *evil*," Natalia protested.

Alexander gave her an ironic look.

"Did we have the same childhood?" he asked. It was a joke, but in actual fact they hadn't. Not by a long shot.

"Fine, okay, but she tries the best she can from her point of view." Natalia shifted Molly in her arms and looked pleadingly at both Alexander and Eugene. "Don't cause a scene."

"Would never cross my mind," said Alexander. "So what convinced the devil, sorry, Mom, to leave her beloved vineyard?"

Ebba and his dad, Gustaf De la Grip, had moved, or fled, depending on how you looked at it, to France after the mayhem last year. What little Alexander had felt for his father had disappeared after those weeks; so many unforgivable things had been said, done, and revealed. As far as Alexander was concerned, his father might as well be dead.

But with his mom, things were more complicated. Largely because Natalia stubbornly insisted on trying to maintain a relationship with their less-than-good-enough mother. And Alexander knew that he loved Natalia more than he despised their mother, which meant he was effectively caught in the middle. It was a near impossible equation.

"Mom came back to Sweden for Molly's christening," Natalia said. "She'll be in town for a few weeks. Please, could you try? She was really upset when you didn't get in touch at Christmas. Or at Easter. It's a huge step for her, to leave Dad in France and come here alone." Alexander rolled his eyes.

Ebba had stopped to greet a friend, and Alexander tried to study her as objectively as he could. Her pale blue dress and the matching hat perched on her blond hair; her smooth skin, and cool perfection. She looked like any other aristocrat. Beautiful and well-kept but nothing more. An ordinary woman. Alexander could still remember the way he had longed for her and her love as a child. Remembered the way she would leave him to go see one of her "friends" while Nat and Peter were in school.

"You mustn't tell anyone," she would say while putting on coral lipstick. "If Daddy finds out, he won't love us anymore. Mommy will cry and we'll have to move and it will all be your fault. You don't want that, do you?"

He had shaken his head.

"Good boy. Just sit here—Mommy will be back soon," she'd said, and disappeared in a cloud of silk and perfume.

He had been just a child, only four or maybe five and he'd loved her with such desperation. Disobeying her, he'd snuck out of the house as she left, hid behind a small bush. It was summer and the leaves had been covered with insects. He could still remember the sounds of their humming. The car seemed to come out of nowhere. The man who stepped out was a stranger, but he kissed Alexander's mother, took her arm, put her in the car, slammed the door. Alexander could only stare at the unfolding scene.

The car took off, creating a small cloud of dust over the long gravel drive. Then there was silence. Not even the insects made a sound. She had gone so eagerly, without giving her young son a second thought.

Alexander remembered he'd stayed behind that bush for a long time, waiting, waiting for her to come back.

He had nowhere to go. His mother was the person he trusted most in the world, the person who should have cared for him. And she abandoned him so easily.

At that moment, he felt he had no one.

Alexander shoved his hands into his pockets, embarrassed by how they were trembling. He fought the urge to leave, looked around for more alcohol. Funny how he had loved her then. Well, that certainly was over.

"Hi, Mom," Natalia said.

Ebba looked as though she was about to give Natalia a hug but made do with an awkward pat on the shoulder instead. She gave Molly, who was happily gurgling away, a smile that actually looked genuine, nodded a greeting to her brother, Eugene, and then looked straight at Alexander.

He steeled himself as her blue eyes brimmed with tears. "Alexander. So wonderful to see you."

He could feel the usual wave of unease approaching, the one he always felt when she hinted at an emotional closeness he no longer wanted. He held his breath, getting used to the familiar scent of her perfume—always White Linen, which he hated.

Things would be so much easier if there hadn't been a period when he'd loved her, he thought, bowing slightly.

"Wonderful to see you too, dear Mother."

If Ebba noticed the mockery in his voice, she showed no sign of it. She simply took another step toward him, entering his personal space. He went rigid. Ebba rarely cared about what other people needed, but today she seemed to realize that she had crossed a line. She paused, blinked uncertainly, and turned back to Molly instead.

Alexander let out his breath.

As the bells in the old Gyllgarn chapel rang, the christening guests gathered in the pews. A female priest led the ceremony, and Alexander was proud that in everything she did, his big sister challenged the prejudices that still held such sway in their class. The music rose toward the ceiling, and for some reason he shuddered. He had enjoyed playing in the chapel as a child, been fascinated at how the sunlight found its way in through the uneven glass, but had also been scared of the way the acoustics caused even the smallest of sounds to echo throughout the entire room. They had spent the majority of their summers at Gyllgarn when they were small, and he had memories of Natalia's long brown hair swaying in a ponytail, the horses she loved to ride, and the children from the nearby village they played with. Some of them were here today—adults now, of course, with their own families. He remembered many of the things they had done as children, but he couldn't remember the feeling. Had he been happy? No matter how hard he tried, he couldn't remember, and that bothered him.

The music fell silent, and Natalia and David carried Molly up to the antique christening basin. The godparents, Natalia's best and oldest friend, Åsa Bjelke, and David's business partner, Michel Chamoun, stood ceremoniously alongside. Molly protested loudly at the water on her head, and her parents hurried to comfort her.

Ebba's eyes glistened, and she dabbed a handkerchief at the corners. Alexander didn't know what to think. Had their mother finally forgiven Natalia for marrying David, the man who'd taken the thing Ebba loved most of all away from her: her position in society? And then Alexander caught a rather nasty smile in one of the pews. A woman in her midthirties had looked over her shoulder and was eyeing him, quite openly. Christ. He hadn't seen that she was here. She was one of *them*. He knew her but suddenly couldn't remember her name. Maybe he had suppressed it. She gave him a raised eyebrow and then started whispering to the woman sitting next to her. Alexander couldn't hear what they were saying, but it wasn't too difficult to imagine, to remember. They both turned around and looked him over, winked at him. He fought against the wave of repugnance that washed over him, tried to focus on the ceremony.

After the christening, Alexander shook David Hammar's hand and congratulated him, grateful for the distraction.

"Good that you came, Alexander," said David curtly. He said nothing more, but there was judgment in that uncompromising look, wasn't there?

Alexander mumbled something about the ceremony being fantastic, but then withdrew; he needed some breathing room, away from his family and the things he imagined he could read on their faces, away from people that made him feel dirty. He snuck out the back, onto the terrace at the other side of the castle, and leaned against a stone pillar, looking out at the water.

"Are you okay?"

He turned. Gina again.

"Just a bit of family overdose. I'll need something stronger than champagne after this," he said, trying to keep his tone light.

He let his gaze wander over her. She wore a simple dress beneath her apron. Soft canvas shoes. "Feel like going out once you're done here?" he asked.

Gina smiled. "No, thanks. I'm flattered. At least I think I am. But I like my job, and it would make things too complicated."

"We don't need to make it complicated," he said flippantly. But it was a halfhearted protest. He didn't want to ruin the relationship he and Gina had, he realized. And besides, she deserved much more than a cynical, disillusioned man like him.

"Plus, I have to study tonight," she added.

"Ah. Sorry, I had no idea you were studying. Which subject?"

"Medicine. My second semester." She said it proudly, but also slightly defiantly, as though she expected to be questioned.

Evidently he was surrounded by doctors these days.

"So you'll be a doctor, then?"

"Yes, eventually."

"Helping people and stuff like that?" He gave her a slight smile.

Gina's eyes narrowed, and suddenly she reminded him of Isobel Sørensen. The same integrity shone in her gaze.

"I need to get back."

"Good luck, Gina," he said. He truly meant it.

She hesitated, bit her lip. "I just think it's everyone's duty to do the best they can. It's never too late for that." With those words, she turned and left.

Alexander stayed out on the terrace. He fished his cigarettes from his jacket pocket, shook one out and lit it, then blew smoke into the clear spring air.

Finally this bloody ordeal was over.

Chapter 6

"What are you doing here?" Leila asked, studying Isobel over the top of her tortoiseshell glasses.

"I worked at the clinic the whole weekend," Isobel replied. "And I've got a load of comp time I need to take. This is my day off."

Leila crossed her arms. "That's exactly what I mean. Why are you here, at Medpax? Shouldn't you *not* be working? Sleeping or reading like a normal person? Doing yoga?"

"I hate yoga. And I hate people who do yoga."

"Yeah, they are rather annoying," Leila agreed. "So what are you doing?"

Isobel showed her the folder she had been leafing through. "Old memories. Did you know I practically grew up here? I used to come after school."

"Is that why you're here today? Nostalgia?"

"I don't know," Isobel said slowly. She had come on a whim, but now she was in a strange mood she couldn't shake. Maybe it hadn't been so wise to come here after all. As a girl she had been so desperately lonely. She couldn't tell Leila that, but she had always come here hoping to feel closer to her mom, hoping that Blanche would notice her. Which she never did. It was rather pathetic that she, as a grown woman, still couldn't get over this need to seek love and attention from her mother.

Isobel wondered whether maybe that was one of the reasons she enjoyed being in the field so much. It was almost unbearable at times, but in some strange way things were much simpler when everything but life and death was taken out of the equation.

"I really am feeling better now," she said, as if to convince herself. "Liberia was tough—the Ebola outbreak was the worst I've ever seen. But I'm fully recovered, I want you to know that."

"I know, you look it. I was worried for a while, but I would never let you go to Chad if I wasn't sure you could handle it. Your well-being is my number one priority."

"Thanks. I spoke to Idris over the weekend," she said.

Idris Toko was the local doctor in charge of the pediatric hospital in Chad. They Skyped from time to time. Idris was glad she was coming back; they made a good team.

"I'm assuming you still have all the visas and vaccinations you need?" Leila asked.

"Yup, so it's actually a pretty perfect solution that I go again."

Isobel spoke French; was used to fieldwork; and had all the necessary stamps, visas, and vaccinations. She would stay for a month while Leila looked for another doctor willing to head out there for longer. And she would get to spend time with Marius again. Was he hoping for her to return? She wanted him to feel that he was important to her, that there was one person who truly cared. It felt important. Not disappointing him.

"It'll be rainy season," Leila said.

"Yes, but that just means it'll be a little muddier."

"One thing I was curious about . . . When did you last have any kind of safety training?" Leila asked, giving her a piercing look. Isobel scoffed.

She had been a volunteer since she was sixteen, for a number of more or less organized groups. Before she'd gone to Iraq to work in a refugee camp on her first mission for Doctors Without Borders, she'd taken a comprehensive preparatory course in safety, among other things. After that, straight after her medical degree, she traveled to Haiti to work amid the chaos following the earthquake there. And working with Ebola had required a whole new level of caution. There was, in other words, very little she didn't already know about safety in the field. And besides, she wasn't some kind of cowboy doctor. She knew that evolution dealt rapidly with careless field-workers.

"It was a while ago," she said cautiously, not liking where this was going.

"I signed Sven up for one—you can take his place," Leila said, confirming her suspicions.

Isobel started to protest, that she was much too experienced, much too senior, much too not interested in going to stupid security courses, but she was interrupted by Leila's cell phone. "It's not up for discussion," Leila said curtly before she disappeared to answer the call.

When Leila came back, Isobel was deep in inventory lists and field reports from Chad. Her grandfather, Henri, who'd died in Chad, had left behind reams of notes in his dry, archaic French. Idris Toko, and all the doctors who had preceded Idris, had also sent regular reports back to Medpax over the years. All this meant three decades' worth of fascinating reading on malaria treatments, cholera outbreaks, and the constant battle against undernourishment. Isobel couldn't help but feel proud. This was her family's legacy, after all.

"Guess who that was on the phone," Leila said from the doorway.

"The pope? The king? I don't know," Isobel replied absentmindedly. She had found an old newspaper clipping. Her mother and grandfather outside the hospital in Chad. Simple buildings. A jeep. A vast, sandy landscape.

"Alexander De la Grip. He wants to meet you."

Isobel looked up from the folder. "Is that a joke? Why?"

"He wants you to tell him about Medpax and explain why his foundation should give us money."

Isobel had been so sure she had blown it. Had actually been relieved not to have to see him again.

"Can't you do it?" she pleaded. "Considering how I acted last time."

Leila leaned against the door frame again. "But he wants to meet *you*."

"I don't know why."

"You must have made an impression on him."

"That's one way of looking at it. It's just that he annoys me."

"This isn't like you, Isobel."

"Fine, I'll go see him. But I just want to say, on record, that I hate this, having to suck up to someone like him just to get money," she said, knowing she had already lost.

Leila snorted. "I just don't understand the issue here. I've seen you fawn over people before. What's the problem?"

"Nothing. Aside from the fact that I'm used to dealing with older men. He's so young," she said, knowing even as she spoke that it was a ridiculous excuse.

Leila gave her an incredulous look. "Alexander De la Grip is rich and he's hot," she said slowly, with emphasis on each syllable. "He turned twenty-nine this past January, so that makes him twenty-two months younger than you."

Isobel didn't ask why Leila had memorized that fact. Leila stored masses of information in her super-brain. She was like a data bank on the people she met, their qualities and weak points.

"I'll give him a call then." Isobel sighed. She wasn't looking forward to that conversation. He would probably be drunk, was no doubt planning to humiliate her in any number of ways.

"No need." Leila turned her wrist and looked at her watch. "He'll be here any minute."

"Here?"

"Now you're just *playing* dumb. Count Alexander De la Grip, Sweden's most coveted bachelor, according to verified sources, is on his way here. And you, Doctor Sørensen, need to be on your very best sucking-up behavior." Leila looked her up and down. "You should know that if you didn't dress like a pious social secretary and didn't criticize people the moment they turn out to be less moral than yourself, you could bring in a lot of donations."

Isobel drew for breath. "I don't criticize people, do I?" she asked, offended. She decided to ignore the comment about her dress sense for the moment. "You make me sound like some anal psych case."

Was Leila right? Was that what she was like? No, criticizing Alexander De la Grip was practically a civil duty, but otherwise she wasn't a moral snob. Was she?

"Isobel, you're the best doctor I have ever known. No one is as good with their patients as you. You're warm, empathetic. If someone is dying or ill, you're the one they want at their side. But even the people who won life's lottery can actually be okay. You can't judge someone just because he was born rich. Alexander De la Grip is a person. More important, he's one we need."

Isobel hadn't realized how obvious it was that she tended to—*oc-*

casionally—look down on people who sailed through life. It was embarrassing. Her entire identity rested on the notion that she didn't distinguish between people, but here was Leila, poking at her most vulnerable spot. Though that was Leila in a nutshell. She lived to push people's hot buttons

"Okay," Isobel mumbled.

"Don't be so hard on him." Leila came into the room and put a hand on Isobel's shoulder. "And don't be so tough on yourself. He looks good, you're single. Try to have a bit of fun."

"You're not telling me I should use some kind of female charm?" If there was one thing Isobel despised, it was women who batted their eyelashes to get what they wanted. "If I start to act like an idiot, you've got carte blanche to analyze me to death."

Leila rolled her eyes. "I mean that if you listen within, you'll realize it might even be fun."

Listen within. It was Isobel's turn to roll her eyes.

"Sometimes I think that psychologists are the worst occupational group in the world."

"Not at all," Leila replied, unfazed. "There are much worse. Politicians. PR types. Passport police. And those are just the ones starting with p."

"Thanks for your input," Isobel said. She was petty enough to make sure she sounded cool and collected. "I'll bear it in mind."

"Isobel . . ." Leila began, but then she shook her head and sighed. "I'll send him in when he gets here."

"No," said Isobel, getting to her feet. "I'll wait in the lobby."

She wanted to take back control of the situation. Leila could be a pain in the ass when she decided to root around in your psyche, but she was right about one thing. Isobel was driven by a desire to do what was right, what was important, and she didn't want to be fumbling about on the edges of morality. It was important to see the bigger picture, and in this instance, that was the future of Medpax. So. She would put on some lipstick and do what she was good at when she really put her mind to it. She would charm that rich good-for-nothing into giving them what they so badly needed. Money.

Alexander wouldn't know what had hit him.

Chapter 7

Alexander looked up at the building on Sibyllegatan, one of the city's most expensive and exclusive streets. A flag bearing the Medpax logo hung from the façade. Fancy address, he thought as he studied himself in the elevator mirror. He hadn't partied the past few days, hadn't even gotten drunk, and he looked refreshed. It felt odd.

Instead of drinking, flirting, and fucking, he had kept to his hotel room and gone to bed early each night. This morning he had taken a long shower, eaten a light breakfast, and dressed in one of his best tailor-made Italian suits.

He ran a hand over his freshly shaved chin and tried to remember when something similar had last happened.

He had literally hundreds of contacts in his phone, some of the world's most sought-after women. They were supermodels, film stars, a couple of countesses, and a princess or two. Lovely, sexy women who appreciated the glamor and the notoriety that the infamous Alexander De la Grip brought with him. Several of them were in Stockholm at the moment. All he had to do was call any one of them, or simply walk down to Stureplan, and he would be set. But he hadn't felt like it. Not since he'd met with Isobel, when he thought about it. That in itself was worth investigating more closely.

Rather than indulging in his usual vices, he had spent the past few days reading up on humanitarian organizations in general, and Medpax in particular. What he didn't know now could hardly be worth knowing. Because that was how his brain worked. He focused on a subject, learned everything, and then quickly got bored of it again.

He straightened his jacket and put a hand on the elevator handle.

Over the past few days, he had gone through all of his mail, come to grips with his finances, delved into aid work, and called a real estate agent. It was profoundly unlike him.

Maybe he was getting sick?

He smiled to himself and opened the door. Well, as luck would have it, he was about to meet a doctor. . . .

The lobby was dark and somber despite the sunshine outside. A young woman with a boyish haircut and a green lace jacket caught sight of him. Alexander walked over to the polished wooden desk. He went all in and turned on the charm.

"Hi there," he said, giving her a brilliant smile.

Her eyes gleamed eagerly. "Hello. My name is Asta. What can I help you with?"

"I spoke to Leila Dibah," he started, because he wanted to meet the woman with the husky voice and the impressive efficiency. Leila had sent to his hotel all the documentation and paperwork he had asked for. No fuss, no excuses, just a straight question about what he wanted, and then he had received it. "But I'm here to see Isobel Sørensen."

Before Asta had time to reply, a black-clad woman with thick, gold jewelry and high heels came out of a wide doorway.

"I'm Leila." She greeted him with a firm handshake. Sensual in a sophisticated way, but also commanding respect, with her piercing gaze and that voice, which made her sound as if she drank whisky for breakfast and chain-smoked the rest of her days away. Words like *flint hard, no nonsense,* and *I eat people like you for breakfast* came to Alexander's mind. He remembered that this general secretary wasn't a doctor, or a bureaucrat, but a trained psychologist. She didn't look like any psychologist he had met before, though.

A moment later Isobel appeared. In contrast to Leila's refinement, Isobel was wearing virtually identical clothes to the ones she'd had on last time they met. Practical and hideous. And yet there was something about her. It was so amorphous that Alexander had trouble putting his finger on it. But Isobel had a presence. Everyone else disappeared into the background when she was around. Maybe it was her height, maybe her flaming red hair. He had never seen a color like it.

"Hi," she said.

And then something unprecedented happened.

Isobel Sørensen favored him with a smile.

A thrill coursed through Alexander's entire body. It began in his chest, moving backward and outward, up his spine, to his hair and arms. It was unreal. The woman had a movie star smile.

"Hello again." Alexander held out a hand, enclosing hers in a firm grip. Isobel's skin was cool, her fingers almost cold, but when he fixed his gaze on her gray eyes, he saw something glittering. Isobel continued to smile, he continued to hold her hand, and they stood like that for a second or two too long.

"Isobel will look after you," said Leila. "Right, Isobel?"

"Of course." She withdrew her hand. She seemed completely un-fazed by what had, for Alexander, been a handshake verging on the erotic. "This way."

Alexander waited politely for Isobel to sit down before he did the same. When she caught him looking at her, she flashed him another smile. Her mouth was fantastic, wide and sensuous, pale pink lips dotted with faint freckles.

"Is this where you work?" he asked, leaning forward slightly and giving her his full attention. He looked her only in the eyes, didn't make the mistake of allowing his gaze to fix on her mouth or move down over her body. Plus, he already knew: long, lithe legs, luscious curves. And then those freckles.

"No, not primarily. I work in a private health clinic. On Valhalla-vägen."

Private? That was unexpected. Private health care was still rare in Sweden, still somewhat of a delicate issue in a country that prided it-self on equal health care for all.

She leaned back in her chair and crossed her legs. She was wear-ing flat, canvas shoes, and he wondered if she was one of those women who always wore flats so as not to be too tall. If so, it was a shame. She would be shit hot in high heels.

"I have a special arrangement there," she said, and Alexander dragged himself out of his fantasies. "So I can leave at short notice."

"Leave?"

"I also work for MSF—Médecins Sans Frontières, or Doctors With-out Borders."

Three jobs. He barely had one. "But it's Medpax you're passionate about?"

She furrowed her smooth brow. "I don't like that phrase, *passionate about*. I'm involved in Medpax in my spare time."

"But how do you manage? With all the work. And being out in the field?"

He had spent the weekend reading about the endless needs out there. She must have seen so much suffering, so many people die. It sounded unbearable.

"I make sure to remember the times things went well for my patients. The sunshine stories. That's the reward, and that's how I cope. Also, you have to have reasonable expectations of yourself."

"And you do?"

She gave him a wry look. One of her feet bobbed. "That depends on who you ask."

Alexander crossed his legs and smoothed his perfectly tailored suit, which had cost so much it could probably support more refugees than he wanted to think about. "It all seems so hopeless."

"Helping people?" Her tone was mild, but he caught the steel beneath it.

"It's so obviously never ending," he said. "Do you never just feel like you want to give up, go home, and have a drink?"

"Often, yes. But each of us has to do what we can."

That was almost word for word what Gina had said to him. It sounded equally naïve coming from Isobel's lips. But it was clear she was serious, that helping people was, perhaps, the most important thing in her life.

Alexander had wondered why Isobel thought so badly of him from the first time they met. It had been last summer. He hadn't been able to understand her hostility when he was trying to come on to her. But now, it was as though he could suddenly see himself through Isobel's eyes. *She* gave up her comfort and her time to help other people. *He* was a superficial rich man with no interest in anything other than his own pleasure. She was practically genetically predisposed to dislike him.

"The worst is when you know you should've been able to save a patient," she continued. "So many you could save if only you had access to what we have in any average neighborhood pharmacy. It's tough."

This entire conversation was tough.

Staying sober and learning about aid, had that really been such a good idea?

"You look different," she suddenly said, studying him closely.

Alexander raised an eyebrow, glad that they had stopped talking about misery and death: "Good different or bad different?"

She made a gesture to his face.

"You broke it," she said.

He automatically raised his hand to his nose. The plastic surgeon had been either incompetent or hungover, because he really hadn't done a good job. Still, most people didn't notice. People paid less attention to things than they thought.

"I used to box. The other guy got a direct hit." It had hurt like hell, actually.

"Do you still do it?"

"Box? No."

He had enjoyed boxing, liked how strong it made him, liked to fight, if he was honest. But there were limits to how often you could have vital parts of yourself broken, punctured, or bruised.

"Probably sensible. Sooner or later, the head takes a hit," she said.

He grinned at her. "I don't use it all that much anyway."

She laughed, an open and sensual laugh that made Alexander's toes curl in his handmade shoes. It was like talking to a completely different Isobel from the woman he'd met so many times before. This version was like the disapproving and angry Doctor Sørensen's sexy twin sister.

"Tell me about Medpax. Tell me why you in particular deserve my money."

"Because it's the right thing to do?"

He gave her a sarcastic look. "You're gonna have to give me more to work with than that."

She nodded; it didn't seem that she had taken offense.

"My mother and grandfather founded Medpax, but I guess you already know that."

"Yes, but tell me anyway. I like to listen."

"They were both brilliant doctors."

"Just like you?"

Isobel shook her head. "No, no, those two have always been special."

"Are they still alive?" he asked, though of course he knew the answer.

"Mom is. My grandfather is dead. He died a heroic death."

"Sounds like there are lots of heroes in the family."

"You have no idea," she said. "My father died a hero's death in a plane crash while he was on a mission for the UN. And *his* father was a Danish war hero. Sometimes it almost feels like it's expected of me, too. That I should die while I'm doing something really heroic, I mean."

A chill went through him, and he brushed an invisible thread from his pants to hide his reaction. "That's so macabre," he said lightly. "I would never be able to care so much about something that I died for it. Other than champagne, maybe."

And sex, he added silently to himself. Especially sex with this fierce woman.

Isobel flashed him that new smile, the one he thought he could easily get used to. She was dangerous when she was like this. She made him want to flex his muscles and lay down prey at her feet. If it was an act, then she was damn good at it. When had he last felt that he wanted to impress a woman so badly?

Don't kid yourself, Alex. You want to sleep with her, that's all.

"The truth is that the money Medpax receives has a direct correlation to life and death. Our hospital in Chad needs everything. Staff, equipment, medicine. The patients' needs are, as you already mentioned, practically inexhaustible. We're a small organization, we have low administrative costs. Most of our staff are volunteers."

"And you? Do you get a wage? Sorry to ask."

"It's okay. No, I'm not paid."

"What do you earn with Doctors Without Borders?" The woman could hardly exist on nothing.

"Around eleven thousand. It's meant to cover expenses only."

"But that's not enough to live on."

"That's why I do temp work at the private health clinic. People with that kind of health insurance can afford to pay me a lot."

If he hadn't been studying her closely, he would have missed it.

But now he saw it. The conflict inside her. Christ. It couldn't be easy being Isobel Sørensen.

"I'd like to apologize for being so rude before," she said. Her voice was as warm as a Caribbean breeze. When she spoke like that, he wanted to just skip all the aid talk and throw her down onto the rug instead. Peel those shapeless, utilitarian clothes off her, uncover skin and her secrets, kiss her, drink in her sultry laugh.

"What do you mean? Specifically, that is," he asked. He had to clear his throat to regain control of his voice. It was clear that Isobel had adopted a new strategy since they'd last met. It was quite thrilling. He was looking forward to seeing how far she was willing to go for his money. Not very nice, perhaps, but then he wasn't an aid organization hero.

"When we met . . ."

"In Skåne, last summer," he suggested helpfully.

She fell silent and furrowed her brow. "Yeah, then too. But I mean . . ."

"On the airplane from New York? Or at the airport maybe?"

She looked embarrassed. "I suppose so. I didn't realize I'd been so rude so many times. What I meant was when we met the other day, at your foundation. I was impolite, and I'm really sorry about that. I'm glad you're giving me a second chance."

He looked at her earnest face and decided that he wasn't going to fall for this little performance at all. All the flirting and the twirling of her hair around her little finger affected him, that went without saying—she was, after all, an enormously attractive woman—but he wasn't quite as easily duped as Isobel seemed to think.

"What?" she asked, smiling, her voice all but a purr.

It was time to raise the stakes. "I thought we could continue this discussion. Over dinner and drinks?"

Her eyes narrowed. "I'm happy to continue here and now." The purr was gone.

"I don't have time. I have to go get my nails polished," he said with a straight face. Judging by Isobel's expression, she didn't have too high an opinion of men who got manicures. "And I have an appointment with my color coordinator. Don't want to end up wearing the wrong tie," he added.

"You're kidding."

Of course he was. "A date. You could tell me more about Medpax and why we should give you money."

Money he knew they desperately needed. Leila hadn't said anything concrete about the organization's financial situation, of course, but Alexander was neither stupid nor without his contacts. He could guess how things looked for them. Columns of red, donors who had jumped ship. It wasn't a pretty picture. He stretched out his legs, showing off the superb tailoring of his suit. He was wearing his signet ring today, bearing the family crest, glittering faintly.

Isobel's eyes narrowed even farther.

"So that's it for Medpax unless I go out with you?"

Oh, she really did want to have her low opinion of him confirmed. But Alexander didn't plan on giving her the satisfaction, had no intention of making her think worse of him than she already did.

"Isobel," he said, "that really wasn't meant as some kind of provocation. I'd like to get to know you better, understand how Medpax works. And call me conceited, but I'd also like the chance to convince you to like me."

"But I do like you," she replied, a tad too quickly.

That might have been the most dishonest thing Alexander had ever heard. "Right, sure," he said dryly.

"But the fact remains—you want a date in exchange for us getting our money."

"No, I've already authorized it," he said. "I did it before I came. The money only stopped because of an administrative error. They made the decision without consulting me." That sounded slightly better than admitting he hadn't signed any Swedish papers for the past six months because he'd been too drunk. "The money should start up again soon. And it's retroactive, too. Someone from the bank is probably on the phone to Leila, telling her the good news now. So if you say no to a date with me, it won't make any difference."

Her face relaxed. "Okay, I'll say no then," she said, sounding relieved. "And thanks, your money will make a huge difference."

"But I'd be willing to give you much more if I could take you out on a real date."

She fell silent. Was motionless.

"Would lunch do?" she asked finally, sounding hopeful. "I'm really busy. . . ."

He shook his head. "Sorry, it's dinner that's on the table."

She bit her lip. Seeing how much she wanted to say no, he had to hide a smile. He didn't normally have to pay women to go out with him. Romeo would have died laughing. But Alexander had found Isobel's weak spot. She *was* passionate about her little organization.

She shook her head. "I can't date a donor."

It was the most ridiculous thing he had ever heard. "Of course you can."

"No."

And with that, he saw it, utterly crystal clear. Isobel *enjoyed* being better than everyone else, being untouchable. Now there was no chance in hell he would give in. What would it take to get her to abandon one of her absurd principles?

He leaned back in the chair. "You don't even know how much you're saying no to," he said slowly.

"Makes no difference."

"Come on, aren't you curious?"

"Is it just dinner and drinks we're talking about?"

"Of course."

Unless you want more, that is. He could easily imagine her naked beneath him. Eyes dark with passion, that husky laugh. Christ, the thought alone turned him on. He shifted in his chair.

"How much?" she asked, her chin in the air. "Purely theoretically. How much would you give Medpax for one single date?"

He hid the feeling of triumph that surged through him. Isobel Sørensen was sitting there, thinking about selling him a piece of her spotless soul.

He loved it.

"Give me a figure," he said nonchalantly.

She studied him. He waited. He was a professional card player. And he had been a paratrooper during his military service. Had lain in pits, behind rocks, alert. If he had to, he could wait for hours, days.

"One hundred thousand," she said calmly.

Alexander didn't bat an eyelid. He had burned more than that on some of his wildest nights. A bit immoral, perhaps, but then he had never aspired to be the conscience of the world.

"Okay," he said. He had the great pleasure of watching Isobel Sørensen lose a bit of her cool doctor's composure.

"You're crazy."

He laughed. "Tell me something I haven't heard before."

She squirmed in her chair. "*Merde,* I should've asked for more."

"Don't push it," he said as he thought that he probably would have agreed to double that amount.

She chuckled, and the throaty sound sent a wave of lust coursing through him.

Maybe he *had* gone crazy after all.

But Isobel was both beautiful and intelligent. That in itself would have been enough to catch his eye. She disliked him, and that was another irresistible challenge. But there was something else about her. Something he caught a glimmer of every now and then, something secret and incomprehensible and maybe even a little chaotic, as though Doctor Sørensen had some kind of power she didn't quite have full control over.

"It's a date, then," she said.

He met her gaze. Her storm-gray eyes sent a thrill through him. It was the same feeling he'd had as a child, when he hadn't learned how to swim but had been nearing deep water where he couldn't touch the bottom. Isobel was a serious woman, one who commanded respect, who held responsibility. In other words, not his usual type at all.

He smiled. "It's a date," he agreed.

This should be fun.

Chapter 8

A s Peter De la Grip looked back at the past year, he often reflected upon the fact that (1) he had lost everything he had once taken for granted: his job, his wife, his possessions. And (2) it was entirely his own fault.

Eight months ago, he had been faced with an impossible choice. To achieve all he had ever worked toward or to atone for a terrible crime he'd once committed. He had chosen the latter, and it had felt damn good.

Until it didn't anymore.

So much had changed since then that he no longer knew who he really was. A life crisis, that was what the therapist he saw over the winter had called it. She was right, of course. But when she started to talk about his childhood and the bullying and his destructive relationship with his father, Peter had left and never gone back.

Maybe that had been stupid. Somewhere deep within, Peter knew that his lack of appetite, his trouble sleeping, and the leaden sensation in his chest were all signs of depression. That it wasn't normal to need all his energy just getting up, shaving, and getting dressed in the morning. Going to work.

He looked up from his e-mail. The workday was practically over, and the office was almost empty; most of his coworkers had gone home without saying good-bye to him. He had never been a particularly popular person, and since he'd lost his elevated position in the world of finance he had been disappearing into the background, becoming an anonymous part of the gray masses. His current job with one of the capital's financial institutions was way beneath his formal qualifications, but Peter was relieved by the low demands it placed on him. His peers enjoyed glittering careers, but he, someone who should have become the board chairman at Investum, the finest company in the nation, was here doing the same job as men ten years his junior. Not that he was complaining; he didn't care. He did his job, assessed credit reliability, approved or rejected loans without making a fuss. The rest of the time, he did very little. Most people he knew, his family included, treated him like a pariah. The exception was, perhaps, his half sister, Natalia. But that relationship was so complicated on so many levels, and he didn't really have any energy left to sort it out.

In the early days, right after The Scandal and his separation from his wife, Louise, his friends had invited him on weekend trips and to dinner, but those invitations had gradually petered out. Maybe they invited Louise now instead of him. What did he know? Or care. The last he'd heard of his ex-wife, she had already found a new man; the two of them were probably better company than the gloomy, brooding, wasted remainder of Peter De la Grip.

Every evening, he found himself sitting in his car, thinking that he should be headed to the gym. But instead he went home to his new, sparsely furnished flat and ended up in front of the TV or the computer. If he was lucky, he would sleep a couple of hours before insomnia caught up with him in the hour of the wolf.

His cell phone buzzed to life on his desk. Peter stared at the display. Alexander. His first impulse was to reject the call from his brother. They almost never spoke, and Peter doubted it was good news on the other end of the line. But his sense of duty won out.

"Hello?" he said guardedly.

"Are you at work? Can I come over?"

They hadn't seen one another since the christening. Not that they had spoken there, just acknowledged one another with a nod. Peter had felt as though he was in a bubble at the ceremony, had felt Alexander's eyes on him the entire time, seen the way people looked at him and then quickly averted their eyes again.

"What do you want?"

"I'll be there in ten," was all Alexander said before he hung up.

He wouldn't have thought Alexander knew where he worked. Goddamn it, he didn't want to see him. He looked out the window and wondered what would happen if he simply got up, left, and never came back to this place again.

Exactly ten minutes later, Alexander was opposite him in the visitor's chair. Alexander was like that, always on time when it mattered. Somehow, it annoyed Peter.

"I need your signature on these, apparently," Alexander said, and held up a plastic folder full of documents.

It was usually the other way around, and Peter had to chase Alexander to sign papers. It was crazy really, that two people who disliked one another so intensely could still be so tightly linked from a financial point of view. Although control of Investum had left the De la Grip family hands when David Hammar took over, they still jointly owned a number of other companies and foundations, which in turn were operated by other foundations. The structures were old, intended to protect an even older family fortune. Not even Alexander, with his lack of interest in everything to do with the family, could quite break free.

"What are they?" Peter asked as he began to leaf through the papers.

Alexander shrugged. "All kinds of stuff. Read for yourself."

Both he and Alexander had people to help them with their finances, who managed their money and dealt with the administrative side of things. But he and his little brother were, perhaps, more alike than one would think. Neither of them relinquished control. Ninety percent of the time, Alexander acted like a self-indulgent playboy, but Peter had seen flashes of brilliance from him, and he had always suspected that Alexander's nonchalance was partly an act for the world around him. Maybe a way to irritate their father. God knew, if that was the case, it had worked. Peter hadn't heard the man say a good word about his youngest son in years.

He glanced at his brother, sitting with one foot crossed over his knee and a bored look on his face. He was dressed in one of his perfectly tailored suits. And Peter knew, since he had once asked, that it cost a thousand dollars every other week to maintain that seemingly ruffled and slightly-too-long haircut. Alexander had always been extravagant. The apartment on the Upper West Side, the castle in Skåne, the over-the-top jet-set partying. Peter himself was wealthy by most people's standards, but it was a Swedish fortune, mostly inherited, managed by one of the traditional law firms. It meant a modest position in the lists of the country's wealthiest, occasional trips to the West Indies, a suitable apartment on Östermalm, a couple of cars, and a wardrobe full of quality suits. But Alexander associated with the richest people in the world. Where did that kind of money come from?

"What did you do with your Investum shares?" Peter asked as he searched his desk for a good pen.

"Sold them. I hated that company. You?"

Peter shrugged. "I was meant to take over, so I didn't hate it. But I sold most of them too."

Alexander bared his teeth in what passed for a smile. "It was a good deal."

"Yeah," Peter agreed. He was on the verge of smiling back. He wondered whether their father had kept his shares. Not that it mattered. The De la Grip family had been irrevocably removed from Investum, and his father would never speak to him again.

"How long do you plan to stay in Sweden this time?" he asked as he signed the document he had just read.

The fleeting warmth on Alexander's face disappeared. He gave Peter a frosty look. "Why?"

Peter was immediately on the defensive. "Just wondering."

"I'm actually looking at apartments on Strandvägen. So you won't be getting rid of me, if that was what you meant. We'll just have to stay out of each another's way. Shouldn't be too hard. If you avoid anything fun, I'll try to avoid all the tight-ass places."

Peter looked down. Did he want Alexander in Stockholm? Did he really need yet another sibling to remind him of just how unsuccessful he was? Wasn't it enough with Natalia, her perfect little family, and her fantastic career?

"Do you have a real estate agent?" he eventually asked.

Alexander gestured to the papers. "Could you just sign them so I can leave? I don't know why I came. I should have sent one of the people from the bank."

Peter studied the broad-shouldered man opposite him. It was like looking at a stranger. Alexander had been so slim and shy when he was younger. A sensitive soul who had cared for all living beings. He wanted to know how Alexander viewed their childhood. The questions the therapist had posed to him had woken so many thoughts about what shaped a person, what had made him who he was. Alexander had been beaten so often by their father when he was little. Peter too. Their father was a tyrant, and their childhoods weren't utterly different. And yet they had become different in so many respects. How had that happened? Which decisions had he himself made that had turned him into the person he was today? Alexander was a social genius, liked by everyone, while Peter felt increasingly lost. He couldn't just blame it on his environment. Maybe he had simply been born bad? A genuinely defective person. One of those people you read about sometimes, lacking empathy, disturbed. Evil. He glanced at Alexander. He was bobbing his handmade calfskin shoe up and down as he looked around without any real interest.

"Do you really like it here?" Alexander asked.

"It's okay."

"But isn't this place really goddamn depressing?"

"It's a job, Alexander. You might have heard of them. Even though you've never had one of your own."

Peter hadn't planned to sound quite so superior, but he couldn't help thinking that Alexander, with his gifts, should start doing something more meaningful. None of them really had to work, not from a financial point of view, but Peter had always thought that you needed to *do* something, and Alexander was so damned smart. After his military service, he had gone to the Stockholm School of Economics, a university Peter himself had never managed to get into. His little brother had proved himself to be financially brilliant, of course. At least before he'd gotten tired of it and headed to London to party instead. Peter, on the other hand, had been forced to fight for every single university credit he'd ever taken.

"I just mean that you're throwing your life away," he said.

Alexander plucked an invisible piece of dust from his jacket sleeve and gave him a look so cold that Peter shuddered. "You being the right person to preach about morality, of course?"

The silence, and the unspoken words between them, spread, engulfed them. Peter could hardly breathe. They had never spoken of . . .

He bent over the documents again as Alexander got to his feet. The low hum of a vacuum cleaner approached.

"Hi there, Gina!" Alexander called through the doorway.

Peter had completely forgotten that Gina had started to clean for the firm in the evenings. Someone, his sister maybe, must have given her a recommendation, and now she was here. Alexander murmured something, and Gina made one of those feminine head movements women typically made when they were drawn into Alexander's force field of charm. Peter himself had always had real trouble with women, and he knew that one of the reasons he didn't respond to the interested looks he still sometimes received was that he was worried he might end up doing something worse than he had already done.

"I'm almost done out there. Can I start in here?" Gina asked. "Empty the trash baskets and things like that?"

"We're a little busy," Peter said, but the moment the words left his mouth, he heard how wrong they sounded, how self-important and condescending.

Her lips tightened. Things always went wrong when he talked to Gina. He didn't know why he felt so insecure around her, why he froze and started to mumble the moment he spoke.

"We're almost done here, Gina," Alexander said, smoothing things over with a wide smile. "It's great to see you. Please, don't let us disturb you."

She looked slightly appeased. When she straightened her apron, Peter's eyes followed the movement. He tried to think of something to say, something casual. But words failed him. Gina had been with his family for several years now, but he had never managed to relax around her. Somehow, everything he said sounded idiotic. And then, when he tried to untangle himself, to show he wasn't all that bad, things just got worse.

"I've signed everything," he said instead. Alexander was leaning against the door frame, smiling at Gina. "You can go now," Peter continued dismissively. "I need to work a little longer." He looked at Gina. "And she needs to work too, so stop bothering her."

Alexander gave him a long look. "You're such a fucking jerk," he eventually said, and snatched up the papers. "Don't let him boss you around," he said to Gina.

Peter shoved his hands into his pockets, refused to let himself be outmaneuvered in his own office. Alexander left, and he breathed out.

"I'm going to leave soon, so you can work in peace," he said to Gina.

She left the room without a word and disappeared into the office. When Peter left half an hour later, there was no sign of her.

Chapter 9

The only good thing about it being Friday was that she would soon have made it through the dinner with Alexander, Isobel thought as she stepped out of the shower.

She must have regretted going along with this crazy idea at least a hundred times by now. She should have said no. It went completely against all of her principles. But Alexander had surprised her, and now here she was: with newly waxed legs and curls in her hair.

What would they say at Medpax if they knew what she'd done? She could tell herself it wasn't weird for her to be going out with him as much as she liked, that he was just one donor of many. But it *felt* weird. She was used to finding creative solutions to the most unexpected problems. Had used her own tights as a bandage, sawed-off broom handles to splint broken legs, and paid bribes to get ahold of vital drugs. But a date like this, did that really fit into the same category? The issue was, she thought as she slathered herself in scented skin lotion she rarely used, that a tiny part of her was looking forward to it.

She remembered how Alexander had looked when they'd met those first few times. As though he had just visited some kind of private hell. That wasn't quite so plain any longer, but there was an occasional flash of it in those impossibly blue eyes, something that made her wonder what he was really hiding behind the charming devil-may-care façade.

She loosened the clip holding her hair up and shook out the curls.

The best thing would be if she could go on the date, secure the hundred thousand kronor, and then get out as quickly as she could.

It would be even better if she had any idea what to wear.

She cast a dissatisfied glance into her wardrobe and finally pulled out a dress she'd bought on sale before a donor dinner a few years earlier. She had never worn it. The thing was, people told her she was beautiful. Not every day, of course, but it happened. And men sometimes did a double take as she passed, at least when she had her hair down and wasn't in a bad mood. She shouldn't be so insecure about her appearance. It was just that her greatest asset had always been her brain. In school, she'd been the tall, weird girl who spoke French and Danish and blushed on a regular basis. She hadn't been bullied, exactly, but she had been an outsider, hadn't quite understood the subtle codes that made certain girls popular and others . . . something else.

And then she had somehow managed to catch up with herself, just in time to start her medical studies. People bloomed at different ages, and she was simply better suited to being a grown-up doctor than she had been a gangly teenager. But her self-confidence with regards to her looks had never quite caught up. And it hadn't gotten any better when she fell in love with . . . She shuddered, rapidly chasing *that* memory away.

She studied the red dress thoughtfully. The price tag dangled accusingly toward her. She had bought it because it flattered her body. It emphasized her waist and legs, and with the right bra it actually made her look quite okay, if she said so herself. But it needed high heels to come into its own, and she had wimped out when it actually came to wearing it, and had chosen a safe dress and low pumps for the dinner. Still, that dinner had gone very well, and she'd managed to bring in a new donor.

This time, there was a hundred thousand kronor at stake. Money that could mean so much to their hospital, to children who had literally nothing, boys like Marius. Medpax wasn't a wealthy organization. The hospital needed everything. Appliances. Personnel. Medicine. She had made her decision to go back to Chad. Was already looking forward to seeing Idris. And Marius. One hundred thousand kronor was a fortune here in Sweden. In Chad it was more than that. It was the difference between dead children and living children.

In the end there was no question.

Alexander was already waiting in the bar. Isobel saw his eyes widen a fraction when he caught sight of her, and then he did something she knew she wasn't supposed to notice. He looked her body up and down, just for a split second, before he met her gaze. He came toward her, like a gentleman, ignoring everything in the room in favor of her.

"Hey," he said quietly.

She wouldn't have thought it was possible, but Alexander looked even more handsome than last time. He had on slim gray pants and a dark jacket, with a tight black T-shirt underneath. His blond hair looked golden against the muted colors. She was far from a fashion expert, but even she could see that he looked stylish, wealthy . . . and hot.

She shook her hair, hoped she didn't have lipstick on her teeth, gripped her clutch beneath her arm, and held out her hand.

Alexander looked down at it for a moment. A smile played on his lips, but then he politely held out his own hand and shook hers.

"Have you been here before?" he asked.

"No, but I've read about this place. I heard it was impossible to get a table."

"Yeah. I felt like I needed to boost my stock a little. Our meetings have been a bit . . . ahem, tense." He held out a hand and she sat down on the stool next to his. "Champagne?"

Isobel heard herself say yes, despite the fact she hadn't been planning to drink this evening. But one small glass, what harm could it do?

She was handed a tall glass of nearly ice-cold Bollinger. They toasted and she took a sip. Sweet Jesus, so good.

"They don't have menus," Alexander said once they'd gotten their table. He had given her the seat with the best view of the restaurant, and she had to remind herself, quite firmly, that she was here for work.

"The chef presents a tasting menu."

Damn it.

"What?" he asked, studying her.

"I'm actually a vegetarian," she said apologetically, not wanting to cause a fuss. "But it's okay. I'm not so strict."

Alexander smiled, and Isobel thought that it was biologically impossible not to be attracted to him. It was as though there were just two poles: attracted to Alexander or dead. It made no difference how much she reminded herself what she *really* thought of him. He was like a force of nature.

"Don't say that. I like that you're strict," he murmured. His eyes were hooded, and his voice had an undertone that went right through her. Or maybe it was just the champagne. The waiter took the bottle from the bucket and refilled her glass. Somehow, it was already empty.

"Could you ask Anna to come out?" Alexander inquired.

"The chef. I know her," he explained once the waiter had disappeared.

Of course he did.

The chef was a young woman with a serious face. Alexander stood up when she approached, and they shook hands.

"My guest here doesn't eat meat," said Alexander.

Anna looked at her. "Fish?"

"Ideally no," Isobel replied apologetically.

"No problem. We'll figure something out."

"Thanks," said Isobel.

"Good to see you, Alexander," said Anna, before she gave them both a quick nod and disappeared.

Alexander sat back down with a pleased look.

He just kept on earning points, Isobel admitted to herself. She was used to finding herself in endless discussions about being a vegetarian, most often with men who enjoyed explaining how wrong she was, but he just accepted it and adapted.

"Is that why we got a table? Because you know the chef?" she asked.

"I'm actually a part owner here. Though it's my best friend, Romeo, who owns and runs the restaurant. I provided the capital when he started his first place. He has several now, all over the world, and I've kept investing. It means I always get a table, which suits me just fine.

Anna's one of the world's best chefs, by the way," he said as the food began to arrive.

A tiny little dish.

Isobel gave him a suspicious look. Was this a joke? She was starving. She had been working hard all week, cycled everywhere. And she had just drunk two glasses of champagne on an empty stomach. If she didn't get more food, she would commit a murder.

"There'll be twelve courses," he said with a glimmer in his eye. "I promise you won't leave here hungry, Isobel."

"If you say so," she said, not entirely convinced. She took a small bite. The taste was sensational, salty and sour, the texture both soft and crispy.

"Why do I get the feeling you don't trust me?" he asked.

No matter how much the pheromones and the alcohol affected her, Isobel still had full control of her brain, and yes, he was right, she didn't trust him at all. He was polite and had made an effort for her, but there was more to trust than that.

She put down her cutlery, picked up her glass. "Do I have to answer that?"

"But I'm so trustworthy."

"You live in New York, don't you?" she asked in an attempt to change the topic of conversation as more food arrived. The dishes were small, modernist masterpieces. She couldn't even identify what most of it was; she just listened to the poetic descriptions and then ate, drank—though more cautiously now—and enjoyed.

"Yeah, for a few years now."

She knew where he lived; several journalists had written about the expensive apartment in Manhattan where the Swede lived alongside princes and multibillionaires. She had trouble even imagining that kind of wealth.

"What do you do there?" She watched as a green soup was poured from a transparent jug.

"Nothing much."

"You don't work?"

Alexander studied her for a moment. He played with his glass. "The official version is that I party hard, drink too much, and sleep too little."

Isobel thought back to all the gossip she had read. She hadn't been able to stop herself. Now she wondered how it felt, to be exposed like that.

"Isn't that true, then?" she asked.

A serious look flashed across his face, followed by something else, before his usual blinding smile reappeared. He shrugged. "I guess so," he said, and Isobel knew he was lying.

In other words, Alexander would rather that she, a woman he clearly wanted to impress, saw him as a superficial playboy than tell her what he really spent his days doing. Apparently she wasn't the only one with trust issues.

She put down her spoon and studied him as objectively as she could. There was more to Alexander than she had initially thought. Most people were multidimensional, after all. He was considerate toward her, was kind to the waitresses, and so far hadn't allowed his gaze to wander to any other woman in the restaurant. That deserved a gold star, in Isobel's book.

"You're a count too, right?" she asked as she bit into a small, fried dumpling. Though maybe Alexander didn't have all that many sides. Maybe he was exactly what he appeared to be: a man who had been given everything in life and didn't think about anything other than his own enjoyment. She almost hoped that was the case. It would make it easier to dismiss him.

He pulled a face. "I hate being called count. I never use my title."

She dipped the last of the dumpling in the spicy sauce. There was a certain self-importance in his reply, of course. Only someone who had been born into privilege could dismiss it so nonchalantly. Still, she decided to let it pass.

"Tell me about your work with Doctors Without Borders," he said.

"What do you want to know?" She set her cutlery down at the side of her plate. She had lost count of the courses but hoped there would be a dessert or two included.

"Anything you want to talk about."

He was giving her attention in order to flatter her; she knew it, but it made no difference. She was here to work, and maybe she was doing the same to him.

"I'm part of a small group of senior field-workers, an emergency pool. We get sent on acute missions at short notice."

"Where to?"

She shrugged. "Wherever we're needed. War zones, natural disasters. Asia. Africa. There was a huge hurricane in the Pacific last month. We get sent to places like that." She thought of Syria, where it was too dangerous for them to work, of the streams of refugees and the camps. The world was an uncertain place for far too many people.

He looked attentively at her, but she hesitated. This was where it was always difficult to find a balance. How much should she tell him? Some people couldn't cope. All the same, she wanted to talk about it.

"Working for MSF involves a few things. There's the actual work in the field, of course. We're often the first on the scene, sometimes in places where there isn't any medical care at all. You see things that . . ." She fell silent.

"That?"

"That shouldn't exist. And I'm not just talking about what people do to one another in war. The illnesses. The children who die because they're too weak, too undernourished."

"It sounds awful."

"Yes. It makes you doubt so much in this world."

"Last time, you mentioned that you can cope because it goes well sometimes."

It made her happy that Alexander remembered. Some people simply wanted to hear about the grizzly stuff, but many of her best memories came from some of the worst places on earth.

"That's what's so incredible. I never feel so appreciated as a doctor as when I'm in the field. To see an undernourished child start to laugh again. To cure malaria, which is an incredibly easily treated illness, really. It's an enormous paradox. You're on your knees, always afraid, almost always crying, constantly feeling like you're not doing enough, but at the same time you're living fully."

His eyes were warm, and Isobel found herself getting caught up in them. He was a great listener. "It sounds as though it can be pretty intense," he said.

"It is. By the end of each trip, you're completely done. You make mistakes and cross boundaries just because you're so tired. And then maybe three kids you're responsible for die, and you happen to go on to Facebook and see someone moaning about the weather, and everything suddenly just feels too much."

He didn't speak, just continued to rest his chin in his hand and look attentively at her. He had the most beautiful hands she had ever seen, big, dappled with golden hair. She had always loved hands, could still remember how she had reeled off the Latin names in med school: *carpus, metacarpus, digiti manus*. The wrists, the palms, the fingers.

"And you get very close to one another in the field," she continued. She heard herself lower her voice, realized she had leaned forward slightly. "In a way you never quite manage at home. It's very special." She fell silent. She didn't normally talk about this part of her life.

"You said that there were several things involved in being an MSF doctor?" he reminded her.

"The other is bearing witness," she said as the desserts started to appear. She chose a small glass and picked up a spoon. It tasted heavenly, of course. Sour berries, caramelized notes. A few grains of salt. She sighed contentedly.

"MSF doesn't take sides in conflicts. We're not armed, we keep away from the military. But we bear witness to what we see. We're a voice for the weak and stand up when crimes are committed. So when I get back from a mission, one of my jobs is to talk about what I've seen and what I've heard. Some MSF doctors run blogs, others write articles or books."

"Yeah, I read some of those blogs and articles these past days. It's hard not to be impressed."

She put down her dessert spoon. Didn't know what to do with the knowledge that Alexander had been reading up on her job.

"What strikes you, out there, is how similar we all are. That grandparents care about their grandkids, parents worry about their children's schooling and their future, people fall in love—it's the same no matter where you're from."

"There are no differences?"

"Well, of course there are. The women I meet often feel sorry for me, for example."

"Why?"

"Because I don't have a husband. It used to cause so much trouble that these days, I tell them that the minute I get home I'm going to get married and have kids. Otherwise I just can't work, because all the focus is on the poor, unmarried, childless doctor."

Alexander laughed.

"I swear. Once, a group of village women even got together to find me a husband. I only just managed to get out of it."

He laughed again, picked up his glass, and sipped from it. "Your surname, though, it's not Swedish?"

"My father was Danish." A stern, absent man who asked about nothing but her grades on those few occasions he came home. With her father, you talked about international politics. And you didn't disagree. "And I've got French heritage on my mother's side," she continued. "But both my grandmothers were Swedes. So I'm just one big ethnic mix of French, Danish, and Swedish."

He smiled. "Not a bad mix."

"I've just been going on and on about myself," she said. "It's your turn."

"What do you want to know?"

What she *really* wanted to know was if Alexander was single, but she contented herself with asking: "How did your foundation end up giving money to Medpax of all organizations?"

He shrugged. "No idea. We give money to all kinds of places. It was probably some kind of tax thing."

And there it was again. The superficial, self-indulgent Alexander she detested. It was almost a relief to be reminded of it.

"I thought you were against aid work."

"No, not at all. Why should I be?"

"Because you said it was pointless," she reminded him.

"I'm not against people trying to improve the world; I just wonder whether it's possible. People are fundamentally selfish, and look out for their own interests."

"Are you talking about yourself now?" she couldn't help but ask.

"I've worked hard to acquire my vices. I like them. And I think most people are like me."

"And yet you plan to give Medpax one hundred thousand kronor after this evening?"

"I wanted to spend an evening with a beautiful woman. It's a purely selfish act."

She remembered all the gorgeous women he had been linked to. Countless, that was the first word that came to mind. There was even a song about him, written by some pop superstar, wasn't there? "You probably could've gotten more for your money, if that's the case," she said ironically.

He laughed. "Ah, Isobel, now you're just fishing. Let me pay you a compliment, my suspicious doctor. The first time I saw you, I thought you were beautiful. Tonight you look completely fucking fantastic. Your hair, your dress—you're easily the most stunning woman in the room. Plus, I get to listen to you talk about your work. Believe me, this date has been worth every cent."

She shook her head. He really was good at this.

When Isobel was twenty, back when she started her medical studies, she had begun to emerge from her cocoon of awkward adolescence. The university environment had suited her better than the claustrophobic high school atmosphere, and she felt happier, more beautiful, and more confident than ever before. For a few wonderful months, she had soared. Her studies, her newfound freedom, her new friends. Everything had just felt easier.

And then she fell in love. Hopelessly and utterly, head over heels in love, with an older man. He was everything she had ever dreamed of, and she had been so terribly inexperienced when it came to love. Unaccustomed to men looking at her, embarrassingly naïve. And so she had made bad choices, allowed him to get much too close, and it had ended in total disaster.

Even today, Isobel was deeply thankful she had managed to finish her studies after the affair ended. She had learned so much from the experience. About love. Men. Sex. But she was thirty now, no longer an inexperienced medical student who wore her heart on her sleeve. She could make the distinction between attraction and other feelings, and life in the field had taught her what she really needed and valued. Kindness, loyalty, and reliability were at the top of her list. She gave Alexander a searching look, and surmised that his list probably looked quite different.

He leaned forward over the table. "This wasn't exactly the reaction I was hoping for. Did I say something wrong?"

She shook her head. "Sorry, I just got caught up thinking about something else. Thanks for the compliment."

"What was it? What caught you?"

She peered down into the jet-black coffee in her espresso cup. "Nothing," she said. Because it was nothing. Even if it defined her entire being.

When they stepped out onto Västmannagatan, it was close to midnight.

"Can you walk in those?" Alexander asked, with a glance at her high heels.

"Yes, I'd like to walk a little."

"I transferred the money," he said, and held up his phone as they passed the bustling Odenplan. A night bus passed.

"Thanks." How she appreciated that he had done it immediately, that he didn't leave her to wonder. She should feel relieved, she thought as they continued down toward Sveavägen, one of the wide boulevards that cut across the city. Should be happy it was over. Shouldn't care that he was clearly done with the flirting for the evening. She took a misstep and wobbled on an uneven patch of asphalt. Alexander's hand shot out, lightning quick, to catch her.

"Careful," he said, letting go of her just as quickly.

Isobel couldn't help it; her mood was plunging. Stupid. But maybe she had hoped Alexander would suggest a drink. She might even have done it herself if she hadn't sat on a too high horse; now she would have trouble getting down. She glanced around. Not that there were many places to grab a drink where they were right now. She shivered a little. When she'd left home, it was warm and sunny, a balmy spring evening. But now she could feel just how thin her clothing really was. She would have to take a taxi. In silence, they turned onto Sveavägen. She would go home, she decided. Drink tea and get on with her *real* life. What had she expected? She was hardly his type; she hadn't given him any reason to believe she was interested in anything beyond this one dinner. And she wasn't interested, she reminded herself.

"I think I'm going to . . ." she began.

"Have you been here before?" he asked at the same time.

Isobel glanced up at the façade, glowing in neon. "La Habana," she read as a door opened and music flowed out onto the street. A woman with long hair and a tight dress came out with a man in an unbuttoned shirt. They were laughing. The man pulled the woman to him and kissed her.

Isobel averted her eyes. "What is it?" She had never even seen the place before; the lettering on the neon sign looked like something from the fifties.

"A Cuban nightclub. Have you ever been to Cuba?"

"No. But I suppose you have?"

She could just see it: Alexander and his golden beauty, sitting beneath a palm tree with a cigar in his mouth; sweaty, suntanned.

There was laughter in his eyes when he looked at her.

"They have dengue fever there," she pointed out.

A glint of humor warmed his eyes. "You would know, of course. But they also have the best drinks and the best music in the world." Loud music came pouring out toward them as the doors opened again.

"Salsa," he continued with the air of a connoisseur, and grabbed the door before it closed. He held it open. The suggestive tones beckoned them in.

"Shall we?" he asked. There was something dangerous in his eyes. As though he was testing whether she dared follow him in, challenging her to try something out of her comfort zone. She hesitated. It was stupid, really. Her entire life was about being able to perform far from safety and comfort. But still. Going to a nightclub with Alexander De la Grip? She was about to say no, completely out of reflex. She couldn't remember the last time she'd danced. And *salsa*. Didn't you need to know the steps? Have at least some kind of sense of rhythm?

But then Alexander raised an eyebrow at her, challenging her. And there and then, on the street outside the slightly faded, old nightclub, Isobel suddenly felt that more than anything in the world, she wanted to stop being sensible, to do something crazy and impulsive. Wanted to unbalance him a little.

Just once, she thought. No one needs to find out.

She held her head high and met his eye.

"Just what I was about to suggest," she said.

And with that, she swept past him, as though she did nothing other than spend time in sweaty nightclubs accompanied by men with dangerous eyes.

Alexander's hand shot out just as she passed. It caught her upper arm, and Isobel blinked. As her shoulder brushed up against his chest, she caught the scent of his aftershave. He leaned in to her until his mouth grazed her hair and her ear. She held very still, a low shiver spreading beneath her skin.

"Bravo, Isobel," he murmured, letting go of the door and following her in.

Chapter 10

Alexander's gaze was fixed on Isobel's softly swaying hips. He liked to see her in that racy red dress, her hair cascading around her shoulders. She looked like a film star from the old days, one of those quick and witty women. And he *loved* that she had allowed herself to be provoked into going to a nightclub. The struggle on her face had been fascinating to follow

The music was loud, and the floor was tightly packed with warm, dancing bodies. He hadn't wanted to take her to Stureplan, the glittering playground of the wealthy and spoiled, where he was sure he would be recognized; he wanted Isobel all to himself, and when he heard the music, he'd known it was the perfect place for them. Still, he hadn't expected a live band, and he felt the suggestive music course through his body. With a smile, he held out a hand to her. She took it and allowed herself to be led onto the dance floor.

He grabbed both of her hands and pulled her close to him. "Just follow me," he shouted into her ear over the music.

She said something that sounded like "Oh, *Jesus*" and then did as he said, cautiously and focused at first, like she was studying some complicated procedure, but then with increasing self-confidence. Salsa was the world's most intuitive dance, and Cuban salsa encouraged physical contact. Alexander knew he was a proficient dancer. The club was warm, and when Alexander took off his jacket, he saw her eyes move over his body. He noticed how her décolletage glistened. Isobel was smoking hot, but she was also an unexpectedly fun dance partner. Not self-conscious, once her initial uncertainty passed, but fearless, bold, and laughing.

The music grew in intensity. It was a quick salsa, hot, almost electrifying. The lights dimmed, hips rolled, hands clapped. Alexander held out his hand and she took it, warm and sweaty but steady. She allowed herself to be drawn in, spun to and from him. He pulled her close once more, pressed her warm body to his again and again. Occasionally she lost track of what she was doing, but he caught her each time, and the more songs they danced, the more often they ended up in perfect rhythm, drawing closer and closer, moving apart and then coming together again with the trumpets, guitars, drums. Over and over, quicker and quicker, until both were breathing heavily, chest to chest. Isobel's hair was damp and heavy, and it snaked over her throat and her arms. One last burst of energy and the music fell silent. Applause broke out.

When the musicians announced they would take a break, Alexander pulled her over to the bar.

"Just water, please," she said, as she wiped the sweat from her forehead and flashed him a brilliant smile. He wanted to lean forward and kiss her lips, lick the sweat from her neck, pull her sensational curves toward him . . .

He was interrupted by a hand on his arm. He turned and saw Gina.

"Well, hello there," he said cheerfully, and gave her a quick hug. "What're you doing here?"

"I'm just here with some friends. What are *you* doing here; is this really your kind of place?"

"Of course it is. This is Gina, my friend," he said, turning to Isobel.

Gina grinned and practically forced her way past Alexander.

"I know who you are," she said eagerly to Isobel. "I saw you dancing and had to come over to say hi. I'm studying to become a doctor—I was at your lecture on refugee medicine."

Alexander wasn't sure he had ever heard the usually taciturn Gina talk so much.

"I remember you," Isobel said kindly, as she shook Gina's hand. "You were at the front, and you came up to me afterward. How do you two know one another?" she asked, with a questioning look at Alexander.

"Gina's part of the family," Alexander quickly replied, not wanting to give Isobel the wrong impression. He turned to Gina. She was essentially ignoring him, gazing at Isobel with worship in her eyes.

A thought struck him. "Gina, you don't work here too, do you?"

She gestured toward a table of young people. "We're celebrating an exam. It's, like, the first time I've been out in a couple of years. But it was a big exam."

"Which one?" asked Isobel.

"The Healthy Human."

"I remember it, lots of chemistry and biology. Tough stuff. Did it go well?"

Gina nodded, and Alexander thought it looked like she was blushing. Serious Gina Adan starstruck, it seemed almost inconceivable. "Really well. But I don't want to bother you," Gina said, giving Alexander a look that clearly communicated she's-much-too-good-for-you before she disappeared.

When the music started back up again, Alexander glanced at Isobel.

"Enough for me," she said. "My muscles are going to hurt tomorrow."

"How are you getting home?" he asked once they were back out on the street. Fuck, he didn't want to say good-bye. Not yet. But it was late and she was a working woman.

"I'll take a cab."

"Okay," he said softly. He raised a hand and brushed a strand of hair from her face. She looked at him, and he leaned forward and kissed her on the cheek. He hadn't planned on anything more than a peck, but somehow he couldn't quite tear himself away from her smooth skin, and so when she didn't move, they remained standing like that until she started to shiver.

"You're cold."

He started to take off his jacket, but she moved away from him.

"No, Alexander, I need to go home now."

He knew that she didn't just mean that it was late and she was tired. It was clear that the statement was an attempt to distance herself from him.

"Thanks for a great evening," she continued. There was nothing but politeness in her voice now—no flirtation, no laughter, no invitation to more kissing or to more intimate dancing. She waved to a cab that was coming down the near-empty Sveavägen. Alexander opened the door to the backseat and she climbed in, said good night, and he closed it.

He watched her drive away, stood like that until the car was gone.

He buttoned up his jacket, shoved his hands into the pockets. Headed toward his hotel. Something had scared Isobel and she had run. She probably thought it was over between them, but Alexander knew better. He wasn't done with Isobel. Not by a long shot.

When Alexander woke the next morning, he had come up with the next steps in his plan. He spent the whole of Saturday on the couch in his hotel room, watching TV, surfing the web, and reading simultaneously. He often found it hard to be still for long periods, had always been easily distracted, but he found it easier to concentrate when the TV was on. After a quick trip to a couple of bookstores, he lay on the sofa and read until long after midnight.

He spent Sunday with his real estate agent, who had broken off his golf plans ("No problem, Alexander, you can call me day or night") to show him some of the apartments he had listed. In each of them, Alexander paused on the threshold of the biggest bedroom. He couldn't help it. He peered into these rooms and fantasized about an extra-large bed, made up with the finest Egyptian cotton, and Isobel naked in it, dressed only in her red hair. Long legs, thousands of freckles, tantalizing curves. He didn't want to take her to his hotel suite—she was worth more than that—but having said that, he wanted her in his bed. And soon.

"I'll take it," he told the real estate agent in the third apartment. The rooms were in a line, the ceilings high and the kitchen modern.

"I have more we can look at."

"I want this one. And I want access immediately. Can you arrange it?"

On Monday morning, he signed the contract and was handed the keys, and by the afternoon he'd contacted the interior design company his sister's best friend, Åsa Bjelke, had recommended. When he set his mind to it, he could make things happen pretty damn fast.

* * *

When Alexander stepped into the private health clinic on Valhallavägen on Tuesday morning, he was in an excellent mood. He'd been for a jog, had a shower, and had a clear goal; he felt practically invincible.

"I have an appointment with Doctor Sørensen," he said with a wide smile and handed his ID card to the receptionist.

She blushed, entered him into the system, and said, "Thanks. Please have a seat."

Alexander was too restless to sit, so he remained standing until Isobel appeared in the waiting lounge.

"Hello, doctor," he said.

She eyed him suspiciously. There was no trace of the laughing, dancing woman of the weekend. She looked stern. "What are you doing here?"

"Why don't you have a white coat? I like women in uniform. I have an appointment," he added.

Isobel cast a questioning glance toward the receptionist, who confirmed what he claimed with a nod.

"Come on, then," she said.

Alexander sat down in the visitor's chair as Isobel took a seat at her desk, placed a hand on the surface, and gazed calmly at him.

"I need medical attention," he said. "That's why I'm here. Thanks for the other night, by the way."

"Yes, thank you. What can I help you with?"

He wondered what Isobel had done over the weekend. Did this beautiful, serious doctor have a boyfriend? For some reason, he had assumed she was married to the job, but assumptions were one thing—*knowing* was something entirely different. Maybe she had a whole host of lovers?

"I'm waiting," she reminded him.

"I bought a flat on Strandvägen yesterday," he said.

"And you're telling me this why?"

"I'm making conversation. Did you know that it isn't actually Africa that needs the Western world's help, but the other way around? We need Africa and its natural resources. By exploiting them for ourselves, we condemn African countries to poverty."

"Yes."

"But did you know that you can get malaria only at night?"

"Since it's my job to know that, yes, I did. People usually get bitten at night or in the evening. Why do you know that?"

"I read a fascinating book over the weekend. A few, actually."

"About Africa?"

"Yes. And humanitarian aid, and Doctors Without Borders. Among others. It ended up being a good number of books. And articles on-line. And podcasts." He rested a foot on his knee. He had looked her up, found a CV. Impressive was an understatement. Specialist here, Harvard education in catastrophe medicine there. And she was still only thirty. Would be turning thirty-one in November. Granddaughter of Karin Jansson Pelletier, the painter and sculptor. "When you asked me what I did in New York, I lied a little."

"I guessed as much."

"Really? You're even smarter than you look. Anyway, when I'm not partying, I'm studying. Psychology, sociology, ecology, anthropology. Pretty much anything that ends with an -ology, actually."

She blinked. "Why?" she eventually asked, as though she had been trying to solve a complex chemical equation but failed.

"I can't say—you'll just think even less of me."

"I could argue that wouldn't be possible," she said drily.

"Nothing is impossible." He gave her an accusing look. "And I thought my stock had gone up."

"From a purely theoretical viewpoint, plenty of things are impossible. And as far as your stock is concerned, it's still pretty unstable. Why only things ending in -ology?"

"I study the subjects my father looks down on. His sons should read economics or law. So I do everything else."

"Sounds childish," she said.

Alexander stretched his legs out in front of him and gave her an amused look. Did Isobel really think he was so easily provoked? He had been called much, much worse things than childish over the years. And he hadn't just read a load of books and articles over the week-end. He had also watched old TV clips. Among other things, he'd found an interview with Blanche Sørensen, Isobel's beautiful ice-queen mother. Again and again, he had seen the way Blanche pursed her lips every time MSF was mentioned. *Cowboys, hippies,* and *irresponsible* were words that recurred whenever Blanche spoke about the organization her daughter had chosen to work for.

"So you've never done anything just to defy your mother, to rebel? Why did you choose to work for MSF again?"

"Touché," she said with a smile.

He laughed and thought that what he wanted right now was to get up, pull her from her chair, and give her a kiss. Instead, he peered around her examining room. She had the obligatory posters of muscles and organs in cross-section on the walls, and a whiteboard. On a bookshelf, a plastic skull sat next to various medical reference books. A stethoscope and blood pressure meter rested on her desk. His eyes fell on a small photo, pinned to the whiteboard with a magnet advertising stomach ulcer medicine.

"Is that from Chad?" he asked as he took a closer look. Isobel was surrounded by laughing children, the stereotype of the white, colonial doctor among dark-skinned kids.

But her laugh was genuine, and the photographer had captured a vulnerability in her face. He wondered who had taken the photo.

Her eyes lingered on it.

"I'm going back there soon."

"Soon? I thought you just came home."

"We're working out the details, but it'll be before summer."

Hmm. Suddenly, he had a deadline to work against. It shouldn't be a problem. A wave of excitement rushed through him. He loved this, the chase; it was the best part. And she had just inadvertently raised the stakes. Isobel was without a doubt one of the most attractive women he had ever chased. Yup, this spring had every chance of being really entertaining. And if he was honest, he had liked all the reading over the weekend, making his brain work. The fact that he enjoyed studying was probably one of his best-kept secrets.

"So, Alexander De la Grip, age twenty-nine, here during emergency hours," Isobel read aloud from her computer screen. She gave him a skeptical look. "There doesn't seem to be anything urgently wrong with you."

He held up a hand. "I've got a box-moving injury."

She squinted without leaning forward. "A what?"

"Can't you see it? A cut."

"You got an appointment for that scratch? With me?"

"I can be very convincing."

"Oh, I'm sure you can. But a nurse could put a Band-Aid on that. From what I can see, the receptionist could probably do it."

"I'm a little disappointed, I have to say. I was imagining how you would tend to my wound, show me some care and sympathy. Aren't you going to put your hand on my forehead at the very least? Are you sure you're a real doctor?"

Isobel smiled. She slowly moved her fingers together until they formed an airy triangle, and her eyes glittered. "I can cut something open if you like. Or sew something up—I'm no surgeon, but I'm very good with a scalpel and a suture needle. Or maybe you want an exam involving rubber gloves and an index finger?"

He stifled a laugh as she looked meaningfully at a paper box of single-use gloves.

"As erotic as that sounds, I think I'll pass."

She laughed. When she crossed her legs, he couldn't help but follow the movement with his eyes. The dancing on Friday had been so hot. Isobel in that red dress plastered to her curves, her hips rocking. The thought alone turned him on. She had on something like a shirt today, and looked cool and professional. The woman really was a study in opposites. Her hair was gathered at the nape of her neck, but loose strands gently framed her face.

"Plus, I don't want to take up vital doctor's time," he continued. He had persuaded the receptionist to give him an appointment, but he suddenly realized that he might have taken it from someone with a genuine emergency. It had been an impulse to call the doctor's office, a joke, but now he wondered whether it was really all that funny.

"My patients here are rarely in great need," she said.

Of course. It was one of the country's few truly expensive private clinics. What did it do to a person, to be thrown between the richest and the most vulnerable? Between Westerners who could get the best care in the world and children who died of simple infections? Why had he never thought about the injustice of his ability to buy Isobel's time when people literally died because they couldn't see a doctor? He shook off those thoughts. This was what happened when you got too involved. Things got complicated.

"I should probably go before I agree to something painful."

"Afraid of pain?"

"Very. It's only normal."

Isobel flashed him a quick smile. Something elusive and private flickered across her face and disappeared before Alexander had time to interpret it. It was as though she had thought of a joke she didn't care to share with him.

"But while I'm here, stealing crucial time from your dying patients, I wondered whether you would go to a concert with me on Friday?" He said it breezily but realized he was holding his breath as he waited for an answer.

She placed a hand on the table and gave him an apologetic look. "I'm sorry, Alexander, I can't."

Can't or won't?

"What about Saturday, then? Opera? Ballet? The Bolshoi Ballet is giving a guest performance."

She shook her head. "I'll be away, in Skåne. A weekend event. Leila and I are chasing financiers. I promised to go."

The woman really didn't do much other than work.

"That's okay." And it really was; he had put the pieces together in less than two seconds. "Some other time then," he said noncommittally. He had the great joy of seeing a flicker of disappointment in her big, gray eyes. So, she wasn't quite as cool as she made out.

But Isobel said nothing, she simply got to her feet and he did the same. She smiled, not her cool doctor's smile but a real, warm smile, and she held out a hand to him. Alexander studied it for a moment. He sighed. The eternal hand shaking she insisted on. He laid a hand on her upper arm, saw her eyes widen, dipped his head, felt his cheek brush against loose strands of red hair, and gave her a kiss. Only another peck on the cheek, but lower down this time, close to the edge of her mouth. He allowed his lips to linger. She was completely still, as though he had surprised her, and his lips brushed her skin, cool and soft and velvet smooth, her scent fresh and with just a touch of disinfectant.

Isobel breathed in and placed a hand on his chest. Reluctantly, he let her pull away, and found himself lost in her beautiful, intelligent eyes; they looked as though they wanted to ask a thousand questions.

"See you later, Isobel," he said quietly.

She blinked slowly.

And that was how he left her, wondering and a little dazed. He wasn't the least bit confused. Fate had clearly decided to be on his side, and now it was game on.

Chapter 11

As Gina made her rounds of the office in the financial building, she listened to a lecture through her headphones. It was what she normally did, record important lectures so she could listen to them whenever she had the opportunity. Some of them she had heard so many times that she knew them by heart. Cleaning flats and offices was a good job from that point of view. She was left to her own devices. The lecture she was listening to right now was one of her all-time favorites: Doctor Isobel Sørensen talking about catastrophe medicine at Karolinska Institutet last fall. Isobel Sørensen. Wow. If she had one wish, it was to be as cool as that woman one day.

Gina had been completely starstruck when she saw Dr. Sørensen at La Habana. And she was *not* easily impressed. As she scrubbed at a particularly stubborn coffee ring, Gina wondered what a woman like Isobel was doing with a man like Alexander. But then again she had never understood why women chose certain men. She herself had never felt more than mild affection for a man. But maybe that was just how things were when you'd lived in fear of being married off until you were eleven, and then had been constantly terrified of being raped by one of the men who helped you flee through Africa and Europe to Sweden. And life in the dangerous accommodations provided to asylum seekers hadn't exactly increased her confidence in the nature of men either.

She moved on to the next desk, gave it a quick rub with a damp cloth, saw the pale children and blond wife framed in gold. She studied the photo thoughtfully. They all had photos just like this on their desks. Wives in pastel-colored cardigans, two or three well-groomed children. Some idyllic landscape in the background. The few women who worked in the office had a man in a suit and nearly identical children in their frames. If she was honest, Gina didn't understand these men at all. The white upper class. The lottery winners. They were completely fascinating—it was as though they knew nothing about life. At best, they were just unconcerned playboys like Alexander. At worst, racist pigs who tried to steer her into a quiet room for a bit of a grope the moment they got the chance.

And then there were men like Peter De la Grip.

Gina glanced to the doorway; she could see Peter at his desk. He had his own corner office, and he was always the last to leave. In a way, she'd long seen Peter as the stereotype for all men in his position. Superior and condescending, unaware of how others in society lived. But then, last year, he had started to change. She cleaned for other families, and she knew what had happened that extraordinary day last summer. People gossiped, and she was used to vanishing into the background. So she knew that he had snapped at the board meeting. That he suddenly had turned against his own family, and that his parents since then refused to have anything to do with him. And that his pale, horrid wife had left him in a fury. It was pretty much all people had talked about for weeks. He seemed to be disappearing into himself. Bad spirits, the women in her village would have said. They were a superstitious lot, and she shuddered when she thought about them and their barbaric customs. By now Gina had studied medicine long enough to know that Peter was probably depressed. Like she cared. Yes, he had lost a lot of things: his wife, his job, his precious castle. But he was still rich. Had everything he needed. To her, he was just weird, with his mumbling and his awkward manner. Irritating. She emptied a trash can and switched to another lecture on her headphones. When she glanced back at Peter's office, he was still there. Soon, his would be the only one left to clean.

She ran the vacuum over the floor. Emptied another trash can. She had counted them once. One hundred thirty-two. Plus the five big bags in the kitchen.

"Gina?"

She was so startled, she jumped. She pulled out one of her earbuds and stared, questioningly, at Peter.

"Sorry, I didn't mean to scare you." Peter fell silent. Cleared his throat. "I spilled water on my desk. I just need to get a cloth. I didn't want to scare you," he repeated.

"I can mop it up," she offered, reluctantly.

"No, no, I'll get a cloth."

She watched him disappear into the kitchen.

She pushed the earbud back into place. But now she couldn't concentrate on the lecture. Did someone like Peter think he was better than other people? Just because he'd inherited a load of money? And if he did, why did it provoke her so much? All she had to do was ignore him. They'd often had discussions like this at home, she and her father. He thought it was caused by her feelings of inferiority. Gina hated that argument. She wasn't inferior to anyone. Her Swedish was perfect. Though they'd only arrived in Sweden when she was eleven, she spoke without mistakes, just like her little brother. No, better—she spoke well and sounded educated. They were in agreement on that, she and her father. They knew that the demands placed on them were much higher than on any native Swede, and they had both studied nonstop once they got their residence permit.

Her father had taken a course in Swedish for immigrants, and coped well in the society that had opened its arms, if not its heart, to them. And that was why she had chosen to study medicine. Doctors were respected. She would be something, someone, and she would do it herself, without being dependent on anyone else.

Gina knew all too well that life was deeply unjust. The idea that life rewarded hard work was crap. She had never seen anyone work as hard as the women in Somalia, and they were hardly rewarded with riches and power. Life was a lottery, and her little family had been lucky, despite everything. Not *lucky* lucky, the way the De la Grip family was, but much luckier than many of her compatriots. Their father had fled with them, away from oppression and threats, and they had made it here. That meant the three of them belonged to the luckier ones. She would never waste the chance she'd been given. All you had, in the end, *all* you had, was your courage and your integrity.

She looked over at Peter's door again. He had already dried the desk and was sitting with his head bowed. She had always been invisible in his world. A silent servant. Peter looked up and their eyes met briefly before he quickly started to leaf through some papers on his desk.

His office was the last one she needed to clean, so she headed over.

"Come in," he said.

She cleaned the room quickly and efficiently, and left as soon as she could.

Once she was finally done for the evening, she rinsed the cloths, changed the bag in the vacuum, and placed the last of the dishes into the dishwasher. It was seven when she changed her shoes and picked up her jacket and purse from her locker. She would rush home—two subway trains and a bus, but with luck she should be home before eight. If Dad had had a good day, he would have made food. If he'd been in a lot of pain or slept badly, she would have to cook for the three of them before she got down to her studies.

The very last thing she did was wash her hands. Just as she had tied the belt on her jacket and was ready to leave, Peter appeared. Damn it, she had been planning to sneak out without talking to him. He reached the door at the same time she did. He had a briefcase in one hand and a thin jacket over his other arm. He quickly moved the briefcase to the jacket hand, opened the heavy plexiglass door, and held it open for her. They took the elevator in silence. She hurried out through the door before he had time to open it too.

Just as they were about to head in different directions, he said, "Bye, Gina. Thanks for today." He disappeared around the corner.

Gina just stared after him in surprise.

Chapter 12

Isobel looked out the train window. They had passed the southern suburbs of Stockholm, and the view outside the train was increasingly green, less concrete. Leila, who had mumbled something about other commitments, had left for Skåne the day before. Isobel didn't know how many people would be there—Leila had been suspiciously vague—but as far as she knew, it was an unusually big event. She scanned the program she had been given, which she was using as a bookmark in the paperback she was trying to make her way through. First, a chance to mingle on the lawn and in the castle grounds, then an official opening, followed by talks in various drawing rooms. The awarding of a newly launched cultural prize would also take place. Between the events, attendees could walk around the castle grounds and view an exhibition of young artists' installations. The whole thing was wrapped up by a ball in the evening, to which certain guests, Isobel and Leila included, were invited. The host was, if she had understood correctly, an eccentric. The theme for the weekend was The Circle of Life: Art, Aid, and the World in Which We Live. Isobel didn't know if she thought it was annoyingly pretentious or actually quite insightful.

Her cell phone rang as they reached Linköping, 125 miles southeast of Stockholm. She fished it up from her purse and answered.

"Hi, Mom."

"I need some help putting up shelves in my living room. You're free this weekend, aren't you? I'd like you to come over," Blanche Sørensen said by way of greeting.

"I'm on my way to Skåne." She had told her mother about the

fund-raiser earlier that week, but Blanche had a tendency to forget anything that didn't directly affect her.

"What are you doing there?"

"Leila and I are speaking about Medpax," Isobel reminded her patiently.

Blanche was silent for a while. "I remember when I used to go to those events. I was a star. I could bring in as many donors as I wanted."

It was true. Her mother had been legendary. Witty and beautiful. It was no accident that Medpax's golden age had coincided with her mother's. She was extraordinary at galas and on TV sofas, hated to be at home.

"I'm planning to invite people over for the Feast of the Ascension," Blanche continued. "That's why I'm putting up shelves and bringing in new furniture. When you come home, you can help me to move the couch. I thought you could come to the party too. You can help me with the food."

Her mother always assumed she would be there to help. But Isobel knew she only had herself to blame. She had lived and grown up with her grandmother for the first ten years of her life. Her mother had been in Paris and visited them at irregular intervals. When her grandmother died, Blanche had moved back to Sweden, but Isobel had always been afraid that her mother would get tired of her and leave again. For many years, her sole desire had been for her mother to need her, want her help, and so during her childhood Isobel had practically bent over backward to please her. As the years passed, her mother had gotten used to Isobel organizing whatever she wanted for her. Except when it came to her job. That was the only area in which Isobel put up a fight and clung tightly to what *she* wanted to do, regardless of the price she paid in criticism and disapproval.

"I'll be in Chad then," she said.

"You didn't say anything about that."

Isobel pinched the bridge of her nose. Two more minutes, then she would hang up. "It only got decided recently. They gave me the date this week."

"Why are you going? Doesn't Leila have anyone else?"

"Sven dropped out. Family reasons."

Blanche snorted. "Doctors today are made of such weak stuff. I suppose you'll have to do it, then. At least it's better when you go out on behalf of Medpax rather than MSF. But Isobel, I'm only saying this for your own good, you really do need to think about your future. *One* field mission is good for your CV, but this constant travel around the world. Everyone else is moving past you. When I was your age, I had already started to write my thesis."

Isobel stared out the window. Sometimes these conversations were so similar that it felt she'd had them hundreds of times before. She assumed there was a psychological term for the relationship she had with her mother, but it was difficult to analyze when you were in the middle of it all. The hardest thing to understand was how other people could see her as so successful when all her own mother could see were faults to be criticized.

"Mom, I need to go through my notes."

"Don't mind me, I'm used to taking care of myself. Your father never had the time either. It's just that my friends' daughters always help them. I don't know why it's so difficult for you to step up from time to time. Think about it. Don't have children, they're so selfish."

Isobel took a deep breath. Well, at least Blanche couldn't be accused of being overprotective. Or of pressuring her for grandchildren.

"I'll call you when I get home. I'll try to come over one evening. I need to hang up now," she said, ending the call before she said something she would regret.

She got up and went to the restaurant car, bought a coffee, and sat back down. Outside, the countryside was slowly changing from coniferous trees and a pale landscape to deciduous trees and golden fields. Skåne was three weeks ahead of Stockholm; down here, spring had long since arrived.

She drank her coffee, threw the cup away, and closed her eyes for a moment. She hadn't heard from Alexander. She assumed that meant it was over between them. What little there had been. Their dinner date, the salsa dancing, his visit to her at work, it had been so . . . nice. Christ, when did she last have so much fun?

But he hadn't called. She looked at her phone again. Brought up his number. It would be so easy to text him a line or two. Instead she put the phone facedown on the table. If she didn't care in the slightest about Alexander, she might have contacted him. Dared to ask if he wanted to go out for a drink. But she had been thinking about him all week, felt disappointed when he hadn't gotten in touch. It was as good a sign as any to step away, this feeling of her control slipping. From an emotional point of view, she couldn't afford to let a man like Alexander into her life. He was too intense, too unpredictable. Had the potential to awaken things she wasn't sure she ever wanted to wake again.

She rummaged for her notes. Smoothed them out, resolute. A weekend in a castle was just what she needed to get away from these unwelcome feelings. They would disappear soon enough. She had even bought a ball gown. She would have *fun*. It was a good plan, and the smartest thing she could do. After all, she excelled at being smart. She sighed.

When the taxi dropped Isobel off outside the castle just after lunch—she actually paused to catch her breath; she hadn't realized that Sweden had castles like this—she was met by the kindly, smiling staff, who asked for her name and then made sure she was shown to her room in one of the turrets.

"There has to be some mistake." Isobel paused, stunned, in the doorway.

The young woman dressed in seventeenth-century costume who had shown her the way—a history student from the university in Lund, she'd told her—looked at a piece of paper. "Dr. Isobel Sørensen?"

"Yes."

"Then this is your room. It's called the Queen Room, because a number of Swedish queens from the last three centuries have stayed here. Breakfast is between seven and ten in the dining room on the first floor."

"But . . ." Isobel began before she realized the young woman had already disappeared.

She went into the room. Huge, pastel-colored oriental rugs silenced her footsteps. An enormous bed in the middle of the room was covered in pink and red fabric; the wallpaper looked as though it had been painted with real gold. Vases of roses were placed here and there, and the breeze from the window caused the thin, embroidered curtains to flutter. Magnificent didn't come close to describing the room.

After quickly unpacking, Isobel went back down the steep, uneven castle stairs. Each step was gently worn down in the middle, thousands of feet, over hundreds of years, having followed the very same route. Outside, people blanketed the paved courtyard. She walked over to the moat and stood there for a moment, peering down into it. Then she saw Leila, walking arm in arm with an older man. Leila was dressed in black, as usual. The man was in a wine-colored suit, a colorful waistcoat, and a silk cravat.

"Isobel! Let me introduce you to our host," Leila called.

"Eugene Tolstoy. We've actually met before," he said as they shook hands. His sharp eyes moved over her.

"I'm sorry, I don't remember," she said. She did recognize him but couldn't quite place him. People were pouring in from all directions, and Eugene's attention was elsewhere before he had time to reply.

Leila let go of Eugene's arm and took Isobel's instead.

"Come on," said Leila. "I want to see the exhibition before it gets too crowded."

They came out onto a lawn. People were already wandering about there. Through the trees, Isobel caught sight of a lake with swans and wild ducks paddling in it. Beneath a fluttering awning, guests studied the paintings hanging from thin silver cables, as though they were hovering weightlessly in the air. Surrealist paintings, remarkably beautiful.

"Eugene has collected art his entire life. He says this boy is a genius," said Leila, standing with her gaze fixed on an image of a huge bird with wings metamorphosing into tree trunks. Identity and outsiderness, Isobel thought. It was sad and beautiful.

"He's only eighteen. Fled from Russia. I mean, the things they do to people in that country. Eugene is particularly protective of all the LGBTQ people, of course. And anyone else who falls outside the norm."

"Eugene is gay?" Isobel asked. They had seemed very affectionate, he and Leila. "I thought maybe the two of you . . . ?"

Leila shrugged. "We've known one another a long time. He's a Renaissance man, and we have a special relationship. We play backgammon when we get the chance. Talk about politics and history. He's related to the old Russian tsars. My parents had relatives close to the Persian throne. We old aristocrats have lots in common."

"Backgammon?"

"It's actually a Persian game from many years ago. The oldest board game in the world. He's very good."

"We can talk about that later," Isobel said with an eye on her watch. "I want to have a look at the room where we're going to speak. Coming?"

"Of course. There's a lot of press here too. It's one of Sweden's oldest privately owned castles, and it hasn't been open to the public before, so the media is curious. We'll make sure Medpax gets plenty of coverage."

"It's great company for us to be seen in," Isobel said as they crossed the luscious lawns. "You've done a fantastic job, Leila."

"How is your room?"

"Never seen anything like it. I'm wondering if I wasn't given the wrong one."

"Of course not, you're an important guest."

"I am?"

"Don't you realize that—" Leila started but was interrupted by a journalist who had recognized her. "I'll come and find you," Leila said before turning to the journalist.

Isobel left to look for the room where the lectures would take place. She shook hands with a few other speakers, greeted a famous professor from Karolinska Institutet—a man she had spoken to many times before and who would be opening the talks. She had a lot of respect for him, and he regularly tried to convince her to come work for him. When they parted, she glanced wide-eyed around the room in which they would be talking. It was at least as grand as the bedroom she had been given. Golden walls, antique furniture, and row after row of chairs upholstered in blue velvet. It was easy to imagine noblewomen sitting there, in their crinolines, whispering behind their fans.

Isobel took out her stack of prompts and decided to go through her speech one last time. She was glad she had come, glad to be able to focus on something. This was just what she needed in order to leave all thoughts of Alexander where they belonged: in the past.

Chapter 13

Alexander took the back stairs to the room where Isobel would give her talk. He had arrived at the castle the night before, but they hadn't seen one another yet. The first thing he did when he got here was to make sure Isobel was given his favorite room in one of the turrets. Then he drank cognac with his uncle and a few other guests, Leila included. After that, when everyone else had gone to bed, he and Eugene stayed up drinking Russian vodka into the small hours. They had talked about the family, a subject Alexander abhorred, and about the castle's upkeep, and then they had listened to some horrid music his increasingly inebriated uncle insisted on calling "your cultural heritage."

First thing this morning, Alexander had gone for a run around the lake, taken a shower, and then mostly made sure to keep out of the way of the staff, who were busy putting up tents, arranging a long table, and making other preparations. He had caught sight of Isobel when she arrived, but she had looked stressed, so he had decided to wait to greet her, despite his impatience.

He opened yet another of the castle's side doors and moved quickly through the rooms. They were cleaned and polished, and he wondered how big the bill would be this time. The idea was that the income from the property should cover expenses, but a castle of this size cost an enormous amount to run, and because Alexander could afford it, he paid every extravagant and crazy bill Eugene sent him. He let two men lugging an enormous table go past him, and then almost crashed into three of Eugene's hunting dogs, which were running around and barking wildly. Ordinarily, Alexander wouldn't have set foot at an event like this. But once he'd realized that this was where Isobel was headed, the temptation was too great to resist. He passed the room containing Eugene's collection of Russian art objects, where they had sat drinking vodka.

Eugene and his sister, Ebba—Alexander's mother—had Russian roots. Alexander's great-grandmother had been the daughter of a grand duchess, his great-grandfather one of the first oligarchs. Their daughter, Alexander's grandmother, had married a Swedish nobleman, and once *their* daughter, Ebba, married Gustaf De la Grip, it cemented their place in the Swedish upper class.

While Ebba loved her Swedish heritage, Eugene had taken his mother's maiden name, Tolstoy, and grown more and more Russian as the years went by. Eugene was also a man of exclusive taste, Alexander thought as he sighed at something that looked like an ice sculpture being carried out. Eugene's events here at the castle often ended up somewhere between legendary and verging on illegal. One New Year's Eve, for example, the fireworks had been a little over the top. Apparently they could be seen as far away as Lund, which wasn't in itself a bad thing. But one of Eugene's guests (a young Russian fashion designer) had, just after midnight, set off a powerful rocket. Not only did it manage to hit the medieval clock tower on a neighboring estate, but it also set fire to it. The clock tower, which had seen medieval kings like Magnus Eriksson and Gustav Vasa pass by, had burned down. Alexander had paid for the rebuilding and had had to donate a huge sum to the vicarage. Eugene had kept things relatively tame for a while after that.

But earlier last fall, an invoice for twelve peacocks and three dozen white doves arrived in New York. When Alexander called to ask what the hell Eugene needed four dozen birds for, his uncle had cheerfully replied that the birds were doing fine and that he was busy building a new scented garden down by the lake. "Vision, Alex, one must have vision. Just imagine how magnificent it will be." Unfortunately, Eugene's garden project seemed to consist primarily of plants that happened to be the peacocks' favorite food (they loved aromatic scents, apparently), and at roughly the same time as Alexander paid *that* invoice, the peacocks had eaten the last lavender plant. The beasts also bred like rabbits, which was the reason the grounds were crawling with ill-tempered peacocks that nibbled at anything and everything.

Alexander stopped to talk to an acquaintance. As usual, Eugene had managed to assemble a motley crew of guests. Representatives of the Skåne nobility, of course (or at least those who still spoke to him after the fireworks fiasco). A handful of the true jet-set—rich, young people, the majority of whom Alexander knew and who had come in by private jet from New York, London, and Moscow to party for the evening before they set off elsewhere, like a glamorous swarm of grasshoppers. Some of Eugene's LGBTQ friends were there, livening up the party, to put it mildly. After Alexander moved on, he caught sight of the more sociable of Sweden's current and former government ministers, those who didn't see too much of a problem in being invited to enjoy free food and drink in a luxurious environment. And then, of course, a handful of people were here to talk about aid. It was a mad mix of people, really, but Eugene was an expert at exciting gatherings like this. Alexander passed one of the kitchens and grabbed a glass of champagne, downed it, grabbed another, and then headed for the drawing room, filled with expectation at the thought of finally getting to see Isobel.

He sat down at the very back of the room as the welcome applause roared. The first speaker was a professor in international health, whose TED talk Alexander had actually watched and enjoyed on YouTube the weekend before. After enthusiastic applause, Isobel came out with Leila. Isobel had on a gray dress with white cuffs and a white collar. Through the window, the sun beamed in, and her hair, gathered in a thick bun low on her neck, shone with all the fiery red tones in the color wheel. The room was packed, he was way at the back, and she seemed to be concentrating, so she didn't see him.

Leila presented herself first, talked about her role at Medpax, its history and what they had been doing in recent years. Then she handed the mic over to Isobel and sat down in the front row.

Isobel stepped forward and seemed to pause to take the room in.

"My name is Isobel Sørensen. I'm a doctor of general medicine. My mother, Blanche Sørensen, and grandfather Henri Pelletier founded Medpax in 1984. I was invited here today to talk about my work as a field doctor." She paused and smiled. The woman had a smile that men would go to war for.

"And to get you to give me absurd amounts of money too," she added with a glimmer in her eye.

The joke made the audience laugh; she had them on her side after that. She took another step forward, closer to her listeners, and swept her gaze over them. "I've seen many children die. But I've seen even more survive. Medpax runs a pediatric hospital in Chad, and I'm headed down there in a couple of weeks. The organization has also been involved in funding vaccination programs, taken part in national public health campaigns, and helped to ensure that under-nourished children have enough food to survive. I'm telling you this because it's easy to feel hopeless." She paused, allowed her words to sink in. The audience was silent. "But if, like me, you've seen the re-sults of such relatively simple contributions, there's no more doubt. All of you gathered here today can make a huge difference. Every one of you can save lives."

She had an amazing voice. Alexander wasn't the only one to be drawn into her force field. The audience sat absolutely still. No one jabbed at a phone or moved restlessly in their seat. Isobel held them all spellbound; she brought tears to their eyes when she talked about the sick children she had met, only to make them burst into laughter at the story of how she and two nurses had once organized a wildly popular spa using buckets of mud and a tub of skin lotion, and then made her audience sit silent in awe as she talked about proud Cha-dian men and their love for their families. She was magnificent. Even he, who had already given so much money to Medpax that his bankers had started to send him questioning messages, wanted to give more. It was a need to impress her, to win her respect. Was she actually get-ting to him? He looked at the straight-backed, self-confident woman up there at the front. If that was the case, it wasn't necessarily a bad thing. Just unexpected.

Partway through the presentation, her tension had vanished, as it always did. Isobel knew that no one probably noticed it, but she was always enormously nervous at the start of a speech. Once she could finally breathe normally, she allowed herself to look out at the audience as she talked and gestured. She wanted to invite her listeners into her life, make them understand how important they could be in creating a better, more equal world. And perhaps a part of her—not that she would ever admit it—enjoyed being the center of attention after all. The thought made her smile, and at that exact moment she caught sight of Alexander, sitting in the last row. Above him hung an oil painting of a fat, old man on a little horse. She suddenly lost the thread. How the devil had Alexander ended up here?

She cast a glance at her watch and continued. Talked about Doctor Idris Toko, so caring to the children in the hospital, so respected among the patients; she talked about the mother who had dared defy the medicine man and come to the hospital instead; and she talked about Zouhoura, the sixteen-year-old Chadian girl whose malaria they had cured and who now went from village to village telling people about the importance of using mosquito nets. She finished at exactly the right time and was met by thunderous applause. Leila clapped hard, looking proud. Alexander stood up and applauded, too, winking and grinning at her, and then she was shown out through a side door by an assistant. She breathed out and heard the next speaker being introduced. And then Alexander came out to her.

"You were fantastic," he greeted her.

"Thanks. I was so surprised when I saw you there, I thought I was seeing things." It still felt completely surreal that he was there.

"Only surprised? Not radiantly happy? Almost ecstatic?"

"That too, of course. But what are you doing here?" Had he come here just for her? Was that even possible?

"It's my castle."

"Why am I not surprised?"

"I don't come here often; my uncle takes care of it. He's the one who organized this whole circus."

"Eugene Tolstoy is your uncle?" But she could see the likeness now: the same blue eyes and blond hair. An air of decadence. A touch of danger.

"Want to go outside for a while? Or did you want to stay?"

Isobel had planned to stay and listen to the others, but being outside with Alexander in this beautiful weather was pretty irresistible.

"How long has your family owned this place?" she asked as they walked across the velvety lawn. Other guests were moving about the park, some with glasses in their hands. She caught sight of a peacock pecking at a magnolia bush. She laughed at the sheer absurdity of it, but Alexander just rolled his eyes.

"It's not a De la Grip castle. I won it three years ago."

"Won it?"

He shrugged. "Poker."

She shook her head. "I never know whether you're kidding or not."

"I usually am. But I really did win it. It had been in the guy's family for generations. You don't really sell this kind of thing, you know; people hold on to these places until they go under, financially. In a way I think he was relieved to get rid of it. Eugene moved in, and that was that. I hardly ever come here."

"Aside from now," she said, and God help her but she was *flirting* with him. How could she not? He had come all this way for her, she suspected that much.

"Are you staying for the ball?" she asked.

"Are you?"

"Yeah. I even bought a new dress."

"What color?"

She pulled a leaf from a tree and twirled it between her fingers. "Green."

His gaze never left hers. "My favorite. There'll be dancing. Should I ask them to play a salsa?"

She shook her head. "It's not a salsa dress. It's a waltz dress."

"I'll ask them to play waltzes all night, then."

"You can't do that." Their eyes locked, and there was a faint buzz in the air. He leaned closer to her.

"Right now, it feels like I can do whatever I want."

Chapter 14

Leila had draped herself on the window ledge inside Isobel's room. She had opened the window, lit one of her slim, black cigarillos, and was now blowing bluish-gray smoke out through the gap, ignoring Isobel's demonstrative coughing.

"Passive smoking isn't nearly as dangerous as they make out," Leila said, unconcerned, exhaling yet another menthol-scented cloud of smoke. She had on a tight black dress and glittering black shoes with bright red soles. With her kohl-rimmed eyes and jewels in her jet-black hair, she looked more like an exiled Persian queen than ever.

As Leila took yet another puff on her cigarillo, Isobel pulled out the dress she had bought. The dress code was black tie, and since the only suitable dress she owned was ten years old, she had bought a new one.

"It's nice," said Leila.

"Thanks."

Isobel carefully pulled on the green dress, shivering slightly at the rustling noise it made. "I don't really get dressed up too often. Other things are more important than appearance," she said, and thought that usually, that was true. She fell silent, embarrassed, and busied herself choosing between a simple gold chain and a pearl necklace, the most expensive pieces of jewelry she owned.

"But now there's a man you want to feel pretty for," Leila stated. "In my professional opinion, that's completely normal. Men are rarely attracted to your brain, after all."

"What an awfully judgmental thing to say."

Leila snorted. "We're talking about Alexander De la Grip, aren't we? Just so I know. The same man who gave me one hundred thousand kronor just to have dinner with you the other day?"

Isobel bit her lip. That still jarred.

"Did anyone say anything about that?"

"At the office? No one knows. It has nothing to do with them." Leila stubbed out her cigarillo on a plate with a golden rim; Isobel was sure that it was both antique and irreplaceable. "I don't really like this," Leila said as she took out the pack again. "Two intelligent women like us, talking about men."

"You want to talk about something more intellectual, you mean? We can always discuss COPD and lung cancer."

"I really don't. I'd rather talk about men, if that's the case. In fact, I can even give you a piece of dating advice right now. Don't talk about deadly lung diseases if you can avoid it. It's rather unattractive."

"You're a psychologist. I read somewhere that psychologists aren't meant to give advice."

Leila took a deep drag. "Maybe, but it's tough when you have so much wisdom to share."

"So what do you think of him?" Isobel asked as there was a knock at the door. She went to open it.

"The interesting thing is what *you* think of him."

A young man, dressed in what Isobel would have described as period clothing, was standing outside. "With compliments from Alexander De la Grip," he said. He held out a flat package.

Leila came over to the doorway and studied the young man's tights-clad legs with great interest. "What is it?" she asked as she stopped ogling him.

Isobel closed the door, ripped off the thin tissue paper, and found a case, old and worn. "It looks ancient," she said.

"Open it."

Isobel lifted the lid. Her eyes widened. Lying on a liner of black velvet were a necklace and a pair of earrings.

"*Mon dieu*. Do you think they're real?" She lifted up the necklace. The green stones sparkled.

"I know what they are," Leila said. She touched one of the enormous green gems. "Eugene told me about them. They're emeralds—

they belonged to Josephine Bonaparte, the first wife of Napoleon and the first Empress of the French. Most of them are in Norway, on the crown jewels, but this set wound up at an exclusive auction, and Eugene bought it."

"So shouldn't they be in some kind of vault?" Isobel turned the necklace in her hands. The stones were a clear, almost poisonous shade of green.

"Yes. He must have gone to get them. What does it say in the note?"

Isobel picked up the little envelope that had been lying on top and opened it.

> *Your dress just begged to borrow these.*
> *A*

Leila grinned. "You've got to give him bonus points for this, Isobel. Turn around, I'll help you."

Isobel waited while Leila fastened the necklace. She put on the earrings and then looked in the mirror. The green stones against her pale skin, the dress, her hair—she had never felt so beautiful in all her life. The set had to be priceless. It was extraordinary. Her fingers grazed the necklace. She *was* happy. But all the same, she wondered. All this extravagance. How could Alexander afford it? Her misgivings had been lulled by his attentiveness, but now they rushed to the fore. The place in Manhattan. The brand-new apartment on Strandvägen. This castle. True, he came from a wealthy family, but still. The last time she checked, you didn't earn much money from taking the occasional course here and there.

"What do you think? Just a superficial playboy? Criminal? Sex addict?" She said it in a jokey tone, but what was it people often said? If something seemed too good to be true, it probably was.

"If there's one thing I've learned over the years, it's that you shouldn't form an opinion of a person too quickly. The first impression is always a lie."

"But I'm asking you for an opinion now, not drivel like that."

"Please. If I only ever said what people asked me to say, I'd never get to talk about anything interesting. But if you asked me, I'd say that you need a man to take care of you."

Isobel shook her head. "I can take care of myself."

"But still."

"He's got no staying power. He said so himself."

Leila snorted. "You can't analyze yourself. He drinks too much and he needs something to focus on."

"And you think that's Medpax?"

Leila gave her an ironic look. "Hardly. He needs something to fight for, a cause, and he just doesn't know it. He gave money to Medpax because he wanted to impress you. Not that I mind. A couple more dates, and we'll make it to Christmas."

"Are things really that bad?"

"Isobel?" Leila's voice was stern.

"I know, I know." Isobel sighed. "I shouldn't take everything so seriously. And it's just one party."

"Mmm, exactly. Just one party." Leila smiled demonically, then took a puff on her cigarillo, holding the smoke in her lungs for a moment before she blew a perfect smoke ring. "Just one party where anything could happen."

Once Leila had finished smoking and Isobel had finally chosen between her only two pairs of evening shoes, they went down the castle stairs. The green dress was snug and formfitting at the top, hugging her breasts and waist, only to fall out in thin layers that fluttered at the slightest movement of her feet. It wasn't hard to feel like Cinderella or a princess. The castle was filled with voices, and they followed the sound to a big room in which trays of wine, champagne, and sherry were being passed. There was something almost decadent about the atmosphere. Expectation, flirtation, and excitement hovered in the air, as though the castle itself was looking forward to the evening and planned to make sure everyone ate, drank, and enjoyed themselves to the max.

When Isobel saw what the other guests were wearing—people were dressed in velvet, lace, and jewels—she was glad she had dressed up. For roughly the tenth time she checked that the emeralds were still there, then took a flute of champagne from a tray, glanced around, and tried to look as relaxed as possible for someone wearing antique crown jewels for the first time in her life.

She saw Alexander before he caught sight of her. He entered the room, and it was as though his corner was lit up by brilliant sunlight. She watched him talk to another guest. He really was absurdly handsome. Muscular and tanned, of course, in the way only the truly rich could afford to be. But it was more than that. It was as if someone had gathered every desirable feature a man could have, mixed them all together, poured the result into some perfect mold, and out came Alexander De la Grip—a pure, unspoiled model of blond male beauty. He was dressed in a dinner jacket and naturally managed to look ultrasexy in what would make many men look like badly dressed waiters. He had told her he had been a paratropper when he did his military service, so she tried to picture him as a soldier but failed. He was just too suave, too glamorous.

The women in the room were drawn to him, as if they were small planets gravitating toward the bright center of the universe. Alexander paused again, chatted with two young brunettes, laughed, moved on, and was stopped again. Over and over, as though he was the very life of the party. Every now and then he cast an almost imperceptible glance over the guests, and Isobel knew he was looking for her.

And then he caught sight of her and halted, his eyes locking on to hers. He cut a path across the room and stopped right in front of her. Long, dark eyelashes amped up the intensity of his gaze. His eyes fell on her necklace, and she felt her breasts strain against the edge of her dress as she breathed.

"You're so goddamn beautiful," he said, kissing her on the cheek. It was just above her cheekbone and lasted slightly longer than an ordinary, polite kiss. She could smell him—he was warm and masculine, and she felt herself tremble. No one could kiss a woman on the cheek like Alexander De la Grip. Then again, he'd probably had plenty of practice, she thought cynically, taking a step back and telling herself to get a grip.

"Hi," she said.

Beneath the calm surface, her heart was pounding hard and expectantly. Her pulse and blood pressure increased, and she knew that her blood was rushing through veins and arteries, pulsing out into capillaries and giving her skin a sheen. He affected her. But Alexander wasn't the first man who'd made her weak in the knees. Ultimately, it was just biology and chemistry—hormones and nerves.

"Thanks for this," she said, noting that her voice still sounded cool and collected as she gestured to the necklace.

"I thought you'd like them. They're so old, it's practically recycling."

"Is it true they're from Napoleon's days?"

He nodded.

There was, of course, an attraction between them. It would have been foolish to deny it. But Isobel was an experienced doctor. So many of her patients had alcohol problems. Alexander's eyes were glazed, and when he put down his empty wineglass and picked up a new one, she knew that he, with his various affairs and his extravagant lifestyle, was a man on the way down the slippery slope toward dependency. Not someone it would be smart to rely on, in other words. But with that said, she couldn't deny that she and her autonomous nervous system were very happy to see him.

"Good evening," Eugene Tolstoy said, joining them. He took Isobel's hand, raised it to his lips, and kissed it. "Ah, Isobel, French jewels become you. Alexander tells me you aren't just a great physician, but a brilliant speaker as well. I must say, it's an honor to have you here as our guest."

Isobel glanced at Alexander. Apparently he had talked to his uncle about her. "This castle is fantastic. I'm so grateful we could come to talk about Medpax's work."

"It is I who should be grateful," Eugene answered smoothly. "So, how is it going? Is there anyone in particular you'd like to be introduced to?"

Isobel was on the verge of replying when she suddenly glimpsed a face she recognized. He was right across the room from her, and she froze. *No.* It couldn't be. The shock almost numbed her. Don't react to seeing him, she told herself. It had been years. Nonetheless, the reaction was physical, and she couldn't control it.

In a daze she felt Alexander's arm on her back. "I'll look after Isobel," he said with a smile in his voice, and she vaguely realized he was still talking to Eugene. She swallowed. Again. Jesus Christ.

"Isobel? Did something happen? You're completely white. Do you feel okay?" Alexander sounded concerned. Damn, he was perceptive.

She took a deep breath, held it, counted to four, exhaled, counted to four. Repeated.

"Do you need to sit down? Water?"

Alexander's arm had tightened protectively around her, and she leaned against him slightly, turned away. You don't faint from fear, she told herself. You go pale and shaky, but you don't faint. And I'm not scared, not really. It's just an automatic reaction.

"I'm okay," she said, managing a thin smile. "Low blood sugar. I'm probably just hungry."

He flashed her a worried look.

"It's fine," she said. "I promise."

"If you say so," he replied, though he looked deeply skeptical. "You looked almost scared. Are you sure nothing happened? You can tell me."

She gave him a calm smile, but if there was one thing she *couldn't* do, it was tell him.

"Alexander!" A couple came over to them. Shook hands with Alexander and glanced curiously at Isobel.

Alexander gave her a questioning look.

She breathed out. It was fine now. She nodded and he introduced her.

"I heard your speech," said the woman. "Do you give private talks? We run an association. An order, actually. And we'd pay, of course."

"Absolutely."

"Then that's that," said the woman. "I'll ask our secretary to get in touch. Good to meet you."

"You'll definitely find them useful," Alexander said once the couple moved away. "If you stick with me, you'll see I can organize more donors than you can manage."

"I'll have to stick with you, then," she said with a shaky laugh.

Feeling herself once more, she turned as Alexander introduced her to another group of people. Maybe she had just imagined the whole thing. What would Sebastien be doing here?

Chapter 15

"Four hundred years, my family lived here. He practically stole it from me."

Alexander turned around and sought out the man who had spoken so loudly. "Lucius, I thought I heard you whining," he shouted, giving the man, Lucius af Kraft, a sardonic look. "I tried to ignore you, but Christ, you're loud."

"De la Grip? What the hell are you doing here?"

"I didn't know I had to tell you when I was coming here. I own the place, after all. What the fuck are *you* doing here?"

Lucius wobbled. "My boss forced the entire department to come, otherwise I never would've set foot here." He pointed at Alexander with his drink. "You took all this from me. My family won't talk to me anymore. It's all your fault. You cheated me out of my inheritance."

It had been a crazy-ass poker night, if memory served him right. The stakes had been ridiculously high. They had all been drunk, and in the end only he and Lucius were left at the table. Alexander had waited patiently all evening, and then finally it happened: He had an exceptional hand. A straight flush. Hearts. He could still remember the symmetrical beauty of it, one of the best hands he'd ever had, well worth the wait.

"I warned you. I told you to quit. Your friends warned you." It was true. He had given the guy fair warning, much more than he deserved. But Lucius had offered his heirloom castle as security, and Alexander had drunkenly accepted.

Lucius snorted. "You didn't have to fucking go through with it."

Of course he didn't. He could've backed down the next morning, when Lucius fell apart.

But no, it was a matter of principle. And he had always liked this place. "No. You lost. I won."

"Alexander?" Isobel's questioning voice interrupted them.

"Aha, and what do we have here?" Lucius's unsteady gaze panned up Isobel's green dress, lingering on her bare flesh.

Alexander hesitated, didn't want to sully Isobel somehow, didn't want her to have to deal with Lucius. But she got in there first, of course. She wasn't a woman who needed a man to introduce her.

"Isobel Sørensen," she said politely, and held out her hand.

"Hi. And what do you do, sweetheart? You don't look like one of Alexander's usual girls." His eyes were still roaming across her body, eventually stopping at her breasts again. A growling sound was building up inside Alexander. He took a warning step forward.

Isobel still seemed completely unfazed. "I'm a doctor. I'm here to talk about aid work."

Lucius made a dismissive noise.

"Charity?"

"We don't use that word. It's aid, or humanitarian work."

Lucius scoffed. "In developing countries, right? That stuff's completely pointless. The world's already overpopulated. It would be better to let natural selection do its thing. It'd be better for everyone."

"Not exactly for everyone, surely?" she replied calmly.

"Didn't the state pay for your education? Shouldn't you be working in Sweden? We need Swedish doctors at home. Let their own doctors take care of them."

"Yes, of course, it would be fantastic if the world worked like that," she replied.

Isobel still looked utterly composed, but Alexander had had enough. "First off, don't talk about things you know nothing about. It just makes you look like an even bigger dickhead than you already are. Second, don't insult a person who is better than you in every way. And third, get the fuck away from her," he said with barely controlled rage.

Lucius simply took another gulp of his drink and gave Alexander a nasty look. They had partied at Stureplan in the past. But Lucius was an asshole without an ounce of honor in his body. Whenever Lucius invited young, party-crazy girls out for drinks, he expected sex in return. And he turned aggressive when he didn't get it.

If Alexander had seen the guest list, he would have crossed out his name.

"All I mean is that we can't keep contributing to overpopulation," he said.

"You really are stupid. And wrong, too. All the research shows that people choose to have fewer children if there's a greater chance they'll survive. They're just like us in those countries. And they deserve medical care."

Isobel cast him a glance from the side.

"What?" asked Alexander, still fuming. Christ, he was mad.

"I was just thinking that I couldn't have said it better myself."

"I still don't know why Swedish doctors are supposed to care about a load of blacks. Aren't there poor people you can help at home?" Lucius interrupted. He was like dog shit on the bottom of your shoe, impossible to get rid of.

"That's enough," Alexander said sharply.

"Alexander, it's fine," said Isobel. "There's no point getting angry. Stuff like this happens all the time."

But her words didn't calm him; he felt even angrier to realize that Lucius's opinions were commonplace to Isobel. And maybe part of him was uncomfortable remembering that it wasn't so long since he'd held similar thoughts himself, that he had been one of the countless people to whom Isobel was forced to defend her decisions.

"It's *my* opinion," Lucius continued with the stubbornness of a true drunk. "We live in a democracy, don't we? I can say what I want."

"Not when your opinions are so idiotic. In fact, I think you should leave now."

"*You* can go if it bothers you."

"You're misunderstanding me, Lucius, but you've always been slow. I want you to leave this house. Take your things and get the hell out of here."

"Are you kidding? We're in the middle of nowhere. And you of all people can't pretend you actually care. I know you, you're completely devoid of morals. I don't know why you're showing off." Lucius glanced at Isobel. "Though I'm guessing it's the doctor you're interested in. I get that." His eyes were on her cleavage. "You know, babe, we've chased women together before. He normally gets tired pretty quickly. I wouldn't mind letting you give me some first aid, if you know what I mean."

"Leave, now." Alexander was surprised he had managed to sound so calm considering the bubbling rage he felt.

"I was invited. My boss goes hunting with Eugene. You can't kick me out."

"Alexander, it's not worth getting into an argument over this. If I got offended every time someone was ignorant, I wouldn't have time for anything else." She gave him an urgent look. "Don't let him ruin the evening."

Alexander pulled himself together. Isobel was right, of course. It was better to let it pass, to be civil.

"It's people like you who are ruining this country," said Lucius. His eyes were unfocused.

Alexander shook his head and placed a hand on Isobel's arm. "Come on," he said quietly. He just wanted to get her away from this creep.

"I don't mean you," Lucius hissed viciously. "No, I mean this politically correct left-wing cunt here."

Alexander didn't even think. He just acted. Swung around. Clenched fist, contact, thud, and then Lucius was on the floor, groaning and with a bleeding nose. His glass had broken; the contents spread quickly across the floor.

A few guests turned to stare at the commotion.

Alexander shook his hand. It was throbbing like hell. Good.

Isobel was standing with her arms crossed. She looked completely unfazed as she cocked her head. "What were you thinking, Alexander? That *violence* would get him to stop being a racist idiot? Or did you think that maybe he would change his mind about Swedish aid policy once you'd floored him?"

"Didn't you hear what he said? I can't let someone talk to you like that. I didn't mean to upset you," he said. He ran a hand through his hair.

"Upset?"

Lucius swore. He was still on the floor, defeated.

"Yeah, you know, by getting in a fight."

Isobel gave him an amused look and calmly studied the heavy blood flow Lucius was awkwardly trying to stop with a tissue. "Last time I was in the field with MSF, I got caught up in a gang fight. It ended with four dead and many injured," she said slowly, almost thoughtfully. "A Congolese nurse and I did what we could, and then they started to fight again. We were practically wading in blood at the end." She studied Lucius. "One drunk partygoer is about as pulse-raising as over-the-counter cough medicine."

She caught Alexander's hand as someone else helped Lucius back onto his feet. One of the wait staff was sweeping up the pieces of glass, and the commotion had already blown over.

She inspected his hand. "Your knuckles are grazed. You fight hard."

"Are you planning on bandaging me up? Now that I've fought for your honor?"

"Even ignoring the fact we don't live in the nineteenth century, I'm not so keen on people fighting for my honor." Her voice was stern, but there was a smile in her eyes. He felt like hitting anyone who ever said anything disrespectful to her again.

"Watch out for him," Lucius said hoarsely as he brushed himself down. "He's a player. Toys with women and then gets bored, fast. Don't think you're special." He waved a hand at Isobel.

Alexander caught Eugene's eye, and his uncle, already on the way over to them, nodded. Lucius would be thrown out. Alexander turned away with disgust. The adrenaline was still rushing through his body. He couldn't explain it; he had never done anything like that before. Hadn't punched someone just because he was rude to a woman.

"Wading in blood. You're cool, Doctor Sørensen, have I told you that?" He held out an arm and she took it. "Hungry?"

She gingerly laid her hand at his arm. "Very. I'm a simple woman. I don't like it when people fight. But if you feed me, I'm yours for eternity."

He laughed, feeling the euphoria that always followed a rush of adrenaline. "To the buffet, then," he said.

* * *

After they ate, Alexander suggested they head outside. The ballroom was warm and overcrowded, and he selfishly wanted Isobel to himself. He grabbed a bowl of strawberries, a bottle and two glasses, and steered her out, away from the parlors. They passed groups of smokers outside but managed to get past them without being stopped. They sat down in one of the sofa groups; Alexander moved one so that its back was to the castle and they could look out at the lake. The night was still light, but the staff had started to kindle fires in large, wide barrels with steel baskets around them.

"I'm really sorry about what happened before," he said.

"It wasn't your fault. It happens more and more often, unfortunately. I try not to let it get to me—it takes too much energy."

"I can't believe you managed to stay so calm."

"You get used to it," she said.

He looked at her, still wondering what she had seen before, when she looked so frightened, but instead of asking he raised a hand and pushed her hair back behind an ear. She blinked slowly, and turned her face to him so that the sun painted her skin golden pink. He leaned forward and gave her a light kiss on the lips. She closed her eyes, breathed in, and remained like that, their lips softly pressed together. A thrill went through him as the chaste kiss set him on fire.

But when Isobel broke the kiss, her eyes were serious.

"Alexander, I need to know. Do you have a girlfriend? Here or in New York? I'm sorry, but I just feel like I need to ask before this goes any further. I don't want to snoop, and I shouldn't read gossip, but . . ."

He shook his head. "Don't believe everything you read."

"But there have been so many women; surely it's not all just gossip."

"No, not all of it. But I'm one hundred percent single at the time being. Otherwise I wouldn't be doing this."

He brushed his mouth against hers once more, nibbled at her lower lip before moving on, grazing her ear. Her ears were so beautiful, delicate, sensitive, and fragrant. He breathed in. God, he loved that scent. Fragrant skin and a whiff of something that could have been antibacterial wash. It was oddly erotic.

"I'm single too," she mumbled.

He gently bit her earlobe. "I know," he whispered. "I asked Leila."

She pulled away and frowned. "For a psychologist, Leila talks a lot."

"Maybe." He kissed her chin and then her mouth, just gentle kisses; there was no rush. "Though I'm pretty good at getting secrets out of people."

"It's no secret that I'm single," she murmured into his mouth.

"Do you have other secrets then?"

She bit her lip and he leaned forward, reached for a strawberry, pulled off the stalk, and handed it to her. He watched her closely as she bit into the dark red berry. The juice colored her lips, and he wanted to lean forward and lick it from her freckled mouth.

"Can I ask you something else?" she said, swallowing the strawberry.

"Judging by your serious look, my spontaneous reaction would be to say no," he said. He would much rather eat strawberries and kiss, drink champagne and look at the stars.

"The money you gave Medpax, that hundred thousand." She worried her lip, and then seemed to steel herself. "Where is it from? Is it clean money?"

Alexander gave her a long look. Her hair fell around her face, glowed in the evening sunlight.

"Are you asking if I'm a criminal?" he asked slowly. "If I'm using Medpax to launder money? Aside from the fact I'm pretty certain it's impossible, just how low *is* your impression of me, exactly?"

She swallowed, though she didn't shy away. "Most people wouldn't just give away a hundred thousand kronor on a whim."

He sighed. He should have known this was coming. "You're right, and you deserve an explanation," he said after a while. He went on somewhat reluctantly. "I come from a wealthy family, as I'm sure you know." She nodded, but he was sure she had no idea how much of an understatement that was. The De la Grip family had utterly dominated the Swedish business world until last fall. They had always been rich, even though that wasn't something you ever talked about, and they were still wealthy. The fact that his father had lost control of Investum had been a huge blow in terms of prestige, but it was hardly as if Hammar Capital had killed them; on the contrary—economically, little had changed.

"So you live on your parents' money?"

Alexander shook his head and tried to remember whether he had ever talked about this with a woman. It was his American life they were talking about now, and that life was utterly his own. Not a De la Grip thing, not an inheritance. His and his alone. And he had never allowed a woman in.

"The fact is, my beautiful Isobel," he mumbled, his index finger tracing the freckles up her arm, "if it can stay between the two us—I have a reputation as a playboy to maintain, after all. I'm good at earning money."

Her eyes narrowed, and he knew that Isobel would never be satisfied with such a vague answer.

"What does that mean?" she urged.

"I've got an inherited fortune and I could live well off it here in Sweden. But the fact is that I earned most of my money myself."

He fell silent. It made no difference how far he distanced himself from his background, how much he spent time with people who boasted about their success, it was in his very bones. You didn't talk about yourself and your income. But he didn't want Isobel to doubt him. The attraction between them had knocked him off balance.

In a way, all people were unique. But Isobel was more unique than anyone else he had met, more of everything. At once strong and vulnerable. Cool and competent, but she also had that fragility he caught a glimpse of every once in a while. The uncertainty that carved deep furrows into her brow. And then her extraordinary beauty, of course. He was on the verge of being obsessed with her appearance; he could lie awake for hours, studying her in his mind, centimeter by centimeter. He wanted her, and if the price was honesty, then he could be honest.

"But how do you earn so much money? Surely not on poker?"

He shook his head. No, it was much more complicated than that. It was strange that he had never spoken to anyone about this. Not even Natalia or Eugene knew everything. Did they also think he was a criminal? He needed to think about that.

"It started with my friend, the one I told you about."

"The chef? Romeo?"

"Yeah. We met ten years ago, in New York. I was on a summer break from the School of Economics in Stockholm and went over there to party. We met in a nightclub. Romeo had just won a competition, a reality show, on TV and was dreaming about starting his own restaurant."

Alexander had been drunk and thought that taking some of his money and investing in a gay Italian chef sounded like the best idea in the world. "Shame you're not Muslim," he'd slurred. "It'd annoy my dad even more." And so, still hungover, he had started the company Golden Griffin Business Growth to give Romeo the start-up capital he needed.

"I invested in that restaurant, and now we've got several, pretty much all over the world. Romeo's a genius." The only thing he regretted today was the ridiculous company name, but it had stuck.

"You mean it's possible to get that rich just by owning a few restaurants?" Isobel sounded doubtful.

He shook his head. "Something else turned up one day, by chance. I met a guy who'd recorded a sound he thought was funny. He said he wanted to create ringtones for cell phones. My company gave money to him, too. It's one of the most-downloaded ringtones ever now. And it just continued. I was one of the first people to invest in games for cell phones."

Golden Griffin had started as a drunken joke, developed into a business, and become something that made him independent of his family.

"I can see problems and potential several steps ahead. It's almost laid out like a map in front of me. It's like poker in that respect."

They had cross-fertilized one another, his card playing and his businesses. Both relied on having the patience to wait for the right moment, on daring to take risks but at the same time staying rational. Ten years ago, mobile and digital solutions had still been unfamiliar and difficult to understand, but Alexander had seen the potential immediately. His company had systematically invested in businesses—sometimes just two guys in a cellar—who developed various digital services, apps, and other solutions. When the cell phone market exploded, first in the West and then in the East, the money had really started to roll in. The Internet: the modern route to inconceivable wealth.

"The money I gave Medpax was lily white—you've got my word."

Isobel looked so relieved that Alexander didn't know whether to laugh or take offense. The idea that she had been wondering about this had never struck him.

"Shame on you, Isobel, for thinking so little of me," he said. He raised his hand, placed it on her neck, and stroked her skin with his thumb. Her pulse pounded beneath his touch.

Alexander would never say it aloud, but in his experience the more beautiful a woman was, the less engaged she was in bed. It was as though beautiful women thought that just *being there* was enough. Not that he was complaining, but it was always more fun with a woman who *wanted* as much as he did. And he was willing to bet that Isobel, the most beautiful woman he'd ever seen, hid true passion beneath her cool surface. He would wager that she was getting wet as they kissed again. That she pushed against the fabric of her dress because the friction of it against her skin excited her. He suspected that the two of them together . . .

No, he didn't want Isobel to have doubts about him, didn't want any unnecessary hurdles between him and the woman he was planning to seduce most thoroughly.

"I'm immoral most of the time, but I'm definitely not a criminal," he murmured before he brought his lips to her collarbone. He heard her rasping breaths, felt how she pressed herself against him, and he whispered, "Happy now?"

"Thank you for telling me," she said quietly.

His mouth grazed hers once more. It was a simple kiss, just lips and breathing, no tongue, but he was in no rush. He loved this, the foreplay, the beginning. He let a hand cradle her face, vaguely aware that new sounds had filled the air and that part of her concentration had shifted away from him.

He leaned forward, but Isobel pulled back.

"Do you hear that?" she asked, a happy smile playing at her lips.

At first, he had no idea what she was talking about, but then he heard it too. Music.

"Don't tell me that's an orchestra?" she said.

"Just a small one. Tonight there is a ball at the castle. And I happen to own an actual ballroom. Want to go in?"

"Absolutely."

He stood up and held out his hand. The seduction would have to wait. "Come on, then. I know for a fact that there'll be at least one waltz."

Chapter 16

Of course he had a ballroom, Isobel mused as she glanced around the extravagant room. Cuir de Cordoue gilded leather hangings were on the walls, huge chandeliers on the ceiling, and everywhere, brilliantly colored arrangements of tulips and other spring flowers. At one end, the musicians were playing. Their polished instruments gleamed, and the guests were already moving across the floor.

Alexander turned to her and bowed formally. "May I?" he asked, and held out a hand. She glided into his arms, a tingling sense of happiness spreading through her body. He had fought for her honor. He wasn't a criminal, he was an economic genius, and he had kissed her as if she was the sexiest and most desirable woman on earth. It truly was a fairy-tale evening.

They sailed out, across the floor. Alexander was, of course, a phenomenal dancing partner. She knew that already, but there was something special about letting him sweep her across a dance floor that was several hundred years old.

"What?" he murmured, pulling her closer.

"It's the second time we've danced together. We're starting to get good at this."

He squeezed her hand and spun them round, round, round.

Much later, after a softly lilting waltz, a fast dance that made her pulse quicken, a polka that made her laugh, followed by another sensuous waltz, Isobel halfheartedly suggested that maybe they should dance with other people. Her mouth was close to his neck, her hand tightly gripped in his. He simply hardened that grip in response.

"No," he said. "I only want to dance with you. I'm not the host, I don't have any obligations; stay with me."

This intensity, this fervor . . . It was so tempting to be drawn in. People were so rarely intense. It was part of the reason she was drawn to field work, that you *felt* so much.

When the musicians took a break, Alexander led her over to the wide-open doors. She was warm, and the cool air that met them in the garden was glorious. They walked away, across the lawn, between the trees. Alexander stopped, put an arm around her waist, and pushed her gently backward until she ended up against a tree trunk. There it was again, that intensity. He placed a palm above her head and leaned in to her. How could she be so superficial that she was turned on by the size of him, his dominant position? But she was. His other hand was at her cheek, and he kissed her, and it was the perfect kiss, exactly as she'd known it would be.

It's really the kisses you want.

Someone had said those words to her, and they were true. Nothing was like the first kiss. And Alexander was so awesome at kissing. Hard lips that turned soft, his tongue, finally playing with hers, and those small bites on her lower lip. His other hand was slowly caressing her waist, her rib cage, moving toward her plunging neckline, his fingers pulling at the material, cleverly working their way in, caressing her skin, making her gasp. She felt his leg between her thighs, and she wanted him more than she had wanted a man in a long time. His mouth covered hers once more, and they kissed, passionately and breathlessly. She placed her hands on his upper arms, loved how hard they felt, and let herself be swept away. She could be young and irresponsible for one weekend, she thought, make out with Alexander De la Grip beneath the stars. The world wouldn't end just because she'd let go for a while.

Until it did just that.

Ended a little.

She heard an indistinguishable murmur of conversation at first. People were headed in their direction. And then she heard the sound she wanted to hear least of all.

A loud man's voice that had, at one point in time, filled her with so many complex feelings, she still had trouble working them out.

A voice Isobel had loved at first, but then had come to fear.

And suddenly there he was, in front of them. Amused look. Piercing gaze. Unconcerned that he had interrupted. But then again Sebastien never did care about other people's opinions. It was what had attracted her to him at first. Before it scared the living daylights out of her.

"*Bonjour,* Isobel."

She hadn't imagined it, after all—Sebastien really was here. Isobel ran her hands over her dress, smoothing it out, and knew that Alexander must be wondering. Sebastien's dark eyes swept over her.

"*Hej,*" she replied in Swedish, creating distance between them by being petty and refusing to speak French with him. He took a step forward, and before she had time to react, he kissed her on the cheek, as though Alexander wasn't standing right beside her. He smelled like he always had, the same aftershave, the same soap, and the memories washed over her. She was twenty again. How was it even possible to react like this? She swallowed, tried to fight the dryness in her mouth, searching for words but failing. And then Alexander stepped forward.

"Alexander De la Grip," he said, and held out his hand to Sebastien. "This is my house, so technically I guess you're one of my guests. Who are you?"

His voice was calm and civil, but Isobel detected hardened steel beneath the polite phrases and courteous movements.

"Sebastien Pascal."

When the two men shook hands, Sebastien didn't quite manage to hide a grimace of pain, and Isobel glanced at Alexander. Had he just crushed Sebastien's hand? Like in some bad film? Alexander gave her an innocent look.

"So, Sebastien, how do you two know each other?" he asked.

"Isobel and I worked together," Sebastien replied. "Among other things."

If Alexander caught the subtext, he showed absolutely no sign of it.

"So you're a doctor too?" he asked, all politeness. But Isobel sensed something wild beneath the smooth upper-class exterior.

"*Oui.* And you, do you work in medicine?" Sebastien asked with a wry smile, as if they all knew the idea was absurd.

"No, not at all," Alexander replied, and Isobel could see him stepping back behind his jet-set façade. She hadn't realized how long it had been since she'd last heard him talk and act like that. As if everything was a joke.

"I'm an international playboy. I'd never have the time or inclination to train to be anything as serious as a doctor. But tell me more about your work together."

He gave Isobel another look, his beautiful eyes devoid of emotion.

"I was her supervisor," said Sebastien. And then his face cracked into a grin that made her skin crawl. "She was a very good student. Very perceptive." He raised a hand and stroked her cheek. She managed not to flinch. "It's great to see you, Isobel."

Alexander studied the dark-haired Frenchman as objectively as he could. Sebastien had to be around forty. No wedding ring. Handsome, if you liked the self-righteous asshole type, radiating competence and confidence.

Alexander took a dislike to him immediately.

And now that the man was standing there, *touching* Isobel, he wished he had squeezed his hand even harder.

Every man worries about how he compares to the men a woman has been with before.

Alexander had read that somewhere. At the time, he'd thought it was ridiculous. Only men lacking confidence worried about things they couldn't change, things that had nothing to do with them.

But now . . . That Isobel had been with this self-important doctor, it was obvious.

He would never stoop to jealousy, never. But there was something that didn't add up. Isobel was rigid, and she hadn't said anything for a long while. In contrast to Sebastien, who just kept talking.

"*Chérie,* you surprise me. He's not your type at all."

"Nonsense, I'm everyone's type," Alexander said.

"I think I need to . . ." Isobel began, falling silent midsentence.

Something definitely wasn't right. Alexander found her hand; it was ice-cold. Sebastien wasn't just some boyfriend from the past. There was something else in the air, playing out in ordinary, everyday phrases. But Alexander had grown up with parents who were experts at communicating via more or less veiled criticism; it would take more than Sebastien's needle pricks to get to him. He put an arm around Isobel's waist, and when she didn't seem to object, pulled her close to him.

"Don't let us keep you," he said firmly to Sebastien. "There's a free bar. Just help yourself. If you'll excuse us," and he maneuvered himself and Isobel past the Frenchman without waiting for a reply.

"Are you okay?" he asked as soon as they were out of earshot.

She took a deep breath, shook her head gently, and gave him a faint smile. "Sorry, I don't really know what happened. It's been a long day."

He led her inside, down a hallway, opened a door and held it open for her. "Let's go in here."

"Where are we?" she asked once they entered the room.

He pulled a small armchair over.

"Sit."

She sank down into it, leaned against the back, and breathed out.

"I'm completely exhausted."

He grabbed a thin blanket and laid it over her knees. He hadn't even thought about it, the tempo she'd been at all day; he had just wanted her for himself.

"This is the small library," he explained, pulling another armchair over toward her. "Do you want to talk about it?"

She bit her lip.

"Isobel?"

"Oh, alright then. I knew Sebastien was here. I saw him earlier."

It was he she had seen when she'd looked so scared. Christ, he had a good mind to go back and knock out a few of the French doctor's perfect teeth.

"He likes events like this. He's a good doctor," she added, almost as an afterthought.

"But a bad person?" He wanted her to agree, to say that Sebastien Pascal was the worst person she'd ever met.

"All people have bad sides."

"You don't," he said.

She laughed. "Of course I do."

He leaned back, stretched out his legs. "Like what?"

"I can be a little judgmental at times."

"Really? I hadn't noticed."

She laughed again, loudly, and he was pleased that the easy conversation was working. The color was returning to her face, and the awful haunted look he'd seen in her eyes was gone. What exactly had this Sebastien done to her? And did he really want to know? Did he want to get mixed up in this?

"You were together?" he asked, because this was Isobel and he did want to get mixed up with her.

She stalled before she answered, with a sigh. "Yes. I was really young. He gave a lecture to our course. Trauma surgery."

Older doctor. Gifted. Of course she'd fallen for him. And Sebastien Pascal didn't look like a man who had any moral qualms about having a relationship with a student.

"What happened?"

She shook her head. "It's really complicated."

"Isn't it always?"

"I guess so."

"Isobel?"

"Yes?"

He studied her face, her generous curves, her long legs. How had she looked at twenty? She couldn't possibly have been more beautiful than she was today. "Did Sebastien hurt you?" he asked levelly.

She didn't answer immediately, just looked straight ahead. Her face was impossible to read.

Alexander waited, his pulse pounding. He was certain he had broken hearts. He had slept with married women for nearly half his life, and he'd often been selfish. But he had never physically hurt a woman. Just the thought of it made him feel ill. It was the one thing that defined him, and it was more important these days than it had ever been. With his family background . . .

"I don't really know how to answer that," she said slowly. She turned to him. "It was all so long ago. I was just shocked to see him, shocked by my own reaction. In a way I'm glad we met, talked. It was good for me. As a kind of closure, I guess."

He exhaled the breath he hadn't realized he was holding. Was her answer deliberately vague? Should he head out, find Sebastien, and beat him up?

"Did you love him?"

She looked down at her hands, pulled at a loose thread on the blanket. "Yes. A lot."

"And now? How do you feel now?"

"Like it's time to look forward. I moved on, of course. It was ten years ago. I've had plenty of boyfriends since then."

"Good to hear."

She laughed. "Oh, come on. I'm sure I haven't had as many as you."

"Nah, I haven't had a single boyfriend."

He smiled at her laugh.

She rested her chin in one hand. "Have you ever been in love? If you don't mind my asking."

He dragged a finger along the armrest of his chair.

"Not in the way you mean," he said. He realized it wasn't just Isobel who had things in her past that were difficult to explain to an outsider.

He had never been deeply in love. It felt like a defect at times, a huge plus at others. He loved the company of women, enjoyed spending time with them, but he always moved on before things got serious.

Isobel nodded without pressing for more. The tension was completely gone from her face now; she looked young and vulnerable. Happy and still slightly ruffled from his kisses.

Alexander leaned back in his seat and tried to look at the situation objectively. She was a passionate idealist and a competent working woman. Sexy as hell. Their kissing had been pure eroticism, the promise of passion beyond the everyday. But she was also a woman with a complicated past that might or might not be over. It was probably now he should take a step back. The stakes were getting higher, and the outcome was uncertain. If he continued, he would just get more and more involved, he knew that. At worst, Isobel might start to have expectations. She could talk about boyfriends and have secrets all she wanted, but she wasn't nearly as experienced as he was, not when it came to this kind of game. Maybe it was time to listen to the warning bells after all? Stop now, while there was still time. Back up before things got too messy and complicated. Before people got unnecessarily hurt.

On the other side of the door, the party was still going on, despite the late hour. At least two dozen women out there would more than happily welcome him into their beds. They would offer him the things he liked most in the world: pleasure and the warmth of physical contact, with no expectations other than a bit of fun while it lasted. Out there, things were certain and risk-free. In here, uncertain and risky. He had always been a smart player. He should get up from his chair, say something superficial and distant, and then back away.

Alexander knew all this as he leaned forward, placed a hand on Isobel's leg, felt her warmth through the blanket and the thin green silk beneath, felt Isobel tremble the way she had earlier when he had touched her. He was about to cross a line he might come to regret later.

Maybe.

"Tomorrow," he said quietly, "would you like to go to Copenhagen with me? We could fly over, have lunch."

"Fly? To Denmark?"

He caressed her knee, slowly, almost thoughtfully. Some of the guests had arrived by private jet. He could borrow one of them. Could take Isobel for a day to her father's homeland. Take her away from drunken idiots and sadistic doctors from her past.

"One of the best restaurants in the world is there," he said convincingly, still caressing her leg. "What d'you say? Can I take you for lunch tomorrow?"

"Copenhagen?" Her voice was quiet.

"It's just lunch—you need to eat."

She nodded, as though what he said was logical. "Yes, I do." She smiled, and her smile sent butterflies through him. He couldn't let go of her yet. He wasn't responsible for her feelings and expectations; he was responsible only for his own. And things would go well between them, better than well. No one would walk away from this disappointed, that he could promise.

She covered her mouth with her palm and stifled an enormous yawn.

"Sorry," she said, embarrassed. "I suddenly have no energy."

He looked at his watch. "It's almost three. Do you want me to walk you to your room?"

She raised an eyebrow.

"I just meant walk with you up to the turret, nothing else," he lied without hesitation

"So you *are* the one who fixed that beautiful room for me. Thanks. You really are a gentleman, Alexander. But if it's okay with you, I'd rather say good night down here."

She put the blanket to one side and got to her feet. He did the same. They studied one another. He wanted to raise a hand, touch her cheek, pull her close to him, but she really did look exhausted. She didn't look like a person who should be going to a field hospital in Chad; she looked like a woman in need of a vacation.

"Good night," she said softly.

"Sleep well, Isobel."

Once she had gone, Alexander grabbed a carafe of whisky and sat back down in the armchair. As he sipped his drink—he actually preferred vodka but wasn't so finicky that he couldn't appreciate an eighteen-year-old single malt—he thought about his next move. He had always been a shrewd poker player. Never careless but never afraid, either. He loved and respected the game. He thought about what Isobel had said. She was a smart woman, and she was right about many things.

But she was dead wrong on one point. If there was one thing he wasn't, it was a gentleman. He played to win. Always.

Chapter 17

Isobel took the last few stairs up to her turret room. After she closed the door behind her, she practically slumped with her back against it.

Jesus.

She took off her heels and sat down on the bed, her mind berating her. *What,* exactly, did she think she was doing? She couldn't get involved with Alexander, she knew that. She wasn't insane.

How could she even think of doing anything other than a bit of flirting? She fumbled for the clasp of the necklace, almost panicking when she couldn't undo it. Eventually, she managed. She got up and put the necklace back in its box, along with the earrings. It was as though a spell was about to break. As though she had temporarily been another version of herself but was now slowly regaining her senses.

There were plenty of reasons why she shouldn't have anything more to do with Alexander, she thought as she pulled off her dress. Hundreds, maybe even thousands of rational reasons. And then a few irrational ones, too.

The intensity. The feelings.

She took off her underwear, washed her face, fetched a glass of water, and then slipped between the ironed sheets in her absurdly big bed. She could still hear a faint murmur and the occasional hint of music from elsewhere in the castle.

She looked out through the window, growing drowsy, allowing her gaze to fall on the night sky and the twinkling stars.

What had she gotten herself into?

And then, before there was any time to react, she suddenly felt a hand over her mouth. Nothing could really prepare you for how it felt, to be almost suffocated by someone else's palm. She wanted to scream but couldn't. She felt her arms and hands being tied, quickly and without mercy. Bone-shattering terror coursed through her.

The fear. The petrifying experience of being totally at someone else's mercy. The horrific sensation of not being able to move without your wrists hurting. She fought the rising panic, tried to scream, to break free, but couldn't. She pulled at her bonds, panicking when she felt them cutting into her wrists. Please, she wanted to say to the man who had taken total control of her body. Please, don't hurt me.

A sob racked her body and then she broke the surface of the dream. Her heart was racing, and she heard her breath coming in shallow gasps. A dream. It was just a dream. She'd had them before. She tried to steady herself. The loss of control was terrifying, she knew that painfully well. But it was just a nightmare. She fell back, pressed a hand over her forehead, and just breathed, trying to clear her head of the last remnants of the violent dream.

She was still lying awake when the sun began to shine outside, when the birds started twittering, and when what she assumed were the peacocks started to make screeching sounds.

When she heard a vacuum cleaner start and caught the scent of freshly brewed coffee, she got up. She took a quick shower and then headed, bare-faced, down the winding staircase. She knew that the castle was full of overnight guests, but it was just seven, so she was one of the few people awake. She followed the scent of coffee and found a kitchen where she picked up a freshly brewed cup and a cheese sandwich from a woman in a striped apron.

She heard the rustle of a newspaper and turned around to see Eugene Tolstoy.

He folded the paper and got to his feet. "Good morning," he said. "You're up early."

She took her cup and sandwich and sat down opposite him.

"Leila is still asleep," he said. "We stayed up late, playing cards and talking."

She took a sip of the steaming coffee—strong and hot. She had completely forgotten about Leila.

"Is everything okay?" he asked, studying her. "I heard you got caught up in a bit of a scuffle yesterday."

"Did Alexander tell you?"

"A little. He sat with us awhile after you went to bed. We don't have to talk about it, if it makes you uncomfortable. But I want to apologize. You're my guest, and I'm sorry it happened to you. None of those men will ever be welcome here again, that much is certain. You mean a lot to Alexander. And to Leila. That means you're also important to me, if you'll allow me to say so, even though we don't know one another especially well."

She smiled at his elaborate speech. "Thank you," she said.

He played with his fragile teacup. "Did you know that I've met your mother?"

"No. When?"

"I met Blanche in Paris in the eighties. I actually met your grandmother, too. Karin Jansson, yes? She was a fantastic artist. I saw one of her canvases at the Tessin Institute in Paris. Have you seen it?"

"A girl with red hair, right?" Isobel smiled and held out a strand of her hair. "It's me."

"I suspected as much. It's beautiful, just like you."

They fell silent, and Isobel drank her coffee as Eugene stirred his tea.

"It's been good to have you here," said Eugene. "I hope you see me as a friend. And if you ever need anything, don't hesitate to ask."

Isobel picked at a bread crumb. "Could you arrange a taxi?"

He gave her a look of surprise. "Are you leaving? I thought you and Alexander . . . ?"

She shook her head. She couldn't begin to deny the physical attraction she felt for Alexander. She was experienced enough to realize it was unique in its nature, and she had come close to being drawn in. But that was the problem. Alexander threatened to free everything she tried to control within herself. First those crazy-hot kisses, melting her brain, setting dangerous feelings loose. Then Sebastien appearing, reminding her of things she desperately needed to keep in the past. And then that vivid dream. Christ, she hadn't had that dream for a long time. It wasn't a coincidence. When she was with Alexander her defenses began crumbling, and she couldn't afford that, simply couldn't. No, she was putting an end to this madness, taking the only logical, the only sane, step she could.

"I need to go home. I have lots to do."

"Does Alexander know? Sorry, it's not my business. But he likes you, I can see that."

She sighed. The day trip to Denmark he'd suggested did sound great. She loved the language, the food, and the culture, and she hadn't been to Copenhagen for years. Alexander's suggestion had been almost irresistible.

"I'll leave a note. I've already rebooked my train ticket," she said.

"In that case, of course I'll make sure you get to the station. If you give me five minutes, I'll drive you myself."

"Thank you," she said. She felt a pang in her chest at the thought they might never see one another again. She liked Eugene, but they hardly moved in the same circles.

Once Isobel was on the train, her forehead resting against the window, her cell phone rang in her bag. Alexander's number appeared on the screen, and she waited until it stopped ringing, sent a text saying she was heading home, and ignored her phone the rest of the way back to Stockholm.

She walked the short distance from the central station to her apartment on the corner of Kungsgatan and Vasagatan. Dropped her bag on the floor, and gazed sightlessly into the refrigerator.

She would never admit it, but Isobel knew exactly what she had done today. She had run, and she was ashamed of her cowardice. She wasn't normally a coward. But the fact was that the last time she had felt something like what she felt for Alexander, the last time she felt such an intense attraction that she had trouble thinking clearly, it had ended in nothing less than disaster.

She closed the refrigerator, went over to the couch, and lay down. She stared up at the ceiling. She had eight unanswered messages from Alexander, but it was best to cut it off now, however much it hurt. Because the last time she felt like this, it had been for Sebastien, and she had very nearly not survived.

Chapter 18

No matter where Peter looked these days, he saw people at work. He hadn't seen the world like that before. People working in kiosks, in restaurants, and behind counters. Serving, cleaning, and tending to the needs of others.

He placed a hand on his desk, studied the back of it, and tried to remember how much cleaning or manual labor that hand had done. They had grown up with staff, he and his two siblings, and he had always taken their presence for granted. But these days he often wondered about all these people whose lives were so different from his own. It was as if he saw life itself differently now. As though a filter had been removed, giving the world new contours, populating it with individuals he hadn't noticed before. He liked to watch them. Some seemed happy and contented, but others definitely seemed weighed down. Why was that? Why were some people happy with their lives while others were unhappy? Where did the difference lie?

Peter watched Gina as she pushed the vacuum over the expensive office carpets. She was one of those who worked hard, who existed in the background. Was she one of the happy or unhappy ones?

He hadn't said a word to her. Not since that evening last week when they'd left the office at the same time and he had spoken to her. He didn't even recall what he'd said, just that she had looked at him like he was an idiot.

Peter got up from his chair. She didn't look up as he pushed the door shut. The dull sound of the vacuum motor grew fainter. He was so tired. He couldn't sleep, not at home, not in his bed, not at night. His mind just kept racing. There had been a time when he was worried because he felt so little. But these days it was the only thing he did: feel.

He sat down on the small couch that somehow had ended up in his office. Heard the faint sound of the vacuum moving back and forth, leaned against the backrest. He would just close his eyes for a minute or two.

"Hello?"

Peter woke and sat upright on the couch, completely disoriented. He blinked, tried to shake the sleep from his brain. When he saw Gina in the doorway, he quickly pulled his hand over his mouth, worried he might have snored or dribbled. Gina's face looked concerned. Her eyes swept over him as though she was looking for a sign of . . . something.

"Is everything okay?" she asked as she wound her earbuds around her cell phone and then shoved it into her apron pocket.

"Yes, sorry," Peter said, smoothing out his shirt and tie. He had no idea how long he'd been sleeping. "What time is it?"

"Eight."

He stood up, feeling stupid just sitting there.

She quickly backed up.

It was probably just the two of them left in the office. Had he scared her? Christ.

"I'm sorry, Gina," he said hurriedly. "I've been having trouble sleeping—I didn't mean to fall asleep here. Sorry," he repeated.

"I'm leaving soon," she said, her chin jutting out. "I just need to eat something. You can go if you want. I'll lock up."

She started to leave, and Peter found himself following her to the lunchroom. He drank a glass of water while she ate from a round plastic box; it smelled spicy, looked vibrant. His stomach rumbled; he hoped she didn't hear it. They stood in silence as he refilled his glass.

"Why can't you sleep?" she eventually asked, as she wiped her mouth and put the box to one side.

"It's been that way awhile."

"My dad has problems like that."

Peter smiled. "How old is he?"

"Don't know. About forty. Or fifty. You?"

"Thirty-six." He didn't dare ask her age, but she looked young.

Her Swedish was perfect, but he could still detect a slight accent he couldn't identify. He wondered where she was from. Was it rude to ask? He had no idea, wasn't sure he'd ever had such a long conversation with a dark-skinned person. Could you say dark-skinned? He was close to breaking out into a sweat, terrified of sounding politically incorrect or worse. He had grown up with his father's prejudices. The man hated everyone: foreigners, blacks, feminists. Peter had never thought about it before, embarrassingly enough, had simply kept his mouth shut and adapted. But things were very different today, and he was genuinely curious about what life was like where Gina grew up. Geography was the only subject he'd enjoyed in school, maybe because the focus wasn't just on numbers and letters but pictures and stories. But he didn't dare ask, didn't dare break the fragile state of noncontempt from her side.

He settled with asking, "How is it you don't know your father's age, if you don't mind my asking?" He held his breath, hoped she wouldn't rail at him.

She turned on the tap, added some dish liquid, and rinsed out her box. "He doesn't know himself. It isn't important in our country. I'm from Somalia. You aren't defined by your age there, or even what you do. You're defined by your family."

Peter rinsed his glass and dried it off, wondering what it would be like to be judged solely by your family. "Is it just you and your dad?"

"I have a little brother," she said, but her voice changed. She didn't like the subject, that was clear. But he didn't want her to stop; he had been starved of any conversation that wasn't about work.

"I have a little brother too."

She smiled but said nothing.

Idiot. Gina'd met Alexander plenty of times.

Gina dried her box, threw away some paper, wiped the counter. Peter realized she was about to leave. He looked at his watch. It was almost nine. Where had the time gone?

"Where do you live?" he asked.

She looked at him as though she wanted to ask *Why?* but answered curtly: "Tensta."

He had never been there, he realized, just knew it by reputation. Built in the seventies, called the Million Programme, once its aim had been to offer reasonably priced housing; today the huge high-rises were poorly kept. Ninety percent of the inhabitants were immigrants, and the project was infamous for violence and crime. "Do you have a car?"

She flashed him an ironic look. "Do I have a *car?*"

"Sorry," he said. "I mean, how are you getting home?" Tensta was on the way to Gyllgarn. He must have passed the area hundreds of times, but it was far. He had no idea how you would get there if you didn't have a car. Train? Bus? It was late already. Was it really safe?

"I get home the same way I've done the past few years," she answered. All the usual contempt was back in her voice. "It's called public transport."

She started to untie her apron; his eyes fell on her narrow waist.

"Are you working some more?" she asked. "Could you lock up? My dad is waiting, and I'm late."

"Of course," he said, ashamed that he might have held her up. "Go on."

Ten minutes later, Peter switched off the lights. He set the alarm and took the elevator down. When he came out onto the street, Gina was standing on the sidewalk. She was on the phone. She hung up, sighed deeply, and caught sight of him.

"Everything okay?" he asked.

She frowned. "Dad called. There are no trains to Tensta tonight. Someone threw fireworks into the tunnels so they're all full of smoke. I don't know how I'm going to get home." She rubbed her forehead wearily. "There aren't any replacement buses. And my dad's having a bad evening, so they haven't eaten, and I need to study too." She shook her head. "Shit."

He was on the verge of saying that she could just take a taxi, but he stopped himself in time. "I can give you a ride," he said. It was impulsive, but as soon as he had said it, it felt right. He had the car, after all. He drove it to work every day, thinking that he might go play some tennis, but he never had the energy. And it wasn't like anyone was waiting for him at home.

"Why?" She looked suspicious.

"I can see you're worried about your dad. It'll be quicker."

She looked hesitant now. She was wearing a thin jacket and had knotted the belt tightly around her waist. When he cautiously glanced at her, he saw that she was bare-legged, wearing thin canvas shoes.

"You'll be home in fifteen minutes," he said persuasively. "The car's around the corner, and I'll drop you off outside your door."

She pulled at her lip hesitantly, but Peter could see he had won. She nodded curtly. "Thanks, that would be great."

They walked the short distance to the street where his car was parked. Peter fished out the keys. If Gina was impressed by the shiny, light gray Mercedes, a brand-new sports model, she said nothing. Peter unlocked the car and opened the door for her. She slipped into the passenger seat.

Peter started the engine and steered out into traffic.

"Music?" he asked.

She shrugged, and he hesitated, didn't want to put on something she was too polite to say she hated. "Why don't you choose the station," he said, solving the dilemma. From the corner of his eye, he saw Gina's slender fingers at the controls. She paused at a commercial channel, and soft eighties music washed over them. He wondered whether she'd even been *born* in the eighties.

"Do you like your job?" he asked, grimacing at his question. She was a cleaner. Of course she didn't.

"It's okay, actually. It's hard work, but I can work independently." She looked down at her lap.

"You said you were going home to study?"

"Yes."

Peter waited, but she offered no further information. He turned off at Norrtull, signaled, and continued north.

"Medicine," she said after a moment. "At KI. Karolinska Institutet."

"Enjoy it?" He had hated school, all those letters dancing on the page, and his father's constant disappointment, the endless comparisons with his brilliant siblings. Natalia, with her head for figures, and Alexander, with his charisma and flashes of genius. Both of them had been moved up a grade in primary school. Peter had needed to fight just to pass.

"I'm only in my second semester, but I always dreamed of being a doctor, and I love it."

"I can hear it in your voice. But managing a cleaning job at the same time—" He knew people who had read medicine; they had studied almost constantly, as far as he remembered.

"I have to. I don't want to take out a student loan, and my family needs the money."

Peter's own concerns suddenly struck him as being first-world problems. Did she support her father *and* her little brother? All while she studied medicine?

"How old are you, Gina? If you don't mind my asking."

"Twenty-two."

He tried to remember what he had been doing the spring he turned twenty-two. Partying. Going on ski holidays. He'd been given a million kronor in shares as a birthday gift.

"Turn in here," she said, pointing to an exit.

He made his way through Tensta, following her instructions. He pulled over when she told him to, and resisted the impulse to get out and hold the door open for her. For some reason, he suspected it would bother her.

She leaned back into the car. "Thanks so much for the ride," she said. He could see that she felt uncomfortable. It *was* an unusual situation.

"It's no problem," he answered honestly.

She flashed him a quick smile before she turned to go. Peter waited. He saw her open the door and disappear into the tall, gray building. He waited for a while, to see if he could work out which floor she lived on. No lights came on.

Chapter 19

Alexander waved to Natalia, who was waiting for him with the stroller by the bridge onto Djurgården, the Royal Game Park, a lush island in central Stockholm. Djurgården was home to yacht harbors, extensive stretches of forest and meadows—a favorite recreation area. He and Natalia used to come here when they were young. Had Peter come also? Alexander couldn't remember.

Natalia waved back, and when he reached her, he gave her a big hug.

"Everything okay?"

Natalia pushed her dark hair from her face and smiled at him. "I'm glad you called. David's gone to the office for a few hours, and it's nice to get out."

"So you only have time for me when your husband is doing something else?"

She rolled her eyes. "Oh, please. You only want to see me when you need something, so don't try to guilt trip me."

Alexander grinned. His big sister was right; he did need something from her. He peered into the stroller where Molly lay, happily sucking on a pacifier.

"She's sweet," he said, and he meant it. "Not that it's so strange, since she's your daughter," he added.

He had always known Nat would be an excellent mother, if for no other reason than she was the opposite of their own mother in all respects. He put an arm around her, and when she leaned into him, he felt an unexpected lump in his chest. He cared so goddamn much about her and was so bad at showing it. If Natalia hadn't been there when they were growing up . . .

He hugged her more tightly. Natalia had represented all that was warm and safe back then. She had always tried to protect him when they were young, had comforted him when he was sad, and played with him when he was lonely. She had been a child too, so there had been plenty of stuff she hadn't been able to prevent, but Alexander was utterly certain that Natalia had nurtured, knocked, and coaxed the few positive traits he had into him. Without her, the emptiness inside would have been unbearable.

Natalia smiled and leaned over the stroller to tuck in her daughter. He watched her confident movements. They had been so close during their childhood, but he didn't think she had ever suspected what he had gone through when they were teenagers. What he had done and what had been done to him. How would she react if she ever found out? Nat had protected him when they were small, but he had also kept some of the worst things from her, the things he was ashamed of.

She glanced up and gave him a quick look. What would she say about the stuff he worked on in New York? She worried about his playboy lifestyle, the scandals, his lack of goals and purpose. She probably thought he took drugs, drank too much. He *had* been close to telling her, several times; the last thing he wanted was for her to worry about him. The problem was that he knew his sister. If he told Natalia, she would nag him about telling their mother and sharing with Peter and God knew what other crap. And then everyone would know, and he would be . . . defenseless. He usually tried not to think about it, but sometimes, like today, his conscience bothered him. It was easier when the family thought he did nothing but party, because if they had no expectations of him, they couldn't be disappointed. The strange thing was that he had told Isobel. They barely knew one another, and yet he had blurted out everything.

"What?" Natalia asked with an affectionate smile.

"Did you know right away, when you met David, that you two could be together?"

She straightened. "No. People always think that in retrospect, but no. It took a while." Her eyes pierced him. "Why? Have you met someone?"

He laughed and shook his head. "I just wondered. Listen, I know I haven't always been the best of brothers, and yes, I did call because I need your help with something. But I hope you know that I'm happy for you—that you have David and Molly. You, my beloved sister, are my favorite person in the world."

"Aside from all the girlfriends I read about every day?" she joked, but he could see delight in her intelligent eyes. He should say it more often, how much she meant to him.

"Aside from them, yeah. Look, the kiosks are open. Can I get you an ice cream?"

They walked along the canal with ice creams in their hands.

"How's the new apartment?" Natalia asked once Molly had stopped fretting and fallen asleep in her stroller.

"It's all painted white, very Scandinavian. No family heirlooms as far as the eye can see. I like it."

After the interior designers had done their thing, Alexander had spent the past few days finishing things off himself. He had bought glasses and china. Candlesticks and bedding. All the while he'd imagined Isobel coming to visit, how he would show her around.

If she hadn't dumped him for good, that was.

A note was all Isobel had left behind when he had come down to breakfast, expecting to whisk her off for their planned day trip. At first, he'd thought it was just a bad joke, but when she didn't answer her phone and simply texted an apology that she was already on the train, he had been forced to accept that she'd actually bolted. With the help of Eugene, the traitor, who'd given her a ride to the station.

Alexander couldn't remember the last time he'd been so thoroughly dumped.

Skåne had been no fun without Isobel, so he'd gone home to consider his next step. He had trouble believing he had imagined the chemistry between them. Light a match and sparks would've flown. But there was something else about her that he hadn't managed to decipher yet. He had caught glimpses of it every now and then, heard it in a tone of voice, a cut-off word, as though she had said too much. No, something else had scared her away from Skåne, and Alexander would bet a fortune on its being some kind of complicated *feeling*.

So, he would just have to come up with a new strategy. He had already planned his next move, and that was where Natalia came in.

"Could you do me a favor? Could you speak to Åsa? I want to take a guest to her and Michel's mega wedding."

Natalia flashed him a suspicious look, and he was reminded that, new mother or not, she was one of the finance world's sharpest minds. "Can't you ask her yourself?"

He groaned. "Have you *talked* to Åsa lately?"

Natalia threw the rest of her ice cream away. "She is a little hard to talk to if you're not a wedding caterer or a dressmaker," she admitted.

Yes, a little hard. If by that you meant impossible. He couldn't chance it, better to ask Natalia. Åsa would never refuse Natalia anything. Åsa Bjelke had been Natalia's best friend since childhood. She had come to live with the De la Grip family after her entire family was killed in a car crash. She had been an eighteen-year-old platinum blond goddess, Alexander had been thirteen and the envy of every male between twelve and one hundred. But their relationship had been far from uncomplicated.

"I've never seen her like this." Natalia continued her musings. "Who would've thought that the queen of cool would turn into bridezilla? But since I'm such a nice person, and since you bought me an ice cream, I'll ask. Michel has two thousand relatives or something like that, so I'm sure Åsa will be happy to have someone else on her side. Who is she? Your plus one. It's not one of your horrendous American bimbos, is it?"

Alexander looked out at the water, suddenly ill at ease. It felt strange, talking to Natalia about Isobel, as though he wanted to keep Isobel to himself. Normally, he had no trouble discussing his female acquaintances. In fact, he quite enjoyed entertaining Natalia and Åsa with carefully edited stories of his escapades. But this felt different, more private. How weird.

"Alex? Spill it."

"A doctor I met. She works for Doctors Without Borders. And for an organization called Medpax."

Natalia used her hand to block the sun from her face. "You don't mean Isobel Sørensen, do you?"

"You know her?" he asked, taken aback.

"Not exactly. But we've met. She's the one who told me I was pregnant."

"Was she?" Isobel hadn't mentioned that. Though, of course, she would be very correct about her professional confidentiality, Doctor Isobel Sørensen. As far as Alexander knew, Isobel could treat all of his family and friends and not say a word about it. Admirable. And somewhat irritating.

"How do you know one another? Did you meet in Båstad?" Natalia asked.

"Yeah, and elsewhere. We've met a few times," he answered vaguely.

He should have known his big sister would sink her teeth in. "How many times? Are you together?"

"We were in Skåne. At Eugene's."

She stopped, looking at him with wide eyes. "Are you kidding me? Eugene met her? You've never introduced any of your girlfriends to the family."

"She's not my girlfriend. Please, Nat, don't make a big thing of this."

She looked like she was ready to burst, but simply said, "I'll talk to Åsa."

"Thanks."

She bit her lip. "Have you heard from Peter?"

"Not recently."

"He seems pretty down," she continued with the stubbornness of an older sibling. But as far as Alexander was concerned, Peter could sink into depression for all eternity.

"Can't you talk to him?"

"Nat, I love you to death, but even you can't fix this. Please. Drop it."

"Alex, there's something else I need to tell you," she said hesitantly. "I met my father."

It was his turn to stop. Last summer, it had come out that Gustaf De la Grip wasn't Natalia's biological father, that they had all lived in a lie. They hadn't talked about it much, but Alexander realized that he hadn't even asked. Had been too preoccupied with drinking. Funny how that worked. You not only forgot the things you wanted to, you forgot everything. "So you found him in the end?"

"Yes." Her eyes turned misty.

She was a family person. The news that she was the result of a lie and a betrayal had been tough for her. It wasn't her fault, of course. It was Ebba's. And Gustaf's. The parents again. Christ, they couldn't do anything right. "Who is he?" he asked gently, knowing this meant a lot to his sister.

She wiped away a tear. "He lives in Uppsala. He's a math professor at the university there."

Alexander chuckled. "Of course you're the daughter of a math genius." Natalia's head for numbers was legendary.

"He didn't even know I existed." She had a sad look in her eyes. "Mom never told him."

"Mom has a lot to answer for," he said, trying but not quite succeeding in keeping the animosity out of his voice.

"I know. But I'm tired of fighting with her. I just want her to be a grandmother to my daughter."

Natalia was a good person. He should tell her about his American life. He was resentful of his parents for lying to them; he shouldn't do the same to her, shouldn't withhold important things. "Nat, there is something I've been meaning to . . ." He was interrupted by a grin and Natalia suddenly lighting up like a supernova, the way she always did when she caught sight of her husband. Alexander couldn't help rolling his eyes. Love made people exceptionally stupid.

"Oh, stop it," she said, and flashed him a grin.

Alexander turned around and waited until David Hammar caught up with them. They greeted one another politely, and David gave him one of his grayish-blue looks, one that seemed to judge, value, and decide, in a split-second, that Alexander hadn't changed—or not for the better, anyway. He would describe the relationship he had with his powerful brother-in-law as neutral at best. Not cold, but definitely not cordial. Alexander had taken an aversion to David last summer, before he and Natalia were officially a couple, and despite the fact that David clearly made Natalia happier than Alexander had ever seen her, it felt like a matter of principle to maintain his distance. Besides, Alexander was convinced that the stony, made-it-on-his-own-merit David Hammar didn't care much for either him or his lifestyle. But both cared about Natalia, so they had a silent agreement to be polite and civil to one another.

David stooped over the stroller and looked at his daughter, now snoring faintly. Even before, David Hammar had been a force to reckon with, one of the most ruthless businessmen Alexander had ever met. As a new father, he was utterly impressive, as protective as a black bear.

"Alexander's bought an apartment in Stockholm," said Natalia, giving Alexander an encouraging look. "If you're going to be around now that David's taking paternity leave, maybe you two can spend some more time together?"

Sure. And hell might freeze over.

"We can talk about that later," David said in a neutral tone.

Alexander interpreted that as a sign that David was about as keen to spend time with him as he was to have his teeth extracted without any anesthesia. And so he grinned, gave David a good smack on the back, and said, "Looking forward to it," before saying good-bye and heading home.

Before Alexander had even made it through the door, he got a text from Natalia saying that it was okay to invite Isobel to the wedding.

He lay down on his new sofa, crossed his arms behind his head, and thought about his next move.

Now he just had to get Isobel to say yes.

Chapter 20

"I'll be there in just over two weeks," Isobel said, studying Idris Toko's face over the fuzzy Skype connection. She could see the hospital office in the background, little more than steel-legged tables with fabric partitions. It was almost impossible for Westerners to imagine how little they made do with there. Isobel put her feet up onto the desk and pulled the laptop onto her knee. She was almost alone in the Medpax office; Leila was in her room, but the rest of the staff had left for the day.

On the other side of the screen, in Chad, half a world away, Idris wiped his forehead with a scrap of material. He was one of the best doctors Isobel had ever met, and one of the few local doctors who had stayed put in his poor, unstable homeland. Most of those who trained to become doctors in Chad eventually gave up and moved to countries where they were paid a regular wage and found security for their families, countries where clan fighting and violence didn't make the situation dangerous, the future uncertain. Chad, the land-locked country in the bull's-eye middle of Africa, was one of the poorest and most corrupt countries in the world. It was also a country of proud men and women, people who lived a hard life, loved their families, and did what they could to survive.

"We need you, but the situation is under control," he said as he adjusted his simple glasses on the bridge of his nose. They always spoke French. Chad was a former French colony, and Idris's French was educated, peppered with Arabic phrases.

"How are things?"

He looked like he had been awake for days. He probably had.

"Three C-sections last night." He shrugged.

"Should I bring anything with me when I come?" she asked. She would stuff her bags with chocolate, cheese, and medicine—that was almost mandatory as a field-worker.

"You got a spare oxygen machine?"

"That bad?"

Idris nodded. A pediatric hospital could succeed or fail depending on its access to oxygen. The machines in the hospital were old and working overtime. But Medpax had hospital salaries to pay and up-keep to fund. They also had bribes to make, to guarantee a minimum level of safety. An oxygen machine cost a lot.

"I'll bring it up at the next staff meeting," she promised.

"Marius is here," Idris said, and disappeared from the screen. A tiny, serious face appeared and Isobel's heart swelled. She smiled, flooded with relief.

"*Bonjour,* Marius," she said. He looked so thin, so tired. But alive.

"*Bonjour, Docteur,*" he said, and waved to the screen.

Idris came back.

"Marius wants some of those Swedish cheese puffs you brought last time, don't you?" Isobel could hear laughter from somewhere off camera. Her eyes burned. *Please, Marius, stay alive until I come.*

"I'll bring lots of cheese puffs," she promised.

Idris nodded, and they ended the video call.

She stayed where she was. It was always such an odd sensation, talking to someone so far away, someone who lived under such different conditions. She rubbed her eyes. It was seven o'clock. She had worked hard the past few days, and should really head home. Or go out. Wasn't Wednesday the new Saturday, or something ridiculous like that? Either way, she ought to *do* something instead of just sitting here, obsessing over things she had or hadn't said.

She hadn't heard from Alexander. That was a fact. And it wasn't the least bit surprising. He had sent messages and called her all day Saturday, but she hadn't replied with anything but short, apologetic messages, and he'd eventually given up. Now it was Wednesday, and she had gotten what she wanted—he had left her alone.

She was ashamed of how cowardly she had handled the situation.

She fooled around on the laptop awhile. Surfed the net. It was almost impossible not to Google his name, but she managed. It was over and that was good. She closed the computer and got up.

Her phone buzzed into life. She looked at the display.

Alexander De la Grip. *Seriously?*

She shouldn't reply. Really shouldn't . . .

Oh, hell, why not?

"Hello?"

"Aha, hi there, Doctor Sørensen. You're alive. How are things?"

Alexander's voice was like the promise of sunshine and adventure straight down the line. Oh my, she liked that voice. The warmth and the laughter in it, but also its strength and stability. This was a man who had fought for her, who had challenged Sebastien, and who had studied aid for her sake. She knew it was partly manipulation on his part, of course, that he had an ulterior motive for everything he did, but still.

"Good. I'm working," she replied, feeling a stupid smile tugging at her lips.

"What else. I'm starting to suspect you don't have a life."

He had a point there. "And you? Are you still in Skåne?"

"Where you left me, you mean?"

Well, she deserved that. "I'm sorry," she said.

"So you should be. But I like it when you apologize to me. You've been ignoring me, so now you have to make up for it."

"Have to?" she asked, trying to sound aloof but feeling her pulse start to race a little.

"Yup. I wondered if you wanted to be my plus one to something."

"Something?"

"A wedding. A friend of mine is getting married."

She couldn't say yes. She knew that, but a wedding . . . Isobel had a soft spot for weddings. "When is it?"

"Saturday."

"This Saturday? That's pretty soon."

"In Storkyrkan, the cathedral," he added. "Dinner at the House of Knights."

Isobel frowned. The only people she knew who got married in the cathedral were royalty. And House of Knights? That was where the nobility had their parties, wasn't it? "What kind of wedding is this, exactly?" she asked suspiciously.

"My friend Åsa Bjelke is getting married to some finance guy, Michel Chamoun."

"Are you kidding me?"

Even Isobel had heard about *that* wedding. It was hard *not* to have heard about it. The society wedding of the year, the media was calling it. World-famous guests from every corner of the globe were expected.

"You can salvage what's left of my ego and grab some food at the same time. I know how grumpy you get when you don't eat."

His tone was humorous, but these were his friends; his entire family would probably be there. She hesitated, knew what she had to do. She needed to plan for Chad. And she had already made up her mind. Taking his call had been a bad idea.

"I'm sorry, Alexander, but I have to say no. It's better if we don't see each other anymore. I wanted to say that, not just send a text or avoid answering. I've made up my mind."

"Are you sure?" His voice was quieter, more serious now. "I hoped we could keep seeing one another. . . . I thought that we . . . I like you."

And I like you. Much too much.

"I'm sure. It's for the best."

"Alright," he said. She heard both disappointment and warmth in his voice, but there was no accusatory tone. This wasn't a man who took his frustration out on others. God, she liked that. He was silent, and Isobel held her breath, not knowing why. She pressed the phone to her ear.

"So, good luck with everything," he said softly. "You're doing a fantastic job; I hope you know that. I'm glad we met. It's been really great."

Isobel, a voice within her cried, *what the hell are you* doing?

"Thanks," she said quietly.

"Bye, Isobel."

She paused, and then hung up before she had time to change her mind. Part of her *had* already changed her mind, but it was too late and she knew she'd done the right thing. She breathed out, deeply. The depressing sound filled the empty room.

"Who was that?"

Isobel jumped at the voice and turned around. Leila was leaning against the door frame, her arms crossed and a jet-black eyebrow raised.

"Not that it's any of your business, but that was Alexander."

"What did he want?"

"Nothing to do with Medpax. He wanted to invite me to a wedding over the weekend. I said no."

"Yes, I heard." Leila came in, pulled up a chair, sat down, and gave Isobel a piercing look. "Let me guess. Blanche needs DIY help all weekend, so you said no to going out with a drop-dead gorgeous man who clearly likes you. To help your mother."

Isobel crossed her arms. It was one thing that *she* was annoyed by her mother, another to hear Leila's criticism.

Leila placed her hands on the table, her shiny black nails drumming the surface. "I'm going to give you a piece of advice now."

"Again? Because I still recall all the others you've given me."

Leila narrowed her eyes. "Call Alexander back and tell him you changed your mind. Live a little."

"I don't know what kind of feedback you normally get, Leila, but your advice really sucks. We just ended it."

Not that they had been together, but it still sounded painfully definitive when she said it aloud.

And it made her ache with longing.

"Don't say that, people pay a fortune for my advice. But you're going to Chad in two weeks, so what difference does it make? Go out with Alexander. You like one another. There are so many sparks between the two of you it hurts the eyes. If it doesn't work out, you're leaving soon anyway. It can come to an end naturally."

The thing was, she had thought along those exact same lines herself. A quick fling with one of the world's hottest men before she went off to work—wasn't that exactly what she needed? She had dated after Sebastien, or a little anyway. A couple of older doctors, a few men she'd met through work. A surgeon. All serious types. Intelligent and interesting. But they were so *dull*. Zero intensity.

"I can't just call and say I changed my mind," she complained now that Leila sat there, giving her foolish hope. Or could she? "We just said good-bye for good."

"There are plenty of things you can't do in this life, I agree with that. But this isn't one of them. Sure, you can."

"Why do you care about this?"

"I wish I knew." Leila stood up. "It's a pain in the ass, being so considerate. It must be an innate virtue. And then all the psychological training on top of that. I'm almost incapable of not caring. I'm going for a smoke. Call him. Before he calls one of his many other women. He's charming, but he *is* a bit of a man whore."

Isobel hesitated, but made up her mind the moment Leila closed the door.

He picked up on the first ring, as though he had been waiting, phone in hand.

"Hello?"

"Can I change my mind?"

Oh, God, please. Surely he hadn't already asked someone else?

"You can."

"Then I've changed my mind. I want to go to the wedding with you."

"That pleases me."

They were silent for a moment, until she asked the only relevant question.

"What should I wear?"

"It's an afternoon wedding, so an evening gown."

Merde. She wouldn't have time to buy anything. And what did a dress like that cost? Could she just wear the green one? She wasn't sure about the nuances of the dress code. Weren't the upper class really sticklers about things like that?

"Isobel? Maybe I can help."

"With what?"

"I know how much you work, and I realize that a field doctor who earns eleven thousand kronor a month to make the world a better place has slightly different priorities from a society girl. So I've solved the whole thing. I know a friend with an atelier. You can borrow a dress there. I already checked. Or, my sister did. She told me you know one another, by the way."

Isobel ignored his last point, pretended that Alexander hadn't talked about her with his family.

"Borrow? Are you sure?"

"It's practically secondhand."

"Okay," she said. "Thanks. I'd love to borrow a dress."

"Isobel?"

"Yes?"

"I'm so happy you called."

"Me too," she said, sounding a bit breathless to her own ears.

"I'll send you the details."

"Thank you."

"It'll be fun."

Isobel felt herself crack a smile. It would be *very* fun.

"Yes."

She wasn't 100 percent sure, but it sounded as though Alexander exhaled before he hung up.

Chapter 21

Gina made an extra pass across the floor with the vacuum cleaner. She glanced over to Peter's office. He looked up, half raised his hand in the air, and smiled tentatively as though he didn't dare give her a full smile. Gina stopped mid-vacuum and awkwardly raised her own hand in a quick response before she looked back down and continued her work. So odd. The next time she looked over, his head was down, bowed over the computer. Only the two of them were left in the office, and he seemed to have plenty to do.

She went to his room and hesitantly knocked on the door frame.

"Hi," he said. "Come in. Is it okay if I work while you vacuum?"

As though she was allowed to have an opinion about that.

"Sure."

Peter was focused on the screen, his eyes darting about it as he wrote the occasional line on a notepad on his desk while she moved around the room.

"Thanks," he said when she was done and had switched off the vacuum cleaner. "Were the trains running again yesterday?"

Gina frowned suspiciously. What did he mean by that? Did he expect her to thank him again? She had already done it, several times.

"Yeah," she replied curtly.

"And today? Running like normal? I'm just asking since it's a holiday."

"It isn't normally a problem," she answered, still unsure of what was happening. Was he making *small talk* with her? Why?

"Were you studying today? Or is class over?"

"There are always lectures. We never really get any breaks. And they expect us to work on the weekends." She nodded toward the kitchen. "I have to eat a little before I go."

He stood up. "Do you mind if I join you?"

Gina shrugged. She could hardly say yes, didn't know why she'd volunteered any information at all. She had always preferred to eat alone. People made comments about her food, and she hated it, but maybe she wouldn't mind so very much if Peter joined her. He wasn't quite as annoying as she used to think.

As Gina heated her food—rice, seasoned with cardamom, cloves, cumin, and vegetables—Peter took off the packaging from a ready-made sandwich. She glanced at the plate spinning away in the microwave and wondered what Peter would say if she told him she had never bought takeaway coffee or a premade sandwich in her life. What did one of those cost anyway, with their glossy cheese slices and crisp salad leaves? Forty kronor? She could make several family meals for that.

She took out her plate. The spicy scent filled the room, but Peter said nothing, just fetched water for them both. He put down the glasses. Went to get a cup of coffee.

"How's your father?"

Gina couldn't help it. Her suspicion was automatic.

"What do you mean?"

Peter picked up his coffee. He drank a lot of it, she had noticed. Maybe that was what affected his sleep. With that thought, she made the connection, recalled their earlier conversation. "Oh, you mean his sleeping? Up and down. It's hard to say what the reason is, really."

She didn't want to say any more than that. Didn't want to tell Peter that her dad sometimes woke with a shout in the night—not as often as he used to, but still. She hadn't told anyone how afraid she had been of those shouts when she was younger. How part of what held her tiny family together was the way each of them tried to protect the others from their fears, sorrows, and worries. They had seen so much. Amir had only been two, but she and her father had experienced horrors they never talked about. It was hard to explain to an outsider.

"Sleep is tricky," Peter said, and Gina saw in his eyes something she had never expected: warmth.

He picked at his sandwich but didn't eat it. He was so much thinner these days. Was it because he didn't eat? There were so many things that caused people to lose their appetites. Depression. Anxiety. Cancer.

"What are you studying at the moment? In your course?"

"The whole first year is about the Healthy Human."

"A whole year?"

"Yeah, there's a lot to know before you can start the next chunk. Illnesses."

He took a bite of his sandwich, chewed, and put it down. Wiped his mouth with a napkin. "Like what?"

She smiled. "Chemistry and biology. All the Latin terms."

"You look so happy when you talk about medicine, I guess you really like it. I was terrible at school. When do you decide what to specialize in?" He picked up his sandwich again. Took a bite, chewed, put it down. She had always wanted to be able to eat like that, so controlled and well-bred; sometimes she practiced Swedish table manners when she was alone.

"You only choose when you're finished. You do an internship and have to get your license. It's a long way off."

She put down the cutlery and took a sip of water. She could let her food digest for a bit, she decided. Could sit and talk with him for five minutes.

"And you? Do you enjoy your work?" she asked.

"Absolutely. It's always been my dream to be a mediocre banker."

She laughed. He had nice eyes when he smiled.

When she stood up, Peter did the same. She washed and dried her things. Wiped her hands on a towel as he rinsed out his coffee mug. He hadn't eaten most of his sandwich, but if she had to say something in his defense, he didn't throw it away, simply put it back in the packaging.

"I need to go," she said.

"Are you free tomorrow? It's a holiday."

"We don't have any lectures. But they asked me to do a couple of hours here, so I'll be in around lunch."

"See you then," he said. It wasn't until she was on the metro that it struck Gina that Peter would clearly be working even though the First of May was a big spring holiday in Sweden.

                                    *   *   *

They ended up in the kitchen the next day, too. Peter finished
working at the same time as she switched off the vacuum, and again
they sat down together. He poured her some water while she grabbed
the napkins and warmed her food. She had a small plate of dumplings today, Dad's samosas, and she debated whether to offer him
one. But he had another sandwich, and she decided to keep her
food for herself.

"Are you headed home after this?" he asked. "Or are you going
out? It's Friday."

She almost laughed.

"No, I'm going home. I don't go out much." She wiped a deep-
fried crumb from the corner of her mouth. Her father made delicious samosas. He helped out, when he could, in the cafeteria at the
cultural center, and his dumplings had always been a big hit. "What
about you? You going out?"

She glanced at him. He was smartly dressed and clean shaven,
and he smelled faintly of aftershave. He looked better than she'd
seen him for a long time. She had actually been surprised he even
turned up today. A holiday on a Friday meant a long weekend, and
not even the most junior of careerists had turned up; she and Peter
were the only ones in the entire office. He had to be going out later,
to Stureplan, or somewhere like that. On her way home from work,
she was often shouted at by rich, drunk Stureplan guys who looked
just like Peter and his colleagues. Sometimes they just made lewd
comments, talked about her various body parts, which was bad
enough. But sometimes they shouted for what seemed like an eternity about how they'd never been with a black girl. Gina would tell
herself she didn't care, but it got under her skin, all the years of comments and glances, and she avoided places where she was 100 hundred percent certain she'd get at least one comment about her
appearance. It was enough that she was often the only non-white
person at work.

Peter shook his head. He had eaten the whole sandwich today.
"I'm not going anywhere. I can give you a ride home if you like. It's a
holiday. The trains surely aren't running like normal."

"That's nice, but you don't have to. I've used public transport my
entire life. I like it."

"I know I don't have to," he said calmly. "But I'd like to, that's why I'm asking. If you want, of course."

She thought of the comfortable car, the quick journey home. Once was nothing, but twice? That was stupid.

She hesitated.

"If it's not too much trouble."

"I kept the radio station you chose last time," Peter said as he steered the car out of town. He was a good driver, calm and patient. It had surprised her last time. She looked out of the window. This part of the journey was her favorite, when they had just gotten into the car and her entire body could relax, when the city passed them by and she could watch it from the outside.

"Are they waiting for you at home?"

"Yes."

"How is that?"

"Good. We're really close."

Dad, Amir, and she—they were a little unit, they completed one another. But she was the strong one, the one who moved out in the big, wide world. They relied on her.

"Sounds nice."

"I worry about my brother sometimes."

She said the words quietly, didn't know where they came from. *Why* had she said it?

"You do?"

She looked away from Peter, out through the window. "He's not sick or anything like that, but he never goes out. He just sits at home. In his room. Playing video games."

"How old is he?"

"Thirteen."

"Then he's much younger than you?"

"Yes, he was only two when we left Somalia."

"So your father, he came alone with two small children? All the way from Somalia? It must've been tough."

"Yeah."

"Your mother?"

"Dead."

Peter was silent as if he sensed she didn't want to talk about her mother. "Doesn't he go to school?" he asked after a moment. "Your little brother, I mean."

Gina pulled at her purse. She had no one to talk to about this, didn't want to worry her father. Peter was unexpectedly easy to confide in. "Yeah, but he doesn't have any friends. I don't know. He gets mad when I try to talk to him about it."

"Maybe it's too much like a performance," Peter suggested. "Having friends."

She hadn't thought of it like that. Her brother's loneliness always felt like a lump in her chest, and she just wanted to help him. To get him out more.

Peter changed gears. They were already approaching Tensta. "Does he want friends?"

"Don't know. He says he doesn't, but I have no idea."

"Maybe he had a bad experience. Makes it easier to be alone."

Gina was silent, her interlocked hands resting on top of her bag. She twisted the simple ring on her index finger. Amir had given it to her, when he was five or six; bought it at the market in Tensta, with his own money. Why hadn't she realized before? That she was only making things worse by nagging him about needing friends. Was it the same for Peter? She rarely saw him talk to anyone. Not at work and not in other social situations, either. The fact was, Peter seemed lonely. So lonely that he might give a cleaning lady a ride home just to have someone to talk to.

"Relationships are tough," he said, his eyes on the road. They sat in silence, listening to the radio. "Are there any Somalian bands?" he asked after a while. "Ones that are famous abroad, I mean?" He had smoothly changed the subject, and she was grateful for that.

"Not really. I'm actually not all that interested in my cultural heritage."

He gave her a surprised glance. "Why not?"

"I see my future in Sweden."

"But you like Somalian food?"

She laughed. "Yeah, a lot."

He pulled up outside her door. "Here we are," he said quietly.

"Thank you. I'll see you at the wedding tomorrow, I guess? I'm working the reception."

"I didn't know that."

She had said yes when the wedding organizer called; the pay was good, and it was nothing she hadn't done before. But now she wondered if it would be awkward. Would Peter say hello, or would he pretend he didn't know her at Åsa Bjelke's super-wedding?

"How are you getting there?" he asked.

She blinked. He couldn't be serious. "You know you can't give me a ride, right? You're a guest. I'm staff. It would be weird."

"But . . ."

"They're paying for cabs," she quickly interrupted him. Her voice was curt, but she couldn't help it. She felt so exposed, and as usual she reacted by lashing out. She hadn't taken the psychiatric class yet, but she knew it was a classic defense mechanism against feelings of inferiority and she *hated* it.

But Peter was a close friend of Åsa Bjelke's; they both grew up in Djursholm, the most expensive and elitist community in the entire country, and they belonged to the upper class, moved effortlessly in the highest of social circles. Just what did she think she was doing, exactly?

"You know that's what I am, right? Staff. A cleaning lady, a maid."

"But you said . . . I didn't mean . . . I thought you liked your work?" He sounded confused. "Gina, did I say something wrong?"

She stepped out of the car, got tangled in the seatbelt, struggled free.

"Bye," she said, slamming the door and heading quickly indoors without looking back.

She had only herself to blame, she thought as she waited for the elevator. She almost hoped he would pretend not to know her tomorrow. She leaned her head against the elevator wall. She was an idiot.

Chapter 22

Isobel looked down at the note with the address on it, and then up at the doors on the street. The signage was practically nonexistent, as though the people who lived here already knew where everything was and had no desire to make things easier for strangers. She had never been to this part of town before, on the edge of Djurgården and near all the embassies. She passed the correct door twice before she realized that the anonymous doorway, next to the big window with nothing but a chair in it, was the atelier. She had Googled it but found nothing. When was the last time she'd heard of a business that didn't exist online?

"Hello?" she called in through a crack in the door.

A curtain moved to one side, and a slim woman in her twenties appeared. Behind her, Isobel could see an unexpectedly large room full of fabric, mannequins, magazines, and changing rooms. Soft music and a scent she identified as fruit tea drifted out toward her.

"Hi!" The woman, who had a pincushion at her wrist and a measuring tape around her neck, held out a hand. "Isobel, right? I'm Lollo Chanel. Come in."

She took a needle from the corner of her mouth and studied Isobel. It was a look that measured and calculated; Isobel could practically feel herself being divided up into centimeters and dimensions.

"Chanel? Really?"

Lollo shrugged. "I guess I couldn't be anything other than a fashion designer with that name. You're a size ten, right? Aside from your bust, I mean. I worked from the measurements you sent, so we can do the final adjustments now."

Isobel had sent her every measurement conceivable, including her shoe size. She saw the color photo Lollo had requested pinned up on a board. So far, this was one of the most surreal experiences she'd ever had.

Lollo's eyes continued their work, moving assessingly over Isobel's hips. "Curves, I like that. Most of my customers haven't eaten since 1970. Did you bring the underwear I suggested? I can't believe that's your natural hair color. And those freckles—I'm so happy the dress shows off so much flesh. Stand there."

Isobel, slightly bewildered by Lollo's rapid-fire monologue, found herself in front of a huge full-length mirror. She peered at herself, straightened her back, and pulled in her stomach as far as she could.

"Do you know Åsa Bjelke? Turn around."

Isobel shook her head. "No, only Alexander. They are childhood friends, right?"

Lollo pulled a face. "Åsa's one of my regulars. I've been bending to her will for ages, wanting to do her wedding dress for years. But now that she's actually getting married and *everyone* is going, she suddenly wants a Valentino. I just couldn't believe it. An Italian botcher instead of me."

"But didn't Valentino do the princess's wedding dress?" Isobel had actually thought the fairy-tale lace dress was magical.

"Yeah, but I'm better; Åsa should know that. What do you think about a really stunning dress? I'm only asking to be polite. You'll have a dress that's better than anything Valentino could even dream of."

"Is this some kind of fabric throwdown? Because if it is, I don't think I . . ."

And with that, Lollo pulled out a hanger holding a bronze-colored dress, and Isobel fell silent midsentence. Not that she knew anything about haute couture, but she had never seen anything like it.

"Wow," she eventually managed.

"Right?" Lollo replied, smugly.

She swung the hanger slightly, and the dress came to life, throwing energy out into the room, flaming color, like a barely tamed spirit.

"It's the best thing I've ever made, and it's perfect for you. No one else will ever be able to wear it like you can. I found some shoes, so it's best you take them. They're Italian. Handmade. You're going to be so tall."

Lollo grinned widely, verging on the maniacal. Her hair was wild, flying in all directions, and she was covered in thread. She looked like some kind of mad, sewing genius.

"I'm not too used to walking in heels," said Isobel.

"Doesn't matter. Take your clothes off," Lollo demanded, pointing to a folding screen. "There's a slip in there."

Isobel went behind the screen, dutifully undressed, and started to open the packaging of the delicate slip. She held it up.

"What's it made of? Air?"

"The best silk in the world. You can't wear pantyhose, or every single seam will be visible," Lollo replied from the other side of the screen. "You should be wearing stockings and a garter belt, of course. It goes with the style," she continued. Isobel could hear the pure desire in her voice. "But it just won't work. Did you put on the underwear already?"

Isobel glanced at the thin bra and the even thinner panties she'd bought. They were silk and Lycra, practically seam-free, and they'd cost a fortune.

"I'm going to freeze," Isobel protested. True, it was a sunny second day of May, but the temperature wasn't much above sixty degrees.

"Probably, but it can't be helped. This is art—you have to suffer a little. Plus, it will look good if your nipples are pert. It's sexy."

Isobel quickly pulled on the thin pieces of underwear and wondered when she'd last worn a G-string. It was the single most idiotic piece of clothing she knew of, but Lollo had demanded a silk thong, and Isobel had done as she said, because she was enough of a woman to want to look good in the most expensive clothing she'd ever wear.

She pulled on the thin slip. "I'm done," she said hesitantly. She felt more naked now that she was wearing the new underwear.

"Come out," Lollo ordered.

"I'm going into the field in two weeks," she said apologetically as she came out from behind the screen's blessed protection. She held a hand over her stomach, feeling more like a teenager with body issues than a cosmopolitan doctor. "I always bulk up a little. And haven't been working out as much as I should."

"Don't be ridiculous. You're magnificent, and you're going to look like a goddess in my dress. Every woman deserves to recognize that side of herself at least once. You just have to go with the flow, my pretty." Lollo took down the dress, and Isobel felt a rush of something close to desire. How was it possible to feel that for a bit of fabric? She held out a hand, brushed the bronze-colored silk. She let Lollo help her into the dress.

Lollo took a step back. "My God, I'm about to start wailing, woman."

Isobel looked in the mirror. The dress did something to her body. There were no visible imperfections, just her best assets being shown off. Her skin glowed like white silk, her freckles were gorgeous and unique, her eyes enormous, and her stomach vanished; she was nothing but breasts, legs, and a phenomenal waist. "Pass me the shoes too," she said, suddenly greedy. She was going to a society wedding, and she was going to have a fabulous time.

Lollo helped her to carefully spray her hair and shape the curls into a film-star style. Isobel touched up her lips and checked that her makeup was still as it should be. Lollo handed her a shawl to put around her shoulders. "But only in the church," she instructed. "This isn't the kind of dress you wear with some modest shawl, understood?"

Isobel nodded obediently.

"What do you think of these?" she then asked. She had, on a complete whim, brought a collection of cheap, beautiful bracelets she'd once bought in the field, shining and Amazonesque in their golden and bronzed tones. They gleamed like a sunset over an African desert. With a single look, Lollo gave her approval.

"Good luck, beautiful. Your car's here. You show 'em!"

Isobel took a taxi to Stockholm Cathedral in the Old Town. The surrounding water glittered as the car passed the Royal Castle before it pulled up right outside the cathedral. The Great Church was one of Stockholm's oldest, built in the thirteenth century. The ceremony would take place at three, and the guests had already started to stream in. She paid the taxi and stepped out, cautious on her sky-high heels. The cobblestones were ancient and uneven, and she took a couple of careful steps. This was historical ground, the site of coronations, royal weddings, and royal funerals. People in formal attire were gathering, blue carpets had been laid out, and huge urns with flower arrangements framed the entrance to the church.

Cars were constantly arriving; she saw people she vaguely recognized from the gossip rags. Actors, musicians, and sports stars.

"Hi, Isobel."

She turned toward the voice and saw a familiar face. She smiled at Natalia De la Grip—or Natalia Hammar, these days—and took a few steps forward.

"Great you could come," said Natalia. It sounded like she really meant it.

"Thanks," said Isobel, pulling the shawl up over her shoulders.

"Did you come with Alexander?"

"No."

He had offered to pick her up, but the rebellious part of her had refused. She wasn't a birdbrain. She could make her way to a church on her own. But now, as she glanced around, Isobel wondered whether she shouldn't have said yes after all. No matter where she looked, she saw couples, couples, couples. Maybe there were no single people in the upper classes? "Jesus, so many celebrities," she said.

"Yeah, Åsa and Michel have a huge network," Natalia said, gesturing discreetly to a man Isobel recognized as a former president of the United States. Impressive.

"He was friends with Åsa's father. And her, over there . . ." Natalia nodded her head toward a woman dressed in blue. She looked distinctly British, in a royal kind of way. "She was a close friend of her mother's. Both of Åsa's parents are dead." Natalia waved to a large bearded man who had arrived with a stunning blonde dressed in a body-hugging dress. Even Isobel, completely uninterested in sports, knew he was a famous ice hockey player. "Friend of Michel's," said Natalia. And so it continued.

The elite of the elite poured in, along with those Isobel didn't recognize, whom Natalia identified on her behalf. When one of the royals arrived with their partner, the press photographers practically started a riot. A couple of super-rich financiers. "Åsa and Michel pretty much know everyone who's rich, famous, and in their thirties," Natalia said laconically as yet another blond corporate princess turned up with her husband. Natalia named a few more counts and countesses. Funnily enough, Isobel recognized some of them from Skåne, but these were a younger, even more glamorous group, if that was possible.

"And this is David, my husband," said Natalia. Isobel smiled at the pride in Natalia's voice as she turned to the man headed toward them.

Isobel greeted David, who gave quite an overwhelming impression, and then peered down at the little baby balanced comfortably in the crook of his arm.

"This is Molly," said Natalia, and their eyes met in understanding.

"A little miracle," said Isobel softly. Tenderly she touched the baby's head. Every baby was a miracle, but Molly was special and Isobel was truly happy for Natalia. Their first meeting had been kind of dramatic. Natalia had been an angry, hurt, and very unexpectedly pregnant patient of hers, and Isobel had not been all that sure that it would work out in the end. But it had. And Natalia looked truly happy. "I'm so glad for all of you."

"Thank you," said Natalia. She squeezed Isobel's arm. "And how wonderful that you are here. With Alexander."

Isobel could feel the younger woman's palpable curiosity, but Natalia was obviously much too well-bred to straight-out ask what was going on between her brother and her once physician. And Isobel didn't offer any explanation, didn't even know where she would have begun.

Suddenly, Isobel felt something pass across her skin. It started as a low hum in the small of her back, shot up her spine, and spread outward, making her tingle. Natalia's attention was on David now, and Isobel closed her eyes, letting the sensation wash over her. It felt as though she were being recharged from within. She had never thought it was possible to *feel* a look. But now she did.

She opened her eyes and turned around, slowly, tossed her hair slightly so that her curls and tresses cascaded around her shoulders and back. She straightened up, making herself as tall as possible in her high, Italian shoes. And she met Alexander's gaze, saw how his eyes dilated when he caught sight of her over the cobblestones and the ancient square.

His eyes shone, and Isobel felt herself being drawn in. She flashed him a smile, gave all she had, all that she had been born with but so seldom used.

His gaze was fixed; he just stared at her, as if she were some kind of goddess. And for a brief while, she was.

It was one of the better moments in her life.

Chapter 23

"Doctor Sørensen," Alexander greeted Isobel. He couldn't stop grinning, or keep himself from doing that uncool thing he despised when other men did it: He ate Isobel up with his eyes; no, he *devoured* her. She was magnificent. Her shimmering dress, her swirling hair, her bold jewelry: thick, exotic, *erotic* loops around her wrists.

Regal like a queen.

He pulled her into his arms and held her tight. Fragrant, luscious curves made his head spin.

"I'm so glad you changed your mind. You look completely amazing," he murmured into her hair. She was taller than most people around them, and Alexander had never been so primitively pleased with his own height. Other men had better watch out. Today, this woman was *his*.

She hugged him back, her arms creeping around his back until he felt the warmth of her body against every inch of him. He caught the scent of something that, for once, wasn't antiseptic. All this softness was quickly demolishing his ability to think intelligently. This thing between them, it was becoming less and less like attraction and more like obsession. He kept hold of her, and thought that he needed to speed up the pace of his seduction, get her into bed soon, otherwise he would probably go crazy. He couldn't explain it any other way. Until the last moment, he hadn't been sure whether she would turn up. He'd been worried she would cancel on him, and now it was clear how much of a difference her being here would make. How pleasurable everything felt when she was in his arms, how gray the prospect of enduring the day without her had been. And then a not-so-discreet clearing of the throat reminded Alexander that they weren't alone. Regaining control he reluctantly pulled himself away from Isobel's embrace and turned to Natalia. She flashed him an amused, big-sister smile.

"Hello, sister of mine," he drawled. "I wish I could say you look fantastic too, but did you know there's puke on your shoulder?"

She snorted. "Wait 'til you have kids and you'll see how easy it is. You're happy so long as your clothes are the right way out."

While Natalia fished for a wet wipe, Alexander shook hands with David. His brother-in-law had Molly in his arms but managed to look like a finance magnate all the same. Natalia rubbed at the stain as her eyes flitted between Alexander and Isobel with unconcealed curiosity.

"Stop it," he snapped at her.

"I'm not doing anything," she replied, but her eyes flashed unrepentantly.

"What?" he asked.

"Nothing. I'm just happy you brought Isobel. I like her."

"She's mine," he said firmly. "Go get your own friends."

"So you're together?"

He hated that—how some women started to map out the future the moment a man and woman exchanged more than a couple of words. Natalia had never understood the appeal of loose relationships.

"Stop assuming things. And stop staring," he ordered. "Aren't you supposed to be with the bridal couple?"

"They are fine—we'll join them in church. Åsa is doing this her own way. I'm intelligent enough to have absolutely no opinions on anything lest there be casualties."

A dark car approached over the cobblestones. A security guard moved one of the barriers, and it pulled up.

"It's Mom," said Natalia.

The car door opened. Eugene stepped from the backseat, turned around, and helped Ebba out. The car pulled away, and Natalia waved to them. Their mother gave Natalia a quick hug and then nodded to David, not completely without friendliness. Molly had fallen asleep in

David's arms, and Ebba carefully stroked her granddaughter on the cheek before turning to Alexander.

He pulled himself together. It was just a matter of keeping up appearances.

"Mom, this is Isobel Sørensen. Isobel, this is my mother, Ebba."

Isobel pulled her shawl up onto her shoulders, smiled a professional smile, held out her hand, and shook Ebba's. "Good to meet you."

"Good to meet *you*, Isobel." Alexander couldn't remember ever having heard his mother sound like that. Almost kind.

"Your mother wouldn't be Blanche Sørensen, would she? If so, I've met her. We were on a committee together once. A wonderful woman." Ebba smiled warmly.

Eugene came over and gave Isobel a big hug and noisy kisses on the cheek. "How nice to see you again. You look fantastic. As always."

"Right, you already know one another," said Natalia. Her eyes were, if possible, even more mischievous when she glanced at Alexander.

Eugene smiled enthusiastically. "We met in Skåne last weekend. Isobel came down to tell us all about foreign aid. Alexander came along too. We had a wonderful time."

Natalia gave Alexander yet another lingering look. "Fascinating."

Alexander gave her a warning shake of his head. It was one thing that he had trouble making sense of his feelings for Isobel but something completely different that his big sister was getting all kinds of ideas.

"Is Mom dying?" he asked instead, once his mother and Eugene had left to talk to an old acquaintance.

"No more than anyone else, as far as I know. Why?"

Alexander studied his mother from a distance.

"Because she's acting like a normal person. She *hugged* you. Are you sure? Brain tumor, maybe?"

"If you came home more often rather than partying yourself to death on every continent, you'd see that she's really making an effort."

"Hmm," he replied skeptically. He had always been a firm believer in the idea that people never changed.

The church bells started to ring. It was time.

"Shall we go in?" he asked Isobel, and held out an arm to her. She linked her hand through the crook of his arm. There were people everywhere, and Isobel wound up pressed against him. The warmth and the weight of her silk-clad breast against his jacket sleeve made him pull her even closer toward him. So far, this wedding was really promising.

There were security guards at the church doors. The press was turned away and the guests checked off. Alexander caught sight of Tom Lexington. Of course Hammar Capital's security chief was there, taking care of everything. Tom was dressed in a dark suit and tie, but if the intention had been for him to blend into the crowd, it hadn't worked. He looked like exactly what he was: a man used to violence and being in total control.

"So this is where you are when you aren't kidnapping people?" Alexander cheerfully greeted him as he and Isobel reached the door. Last time he'd met Tom Lexington had been when Natalia and David got married. Alexander had been marinating himself in vodka when Tom had arrived in a helicopter to haul his ass back to Stockholm and the ceremony. Not Alexander's most dignified moment.

Tom gave him a dark look. A beige wire ran down one side of his neck. "Yeah, well, always nice to be at a wedding where the guests come voluntarily for a change," he replied drily.

Once they were inside, Alexander waited as Isobel and his mother, now with Molly in her arms, sat down on the bench before he sat down next to Isobel. Natalia was matron of honor and David the best man, so they would be walking to the altar behind the bride and groom.

The church filled up. Not least with Michel Chamoun's many relatives. Adults, children, and grandparents took their places, and the guests' murmur rose to the ceiling.

"Isn't that your brother?" asked Isobel.

Alexander saw Peter approaching, alone. He slowed down, saw them sitting there, and allowed his gaze to wander over them all before he turned and sat at one side of the church.

"Isn't he going to sit here?" Isobel asked.

"He does what he wants."

This time, she gave him a searching look.

"Sorry, I didn't mean to sound blunt. We don't really get on. It's complicated."

"Okay," she said softly. She let her gaze wander, looked at five-hundred-year-old gilded statues. "Can you believe I've never been in this church before?" She pulled her shawl tight again, and the movement caused one of her legs to graze his. He looked down, saw how her silk-clad thigh rested against his own. He wanted to reach down and place a hand on that leg, high up on her thigh, spread out his palm, caress the smoothness beneath it, bend down and kiss her mouth. He knew the kisses they had exchanged inside and out, remembered how she tasted, what she sounded like when she got excited. Did she think about it too? Did the fact she had changed her mind and come to the wedding—that she'd even gone to see Lollo and borrowed that stunning dress—mean she wanted more of him? And if so, when?

He hadn't even heard the music start, just saw everyone get to their feet. He quickly did the same, and just had time to smooth his suit before the bridal couple came down the aisle. They were a striking pair, walking side by side, Åsa Bjelke in white and her husband-to-be, Michel Chamoun. Natalia and David walked behind them.

Next to Alexander, Isobel sighed and Ebba dabbed at her eyes. Åsa *did* look beautiful. Her white-blond hair was fastened in a simple, low chignon. With a long white veil, a slim, snow-white dress, and a completely white bouquet, she looked almost virginal. Alexander couldn't help but find that amusing, considering all of her former, rather infamous escapades. But she looked happy, so maybe this really was what she wanted. To promise loyalty to one person for the rest of her life. He winked at her as she passed. Her turquoise eyes twinkled, a smile played over her lips, and with that, the couple had passed.

"She's the most beautiful bride I've ever seen," Isobel whispered. Alexander rolled his eyes. There was something about women and weddings he would never understand.

The bridal couple made their way to the pastor, Natalia and David stood on either side, and the guests sat back down. The ceremony was in Swedish, English, and French. Alexander half-listened, his gaze wandering across the room. When he heard a stifled sniff from his left, he couldn't help but smile. He himself wasn't particularly moved—this whole business with God and vows wasn't his thing, but he had been to enough weddings to know two things: Women always cried, and they never had any tissues with them. He pulled out a small packet from his pocket, took Isobel's hand, and handed it to her.

"Thanks," she whispered.

Bonus points to Alexander, he thought with satisfaction.

For over three weeks now, he had been chasing her. He couldn't remember the last time it had taken him this long to get a woman into bed, and he was starting to get impatient.

Isobel wiped her nose and rested her hands in her lap. Alexander reached out and took one of them. He had planned only on touching it, maybe raising it to his mouth and kissing it gently, whispering something clever and humorous, but she clasped it tightly and they sat there, hand in hand. He looked straight ahead. He should find this corny and lame. And maybe he did.

But if that was the case, why didn't he let go?

Chapter 24

"You know, I've never been here before either," Isobel said as they slowly walked up to the pink palace that was the Swedish House of Nobility, or House of Knights. The palace lay at the outskirts of the oldest part of the Old Town. Across the glittering water was a view over the modern Stockholm, but here, in the velvety green symmetrical garden, it was like being transported back to the seventeenth century. When Isobel tilted her head, she saw golden statues at the rooftop. Huge pots of pink and white flowers wafted the scents of spring and summer. It was simply gorgeous.

"It has a rather dramatic history," Alexander said as they walked up the wide stairs leading to the entrance.

"I bet it does." Isobel could practically feel centuries of power struggle, murderous intrigue, and royal gossip surrounding her.

They entered a huge hall with marble columns and tall staircases. The hall was quickly filling up with the glamorous wedding guests. Heels were clicking, and jewelry sent sparkles in every direction. Discreet security guards flitted around the place, and every now and then the room would explode into laughter, the sound magnified by the high ceilings.

"The upper class excels at this kind of thing. No one can party like we can," said Alexander as they continued through the rooms.

Isobel knew that only Swedish nobility had access to this house. Åsa Bjelke, whose ancient family crest occupied one of the most prominent places in the hall, had of course rented the entire building for her wedding dinner. Slowly they moved into the great hall. Alexander's presence was tall and comforting, and every time she leaned into him, a shiver ran down her spine. The whole experience was magnificent.

"Oh my," Isobel breathed. Enormous chandeliers hung from the richly decorated ceiling. Ancient golden furniture and silverware gleamed. It was like entering another era. A more wicked, sensual, and opulent time.

She gave Alexander a slow smile, and noticed how he reacted to it, was drawn to her as though she were a flame and he were . . . whatever might be drawn to flames. This was fun. She had never been much good at flirting, but with Alexander it was the same as when they danced: He was easy to follow and made her feel like she was skilled and sophisticated. Desirable.

His eyes swept over her. His hunger was flattering.

"Did I tell you your dress is . . . I don't know what to say."

She remembered Lollo's instructions and pulled off the shawl, slowly, revealing her skin and décolletage. Without the shawl, the dress was a little too sexy for the occasion, but she didn't see being appropriate as her role for the evening.

Alexander's eyes widened in an extremely complimentary manner. It was possibly the most delicious foreplay she'd ever been part of.

Had she ever been as attracted to anyone as she was to Alexander? He was hot, of course, but there was more to it. His obvious interest in her was so flattering. Even if it was just a game on his part, a strategy to get her into bed—and she was cynical enough to realize that was probably the case, that he hadn't fallen victim to love at first sight—his gaze, always following her, sometimes with a smile in his eyes, sometimes with a predatory hunger he didn't bother to hide, his undivided attention and his absolute concentration on her . . . It was intoxicating.

Leila was right. She needed this. Plus, she was older now; it wouldn't be like with Sebastien. In the past, she'd always been drawn to older men, and it didn't take a high IQ to realize that they were all father figures. She wasn't proud of this tendency, but that was just how it was. Her father had been strict, moral, and distant, and she was usually drawn to men like him. It was basic psychology. But she had never felt this kind of heat for anyone, not even Sebastien. He had been a young girl's first infatuation, a projection of all that was possible, a fantasy.

But Alexander was just . . . Alexander.

The bridal couple entered the room, and the guests began to applaud. The toastmaster, a tall woman Isobel recognized as a news anchor, gave a toast to the newlyweds as the waitstaff brought out more champagne. Isobel sipped her glass, absurdly moved by the speech. She didn't even know these two, but it was all so splendid. She caught Alexander's amused eye and suddenly remembered something he'd said about love once. It was like religious fanaticism, he'd said, made people act like they were crazy. Maybe he was right.

Unexpectedly, she caught sight of a familiar face among the guests.

"Hi, Gina," she called.

The young woman's face lit up. "Doctor Sørensen," she called back, pushing her way through the crowd with her tray ahead of her.

"Please, call me Isobel. How are you?"

"Stressed," Gina replied, gesturing with her head toward the tray of glasses. "I'm sorry, I don't have time to stop and talk, but let me know if you need anything.

At dinner, Isobel found herself a few tables away from Alexander. Of course she had known they wouldn't be seated together. She had always found this Swedish custom rather odd—that couples, with the exception of a newly engaged couple, were always seated far away from one another. As if they couldn't have anything to talk about. Actually, the only time a married couple ever sat next to each other was at their own wedding. Alexander was close to the bridal couple, and she noticed his neighbor was a cute brunette. He politely held her chair out for her before sitting down himself. He said something to the woman on his other side, a heavily pregnant Swedish businesswoman Isobel had recently read about in a glossy magazine.

Isobel was between a young guy named Axel with a neat beard and a Gothenburg accent, and a man in his forties. He introduced himself as Christer and said he worked for a publishing house. He immediately began to compete with Axel for her attention.

"There's no one more self-obsessed than male authors," Christer said, taking a sip of a generously sized dry martini. "Except for female ones, of course," he added. Isobel burst into laughter.

The three of them were soon drawn into an intense, lively conversation about books, the publishing world, and what Isobel could only describe as tall tales. They made her laugh so much she had a pain in her side before they even finished the starter. The toastmaster got back to her feet and introduced the evening's first speaker: Natalia Hammar.

Natalia began by talking about how Åsa had lived with the De la Grips after her entire family had died in a car accident. Isobel hadn't known about that, and she studied the elegant bride. Åsa looked like a Hollywood star sitting next to her hot gangsteresque husband. Who was she underneath? Natalia continued, talking about how Åsa had brought champagne to the maternity ward when little Molly was born and how she'd *sworn* never to do something so bourgeois as to get married, right up until the day she announced she was planning on having the biggest wedding Stockholm had seen since the crown princess got married.

The applause after the speech was deafening. Isobel saw Alexander get to his feet, head over to his sister, and plant a kiss in her hair.

As the main course was served, a waiter bent down to Isobel.

"One more vegetarian, right?" he asked.

She glanced over at Alexander.

He was listening to his neighbor, but it was as though he knew he was being watched, because he raised his head and over tables, clinking glasses and expensive flower arrangements, their eyes met. Everything around her fell silent, and she imagined she could hear his voice, feel his touch, read his thoughts.

Thanks, she mouthed.

He smiled and lowered his head in an ironic bow.

He was so considerate she didn't know what to think. He insisted on maintaining that superficial façade, but when had she last been with a man who remembered small details like that? A man who loaned her crown jewels and gave her tissues and arranged food and gazed at her across the room? If it was a game, he was extremely good at it.

The next speaker was David Hammar.

Isobel had thought he seemed like a stern, impressive person, but the speech he gave was a hilarious account of Åsa and Michel's love story, which had clearly begun many years earlier and then blossomed the previous summer via a huge number of text messages, arguments, and passion. By the end of his speech, people were slumped on their tables in fits of laughter.

The speeches continued and toasts were made, and by the time the main service was cleared away, her two neighbors were drunk and their joking was getting risqué.

She looked up and realized that Alexander was watching her again. She smiled at him before being drawn into another nonsensical conversation with Axel and Christer.

With dessert, Alexander stood up and made a speech to Åsa. He was drunk, but not too much. Isobel could see that his eyes were glazed over, but he seemed happy, and his speech was hysterically funny. He sat down to laughter and applause, and raised a glass in Isobel's direction.

The next time she looked up, when the coffee was served, Alexander's seat was empty. She blinked, wondered where he was. And then she heard his voice at her side, low and commanding, talking to her neighbor.

"Swap seats with me."

"But . . ." Axel protested.

"No buts. Go. Now."

Axel got slowly to his feet. Isobel flashed him an apologetic smile, and Alexander slipped into the chair next to her.

"That wasn't very nice."

"It's my firm belief that niceness doesn't count for much with women."

She shook her head. If there was one thing she had learned, it was this. "Actually, kindness is the important thing."

"Is it? Why?"

"Without kindness, there's no trust."

"And is that so important?"

"You know it is."

The wedding cake was brought in—a huge, white confection.

"They seem so in love," Isobel said as Michel kissed Åsa for something like the hundredth time in a row before they started to cut the cake.

Alexander simply shook his head.

"Have you really never been in love?" she asked.

"Maybe once," he replied.

She only had herself to blame. She had asked, and now she had to accept the slight pang of jealousy. Who had he loved? Who had been unique enough to be loved by Alexander?

"Who was she?" she asked.

He leaned forward and gave her a serious look. "I've completely forgotten. I must've repressed it. Too painful, you know?" He fell silent, a pained look on his face. She leaned forward, holding her breath.

"She was in my course at the School of Economics. She liked graphs, and I thought it was sexy. I was so in love, it hurt. Worst morning of my life."

Isobel laughed loudly. Relieved.

He really was the epitome of a total player, the way he sat there, looking at her, a satisfied expression on his face. She smiled at him and blinked slowly, calculating. How hard could it be to seduce him tonight? He cocked his head. Watched her as though he were a hungry lion and she were a passing gazelle.

Not hard at all, she decided.

Chapter 25

He was too slow, that was the problem. That, and the fact he hadn't punched out Isobel's neighbor when he had the chance. Alexander crossed his arms and looked out at the packed dance floor. This was what happened when you didn't act quickly. You had to watch the woman you were dying to fuck waltz across the floor in the arms of her bearded tablemate. The pair swept past, and Alexander caught sight of a malicious grin on the face of the man.

Alexander had danced with his neighbor and then the bride, but now he had fulfilled his duties as a guest and *he* wanted to dance with Isobel. Truthfully, he wanted to go home and have sex with Isobel, but if she planned on dancing half the night away, he was enough of a gentleman to wait.

The next time she swished past, she was dancing with Eugene, and Alexander caught a wink from his uncle. He gave up and went to sit with a group of Åsa's wilder friends. The table was covered with ice buckets and glasses, and he picked up a glass of Pommery and tried to spot Isobel in the crowd. She was dancing, laughing, with another man, and Alexander thought that the novelty of feeling jealous was rapidly wearing off. He had never been jealous before, and he had to say it sucked. He poured more champagne, stretched out his legs, and watched the dancers. The music had to end at some point.

Eugene came over, sat down, and flashed Alexander an amused grin.

"Here you are, looking cheerful," he said.

Alexander pulled an irritated face.

Eugene poured some champagne and drank it with a satisfied sound.

"People should get married more often."

"If that's a dig at me, you can forget it."

"It wasn't a dig. It was a reflection. So. On a completely different note, which really does have nothing to do with my wanting you to find a girl to marry, what have you done with Isobel?"

Alexander gestured toward the dance floor, the music fortunately stopping. Isobel caught sight of him. He got up as she came over, and she sank into the armchair next to Eugene.

"I need to sit down. These shoes are killing me." She stretched out one leg, and Alexander was transfixed. He had never thought of himself as a leg man. More a breast and ass man. But Isobel's legs . . . In those shoes, they looked like they were made to wrap around his waist. And she didn't even seem to realize just how incredibly hot she was.

"Want something to drink? Champagne?"

Or would you rather go home, let me undress you, kiss you?

"Water would be great." She smiled.

He got up. "I'll get you some water, but you have to promise me something."

"What?"

"Stay here until I get back. Sit right here. No dancing."

She flashed him that smile, the one he wanted to catch in the palm of his hand and carry with him wherever he went. "I promise," she said.

Eugene's grin grew even wider.

Since all of the waitstaff seemed busy serving drinks and clearing glasses, Alexander found his way to a little kitchen and went in. There were piles of trays and porcelain everywhere, but he found a cupboard full of clean glasses and took one out. He sensed a movement out of the corner of his eye, and when he turned around he saw Tom Lexington smoking on a little balcony.

"Everything okay?" Alexander asked as he turned on the faucet. He looked around for a carafe or a bottle he could fill and take with him.

"Yep," Tom said, breathing out smoke.

As Alexander turned off the faucet, they heard some kind of noise. "Did you hear that?" he asked as a shout rang out.

Tom flicked the cigarette away, pushed his earpiece into his ear, and listened. Alexander went toward the door and pushed it open. A disturbance he couldn't quite define was spreading across the far end of the ballroom. Most of the guests were acting as normal, but Alexander saw a few people moving toward one of the doors. He heard another shout.

The seats where Isobel and Eugene had been were empty. He couldn't see Isobel anywhere. Tom pushed his way through the crowd, and Alexander strode after him. His entire family was here, everyone he cared about, but he had only one thought: Was Isobel safe? And then he saw her. She sat next to a man lying flat on the floor. Her dress was pushed up to her thighs, and she leaned over him, her hand at the side of his throat.

"What's going on?" Tom's commanding voice cut through the noise.

Isobel looked up. She swiped her hair from her face, caught sight of Alexander, and then looked to Tom.

"Call an ambulance. He can't breathe, it's an allergic reaction."

Her voice was razor sharp, her eyes steady. "Alex? Are you there?"

"Yeah, what should I do?"

"Find Gina."

She bent back down again. Said something to the man, whose chest was heaving with difficulty. Tom already had his cell to his ear. Alexander turned around and saw Gina in the doorway.

"Let her past," he ordered, holding out his hand and pulling Gina through the crowd and over to Isobel.

"There should be an adrenaline pen in his jacket. Can you find it?" Isobel asked. She was so goddamned cool, her voice utterly unruffled. In the midst of chaos, Isobel was rock steady. If someone had set off a bomb in the ballroom, she would be exactly the same, he thought. Level-headed, focused on helping.

Gina rushed away.

"Tom's called an ambulance. What can I do?" Alexander asked.

"Get people out. Ask someone to get a first aid kit. Gina?"

Gina had returned with an EpiPen. She had already taken off the cap. Together, they undid the man's trousers. Gina jabbed the needle into his thigh and then pushed the plunger as Isobel continued to talk to him.

Alexander had started to lead people out when Michel and David appeared.

Alexander nodded to them and to Peter, who had also appeared in the doorway.

"Gina and Isobel have everything under control, the ambulance is on the way, and here's Tom with the first aid kit. Can someone get a blanket?"

David turned on his heel and disappeared.

Isobel took the bag and rifled through it. David came back with a blanket, and they spread it over the man while Gina made a cushion from one of the seat cushions and a tablecloth. She placed it under his head.

Alexander heard Isobel asking brief, quiet questions.

"Do you know where you are? What's your name?"

"At a wedding. Fares Nassif."

"Okay, Fares. I'm a doctor. You had an allergic reaction; we gave you your EpiPen, and you're already breathing better. I'm going to put in a drip now. Did you come with anyone?"

Michel kneeled down next to them.

"He's my cousin," he said quietly. "Should I get Nour? His wife."

"Yes, please."

Michel returned with a woman, who put her hand to her mouth and sank to the floor next to Fares.

"Does he have a history of any other illness?" Isobel asked as she took out a cannula and carefully pushed the needle into Fares's arm.

"No." His wife blinked tightly, again and again.

"Gina, you take over here," Isobel said, and as Gina busied herself with the drip bag, Isobel took the woman's hand. Alexander brought over a chair, and Isobel sat Nour down in it. Isobel looked at Alexander. "She's probably in shock, but everything seems fine. Did you hear that, Nour? Your husband is feeling better already. But he needs to go to the hospital, just to be on the safe side. Do you want to go with him? Is there anyone else to help you here?"

"I'm okay."

Nour bit her lip and straightened up. Alexander saw that the color had returned to her face. "I'll go with him," she said firmly, and at that moment two paramedics came in with a stretcher. Isobel talked to them, with brisk technical words and terminology that sounded as if it belonged in a TV show. Fares was given an oxygen mask and held his wife's hand. The scene still looked dramatic, but there was a sense that the worst was over.

Tom came back; Alexander leaned against the door frame and grinned in Isobel's direction. She was still debriefing and instructing the paramedics. "Isobel's with me. Impressive, isn't she?"

Tom fixed him with his dark eyes but said nothing.

The paramedics and the stretcher were escorted out by Tom and his staff, and the room slowly emptied until only Isobel, Gina, Alexander, and Peter were left.

"I'll give Gina a ride home once she's done," Peter said.

Alexander gave him a disconcerted look. "Is that fine with you, Gina?"

She simply nodded. "Yes."

Alexander watched them leave the room together. Once *that* surprise was over, he turned to Isobel. She was sitting in a chair and seemed to be breathing deeply.

He picked up an overturned chair and smiled at her. Her hair was ruffled and her dress was creased. "Do you want to go home too? Should I call for a car?"

"Do you think that would be okay with the bridal couple? If we leave the party before them?"

"You just saved Michel's cousin's life. As far as they're concerned, you've got a free pass to do pretty much whatever you want."

Isobel slumped into the backseat. She rested her face in one hand and sat that way as the car left the Old Town, passing over a bridge.

"I'm still coming down," she said after a while.

"I couldn't tell," he said. He stretched out his arm along the back of the seat.

"The thing is, it doesn't make a difference how good a doctor you are. If we hadn't found that needle, he wouldn't have made it."

"But he did."

"Yeah. His wife said she'd let me know how it goes, but I'm not worried."

She leaned her head against his arm, and Alexander rested a cheek on her hair. It wasn't cool to start seducing a woman who'd just saved someone's life, he knew that, but at this rate he'd be gray by the time he got Isobel into bed. He closed his eyes, breathed in the scent of her. This wasn't what he'd hoped for, but with Isobel, nothing went as expected. She moved, and her cheek ended up against his collarbone. A silk-clad knee brushed against his trouser leg. A soft breast rested against his chest. He swallowed. The air in the car disappeared, and his pulse started to increase rapidly. Isobel moved again. It was as though she couldn't find a comfortable position. This time, one of her hands ended up on his thigh, high up. He would have no choice but to move her, he thought dizzily. He was getting aroused. It was embarrassing. But he was dying for her. He couldn't remember when he had wanted a woman this much. He twisted, but she followed his movements, ending pressed up against him.

"Isobel," he heard himself exhale harshly.

She slowly turned her head until their faces were almost touching. As the car passed beneath a streetlight, he caught a glimpse of her freckles, sprinkled like a translucent powder across her nose and cheeks.

"What?" she asked. Her voice was husky and low.

He bent down and kissed her lightly on the nose. "You have freckles on your forehead," he mumbled before thinking that it had definitely been a mistake to kiss her, to breathe in the scent of her, to put an arm around her so that the touch of her skin made every single inch of him buzz with electric anticipation.

"Are you tired?" she asked, blinking slowly. She licked her lips, and they shone. He stared. "Or do you want to continue the evening?"

Alexander had never missed an invitation in his life, wouldn't have thought it was possible, but it took a moment before Isobel's words, tone, and questioning look caused the pieces to fall into place.

"Aren't you . . ." he started. He stopped to clear his throat. "I thought you were tired." His hand caressed the smooth, smooth skin of her bare arm.

"No," she replied, her beautiful eyes glittering. "Saving lives doesn't tire me out. The opposite, actually." Her cell phone buzzed. She took it out and read the message. "All okay. They're keeping him overnight, but it doesn't seem serious." She put the phone back in her bag. "Where were we?"

"You wanted to continue the night with me, Doctor Sørensen. Do you want to come home with me? There's a rumor I've got a well-stocked bar."

She stretched, like an elegant jungle cat.

"Of course you do," she said. "A tiny little whisky would be nice."

"You like whisky?"

He wouldn't have thought it, but suddenly he could see her before him, naked, on a leather armchair, a mature whisky in one hand and a fat cigar in the other.

"Alright, Alexander, you can show me your place. And your bar." She paused. "And the rest, if you like."

And with that, Alexander almost forgot his new address.

Chapter 26

When Isobel looked out the window next time, the cab had pulled up outside an almost laughably posh address. Alexander paid, they climbed out, and he guided her toward the door.

"Looks expensive," she said.

"I like expensive," he replied, chuckling.

He laid a hand in the small of her back. He was so good at making her feel special, desirable. How many times had he done this exact same thing? Pursued a woman until she went a little crazy, could think of nothing but sex?

She stepped into the elevator. Maybe she shouldn't be attracted to a jet-set playboy with dubious morals. She did know that this was just what Alexander did. It made no difference that he'd read up on Medpax or gave millions to young Internet entrepreneurs. He spent most of his time on seduction and conquest. And it made no difference that she'd seen a different side of him, knew that he undoubtedly had his own secrets, that he could be both smart and kind when he wanted to. She knew what he was at heart. A player. No one could change that quickly. And yet. Here she was.

The hall inside the apartment smelled clean and fresh, and Isobel reminded herself that he was a man who had staff to decorate, clean, and do his bidding.

He put down his keys on a chest of drawers and looked at her, silent and searching.

"Everything okay?" he asked.

She smiled, took a step toward him, laid a hand on his solid chest. "Very okay." Maybe she *shouldn't* be attracted to Alexander, but she was, couldn't even remember when she had last been close to something like this. An expectant thrill rushed through her. She didn't care if he was playing some kind of game, because she could decide how much of herself to give. Maybe this was just what she needed. The knowledge that it would never be more than sex and eroticism, the knowledge that the very worst that could happen would be falling for a man like Alexander. As luck would have it, she never fell easily.

"I just need to go freshen up."

He showed her to a bathroom, where she rinsed out her mouth, washed her hands, and stared at herself in the mirror. She had to think hard to remember when she'd last slept with someone. After Sebastien, it had been a while. An aid worker in Paris last summer? Could it really be that long?

When she came back out, he put an arm around her waist, drawing her in for a kiss. Ah, he was so very good at kissing, so bold and assertive. And he must have more than one bathroom; he tasted of toothpaste. Maybe she could fall a little, just for one night?

"Come on," he said, taking her hand and leading her through the enormous apartment. His grip was firm and his voice steady, but Isobel had seen his pupils darken with desire, felt him harden and her own body react.

She came into a huge living room, took a step in as he paused behind her. She noticed the big couches, the bookcases, and an oversized rug, soft as cashmere. She wouldn't be a bit surprised if it really was cashmere. If anyone owned a large, fourteen-foot square rug made from an impractical light-colored wool, it was Alexander De la Grip.

"What do you think?" he asked nonchalantly.

She turned back to him. "It's so cozy."

"You sound surprised," he said with a laugh. But she saw both relief and happiness flash in his magical eyes, blue as arctic ice. Or was it Antarctic? She wasn't sure, had always gotten the two poles confused. Her opinion obviously mattered to him.

Alexander walked over to a sideboard covered with bottles and carafes, pulled a cork, poured whisky for both of them, and held out a glass to her. Isobel sat down on the couch. It was deep and soft, and she had expected him to sit down next to her, to start seducing her, but he chose an armchair opposite, stretched out his long legs, and studied her over the edge of his glass. She crossed her own legs, heard the faint rustle of silk, and saw his eyes glimmer. She had always thought blond men looked boyish, but there was nothing immature about this man. His broad shoulders and hard legs strained against his clothing, and his features were masculine and commanding. Isobel really believed that sex should be about more than just bodies and physical attraction, about closeness and intimacy, but suddenly she could hardly wait until she got to see him naked.

"What on earth are you thinking about right now?" he asked, and she realized he had been silently watching her.

"Just wondering what you look like without clothes."

He sipped his whisky before putting down the glass.

He rested his hands and arms on the armrest, widened his legs. She could see he was aroused.

"What do you want to know?"

The hair all over her body was on end, standing at attention.

"Do you have any tattoos?"

Ordinarily she hated tattoos, but she decided that Alexander was a man who could get away with even that. But he shook his head. "Do you?"

"No," she said with a snort. "I'm a doctor."

He raised an eyebrow. "And doctors never have tattoos?"

"We think ahead and analyze things far too much; we don't do impulsive things."

"You're here."

She took a sip of whisky. It was fantastic. She loved its smoky taste, and it was the right kind of accessory when, for once, you were pretending to be a sophisticated creature.

"Coming here was a considered choice."

"I see." He looked like a fallen angel, sitting there with his ruffled hair and his damaged nose. An angel who had fallen, hard, and then had to do whatever it took to survive.

"So what do you think of piercings?"

"You have one?" she asked. "Where?"

"Guess."

"No, I hate guessing games," she said. Maybe it was the liquor, maybe it was the excitement she'd read in his face. It made no difference if she was just one of many. Right now she was the chosen one, and he made her *feel* it. Was there a more powerful aphrodisiac than that?

"Show me," she ordered.

He undid his fly, unbuttoned his shirt. She couldn't take her eyes off him. He opened his shirt, revealing his chest.

Ah. There were definite advantages to younger men.

"How the hell do you get a body like that?" she said, her eyes greedily working their way over him, remembering anatomical posters and thinking that this man was the godfather of all anatomical sketches. His stomach muscles were hard, vertical and horizontal, and his pecs swelled. He had golden hair on his chest—she liked that he didn't bother with stupid waxing. A thin line of it disappeared into the waistband of his pants. She saw the gleaming ring in his nipple. Glossy and fat. She would never have believed she'd be turned on by a golden ring in a man's nipple.

"Come here," he said. "Come and feel it."

She stood up. "It's not like I've never seen one of those before," she said as she sat down on the armrest next to him. He placed an arm around her, and she ran one of her hands over his chest. She paused above his heart, feeling its steady rhythm.

His arm moved up, along her spine, and beneath her hair. He cupped her nape and pulled her toward him until she ended up in his lap.

"No," she mumbled. "I'm too heavy."

He responded by wrapping his other arm around her like a vise, and then he kissed her. It was the kind of ravishing kiss she liked the best, with clever tongue and nibbling and hardness, and soon she was half-draped across his fit and hard body, inelegantly, with her dress twisted around her legs and one of his hands between her thighs. He cupped his hand against her panties, and she pressed against him. God, it had been so long since she'd felt this way, and it was much, much better than she'd dared to hope for. Say what you liked about amoral playboys without any kind of conscience, but he knew what he was doing and it was glorious, she thought dimly as they somehow ended up on the floor. He kissed her shoulder and searched for the opening of the dress, his hand sliding over the fabric.

"There are buttons down the back," she instructed, breathlessly.

He flipped her so that she was on her stomach, and she smiled into the cashmere at how wicked it felt. He started to unbutton her dress.

"Careful. It has to go back."

He gingerly pulled it off, and her shoes. Isobel attempted to turn over, but he placed a hand on her back.

"Stay there," he said, putting a hand on her ass. "So goddamn sexy," he said. His voice was heavy. His finger brushed against her G-string—she felt as though it had been worth wearing it all day when he so clearly liked it. He pulled at it gently, and she panted into the soft rug.

"Good?" he mumbled, his fingers gliding over her, tracing her back and spine, making her shiver in anticipation.

They helped one another to take off her panties and bra. His eyes were fixed on her breasts, and then he was on top of her—he was naked too, she didn't even know how—and then they were wrapped around one another, and all caution vanished, nothing but hands and fingers and tongues in union.

But when he moved between her legs, she came back to her senses.

"Not without protection." She should have brought this up earlier. He wouldn't care, of course. He was a man, irresponsible, he . . .

She propped herself up on her elbows. "We need to use a condom. STDs aren't a joke."

He pushed back a strand of her hair, kissed her, and bit her on the ear.

"If that's your idea of dirty talk, you're pretty bad at it."

"I think about stuff like that," she huffed.

"Do you?"

"I keep an eye on things."

"Not on everything," he said. "I put one on about sixty seconds ago." He moved, and she looked down. He was right, she hadn't noticed a thing. That had never happened before.

"I'll take it as a compliment," he said. "I don't know what you think of me. I probably don't want to know, but I know what I'm doing here. Lie down so I can finally fuck you."

She obeyed. Her thighs and lips obediently parted for him, and he kissed her as he entered her, filled her, took her. She closed her eyes as they made love on the soft rug, wrapped her arms around him, held him close. His chest rubbed over her nipples, and she bit his shoulder, bucked under his determined thrusts, felt his climax approach before he came, violently, and held her so tight she almost lost her breath.

"Of all the places I'd imagined us making love, the floor wasn't the one that came to mind," he said afterward. He was still holding her tight, nuzzling her.

"You fantasized about us?" she asked. She lay with her head above his heart, his warm skin against hers, and felt like there was nothing more she wanted from life right now. His hand stroked her back, and he had that kind of deep voice produced only by satisfaction, relaxed, comfortable.

"You haven't?"

"No," she lied. He laughed.

"You didn't come?"

She hesitated. "No," she eventually said. But she had been close, and making love to him had been fantastic.

"Why not?"

"It's just the way it is."

He turned and looked at her. "It sounds like it happens a lot. Why?"

"Can't we just lie here like this?" She didn't want to talk about sex. Not with Alexander, and not about what she liked or didn't like. Under no circumstances was she so stupid as to even *think* of letting him in. There were no limits to what damage a man like him could do. It was one thing to maintain a distance but something completely different to lie there in his arms and feel tempted to tell him things she had promised herself never to talk about again. She stroked his stomach.

"It's an important question, though. Coming is half the fun."

"It felt great, isn't that enough? Plus, there's a difference between men and women."

He snorted. "What century did you say you were born in? If you don't talk, then you never learn what the other person wants. Sex should give something to both people. Do you usually come with other men?"

She was almost starting to wish she had lied. Or faked it.

"I'm more than happy," she said primly, trying to pull away.

His grip tightened and he pinned her close to him. "I don't believe that."

"I'm sorry, Alex, but do we have to talk about this?"

He was silent, but she felt him relax.

"Fine, then, we don't have to talk about it," he said. "Not right now. Are you hungry?"

She was on the verge of saying no when her stomach growled.

He smiled, stood up, held out his hand, and pulled her up as though she weighed no more than a stethoscope.

Alexander started to take things from the refrigerator while Isobel leaned back against the kitchen island. He had pulled on a pair of thin trousers and a V-necked shirt, and of course he still looked like a *Vogue* model. Isobel had wrapped one of his light blankets around her.

He held out a glass of some kind of super-luxurious mineral water and then continued to move pans, put things on plates, and remove food from the refrigerator, which looked more like a complex space station. He dropped some butter into a sauté pan and started to cut vegetables. Isobel glanced at the clock. She liked that he was cooking for her at three in the morning.

"Are you some kind of kitchen god?"

"My best friend is a chef. Plus, I took a course once. In Paris."

Of course. His kitchen was fully equipped; she wasn't sure she had ever seen bowls like his. He placed plates and cutlery on a tray. The dish, pasta with tomato sauce, cheese, garlic and basil, smelled and looked fantastic, and she wolfed the food down.

After they ate, they sat down on the sofa again. This time, he sat next to her. He kissed her shoulder, breathed onto it. He was so nice. The words came from nowhere, but he *was* nice. Surprisingly solid under that frivolous surface.

He had handled the entire situation with Michel's cousin so well. She was trained to respond to emergencies, but he hadn't panicked, hadn't started to act irrationally. People who were reliable when it really mattered were so uncommon, something she really valued. Plus, the sex had been fantastic. It didn't matter that she hadn't climaxed—that wasn't important to her, not with her history. The important thing was that she enjoyed being with him. Felt comfortable and relaxed. She scratched her forehead as her thoughts whirled. There was so much Alexander didn't know about her, that he would never know, that he never *should* know. Luckily she was leaving for Chad soon, so she just had to keep her mouth shut for now, not give in to stupid impulses of sharing inner thoughts with him. It scared her how much she liked talking to him. Christ, this whole casual sex thing was much more complicated than she'd thought.

Chapter 27

Alexander studied Isobel on the couch next to him. She had disappeared into herself again. Whatever she was trying to work out in that brilliant head of hers clearly required a lot of frowning.

"Isobel? What is it?"

She looked at him. Pulled an apologetic face.

"Sorry. It's nothing."

Her head was cocked. Her hair fell around her shoulders. She had pulled her feet up onto the couch and was squeezing her toes. Yeah right, nothing.

"Hurting?" he asked with a nod toward her feet.

"I don't think I was made for heels."

"But you looked so damn hot in those shoes. Give me your foot," he said.

She gave him a suspicious look.

"Even though it might sound like it, I don't have a foot fetish. Give it to me."

She tentatively stretched out her leg toward him. He took her foot and started to gently knead it.

"You have pretty feet. Maybe I'm a bit of a fetishist after all. What do you think about this?"

"It's nice."

He took her big toe between his forefinger and thumb. "Do you like when I squeeze it like this?"

She shook her head. "Not so much."

"What about this, then?" He pushed his thumb into the arch of her foot, and she groaned.

"Yes. Keep doing that."

"See, not so hard, is it? You say what you like and you get it."

She gave him a disapproving look. "You're really stuck on that."

"I think it's important for you. Having an orgasm is a feminist act. But it's important to me too."

"Why?"

"Don't you see what a weird question that is? Why *wouldn't* I want it?"

Who had taught Isobel to be content with less than she deserved? And why in hell had she gone along with it?

She pushed back red tresses that were falling around her face and seemed to be thinking. "I think it's about control. I have trouble letting go."

No shit, Sherlock. Isobel had to be the most controlling person he'd ever met.

"And the moment you say that, people always start to press and squeeze and perform and show off," she added, then quickly falling silent, as though she'd said more than she meant to.

"By people, I'm guessing you mean your lousy lovers? Give me the other foot."

He pressed his thumb into the arch again, and she moaned lustily.

"Massages are often better than sex, if I'm honest."

But he didn't fall for that. "Now we're getting somewhere. Honesty. If you turn round, with your back to me, I'll do your neck, too."

He saw uncertainty flash across her face, as though she couldn't comprehend his doing something for her without an ulterior motive.

"Come on, Isobel, you know you want to. I have magic hands."

She hesitated, but then turned around on the couch so that she was facing away from him. Alexander pushed down the blanket, placed his hands on her shoulders, and worked his fingers in beneath her hair.

"God, that's so good," she mumbled as he worked away.

Alexander leaned forward, bit her shoulder. She trembled. So, she liked that. He continued massaging her neck, worked his way down her shoulders and back. Her skin was soon glowing, and she was making a faint humming sound. He allowed one of his hands to creep round, cup her breast, massage her nipple. She didn't say anything, but he heard her breathing change. She raised one arm and put it around his neck, pulled him close to her. He got up, onto his knees, hard against her back. He bent down, still cupping her breast with one hand and working his way down her stomach with the other, cupping her red curls.

She was wet, and she breathed heavily in his ear. She definitely liked this.

"I want to make it nice for you," he murmured.

"It *is* nice."

"Lie down, on your back."

His couch was one of the deepest models, and Alexander moved down alongside her, didn't want to ruin the moment by suggesting they go to the bedroom.

"Show me how you want it. Show me with your hands," he said, taking her hand and placing it over his own. "Touch yourself."

At first, she lay still.

"Do it, Isobel, please."

She slowly moved her hand along her thigh. He followed her movement and carefully parted her legs. She turned her head, looking wide-eyed at him.

"Keep going, don't stop. I want to watch."

Isobel's hand wandered up, over her stomach, and then back down, slowly. She closed her eyes, raised her legs slightly, and grazed the inside of her thigh.

"Go on," he mumbled hoarsely, quickly pulling off his clothes and lying back down beside her again. He placed one hand on the inside of her thigh. She was as smooth as silk. He pulled her apart a little farther.

"Yes," she breathed. Her hips moved. "Come."

He got up and lay down on top of her, resting on his hands. She still had her eyes closed, as though she were in a world of her own, and he studied her face—the long eyelashes, the tightly closed eyelids, the high cheekbones—before he pushed her legs farther apart using his knees. He heard her pant, and made a mental note.

"Keep going," he said. She was breathing more heavily now. He entered her, and she let out a moan and her eyes flew open. He loved her eyes, he thought, as he started to move inside her. But this wasn't about what *he* wanted, this was about forcing Isobel Sørensen to let go a little. He pulled out.

"What're you doing?"

A good question. Why did he care so much whether she came? If it felt good for him, why was it important that he was better than all her previous lovers? The simple answer was, of course, vanity. The more complicated answer . . . was something else.

"You know what I want," he said. "I want you to touch yourself, and I want to watch. You like it, I can see that."

"You're pretty stubborn, you know that?"

He lifted her hand to his mouth. He took a finger, put it into his mouth, and sucked it. She liked that. He took the next finger too, sucked on it, knew that it zapped every single erogenous zone in her body. He pulled the finger from his mouth, cupped her hand in his, and held it to his chest.

"I'm planning to fuck you now," he said in a low voice as he rolled on a new condom. "And you're going to keep touching yourself while I do it. And if I do something you really like, you're going to tell me. Okay?"

He waited until her right hand crept in between her thighs again. She closed her eyes and part of him felt regret. But then he followed his intuition, took her middle finger, and started to suck it again. She shuddered. He pushed back into her, studying her carefully. Whenever he was gentle a frustrated look appeared on her face, but whenever he was rough she began to move her hips. So, she liked it a little rough, his Isobel. He moved more firmly, angling himself so that she had better access with her hands. She was sweating now, her head rolling back and forth, gasping sounds coming from her lips. He took her with much more force than last time. She was breathing heavily, and then she raised her hips and came with an unexpectedly explosive orgasm, and it was so fucking sexy that it tipped him over the edge too. He came with a force that shook him, that rocked through him, that made him grab her and hold on.

"Isobel," he panted into her neck.

She simply breathed, her heart thundering beneath him.

He collapsed next to her, his body shaking. He turned so he could see her. She was sweaty, her hair plastered to her forehead. Gently he pushed it away, kissed her, lay face-to-face, kissed her mouth. He looked more closely.

"Are you crying?"

"No. Maybe. A little. I'm just a bit shocked. No, not shocked. Surprised."

"Can I ask you something?"

She shook her head. "Absolutely not."

"When did you last come?"

"The other day."

He laughed. "With a man. Isobel, when did a man last give you an orgasm?"

She closed her eyes, shut him out in the way she always did. He waited. She sighed.

"It's not so easy for me. I don't know why it matters to you. If I'd known you talked so much, I never would've followed you home."

He snorted. "You practically threw yourself onto me."

"Yeah, yeah."

"It's for my own sake. The more orgasms you have with me, the more often you're going to want to sleep with me. Basically, it's a deeply selfish act. I'm selfish, we've already established that. You're the idealist. I'm the cynic."

Isobel laid her chin on his chest, played with his gold ring with one of her long, sensitive fingers.

She talked about control and safe sex and rationality as if they were the most important things in the world, but there was more to her, beneath the sensible surface. She'd been so wet when he was a little rougher, told her what to do. She got turned on when he talked dirty, and she might sneer at the luxury and glamor of his lifestyle, but she *liked* it.

He supposed it ought to make him happy. He pulled her close and kissed her. It was best when they were making out or making love. Only when he started to think did things get unclear in his mind.

"Should I get you something to drink?" he asked.

She shook her head slowly. "You should stay right here," she said. "I need your chest to rest my chin on." She kissed his skin, then stuck out her tongue and licked the gold ring. "I think I will have to reassess my thoughts on piercing."

How many women had he seduced, only to end up in this same position? Women who liked the idea of Alexander De la Grip, who enjoyed the glamorous surface, but who didn't know him deep down. He had seen exactly that satisfied, contented look so many times before, and he'd never had a thing against it, quite the opposite—it had actually been his goal.

Women saw him as entertainment, as some kind of sexual conquest. He knew exactly what to do to get a woman to come. Not even Isobel and all of her "secrets" had been beyond him once he'd made up his mind. And now she was next to him, purring like a cat.

She wasn't even the first woman he'd ordered to touch herself to climax. Sex was a fundamentally lonely activity. He'd always told himself that he had no need for closeness and had never felt shut out when a woman closed her eyes and came on her own. So. He had given her exactly what she wanted and he had found release. She was humming with contentment and he was satisfied. He really was.

Isobel had no other expectations of him than this.

He hadn't had any other expectations.

All was as it should be. All.

Chapter 28

Peter glanced at the clock, wondering where Gina was. When he'd given her a ride home after the wedding reception, everything had been as usual between them. He had tried to keep an eye on her during the party, constantly worrying that someone might try to accost her. He knew what men were like—especially drunk men from his own social class. He'd felt as if his heart were in his mouth the whole time. He hadn't drunk alcohol, had barely spoken to anyone, had done nothing but watch out for her. And then that surreal episode with the man getting ill.

She had been fantastic. But when he'd praised her in the car, she hadn't wanted to take any credit, had just talked about how she admired Isobel Sørensen. Whom his little brother seemed to be dating.

Peter peered out the doorway of his office. He had hoped everything would go on as normal, but Gina hadn't been in yesterday, and she wasn't in today either, and now he didn't know what to make of it. Had something happened? He looked at the clock again; it was past six. He got up and went to the kitchen. Still no Gina. He opened the refrigerator to see whether her food was inside, if she'd arrived without his noticing, but no, nothing but half-empty cartons of Thai food and a variety of protein shakes.

He headed over to the reception desk but didn't dare ask any of the receptionists if they knew where she was. He really wanted to call or send her a message, just to check if she was okay, but they hadn't swapped numbers, so he didn't feel like he could, even if he did manage to get her number.

Had she quit?

Without saying anything?

An hour later, the office was empty. Spring had arrived, the cherry blossoms in Kungsträdgården park downtown were in full bloom, and people used any excuse they could to sneak off out into the sun. When he went down for the third time, the night staff were already in place in the lobby. He waited, drumming his fingers, while the receptionist made small talk with a guard. Could he ask if any cleaners would be in today?

He was just about to head back to his office when he saw the elevator doors open.

It was her.

She was rifling around in her purse, looking for something, and Peter stilled. Gina looked up at the exact same moment he regained his wits. He hurried over and opened the door for her before the receptionist had time to buzz her in, before she even had time to get out her pass.

"Thanks," she said.

"Hi, Gina." He tried in vain to come up with something intelligent to say, something easygoing, or at least something normal. She gave him a questioning look.

"Is everything okay?"

"Yes. It's just, you weren't in yesterday," he said. "I was a little worried."

"I was off yesterday. I studied and had some classes. Everything's fine."

"Good to hear."

He held the next door open for her and waited while she hung up her jacket.

"And your brother? He's well?"

"Yes."

"And your father? How is he sleeping?"

"Really well, actually." She changed her shoes and hung her purse in the locker.

"And you're well, you said?"

She closed the locker door and gave him a questioning look. "I'm good. Are you alright?"

"I'm great. The wedding was nice. Did you know Alexander is dating Doctor Sørensen?"

"I guessed as much."

"He's fine, by the way. The man you helped. I called Åsa to ask. I thought you might want to know."

"Thanks. Isobel sent me a message." She flashed him a grin. "Just between us, and I know it sounds awful, but it was so damn cool. Isobel did most of it, but still. I almost felt like a real doctor. Do you think I'm terrible for saying that?"

"I think it's a sign that you'll be an awesome doctor someday. Is the vacuum heavy? Here, let me get it for you."

"Thanks."

She stood there in silence, shifting on her feet. "I need to start work."

"Of course. See you later."

Peter went back to his room.

He would work until Gina was done. She normally cleaned for around two hours.

In the meanwhile he hoped he could come up with a convincing excuse to give her another ride home.

Chapter 29

"Hi, my name is Tyra and I'll be leading this training day, the first of two."

Isobel tried to concentrate on the speaker, who had begun with a load of practical information about the safety course. Tyra was a short-haired blond woman, an army officer, and what she said was both interesting and relevant. But Isobel, who was usually an excellent student, was having trouble focusing on the course outline.

"We'll be here for two days. This morning we'll talk about safety and culture in the countries you'll be visiting."

Isobel's mind drifted away; she couldn't help it. The sex with Alexander had been insane. He had been fantastic. Passionate, challenging, dirty—a woman's wildest wet dream. The best lover she'd ever had. She drummed her pen on the notepad, considering the blunt fact that Alexander De la Grip was probably the best lover *any* woman had ever had. He enjoyed sex, he was focused on his partner, and he was impressively experienced.

They had eventually fallen asleep. Woken up, showered, made love, made out again. She had walked around in one of his T-shirts, and he'd made cappuccino with his sophisticated-looking coffee machine, and yes—it had all been like something out of a feel-good chick lit movie. She hadn't gone home until Sunday evening, after they'd kissed and made love and kissed some more.

She had gotten caught up. Or maybe she'd just relaxed. Definitely left doors ajar that had long been closed. And yes, it had been magical. And worryingly intimate.

Well, it didn't look like *intimacy* or getting too close would be a problem. As far as Isobel could tell, she had been dumped.

"You don't need to write this down; we'll give you a folder with all the information. Except the stuff that can't leave this room for security reasons," she heard Tyra say.

Isobel looked up. The whiteboard was covered with writing and arrows.

Tyra gave the class a stern look. "Tomorrow we'll spend the whole day on hostage situations."

Isobel nodded and then immediately disappeared back into her thoughts. So, she'd been dumped. Alexander hadn't been in touch at all Sunday evening, and finally she'd decided that women could send texts just as easily as men could. Well, *that* had been its own special kind of humiliation. Sending a quick text to Alexander, and then worrying that she'd been too brief and so sending another, accompanying message. And then waiting. She broke out sweating just at the thought of it. His reply hadn't come until Monday evening, almost twenty-four hours later. Curt, as from a distant acquaintance. Impersonal, as though from a salesman.

She had spent an entire night and day interpreting every word, punctuation mark, and new line in that message. But it made no difference how many times she read it; she came to the same conclusion every time. She was dumped. For him it had been a one-time thing, and now it was over. Welcome to the twenty-first century. Thanks very much, grow up, move on.

Isobel drummed her pen against her notebook so hard that one of her coursemates, an award-winning journalist she had always admired, shushed her quietly over her shoulder.

"Sorry," Isobel whispered. She made a halfhearted attempt to listen to the speaker, but she lost the plot somewhere around the words "Things to consider in Muslim countries."

She wondered whether Alexander had already left Sweden. That was probably the most likely explanation; he had talked about going back to New York. And she really hadn't expected it to continue. Just the opposite actually. Hadn't she had sex with him precisely because she knew he would vanish? Yes, she firmly reminded herself. That had been the plan, and she'd been well aware of it. It just kept slipping her mind.

After the introduction—she would have to borrow someone else's notes—they took a quick break. Isobel did her best to focus afterward, but the subject was trauma medicine, and if there was one thing she knew about, it was saving the heart and lungs and stemming the flow of blood. She tried to look as though she was listening to the ambulance driver who was demonstrating how to apply a tourniquet to a shot-off leg. It did actually capture her interest. She had met plenty of people injured by mines, and she managed to brush aside all thoughts of teasing blue eyes, hard muscles, and crazy-good sex until lunch.

She would do better during the afternoon, she decided as she followed the crowd toward the lunch room. After all, she would be headed to Chad soon and Alexander would be long forgotten. Anything else was madness. Life would go on like it always had. It had to.

Alexander looked up over the lunch menu. He hummed in agreement with what his lunch date had said, though he hadn't heard a single word of it. He had reserved a table at one of his old hunting grounds, Riche. The service was fast, the food a combination of French bistro and Swedish fine cuisine, the atmosphere in the nineteenth-century surroundings cozy but not too secluded. He glanced around, searching for a waiter. If he was going to make it through this, he would need a drink.

"I was a little surprised you answered my call. I heard you were in Stockholm, but it felt like you were avoiding me," his date said, pouting her lips. She had a sexy mouth. Small and glossy and pink, like bubble gum. She had reapplied her lip gloss three times since they'd arrived.

"That's why I felt it was time to make it up to you, Qornelia," he said smoothly. It was automatic, getting into this kind of talk. *I should be happy now,* he thought as he focused on Qornelia's account of her latest sponsors. She was a former reality TV star, a so-called entertainment profile these days, and she had some kind of clothing label. Or maybe it was makeup or purses? He didn't have the energy to remember.

"That's so nice," she cooed. "And I know I can say this to you without your taking it the wrong way, but it's good for me to be seen with you."

"Of course," he mumbled.

She launched into a monologue about the celebrities she'd met over the past few weeks, the events she would be invited to, and the holidays she was trying to get sponsorship for, but he found it so goddamn hard to drum up any interest at all. He didn't really understand it, why he was suddenly so annoyed by her superficiality. It had never bothered him before.

"Two vodka tonics," he said when the waiter came over to their table.

"No hard liquor for me," said Qornelia. She moved consciously, showing off her perfect little body. "It makes you so fat."

"They're for me. Champagne for my beautiful friend," he said.

Qornelia giggled. "Oh, Alexander."

He emptied the first glass in one go and breathed out. He held up the second one, showing that he wanted to order another.

"What should we eat? Oysters?" Qornelia asked.

"Have what you like."

Her eyes shone. She couldn't be more than twenty-five, but her facial skin was so flawless he knew that she must get it peeled in one of those clinics his mother went to. He didn't know why that bothered him either. He had never cared what women did with their appearance. This was what happened when you spent time around people with passion and conviction. You ended up with strange ideas. But it would pass. Isobel had been a challenge he'd set himself, and one he'd successfully conquered. It had taken longer to get her into bed than he'd calculated, but it had been worth the wait—it had been pretty damn magical. And now that they had slept together, it was time to move forward. They'd both known it, hadn't they? That they would have sex and then go their separate ways? The only thing that really mattered to her was her work, for Christ's sake.

He drummed his fingers on the white tablecloth. He had been in Sweden for over a month now. Maybe that was why he felt so antsy. He was restless. That had to be it. He'd seen his family, his niece—even his mother, for God's sake. He'd signed his name on a ton of documents and he'd managed not to strangle Peter. Fuck, he practically deserved canonization.

Qornelia closed the menu. "I'll take the entrecôte. But just the meat. No sauce, no carbs." She smiled at Alexander. "It's the most expensive thing they have. And I love meat."

"I'll take a risotto," he said to the waiter.

She looked at him with wide eyes. They were framed by absurdly long eyelashes and perfectly sculpted brows. "But that's just rice, isn't it? Sounds pretty boring."

"I feel like vegetarian food," he said.

She pouted again. "Please, Alexander?" He felt a gentle stroke beneath the table. "It's not like you to be so boring. Come on. We said we'd have fun today. Since when is rice fun?"

She was right. What the hell was he doing? He closed the menu with a snap. "Two entrecôtes."

"I'm so full," Qornelia groaned as she put her cutlery to one side. She hadn't even eaten half her serving.

"There are children starving in Africa—aren't you going to eat that?"

She burst into laughter.

"Send it to them, then. Are you getting another drink, or do you want to move on?"

She leaned forward over the table and laid her hand on top of his. She had long, pink false nails. Her entire being was completely flawless; it was like she was made of porcelain. Or plastic. But she had been flirting shamelessly their entire lunch, she laughed continuously, was sexy, carefree, and interested. His usual type, in other words, and so he forced himself to smile back at her, refused to let his strange mood take over. It wasn't Qornelia's fault he was suddenly annoyed at everything and everyone.

"I bought an apartment. On Strandvägen. Maybe we can continue there?"

Her face lit up. "You mean it?"

"There's a well-stocked bar. Champagne in the refrigerator."

Fresh sheets on the bed.

He paid and pulled out the chair for her. Smiling smugly, she took his arm and leaned in to him.

"I'm looking forward to seeing your place."

"Is there anything particular you want to do there?"

She pressed her breasts against his arm.

"I'm sure we'll think of something," she purred.

"So, what do you have against kids in Africa?" he asked as he held the door open for her.

Qornelia swished her long, glossy hair. It fell so perfectly over her firm, narrow shoulders that he knew she must have extensions. Her pink lips and almost glow-in-the-dark teeth were on display with her laughter.

"Other people's problems aren't for me. They can look after themselves. I've got enough to worry about in my own life."

She laughed, and he did so too. It sounded hollow. But the emptiness he felt wasn't some kind of incurable condition. He knew exactly how to treat emptiness, and he had just prescribed himself a Qornelia. If it didn't work out, he would just have to try harder. And drink more.

Chapter 30

Oh, but she had done something really stupid last night, and today she was paying the price for it. Isobel slumped against the wall, waiting to be let in to the course room for their second day. She said hello to a few of the other participants, and then withdrew into herself.

Yesterday, against her better judgment, she had Googled Alexander just before she went to bed. It had been an impulse and so goddamn idiotic. She'd *known* it was a mistake and yet she had done it. And sure enough, she had found brand-new pics of him, eating lunch at Riche with some incredibly attractive, incredibly young woman. The pair had been holding hands, leaning in close, toasting one another. Definitely more than an ordinary lunch. They had been spotted, photographed, and ended up on social media. Stockholm's jet-set prince and some Stureplan personality. Of course there were photos on Instagram.

It hurt so much, even though it shouldn't. Alexander had succeeded in making her feel singled out, special. But it had been a game from the start, and now, rather humiliatingly, Isobel had to accept that she was just one of the many women Alexander had chased, slept with, and dumped. And she did accept it. Couldn't he just have waited *a little* longer, though?

Once inside the classroom, she headed for the back. She had slept terribly, of course, and all she wanted was to close her eyes and disappear somewhere dark and quiet.

A tall, tanned man came into the room. Straight-backed, an excessively serious look in his eyes.

She scratched her nose and wondered whether Leila would find out if she skipped the course. It was a rhetorical question, of course; Isobel had never skipped a class in her life.

"My name is K-G. Yesterday you talked about safety. Today I'm going to teach you how to act when safety disappears. If you get abducted or captured."

He practically roared the last few words, and Isobel's mood sank further. She had met his type before; the refugee camps and bases were teeming with them. Macho military men who just *had* to show who was in charge.

"You won't be rescued, for a start. You have to understand that rescue operations are prohibitively dangerous. In that kind of situation, the most common outcome is that the hostages die, so it's pointless."

People were silent, and Isobel had the unfortunate impulse to laugh out loud. She looked down at her notepad and thought that she had liked Tyra more. K-G started a PowerPoint presentation.

"The phases of capture," he bellowed.

She studied the headings. They were fine, in theory, but she knew from experience that when you were captured, your pulse would be close to one hundred beats a minute. You got tunnel vision and were so afraid you didn't think logically. The likelihood of remembering what you'd once read in a PowerPoint presentation somewhere in Stockholm was virtually zero.

"Is there anything else we should know?" The blond reporter had spoken up.

Yeah. Don't get captured.

"They'll almost certainly try to dehumanize you, so try to get them to see you as a person. Keep clean, if possible, as neat as you can. Remind your kidnappers that you have a family, that you are valuable. Try to stay alive—captivity can be long. Be polite. Try to learn their names, which of them you should avoid for being crazy, psychotic, or high. Who could be an ally."

"Should you tell them who you are, what you do?"

The reporter again. She typed out everything K-G said on her iPad, her fingers making a constant tap tap sound against the screen.

"It's good to convince them you're worth money. That you will be useful."

People started to raise their hands now.

"How long are people held hostage?"

"Some are there for years. Two to three months is seen as a short amount of time."

"What about rape?"

K-G frowned and put his fists at his hips. "You should count on torture. Rape too, unfortunately. Even if it's not quite as common as you might think, particularly in the Muslim countries. We'll talk more about that after lunch. Any more questions? No? Let's move on."

Isobel looked down at her notes as K-G continued. She hadn't asked any questions.

She studied the words she had written.

Hostage. Torture. Rape.

And she had thought this wouldn't be any fun.

It was probably a bad idea, coming here, Alexander thought as he walked through the front door and pressed the button for the elevator. But he hadn't been thinking clearly when he'd called Leila, and now he was here, on the way up to some kind of training room, to look for Isobel.

He leaned against the wall of the elevator and waited for a wave of nausea to pass. He couldn't remember when he had last been so hungover. It struck him that it must have been that time Isobel came to his office. Could that really have been a month ago? He had taken it so easy the past few weeks that he'd lost some of his tolerance to alcohol. But yesterday he'd done a month's worth of drinking, making his very best efforts to completely empty his bar. So now he felt the way he deserved to.

The elevator doors opened. He came out into a hallway full of numbered doors and a wall-mounted information board showing what meeting was taking place in each of the rooms. A door opened. A bearded man came out and turned off toward the restrooms. Alexander headed for the door, pushed it open, and peered in. A dozen or so people were listening to a tall, arrogant man gesturing exaggeratedly at a whiteboard behind him. Cropped hair, tanned, combat pants. *Ex-military*. Alexander could spot one from a mile away. Black T-shirt with a company logo. Sunglasses hanging from his collar.

The man caught sight of him.

"Can I help you?" His voice was loud.

Alexander's eyes swept across the rows of seats. Saw red hair and got the information he needed.

"Didn't you see this room was booked?" The military man was almost yelling now.

Alexander just ignored him and pulled the door shut.

Leila had said the course lasted until six.

At two minutes past, he heard the scraping of chairs moving, and he opened the door and put his head in again. The ex-military man spotted him. His face was decidedly less friendly now.

"Are you still here? Are you looking for something?"

But he had found her. "I'm looking for *someone*. Isobel?"

She looked up from whatever she was doing and froze.

"What are you doing here?"

She sounded about as welcoming as the course leader. But it was a good question.

He had been thinking about her. Had sat with his phone in his hand and been on the verge of calling her at least twenty times since they'd parted on Sunday. Why hadn't he just called? He had no idea, just knew that he'd thought it was better to let things die off before they got too serious. It still felt like the smartest move. And yet he was here.

"Are you done? Can we go sit somewhere?"

Her entire body seemed to be saying she'd rather not.

"It's been an intense couple of days. . . ." she said.

"Please? Just for a while. We can go somewhere nearby. Do you have your bike?"

They ended up in a sidewalk café on a street near Stureplan. The evening was sunny and warm, and there were people everywhere. Isobel locked up her bike, sat down on a chair in the shade, and ordered a coffee and mineral water.

"How did you know where I was? Leila?"

He nodded. God, he hadn't realized how much he had missed her.

"I just wanted to say hi, see you."

Isobel's eyes moved over his face. He hadn't shaved that morning and assumed he looked exactly as bad as he felt.

"Are you drunk?"

"No," he answered honestly.

She gave him a skeptical look. A doctor's look.

"Hungover," he admitted.

"Right."

Her foot bobbed up and down, and she drummed her index finger on her cup. Not a good sign.

"Isobel, I . . ." he started, only to be interrupted by an enthusiastic shout.

"Oh, my *god,* Alexander! Hiiii!"

He reluctantly got to his feet. "Hi, Petra," he said. She was an old friend from school. One of the many women he flirted with as if by reflex.

Petra threw her arms around his neck and gave him a long hug. Automatically he hugged her back.

He could feel Isobel's eyes on them, sensed she was on the verge of getting up to leave.

He'd chosen a bad location. If his brain had been working, he would have taken Isobel someplace else.

"Really good to see you, Petra, but I'm kind of in the middle of something. . . ." he said, backing away from her, feeling oddly self-conscious.

"Oh?" Petra flashed Isobel a curious look, and then smiled at Alexander. She leaned forward and gave him a kiss on the cheek. "Call me sometime," she whispered, and disappeared.

Alexander sat back down.

Isobel gave him a blank look.

"Sorry," he said.

"For what?"

Her face was completely calm. If he hadn't studied her closely, he wouldn't have noticed anything other than the cool exterior. But the storm in her eyes gave her away.

He shrugged. "For everything, I guess."

For being a shit, for not treating you like you deserve, for not being able to leave you in peace even though I should.

"I thought you were in New York."

"Nope, still here."

Her eyes flashed, and he wished he was able to interpret what that meant. But he had hurt her, he could tell. The very last thing he wanted to do.

"So. What did you do this week?"

That cool, passionless voice again.

"I had a few things to take care of."

"Things?"

Her tone was neutral, but he heard a hint of something. It took a moment before he realized what it was. Anger. But why? They hadn't made any promises. And it was four days since they'd parted, not four *weeks*. Wasn't she overreacting a bit?

"I just wanted to see you," he said. "That's not strange, is it? I like you, Isobel. I hope I've made that clear."

She gave him yet another cold, gray look.

"Maybe we could go out. There's time. You aren't leaving until next week, are you?"

She paused, studying him, and he had the feeling he had said something stupid.

"You're thinking we'd get together again? Before I go to Chad?" she said slowly.

"Yeah, it would be nice. We could go out and eat?"

"Like maybe dinner, you mean?"

Something wasn't right. He hadn't been counting on her over-flowing with happiness, but he had a feeling he'd missed something vital.

"Isobel, I'm sorry I didn't get in touch. But I'd like to see you again."

She cocked her head.

"Just have a bit of fun, right? See where we end up?"

"Exactly," he said, relieved.

She shook her head. "This was a mistake."

"There's something wrong with that, you mean?"

"Not at all. It's your life, you live it how you want. But I feel pretty done with all this." She waved a hand, covering him, her, the table. She smiled a cheerless smile. "So you'll just have to find someone else to eat dinner with. Or lunch. See where you end up."

Fuck. She'd seen Qornelia and him.

"I can explain. It was . . ."

She held her hands up in the air, as though she was stopping a car. "You know, that's probably my least favorite expression. Nothing good ever came after 'I can explain.' And honestly, you don't need to. I think I understand pretty well as it is."

She stood up and adjusted her purse on her shoulder.

What the hell?

"Are you really leaving? Just like that?"

"Yes."

"Jesus, Isobel, you're overreacting. Sit down."

She raised an eyebrow. "Well, there's surely nothing a woman appreciates more than being told she's overreacting."

"I didn't mean . . ."

"Bye, Alexander."

With quick steps she left the table. He wanted to say that he hadn't meant to sound like an idiot, that he wanted to make it up to her, that he *felt* things. But instead he watched her unlock her bike, drop her purse into the basket, and cycle off without looking back. The last thing he saw was a blaze of her fiery hair in the sun before she turned a corner.

He stared at her untouched coffee.

Well, this had been a catastrophe from start to finish.

"Everything okay?"

He nodded to the waitress.

"Check, please." He took out his credit card, laid it on the table, and pulled out his cell.

He scrolled through his speed dial numbers, chose one, and rested his forehead in his hand while he waited.

"It's me."

"Alexander? Been a while. How're things?"

"I've had enough of Sweden. I'll be back tomorrow."

"About fucking time," said Romeo. "I was starting to think something had happened."

He entered his PIN, left a tip, and got up. "Nothing happened."

Nothing important, anyway. I just ruined something I should've been careful with. And I've had it.

"I'll send a car to the airport. Let me know the time. And Alex?"

"Yeah?"

"Welcome home."

Chapter 31

"That's it, then," Isobel said to the director of her clinic at the private health center. It was her last day. She had written and signed all her notes, finished off all her tasks, and sent all electronic prescriptions. She held out a hand to her boss, Veronica, a tall, gray-haired physician.

"See you when you get back," said Veronica, giving her a firm hug instead. "Good luck in Chad."

Isobel got on her bike and set off. The sun warmed her back, and she stopped midway to take off her thin cardigan. When she arrived at Medpax, she locked up her bike and headed in.

"Hi, Asta, how's the pollen allergy?"

The receptionist sneezed in reply. Her eyes were red and swollen.

"Let me know if you need a prescription. Is Leila here?"

Asta sneezed again and then gestured to the meeting room.

"It's just you and me today," Leila said as she went in. "How was the course?"

Isobel put down a stack of papers on the desk, then reached for some water and poured herself a glass. "Theoretical. Lots of going over stuff I already know. Some of it was good, I guess, but if we don't have much money, it probably wasn't the best use of funds."

She knew how much even a theoretical two-day course cost. Those who could really afford it sent their people on practical courses. A week of role-playing and exercises. Thank God she had been able to avoid that.

"How was it for you? Distressing?"

"No," she answered curtly.

Maybe she was lying and repressing. Maybe Leila realized it.

Leila studied her, so she drank more water, looked out across the table, and steeled herself for the question she knew was coming.

"Did Alexander show up?"

"Very briefly."

And then Leila did something Isobel hated. She *waited*. She had seen it before, how Leila got people to talk. She would say nothing, just watch and wait for them to continue, to go deeper. She was on the verge of starting to tap her foot, but managed to resist. It was only a week since Leila had told her to go to the wedding and have a bit of fun. As unbelievably naïve as she was, she had thought she would be able to handle what came next.

Leila gave her a searching look. "Want to talk about it?"

Isobel shook her head, violently. But she wasn't angry at Leila; she was angry at herself. That she, despite her hurt pride, hadn't been able to ignore how good Alexander looked. That Alexander, despite being unshaven and hungover and evidently someone who slept with every silicon-enhanced celebrity bimbo who crossed his path, was still attractive to her. It was so humiliating to realize that she was turned on by a man like that, to admit that the best sex she'd ever had was with a man who essentially stood for everything she disliked most. *But he has another side, Isobel, you know that, and that's what hurts the most*.

"Not really," she said. "There's nothing to talk about. There's nothing between us."

In a way, she was glad he'd done what he had. It made it easier to get over him. When he acted like the player she knew he was.

"If you say so," said Leila, looking deeply skeptical. "I just wondered if you knew why he'd suddenly left for New York?" Leila's tone was easygoing, but Isobel knew she was indulging in one of her favorite pastimes: snooping.

"He's there now?" She didn't know why she felt hurt by the news.

"I called him, and he was in New York when he answered. He sounded down. And you look like an abandoned foal every time I mention his name. Are you sure everything's okay?"

Isobel looked out the window. Medpax had cut back on cleaning costs, and flecks of dust danced in the sunlight.

"Aside from the fact I'm going to my mom's for a formal dinner, everything's under control."

She hadn't had time to come up with a good excuse when her mother had called the day before, not so much to invite her to dinner but to order her to come. Now it was just a case of biting the bullet.

"By the way, did you know my mom and Alexander's know one another?"

Ugh, it was hard to say his name so nonchalantly, especially to Leila, who was practically a mind reader.

"No, but it doesn't surprise me. Blanche and Ebba De la Grip move in roughly the same circles. I haven't met Ebba, only Eugene. I didn't even know Alexander was his nephew. You Swedes all look alike. I have trouble telling you apart."

"Eugene is half Russian. I'm a quarter French and a quarter Danish, so I'm going to ignore that."

"Yeah, yeah, Europeans then. Does that mean Ebba is going to your mother's tonight?"

"No, it was just a question. My mother's old friends are coming. I promised to help serve."

She managed to hold back a disloyal grimace.

But she knew exactly what she would hear.

"My daughter is still trying to figure out her life."

"She gets that frame from her father; on my side, the women are slim and dainty."

"She used to eat meat, of course. I don't know what's come over her."

"You could always say no," said Leila.

Isobel flashed her an amused look. "Sure."

She needed to get home and shower before she cycled up to her mother's apartment by Karlaplan, the snobbish address where the youngest of the royal siblings used to live. If she pretended it was a complex field task she had to tackle, if she didn't drink, held her tongue at all her mother's digs, and didn't allow herself to be provoked into any kind of argument about humanitarian work, feminism, or politics, then maybe she would be able to leave by ten.

After she said good-bye to Leila and a sniffling Asta, Isobel took the stairs back down. She looked up as she fastened her helmet. The trees were blooming, all cherry-pink and apple-blossom-white, the air was cool and smelled fresh. In two days, she would have swapped all this bright airiness for something entirely different. Sticky heat, the insects that came with the rainy season, and the typical red Chad landscape.

A cheap, long-haul flight, an overnight transfer in Addis Ababa, and then she would be in one of the poorest countries on Earth. Hardship, death, and near-unbearable heat awaited her there. She would work around the clock, see maybe one hundred acutely ill patients a day, armed with nothing but a stethoscope, experience everything from intense joy to bottomless sorrow, and be thankful for every minute she hadn't been struck down by cholera.

She climbed up onto the saddle and glanced back before cycling off. She wondered what it said about her that she could hardly wait to get away.

She knew what it meant as soon as they came for her. And there were so many of them. She was alone, still a child in so many ways, with nowhere to run. The fear when they came, when they surrounded her, was the worst she'd ever known. Every bone in her body, every muscle, wanted to run. But it was a futile wish. They forced her down on a striped rug, she would never forget the feeling of the floor beneath her, the soft rug and the bumps in the floor beneath it, how they held her down. There was no one who would help her, no one to hear her cries or even to care. After all. She was just one of many girls it happened to. All the time.

Chapter 32

"And then he called to say his wife liked Louise better and that he was sorry, but he couldn't hang out with me anymore."

"But what did you say to him? Wasn't he your friend? Weren't you sad?"

"Not as sad as I thought I'd be. I guess I always expected them to take Louise's side anyway. But I went and took a leak in his wife's kitchen garden one night. On her basil."

Gina burst out laughing.

"Sounds fair," she said.

Peter nodded. "I thought so. You're the only one who knows. Not even my therapist got to hear about that, even though it was her idea."

"Your therapist told you to pee on a garden bed?"

Peter shrugged. "She said I should express my feelings. It was a loose interpretation, I guess."

Gina put her hand to her mouth and felt the laughter bubble up in her again.

She liked that Peter didn't say a single derogatory word about his ex-wife, not even when he had the chance. Gina had met Louise many times, and she would have had plenty of sympathy for Peter if he was resentful about the way he had been shut out of their old community. But he never said anything negative about her, and Gina admired him for that.

The laughter ebbed out and left behind a warm glow in her body. She was starting to get addicted to this car and their journeys. She liked that Peter made her laugh. There had been far too many times in her life when there was nothing to laugh about. She glanced at him in profile. Peter looked happier and better rested than he had in a long while. The new clothes he wore fit him much better than the old ones. Still suits and shirts, of course, but the cut was more modern, and he usually took off the tie in the elevator when they left the office. He smelled good, too. She turned toward the window on her side and relaxed into another smile. Outside, the familiar buildings and roadworks went by. Peter swung into the lane for Tensta. It felt as though the journey went more quickly every time they did it.

"Guess what?" she said.

"What?"

"I've never been any farther north than this road."

"But you've been to Gyllgarn Castle."

"I mean farther away. There has to be a world beyond Gyllgarn."

For half of her life, she had seen the road signs. Oslo. Enköping. Dreamed about what lay at the end of the road.

"Though this road, the E18, the European road number 18, doesn't really go north," said Peter. "More west. It would actually go straight through Norway and all the way to Northern Ireland. And then to Saint Petersburg in the other direction." He grimaced. "Sorry, I didn't mean to sound like a know-it-all. I've just always liked geography."

"You never sound like that. And besides, I like it when you teach me things."

She fell silent, embarrassed.

He looked straight ahead, and the silence stretched out. Then he smiled.

"Want to go a little farther?"

"Now?"

"It was just a thought. I don't know where it came from. I didn't mean . . ."

But she nodded eagerly. "I do. I really do. I was just a little taken aback."

He changed gear, and they sailed past the high-rises of Tensta on the left and a nature park on the right. Her father was out with a friend, Amir would be at the youth club for a few hours—there was a disco. For once, Gina had a couple of precious hours all to herself. The car sped on, along the highway. Suburbs rose up and then disap-

peared, gas stations and exits, and the sparkling feeling in her chest
stayed put.

"Why did you have therapy?" she asked.

"It was after the divorce. I had some things to straighten out."

"Have you done that now, then?"

"Don't know. It depends on who you ask. There are some things I
definitely haven't finished working on."

She waited, but when he didn't continue she simply said, "I met
with psychologists in the refugee house. I didn't like them." She still
had trouble with that profession, to be honest. She wasn't looking
forward to the psychiatric part of her course.

"I only went once, but she was okay. Not judgmental."

"That's good." If she ever met a nonjudgmental psychologist,
maybe she would change her mind.

They passed a sign for Sigtuna, a small town with its roots in medieval times. And suddenly Gina knew exactly where she wanted to
go. She had wanted to see it for the longest time. So when the brown
road sign appeared, she pointed to it. "Can we go there?"

"Wadenstierna? Sure."

"I love Swedish castles."

"You know, a distant relative of mine used to own it, hundreds of
years ago." He bit his lip. "I didn't mean to brag. Sorry if that came
out wrong."

He did that. Often. Thought about how the things he said to her
might sound wrong. He'd never cared in the past.

"I suppose it's not entirely your own fault that you're a white man
with upper-class privilege," she said lightly, wondering if she'd ever
said anything so flip before.

"But the castle is owned by the state now. Do you want to go in, or
just look from the outside?"

"The outside."

"Then I know the perfect spot."

They drove through small communities, past fields full of sheep
and horses, and increasingly smaller houses, country estates, and summer houses.

Gina studied the unfamiliar landscape. No one knew where she
was. It was a strange feeling. But she wasn't afraid; she felt safe. What

a difference it made when you felt comfortable with someone, not afraid of what he might say or do. She was so often prepared for shouts and violence. Ordinary people could shout that they didn't want the likes of her here, in Sweden, she should go back home. But Peter was so careful with her, cautious and respectful.

He turned off and they ended up on a bumpy forest road. The car bounced around, and every now and then something thudded against the chassis.

"Didn't it say this was a private road?" she asked.

"Yeah, strictly speaking it's not exactly legal to drive here. But just wait, you'll see. Look."

The forest had opened up, and they drove out onto a little hill. She looked out. On the other side of the water, the white castle came into view.

"Wow," she breathed. She had seen pictures of the fairy-tale-beautiful Wadenstierna Castle before, but not from this angle. It was majestic, enthroned on its promontory. Flags fluttered from its turrets. "It's so beautiful," she almost whispered. Of all the Swedish castles, this was her favorite. "Have you been inside?"

"I went to a wedding there once. They've got a nice collection of portraits. What is it you like about Swedish castles?" he asked curiously.

"The feeling. The history. The pictures of everyone who lived there."

"I'm sorry, but I don't know much about Somalian history."

She laughed. "Me neither. Dad is always moaning about that, but I'm just not interested."

"Maybe you will be when you're older. I do know what you mean, though. My mother has Russian heritage."

"Do you speak Russian?"

"If I have to. It's really rusty, though. Are there any famous Somalians? Anyone I should know about?"

"I think the most famous is a woman. Waris Dirie. She's a model. And an author. She wrote a book about her childhood in Somalia. Have you heard of it?"

"Don't think so. What's it about?"

"Her childhood. And genital mutilation. It's pretty widespread in Somalia. Nearly all women are mutilated."

Peter flashed her a quick look, and Gina fell silent. This wasn't a subject she was comfortable with. She had come to it by mistake, and it was much harder than she had expected. It awoke too many painful memories.

"Gina, I . . ."

"No, please. I don't want to talk about it anymore."

"Sorry."

She smoothed her skirt over her knees and tried to find her way back to how she had felt earlier. This had been one of the best evenings of her life. She wanted to keep that mood, not talk about terrible things she couldn't change. Things a person couldn't possibly understand unless they had gone through it themselves.

But the silence spread irreparably between them as they headed back to the car.

Peter's brow was furrowed, and he looked as though he was deeply focused on driving. His hands gripped the wheel. Gina sat still.

They were silent for the rest of the journey.

As though each of them had lots to work through, and needed to do it alone.

Chapter 33

"So, what's her name?" Romeo asked. He looked at Alexander through half-closed eyes. The music pounded around them. Far below, the Hudson River flowed by, and the roof terrace pulsed with party-seeking guests.

"Who?" Alexander asked, as his gaze swept across the bar.

"The woman you met who's so interesting you haven't flirted once since we got here. It's not like you."

Alexander shrugged. He looked at the drinks menu. The day before, he had drunk every cocktail he could think of with vodka in it. The day before that, he'd stuck to champagne. Today, he had decided to work his way through the drinks list in alphabetical order.

"What was wrong with the last one?" asked Romeo.

"She had straight hair."

"The actress yesterday?"

"Her laugh was all wrong."

Romeo scoffed.

"I'm just not in the mood," Alexander snapped, downing his Cosmopolitan. What started with D?

"Dry martini," he said to the barman. He cast a look at Romeo. "Want one?"

"I'm still on my Caipirinha. And I haven't recovered from the Appletini, either. Maybe you should slow down a little?"

"Why?"

"Because your liver needs a rest. Besides, I have to work tomorrow. I can't afford to drink myself to death."

He had to work too. He had mismanaged his affairs back here in the US, gotten behind while he was in Sweden. Fuck. Everything was falling.

"Her name is Isobel," he said, rubbing his brow, beating down the hollow feeling. "I met her in Stockholm. She laid into me, and that's that."

Romeo smiled. "So what does she do? This angry Isobel of yours."

"She's a doctor."

Romeo raised an eyebrow. "Really?"

"Yeah," said Alexander. The waiter came back with his cocktail and he drank it in systematic mouthfuls, trying not to taste it. He hated gin. But he had been thinking about Isobel constantly for a week, and alcohol was the only thing stopping his brain from running amok. He hadn't planned to mention her to Romeo. But when had something he'd planned gone like it was supposed to these past few weeks? Plus, it actually was a relief to talk about Isobel, to say her name aloud.

"She's beautiful. And funny. Smart. Dedicated. I've never met any-one like her."

Romeo cocked his head and studied Alexander.

"What?" Alexander asked. He was finally starting to feel the alco-hol. Maybe he ought to take it easy, not lose his judgment. But then again, fuck it. He downed the last of his drink and ordered a vodka tonic. Fuck the alphabet, too. He'd ruined things with Isobel and now he would drink until he didn't feel like an asshole. Awesome plan.

Romeo's gaze tracked a thin, dark-haired man. The man turned, caught sight of him, and raised his glass.

"Someone you know?" asked Alexander.

Romeo smiled into his glass. "Not yet. So that's why you've been so damn weird. You've gone and fallen hard. About time, man."

"That's what I like about our friendship, you're so empathetic."

"At first I thought you had cancer or something, you were acting so weird. I'm just relieved."

Romeo's analysis was absurd, of course, but still interesting on a theoretical level, Alexander supposed. Had he fallen for Isobel? He could see how it might sound that way. But he wasn't the type to fall for anybody. He sipped his drink. Although if that really was the case, he should've forgotten her by now, shouldn't he? They'd fought and then he'd gone halfway around the globe to find something else to think about. He should've forgotten her and moved on already. It had never been a problem before. He shouldn't be lying awake at night, still jet-lagged, going over everything they'd said. Shouldn't find himself smiling when he suddenly remembered something she'd done. Shouldn't be ashamed of how he'd behaved.

Shouldn't feel so . . . Hell. Shouldn't *feel*.

He emptied his glass.

"Another?"

"But with more vodka and less tonic," he instructed the barman.

He was going to end this madness. Now. He had always been able to switch off, it was just a matter of attitude and will. And distraction, of course.

So when two giggling women came over to him and asked if he really was Alexander De la Grip, and whether they could take a selfie with him, he smiled widely and invitingly.

"We're Swedes," they said.

"The best kind," he replied, pulling each of them onto a knee. They fell, laughing, toward him.

"Isn't that Romeo Rozzi?" one asked with wide eyes.

Romeo bowed slightly. "*Ciao*."

The women giggled, and Alexander wrapped his arms around them more tightly. "Don't worry about Romeo, he's gay. Hey, wasn't there someone you wanted to get to know in the bar?"

Romeo shook his head. "You going to manage, then?"

Alexander placed a hand on one of the women's thighs. He looked deep into her eyes.

"Go, I'll be fine."

The woman responded by pressing herself against his crotch. She was small and dainty, giggly and toned. Her friend was exactly the same. If he wanted to think about something other than serious doctors with gray eyes and a million freckles, this was the right way to go.

"So what do you think, a bottle of champagne?" he asked.

The women clapped and squealed.

Romeo left him with a look that seemed half amused, half concerned.

* * *

Alexander woke the next morning completely disoriented. His heart pounded. He had dreamed something. He took a deep breath. Home. He was home. With jet lag, a hangover, and nightmares, but no heart attacks. He looked around. He was alone, thank God. There was a vague memory of Romeo in the elevator with him, putting him in a taxi and sending him home.

He rubbed a hand over his eyes and waited for his pulse to slow before he climbed out of bed, staggered to the kitchen, and drank some water. With the glass in his hand, he studied the New York skyline from the kitchen window. Normally, he loved this apartment, loved being in New York, but the past few days had been a total waste. He hadn't done a thing. Hadn't been to the gym, hadn't done any work. What was the point of partying and drinking if it didn't even help? If he couldn't feel calm here, where the hell should he go? He stared out. There was no point going on like this.

He felt for his cell. Found the icon for the clock app and clicked on a world clock. Isobel had to be in Chad by now. He had saved the time for N'Djamena, the capital. He stared at the screen. It was morning there. He had been on Google Earth. Seen the barren landscape. Wondered what it was like there. The sun was shining; the temperature was probably well over one hundred.

He put down his cell. Picked it back up again.

Dialed a number, waited impatiently.

"Yes, this is Leila."

"Alexander here. De la Grip," he added. "I'd like to have Isobel's Skype name. Can you get it for me?"

Silence.

"Leila?"

"You know you can't order me around just because you gave us some money."

He snorted. "And *you* know that I most certainly can."

More silence.

"I like Isobel. She might seem strong and tough. I don't know what's going on between you, but she's a complicated person," Leila said.

"I know."

"Call after six tonight, her time. They have a curfew then, so she should be back at the base. I'll send you the username. And Alexander?"

"Yeah?"

"Think very carefully."

Yeah, well, it was probably too late for that.

"Bye," was all he said.

Her message arrived. He would take a shower. Drink some coffee. Think.

Chapter 34

Time flew when you were in the field, Isobel thought to herself as she realized, between patients, that she had already been in Chad five days.

"Breathe in." She spoke in French to her patient, a four-year-old boy with feverishly bright eyes and a high temperature. Medpax's pediatric hospital was in the middle of nowhere. Their patients mostly came from the villages dotted around it. Sometimes they had patients from any of the nomadic groups that lived in the desert. Families often walked for days to get there, and the children who came with them were almost always in a bad way. One of the biggest concerns was that people waited too long and arrived at the hospital too late. In the worst cases, the children died immediately upon arrival. When that happened, sometimes the doctors were blamed. The attitude toward medicine was almost medieval from a Western point of view, with all the superstition that accompanied it. Much of Medpax's long-term work was going to the villages and talking about the benefits of taking children to the doctor instead of using the shamans and their downright dangerous methods. *I hope I made a difference,* she thought, because the children who died here were mourned just as deeply as they would be back home. It was just that Chadian parents had to have strategies for outliving one or more of their children, because it happened so often. But a Chadian parent's grief was just as deep and painful as any Westerner's. *"Très bien,"* she said, and then moved on. She examined a six-month-old baby with breathing difficulties. Undernourished and with a lung infection. That was the most common diagnosis here.

"Did he have diarrhea?" she asked in French.

The mother, a girl who didn't look much older than sixteen, nodded.

"We'll give him a drip," Isobel said to the nurse, then gave the mother a reassuring smile. "You can sit with him. And you will get something to eat."

"*Merci, Docteur,*" the mother whispered.

Isobel moved on again. She had at least twenty more patients to see. She had met some of them the past fall, and their joy at seeing her again was mutual. A broken arm that had healed as it should, an undernourished child who had grown bigger and could now smile at her. But some of those she had met and treated last time were dead now. Car crashes, famine, and infections killed many in this country, one of the hardest places to live on earth. But the majority of today's patients were new, part of a never-ending stream. She wiped the sweat from her brow. There was no thermometer, but she would have been surprised if the temperature was much lower than 115.

After she dealt with the morning's new patients, malaria, lung inflammations, and wounds that wouldn't heal in the constant heat and humidity, she went by the doctors' office. It consisted of a table and a generator-powered refrigerator behind a curtain. She opened the refrigerator. Like everything else, PET bottles were in short supply, but she had bought some juice at the airport, kept the bottle, and now refilled it with filtered water regularly. She drank it in slow gulps.

The curtain flapped and Idris joined her.

"How's it going?" he asked.

"I saw to that painful abdomen. Put in a drip. How was the C-section?"

Strictly speaking, it was a pediatric hospital, but the woman had urgently needed the operation and there hadn't been time to send her to the bigger hospital in N'Djamena. The journey took three hours by car, but their patients didn't have cars. Or phones. Or radio equipment. Most of them had nothing.

"It went well." Idris checked the time. "But it's almost six. You have to get back."

That was the frustrating thing. Needing to leave the patients, not knowing how many would make it through the night. But breaking the curfew was madness, and not something she wanted to do without good reason. A dead doctor did no one any good.

"Are you working tonight?" she asked.

"Yes."

Idris worked harder than anyone Isobel had ever met. He was at the hospital every day and every other night. Month after month. The hospital also had some local staff members, and their level of knowledge was much higher than many people back in Sweden realized. Once, when Isobel asked Idris what his specialty was, he laconically replied, "Everything." Doctors in Chad needed to know basic medicine, be able to perform a C-section, operate on an appendix, and deal with tricky breech births immediately after they finished their education. The country had fewer doctors per inhabitant than any Western country; the doctors were responsible for far more patients. All of this created hugely knowledgeable doctors. But it also led to one of the most serious problems of developing countries: a terrible brain drain as trained doctors fled to nations with better working conditions.

"We're completely full. Let's hope nothing happens."

And by "nothing," he meant anything from a serious traffic accident to a conflict, to an outbreak of cholera. Or worse.

That was often too much to hope for.

"*Inshallah*," said Isobel.

Idris, who was about as much of a Christian as she was, nodded in agreement.

Her driver, Hugo, who helped out with everything from driving to cleaning in the hospital, gave her a ride back to Massakory, the village where she was staying. People at home always asked how far apart things were in Chad. How far is it to the capital? How close is the village to the hospital? But those weren't relevant questions down here. What looked like a ten-minute drive on the map could easily end up being a bumpy, shaky, eternal-feeling journey that took an hour. Maybe the road had washed away. Or a tree might've fallen, or a new roadblock had appeared. You never knew. But today, the trip took less than fifteen minutes, and it passed without incident.

"I'll pick you up in the morning," Hugo said, and he disappeared off into the Chadian evening to the sound of a muezzin. Isobel greeted the guard—everyone who could afford one had a guard in Chad—and went into the building. She was covered in sand. It came on the wind from the Sahara and mixed with sweat to produce a coating on the skin. She washed herself as thoroughly as possible, changed to a clean T-shirt, and went to the kitchen. She was given a bowl of food by the cook, a woman who looked around forty, but who Isobel knew was younger than she was, and supported her six children by cleaning and cooking for the few Westerners who came to Massakory.

"Merci," said Isobel. It was the same meal as ever: bean stew with onion and something that looked like tomatoes. People often thought that food in African countries automatically meant fresh mangoes and luxurious fruits, but here in Chad, there was practically nothing to eat.

After she ate, she took out her computer and headed for the corner of the house where, if she was lucky, she could connect to the Wi-Fi. The Skype icon told her she had an incoming message. She clicked on it and opened the window. Assumed it was Leila. She read the message.

Alex Grip would like to add you as a contact.
Accept. Decline.

She blinked. Hesitated. Was it really Alexander? What could he want?

She accepted with a click. Waited, her hands clasped over the keyboard.

When the call came in with the usual bubbling sound, it was a video call. She clicked the green icon and waited.

Alexander had been waiting for the Skype call for two hours. Chad was in the same time zone as Sweden, which meant that Isobel was six hours ahead of him. According to Leila, the curfew came into force at six her time, and so he had sat there, staring at the screen, since twelve New York time. He had briefly gotten up to make some coffee, and when he came back, she had accepted.

The screen flickered, and then she was there. It felt like he could breathe normally for the first time in hours. He hadn't been entirely sure she would want to talk to him, but now she filled the screen in front of him.

"Hi, Alexander."

She had on a white T-shirt and her hair was in a ponytail. Some-where behind her, the sun shone, and he could see plain concrete walls and faded posters bearing the UNICEF logo. She didn't smile, just gave him a cautious look.

"Hi there. How are you?" he asked.

"I've had a few long days," she replied lightheartedly, taking a sip from a bottle of beer. It suited her, drinking beer. "And you?"

"I'm well." It was true. Now that he had her in front of him, he felt better than he had in a long while. "What are you doing?"

"Not a lot. There's a curfew in the evenings, and at night it's too dangerous to go outside. Between sunset and sunrise, I have to be here on the base, so I drink beer and try to relax. Gather my thoughts."

"Is it safe?"

She raised an eyebrow. "Thanks for asking. It's fine right now. There was some fighting in a neighboring village, but nothing here."

"Where are you staying?"

"Medpax has a house at a compound here. I'm staying here alone, but there are some Red Cross people next door. We play cards some-times."

"How are things with the kids?"

"Today was a good day. No one died."

"I'm really sorry about the last time we met. Do you have time to talk for a minute?"

"Wait, let me put my earbuds in."

He watched her plug the simple white earbuds in, first into the computer and then her ears. It felt strangely intimate. The knowl-edge that his voice was now going straight into her ears, wouldn't be heard by anyone but her. She nodded when she was ready. He moved closer to the screen.

"I know what you think, but I didn't sleep with that girl."

"Okay," she said, but he saw the doubt on her face. He wished there was some way he could show her he was telling the truth. Two seconds after he and Qornelia left the restaurant, he had put her in a taxi and sent her away. Had known the whole time that she wasn't the one he wanted.

"I just wanted you to know that. And I'm sorry I . . . I don't know. That I acted like an ass."

That I feel something I've never felt before, and it's scaring the shit out of me.

She smiled slightly. "Thanks for letting me know. I'm glad you got in touch."

The picture started to jump.

"Alexander?"

"Hello?"

"The Internet is overloaded here, so it's going to go off. Do you hear me?"

The picture froze and jumped again. "You're disappearing. Take care, Isobel. I'll call back tomorrow, okay?"

He heard her reply: "Yes."

The call ended.

He closed the laptop. Stood up. Looked down at New York, sprawled out beneath him. He would go out for a run. And give Romeo a call. It was time to pull himself together.

Chapter 35

Hugo was outside, waiting for her the next morning. He flicked his cigarette butt across the street, and Isobel watched it bounce on the red sand. The village was made up of simple two-story buildings constructed of concrete, and a lot of smaller mud houses. Thin-looking animals and hardworking people lived peacefully alongside one of the world's largest populations of insects. In the capital, N'Djamena, where practically all foreigners lived, there was a university, luxury hotels, and a business center, but here in Massakory it was like traveling hundreds of years back in time. There were barely any shops to speak of and practically no running water. Local health care consisted of a medicine man who treated his patients with—ineffective at best, and deadly at worst—household remedies.

"*Bonjour, Docteur,*" Hugo said, opening the door for her.

She climbed into the car, and Hugo steered the rattling jeep out of Massakory. They were in luck today, too. The road hadn't been washed away by rain, and they didn't pass a single roadblock.

Isobel peered out of the wound-down windows. The car lurched, and she steadied herself with a hand on the roof.

"One of the oxygen machines just died," Idris greeted her when she arrived at the hospital.

"*Merde.*"

It had only been a matter of time, but they needed those oxygen machines.

"I'll prioritize it when I talk to Leila," she promised, but wondered whether it would make much difference. How much did an oxygen machine cost? And if Medpax could somehow afford it, how would they even get it down here?

"Rounds?" she asked.

Idris picked up his notepad, and together they got ready to do their morning rounds.

"*Docteur!*"

Isobel turned toward the voice, her face breaking into a smile as she crouched down. She held out her arms. "Marius!"

She had looked for him every day, asked the staff and Idris about him. Finally. She embraced him, held him tight, noticing how thin he felt, his slight boy's body, all bones and no subcutaneous fat. She blinked away the tears that burned at her eyes, allowed herself to be filled with relief and thanks.

I was afraid you had died.

She hugged the boy longer than she should, tried to transfer some of her energy.

She held him at arm's length, her eyes moving over him, and noted the healthy whites of his eyes and his clear skin. He was undernourished and had that same haunted expression she'd almost only ever seen on orphaned and homeless children, but otherwise he looked healthy.

"Are you well?" she asked, knowing that Idris was impatient to get started. There were over one hundred patients admitted, and he needed her. To an outsider, it might seem heartless to have no time for a hug, but she knew better. Idris always weighed things up, and one hundred sick kids were simply weightier than one lonely boy.

Marius held up a hand and showed her a tiny scrape.

She looked at it. "Can you wait for me? Stay here and I'll put a Band-Aid on that. Plus, I have a gift for you." It was against all rules, of course, against all principles. Growing close to the local population, giving gifts. Everyone knew it led to complications. "Wait for me," she said, and stroked his cheek, knowing that she was the only one Marius had. She got up and hurried away after Idris.

Their rounds took several hours, and it was only long after lunch that Isobel had time to sneak back to the office again. Marius was underneath a table, playing with some stones. He stood when she came in and flashed her a cautious look, as though he needed to make sure she wasn't a threat, before his shoulders relaxed and he gave her a lopsided smile. She gave him yet another hug.

"Did you eat?" she asked, studying his too-short trousers and threadbare tank. Marius nodded, but she knew he probably did it only to reassure her. His trust in other people was virtually nonexistent. That was just how things were when you lived without any kind of security whatsoever. She had met many street kids in her time, seen small children starve to death, four- and five-year-olds forced to make it on their own in the world, seen undernourished nine- and ten-year-olds sell their feeble bodies for food and drugs. It was a reality that, as a field-worker, you just had to accept if you wanted to make it through your work. But to her, Marius was different. She didn't know why she was so attached to him. It was just something that happened with some people.

She took out the plastic bag she kept in a locked cupboard in the office. Each morning she had brought it with her, and every night it had followed her back to the compound; she'd guarded the bag as though it were full of gold. She handed Marius the cheese puffs. It was such an impractical gift—they took up room in her luggage and weren't nutritious at all—but Marius's happiness was worth it. She gave him a small chocolate bar, too. At least that contained some fat and a few minerals, she thought, hoping he would manage to keep hold of it. She had brought ten, and planned to hand them out over the course of her stay.

"Where do you live now?" she asked as she quickly cleaned his scrape and put a Band-Aid on it.

He just shrugged in reply. He started to eat the cheese puffs one by one, chewing slowly with his eyes blissfully closed. *I have to go back to the ward soon,* she thought, as she swallowed the lump in her throat. How could life be so unfair? She really didn't understand.

"Marius?"

"Oui?" He looked at her with those intelligent eyes of his, always like a knife straight through the heart. He was so kind and considerate, one of those boys who would rather play and daydream than kick and fight. A child who, if there was any justice in the world,

should have the chance to develop and go as far as he wanted. Instead, he lived on the street, and she could see the fear and forlornness deep in his eyes, and it broke her heart every time.

"I'll be here at the hospital for a while—don't go disappearing, okay?"

"*Oui,*" he repeated, and she hoped he would come back to the hospital, that she would be able to feed and keep an eye on him for the few weeks she was here.

A stressed voice called out for her. "*Docteur?*"

She knew she needed to rush off, that this was a luxury she couldn't afford. The last thing she heard was the rustle of the bag of cheese puffs and Marius's quiet munching.

After a long afternoon in the hospital, a shaky car journey back to the village lay ahead of her, followed by the usual stew.

Isobel washed quickly. The inhabitants of Massakory were almost exclusively Muslim, and they were so clean that she always felt a little like a filthy Westerner, so she made sure to scrub her hands, feet, and face as often as she could. She took out a clean T-shirt, ran a brush through her hair, and brushed her teeth before sitting down at the laptop again.

Her bedroom was little more than a hard bed, a footstool, and a mosquito net, so she preferred to sit in the lounge. The cook was outside the house, smoking. Smoke flowed in through the mosquito net. She could hear voices outside, the occasional shout, but otherwise silence.

When Alexander called, she answered immediately.

"Hi," she said.

He looked shamelessly fresh, as though he'd just showered. She could see expensive furniture and huge windows behind him, bright and clean and Western.

"How are you?" he asked. She was drawn into his smile.

"Good," she replied honestly. It had been an intense day, both physically and emotionally, but they always were.

"No one died today either. It's a huge relief."

She had been there almost a week now. In three more, she would be replaced by a Belgian field doctor. If all her days were like this, it would be one of the best trips she'd ever made.

"But we lost one of our oxygen machines," she added.

"Are they important?"

"Yeah, they're absolutely vital. You can treat so many problems with oxygen; the equipment is easy to use, doesn't require any training. They're our best friends. Children will die if we can't replace it."

"Jesus."

"I know. It's frustrating."

"Is there anything I can do?"

"You don't have a spare oxygen machine lying around?"

"I'll check, but I don't think so."

She laughed, leaned in toward the screen, and rested her chin in her hand. She could see shining stainless steel worktops and a bowl of brilliant green apples. He was in the kitchen.

"Tell me what you ate today."

"You want to talk about food?" he asked, sounding incredulous.

She nodded. "I can honestly say that about ninety percent of my free time here is spent fantasizing about food."

"Pancakes with strawberries and maple syrup."

"American pancakes? God, that sounds good. More."

"I had pizza yesterday. A slice from my favorite place, a little hole in the wall. I sat in the park with my friend Romeo and ate it. Big, long strings of mozzarella."

Isobel groaned. "Know what I miss most?"

"I'd like it to be me, but I guess it's something edible. Tell me."

"Coffee. Hot, black, freshly brewed coffee. With white bread. There's no bread down here."

Alexander laughed. His eyes glittered, and she knew he was thinking about the time he'd made food for her. When they'd laughed in his kitchen in Stockholm. When they'd made love.

"What did you do yesterday?" she asked, and studied his face. "Did you go out?" She had no right to ask, but she did it anyway.

He shook his head. "No. I've got a lot of work to catch up on. I've actually decided to take a break from the partying."

"You have? Why?"

She twisted a lock of hair around her finger, told herself that the tingling feeling that pulsed through her body was tiredness, stress, or something like that, not a glimmer of hope, a feeling that things hadn't ended but started over. He had sounded honest yesterday, and she had decided to believe he was telling the truth, that he hadn't slept with the bimbo.

"Because I think it's time."

Alexander watched Isobel smile and knew that he'd passed a fork in the road when he'd decided to dramatically reduce his drinking. The thought had come to him as he jogged in Central Park that morning. Just like that. And he had made up his mind. For his own good. He had been living in some kind of limbo since last summer. He hadn't thought about it before, but once he did, it was clear.

Last summer when he learned Natalia wasn't his father's child, he had gotten definitive evidence that his mother had been unfaithful. Long before, he had suspected. That was why he'd hated infidelity his whole life. It was one thing to sleep with married women, but something completely different to be the one who was unfaithful, and he had never cheated on anyone. Still, he was petrified of being like Ebba, with her constant need for affirmation; terrified of having inherited the worst traits of his beautiful, superficial mother. After it came out that Nat was the result of her infidelity, the dramatic revelations had kept on coming, and he had started to lose the footing he thought he had created for himself.

That was the superficial reason he would be ready to give to the few people he cared about. Natalia. Romeo. Maybe Åsa. Maybe Isobel, if she ever wondered why he'd acted the way he had, with women and alcohol. But then there was the other thing. His childhood. He had never really believed in being able to repress things. But he had done and experienced things he had buried so deeply, he'd thought they were gone. Now something had happened. The fact was, he was an adult. He could *choose* to move on. He wanted to, for his own good, and when he saw Isobel's cautious smile at his words, saw that he hadn't lost her trust, it felt even more worthwhile. It felt fantastic.

"I have to go," she said from her side of the screen.

The picture had started to lag again.

"I'll call tomorrow," he said, and knew that he'd already started counting down the hours until they would talk again.

Once he hung up, he picked up an apple and grabbed his sunglasses from the kitchen counter. He shoved his credit card into a pocket, took the elevator down, said hello to the doorman, and pulled out his cell. He called Romeo.

"What are you doing?"

"Fighting with one of my chefs. Fucking divas."

"*You're* a diva. Want to go shopping?"

"What're you buying?"

Alexander thought about the gifts he'd bought for women over the years. Flowers, of course. Necklaces and jewels. Clothes, holidays. He had probably used his credit card for almost anything there was. But there was one thing he had never bought for a woman before.

"I'm going to buy an oxygen machine."

"It's Sunday. Aren't the oxygen machine shops closed?"

"That's why I have the big credit card with me. You coming?"

"You sound different."

"Yeah. Well, I *am* different."

Chapter 36

The next day, the shit hit the fan.

"The twins died last night," Idris said when Isobel arrived at the hospital. He was on the stairs, smoking, looking tired.

"*Merde.*" They had delivered them the day before, by C-section, and they had been horribly small. "How's the mother?" she asked.

"Her family came to get her." He let out smoke, stared into the distance. "Do you feel it?" he asked after a while.

Isobel nodded. It was there, an unease, palpable in the air. A new silence, a low pressure, an absence of sound. A foreboding that something was about to happen.

"Some of the staff have disappeared," he said, taking another drag.

That was often how it started. The locals were the first to know. A rumor, spreading quickly during morning prayers. Men, secretly arming themselves. Women, seeking shelter for themselves and their children.

She followed Idris into the hospital, wondering where Marius could be. It was warmer than before, and she slapped her neck. Was it her imagination, or were the insects biting even harder today?

"We have a lot of patients," Idris said as he washed his hands. He clutched his notepad. "I need to go back to ICU. Can you look into this?"

He gave her a handwritten note.

"What is it?"

"They came in this morning. Boy. Two years old. Trouble breathing. They've walked for days."

"So far? Where from?"

"The desert. His blood count isn't good." Idris shook his head. "They should've brought him much earlier."

"I'll take it."

Idris disappeared, and Isobel left to find the family. She quickly greeted the father, Muhammed, a tall, serious man with a tattoo of a bird's footprint on the entire left side of his face. The mother, Halima, who didn't look a day older than fifteen, sat with the boy in her arms.

"What's his name?" Isobel asked softly as she glanced at her patient.

"Ahmed," Halima whispered. She was dressed in a piece of colorful fabric, dusty with sand. She had a tattoo similar to her husband's on her cheek.

As Isobel examined the boy, he was silent. That was never a good sign. A child who cried, protested, or screamed was a child who still wanted to live. When Isobel tried to give him an injection, he was so dehydrated she couldn't get the needle in.

"Medicine," the father snapped. "My son needs medicine."

Yes, Ahmed needed medicine. And nourishment. If only they had been able to get him here earlier.

She filled a pipette with a nutrient solution and gave the parents what she hoped was a reassuring and confident smile.

"Give him this. A drop at a time until it's finished," she told them, hoping it would be enough.

"Where are you going?" the father asked, blocking her way. "You're the doctor—you have to stay. Help my son."

"I will come back. Give him the drops. I need to see my other patients. I'll be back as soon as I can, I promise."

Muhammed stared at her, but then moved out of the way. Isobel smiled encouragingly at Halima, who had already started to give Ahmed the solution. She moved on to her next patient. And then the next. She met with mothers and grandmothers, fathers and siblings, and of course with sick children. Listened to their hearts and lungs. Prescribed medicine, injections, and oxygen. Gave instructions to nurses and tried to have a smile for every tiny child she met, an encouraging word for every parent. Coming to a hospital run by Westerners took a great deal of courage, and she acknowledged that fact.

Being a young mother, daring to seek Western medicine for your child instead of going to the local medicine man was an act of bravery.

"Hello, Fatime," she said to a young mother in her twenties. Fatime had clever eyes, looked tired but resolute, and had her own mother in tow. Fatime had a two-year-old in her lap.

"My daughter, Zara," she said.

Isobel examined the petite Zara. She was two years old but weighed less than a one year old. Her complexion was pale and she was coughing, but she gave Isobel an angry stare when Isobel measured her upper arm. Isobel smiled. An angry child meant there still was hope.

"Your daughter is strong," she said.

Fatime nodded and smiled faintly. "Very," she agreed.

"How many children do you have?"

"Four."

Isobel didn't ask, knowing that if Fatime had four living children she'd probably buried as many. She listened to Zara's lungs. Prescribed medicine for her. "She has a fever, and she is underweight. We need to keep her here, for observation."

Fatime nodded in agreement, and relief rushed through Isobel. Sometimes it was difficult to get them to stay. But Fatime seemed intelligent and strong-willed. Maybe this little girl would survive.

"I will come back. Please, eat something. You have to be strong. For your daughter."

Fatime nodded regally. "Thank you, Doctor, I will." Their eyes met in one of those wordless connections. Two women, born in different parts of the world but with the same determination to keep this little girl alive, to make a change.

Isobel left the family and continued on with her work as the scorching Chadian sun climbed the sky.

When Isobel came back to baby Ahmed and his family, the little boy did actually seem slightly more lively. This time she managed to get the needle into a vein, and she set up a drip. Maybe little Ahmed would make it after all. She stroked his head, nodded to his parents, trying to instill some hope, and then left again. This was a frustrating aspect of her work, that she never had time to stay, that the overwhelming stream of patients forced her to be hard, made her seem uncaring, when in reality it was all about trying to be there for as many patients as possible. She worked without break all day; the hospital was completely full, and there were two small patients in almost every bed.

Next time she came back to Ahmed and the family, it was already afternoon. She had seen over a hundred patients, hadn't had time to eat, barely had time to drink, and was covered with dust and sand. Ahmed was wrapped up in a foil blanket.

"How is he?" she asked the nurse, who slowly shook her head.

His breathing was hoarse, and she prescribed oxygen for him, profoundly thankful that the last of their machines still worked properly. She checked the small boy's pulse and temperature. Listened to his faintly beating heart. Shone a light in his eyes, finding no reaction. There was nothing more she could do, not here in Chad anyway. Had she been at home, she knew she could have saved this child. But now, despite the drip, despite the blanket, even though she'd done all she could, the baby had started to disappear. Slowly and silently he was slipping away, dying before their eyes. His tiny head fell to his chest, which was no longer moving. She listened with her stethoscope, though she already knew it was over.

She laid a hand on his little body, felt the warmth slowly vanishing, before she braced herself and turned around to face the parents. She looked first Muhammed and then Halima in the eye, and shook her head.

Halima put a hand to her mouth and started to sob silently.

Isobel felt the tears well up in her own eyes. It was so horribly unfair.

"He was doing better before we came," said Muhammed. His voice was taught, his face drawn. They were a proud people, Chadians, but this father was on the verge of crying.

"He was very ill," Isobel said gently, wishing she had some way of easing the brutal blow of losing a child.

Muhammed took a step toward her. It was a sudden movement, but she wasn't scared. Not yet anyway.

"He died when we came here," he said through clenched teeth. Anger flashed in his eyes.

"Your son was very sick," she said.

He took another step toward her and suddenly there was a knife in his hand. Isobel froze. Weapons were forbidden in the hospital, but it must have been hidden in his clothes. He held it up to Isobel's face.

"I'm sorry," she said, trying not to flinch, to sound calm. Could anyone hear them?

"You killed him. With your medicine."

She started to move toward the curtain, hoped someone would get there before the situation got even more out of hand.

"Please, put down the knife. I did everything I could. He got the right medicine, but he was weak. His heart couldn't cope."

She had been in threatening situations before, but you never got used to having a knife waved in your face.

Muhammed's eyes narrowed, and she wondered whether she would have time to push him away before he managed to stab her. Goddamn it, he was too close. *Merde, merde, merde.* She didn't dare look at Halima. How could they have missed the knife? Everyone carried knives here, but the hospital had guards—it was their job to guarantee safety.

"Docteur!"

Marius. "No, Marius. Go," she said.

Muhammed turned his head toward Marius. Waved the knife, said something in Arabic. Isobel didn't dare to move, afraid now for Marius more than anything. "Don't hurt him," she pleaded.

Suddenly, the curtain moved back and Idris came into the room.

"Enough," he said calmly. He moved his considerable frame between Isobel and Muhammed. "She's a good doctor. She did all she could. Your son was ill. He is with Allah now."

Muhammed gave her a look so full of hatred she actually shuddered, but he slowly lowered the knife. She nodded to Marius and he turned on his heel, disappearing again. Thank God he was safe.

Idris held out his arms as though to protect her. "Go on, Isobel, I have this."

"Are you sure?"

"Go."

Isobel backed out of the room and walked on shaky legs to the office, where she slumped into a chair. She took out her water bottle, drank, and closed her eyes. The sun was setting, she realized, and at that very moment she heard Hugo's voice.

"*Docteur?* We must leave. The streets are not safe tonight." He sounded stressed, and his eyes darted.

"Is it that late already?" She hadn't even had time to eat today.

He gave her an urgent look. "Come."

She stood. Caught sight of a shadow from the corner of her eye. It was Marius; he stared at her with wide, frightened eyes. Jesus, he'd just been threatened with a knife. He must be scared. Where would he go tonight?

"*Docteur,*" the driver repeated.

She hesitated.

Idris came into the room. "They left. Go home now, sleep," he said calmly.

Isobel glanced around for Marius, but he had vanished into thin air and was nowhere to be seen. She gave up. With a heavy heart, she climbed into the car.

When she got back to the house, she took out her cell and headed for the corner where the Wi-Fi was strongest. Miraculously she had a signal. A satellite must have just passed over. She called Leila.

"Did you hear anything?"

"No, what's going on?"

"I don't know. But it feels unstable. Could you check with the State Department? And with the security company?"

Leila promised to get back to her, and Isobel hung up, completely drained. When you went on trips for MSF, there was a huge safety apparatus behind you, but Medpax was small and she had to trust her own experience and whatever Leila could do from home. Unease crept through her.

The cook came over and placed a bowl of stew in front of her. "*Merci,*" said Isobel.

She switched on her laptop. Opened Skype.

Alexander must have been waiting for her to appear, because he called immediately.

"And how are things in Chad?" he asked with a wide grin.

Isobel blinked rapidly, fighting the tears that were welling up. She had hoped to put her feelings to one side, not give in to them until she went to bed and could cry in solitude. But now they just bubbled up, like a physical reaction. It wasn't something she could control, and from one second to the next, something within her just snapped. She couldn't utter a single word as her tears fell uncontrollably.

"Isobel," he whispered softly from the other side of the world. "What's happened? Are you okay?"

She wiped her eyes, but the tears continued to roll down her cheeks and she couldn't do anything about it.

He stayed silent as she cried. She grieved for the lives she hadn't saved, cried for the little boy who'd died, those lives she wasn't able to change. The abandoned and constantly frightened Marius. Her fear with the knife pointed at her. The poverty that made people do desperate things.

"Life is just so hideously unfair," she sobbed.

"Yes."

She dried her tears, tried to compose herself.

"Sorry," she sniffed.

He held out a hand. It looked as though he was stroking the screen, as though he was trying to touch her. She placed her hand close to his.

"Thanks," she said. "Thanks for calling." He had no idea how much it meant that he just let her cry, that he didn't try to soothe. That he just was there, steady, calm.

"Do you want to talk about it?" he asked.

She shook her head. "Not today. It's too fresh."

"If you knew what a hero I think you are."

"No, don't say that word. I hate it." She was no hero, she was just an inadequate doctor.

"Okay," said Alexander.

"I'm so tired."

"Go to bed. I'll call tomorrow at the same time."

She sniffed again. "Thanks."

Isobel had trouble sleeping. She lay awake, listening through her mosquito net, imagining she heard things, whispers in the night, drums in the distance.

When she came down in the morning, it was dead silent, no sign of the cook. Neither Skype nor her cell would work, so she sat down and sent Leila an e-mail instead.

How the hell had people managed before the Internet, she asked herself as she waited for an answer. It came almost at once.

Preparedness has increased. The situation is seen as unstable. You should start to think about heading home.

Isobel read those short few lines. When had the situation in Chad ever been anything but unstable? She didn't want to leave. It might even be over by tomorrow.

I want to stay.

She hit SEND, closed the computer, and went out to see if Hugo had arrived. When he approached, his face looked haggard and, as she climbed into the front seat next to him, she could sense the stress in the vehicle.

"Thanks for coming," she said.

"It's dangerous now," he clipped out.

They had traveled this road every day for over a week and never been stopped.

Today, the road was blocked. A cart stopped them from passing. Two men, armed with automatic weapons, waited alongside it.

Hugo swore and pulled over.

Isobel studied the roadblock, feeling her pulse skyrocket.

Dangerous, so terrifyingly dangerous.

She didn't dare look at Hugo as the two armed men, no more than teenagers, came toward them. One stopped in front of the car and the other came over to the window. He stuck his head in and looked around.

Isobel averted her eyes, made herself as invisible and unthreatening as she could, let Hugo do the talking.

"Where are you going?"

"The hospital."

"Who is she?"

"Doctor."

She held her breath. Counted the seconds in her head, conscious of the smell of fear and adrenaline.

"You can go," the man eventually said, and motioned for his friend to move the cart. They drove slowly past, and Isobel could barely breathe.

But they left without incident, and when Hugo stepped on the gas, the pedal to the floor, she leaned back in her seat and breathed out.

When she looked at Hugo, she saw that his knuckles were white.

"Bonjour, Docteur."

One of the hospital's anesthetic nurses came out to meet Isobel when the car stopped and she climbed out.

Hugo rushed off so quickly, she didn't even have time to say good-bye.

"We didn't think you would come today. Have you heard about the fighting in the neighboring village? People have been killed. We've already received casualties."

"Here?"

"They don't care that we're a pediatric hospital. But Doctor Idris will be pleased you are here."

Fighting.

Isobel knew what that meant, had seen it far too many times. Raped women. Wounded men. Terrible wounds from machetes and guns. Injured children.

"We'll have to put them in the hallways," said Isobel. "Do we have blankets?"

Side by side with those of the staff who hadn't fled, she dressed wounds, put splints on legs, and stitched up injuries. She had no time to think of anything but her next patient, no time to be afraid. She just worked, methodically, washing blood, sewing, trying to be a beacon of strength in the stormy sea of blood, trauma, and chaos.

When the sun began to set and Hugo failed to appear with the car, it was an easy decision to stay in the hospital overnight, although it was against all safety regulations. Isobel and the rest of the staff took turns sleeping a few hours every now and then. The stream of injured people petered out toward dawn, but the hospital was so full that there was barely room to move between the patients. The stench from bad wounds and the screams from the patients were a blanket of anguish over the hospital.

"We need to start to discharge the people who can leave on their

own," Isobel said, forcing her voice to be steady, refusing to give in to
fear and worry.

Idris nodded. His face was gray. He was sneezing.

"Are you ill?" she asked. He looked awful.

But then so did she probably.

"I'll start to discharge people. Do you think we can hope the
worst is over?"

"Hope is free."

"*Docteur* Isobel?"

She turned toward the voice; it came from one of the local staff.
"*Oui?*"

"You have a message in the office."

Isobel headed over.

Knew what she was about to hear before she even sat down. She
picked up the satellite phone.

"Hi, Leila, how are things?"

"You're coming home tonight. I've managed to talk my way into
getting you an empty seat on one of the Red Cross planes."

Shit, I don't want to go.

"That's an order," Leila said, as though she had read Isobel's
thoughts. "Not negotiable in any goddamn way. You're coming home.
Don't even think about arguing with me."

Idris had come into the office, and he gave her a questioning
look. It wasn't so strange. Leila had shouted so loudly across the line
that Isobel's ears rang. She placed a hand over the mouthpiece.

"She wants to send me home."

"I thought so. She's right. You're White, Western. And a woman.
It's too dangerous. Go. We'll cope."

"But the patients?"

Just give me a sign, any sign, and I'll stay.

"*Non,* Isobel," he said firmly. "It's time."

He stood up and held out his hand. She did the same and gave it
a firm shake. Long.

"*Au revoir.*"

See you again.

She hoped he was right.

Today Hugo was waiting outside the hospital as though nothing
had happened. She didn't dare ask why he hadn't come the day be-

fore. Didn't ask how he knew she would be leaving today. She just sat in the car and allowed herself to be driven back to the village. The feeling of defeat was like a bad taste in her mouth.

There were no roadblocks this time.

The road was empty, as though there had never been any teenagers with automatic weapons and empty eyes, and they arrived in Massakory without incident.

Isobel went into the building, gathered her bags, left as much money as she could for the cook, if she were to come back, and then stopped. She thought of Marius. If things were different . . . But it made no difference how unfair life was, how much it hurt. There was nothing she could do for him now. He was one more in an agonizing line of children she'd had no choice but to abandon. She left the chocolate bars behind, went out, and got back into the car. Ten minutes later, she and Hugo were on their way to N'Djamena and the airport.

Alexander couldn't sleep. Isobel hadn't answered on Skype the day before. Leila had talked about unrest. It was as though his body wanted to turn itself inside out with worry. He had spent hours Googling field doctors and conflict, but he'd had to force himself to stop.

Now he just stared out of the window.

Waited.

The phone rang. It was Leila.

"Yes?"

"I'm bringing her home. The rebels tried to take the neighboring village."

"Where is she now?"

His mouth was so dry he had trouble talking.

"Wait," Leila said, and disappeared.

He waited. Focused on breathing. On not freaking out. He pressed the phone to his ear, tried to force Leila to hurry, to tell him what was going on.

The rebels tried to take the village.

What the hell did that mean? Was there a war going on? It was surreal.

"Hello?" Leila returned.

"What's going on?"

"Isobel is on her way back. I just got confirmation. She's traveling with the Red Cross from N'Djamena; they had a plane to Paris, and she got on at the last minute. There was a bit of chaos, but it seems to have calmed down now. I talked to Doctor Idris Toko. The hospital is secure. It was some kind of power battle between two clans. It's over now."

"But Isobel is still coming home?"

"Yes. Definitely. She's spending the night in Paris and gets to Arlanda Airport the day after tomorrow."

Alexander hung up.

And then he started to pack.

Chapter 37

"She wanted to show how she'd been cured of her fear of needles, but as soon as the teacher took it out, she fainted," Gina said with a laugh.

"Needles *are* horrible," Peter replied, though he was laughing too.

He switched on the kettle, then took out two tall glasses and added the tea bags. Red chai tea for Gina, ordinary black tea for himself. Once the kettle was hot, he poured in the water, leaving room for milk in her glass, and added three sugar lumps for her.

"You'll get cavities," he said as he dropped the last sugar cube into the tea and watched it dissolve.

"Nah, I won't. I've got strong teeth, plus I always floss. Could you pass me a plate for these?"

She held up a tub of her father's small dumplings.

The thought of them made Peter's mouth water.

He handed her a plate, found some side plates and napkins, and filled two glasses with water.

Gina fetched spoons and milk, then laid out the dumplings.

"Looks so festive," she said. Her eyes caught the pink roses he had given her, and she blushed slightly.

"Well, we have something to celebrate," he said, his voice happy and hearty, not wanting to embarrass her. He handed her the glass of tea. "Here's to passing your exams."

She sipped her chai tea and set the glass down next to her plate.

Peter put the sandwiches he'd bought onto a chopping board and cut them in two. Gina didn't like Swedish cheese, so he'd brought one with French brie cheese and one with Swedish skagenröra—

shrimp, mayo, and dill, which she claimed tasted like fish but devoured every time.

He stole furtive glances at her, loved to watch her quick, almost hasty movements as she grabbed some cutlery and closed cupboard doors with a bang, always waiting for her to burst into laughter.

She laughed more often these days.

He did too.

They sat down at the table. He had to stop himself from running over to pull the chair out for her, but he simply sat down and clasped his glass of tea. In truth, tea wasn't his favorite, but Gina drank it, and at some point these past few weeks Peter had made the decision to broaden his horizons and try new things. So now he drank bitter hot tea.

Gina poured even more sugar into her glass, stirred it quickly with a spoon, and reached for the skagenröra sandwich. She ate it by breaking the bread into smaller pieces, scooping the filling with a spoon, smearing it onto the bread, and putting the lot in her mouth. She ate the accompanying vegetables on their own. Slices of gherkin, sprigs of dill, and pieces of tomato.

Peter smiled.

"What?" she asked. Daintily she wiped her mouth.

"Nothing," he said. He bit into a dumpling. Crumbs fell to the table. He would never have thought that happiness could come in the form of crisp, golden flakes of pastry.

"Aha, what's going on here, then?"

Peter looked up toward the voice.

It was almost half past eight in the evening, and he and Gina were the only ones left in the office.

The man who had appeared, Dag Billing, was one of Peter's least favorite coworkers. Peter wiped his mouth. He saw Gina lower her gaze, put down her sandwich, and sit utterly still, as though she had been caught doing something she wasn't allowed.

Dag had his arms crossed. His eyes lingered on Gina before he gave Peter a knowing grin.

"Nothing is *going on*. We're just having a break," Peter said, though he suddenly felt annoyed at himself. When had he become someone who needed to excuse himself for what he did?

"A break? Is that what it's called these days?"

"What do you want?"

"I forgot my cell phone. But now I've got a craving for some chocolate. Dark chocolate, if you know what I mean."

Peter leaped to his feet. "That was really fucking inappropriate."

"*I'm* inappropriate? I'm not the one in here, drooling over the cleaner."

Dag's eyes moved across Gina's body, up and down, stopped at her breasts.

"Though I get it. There's just something about black women."

Gina abruptly got to her feet.

"Gina, wait," said Peter.

"I have to go," she said.

"No, he's the one who should go."

But Gina bowed her head and tried to leave. Dag reached out a hand and laid it on her arm, stopping her. "Maybe you can go clean my desk. I'll come and inspect it in a minute?"

"Let go of her," Peter said as Gina pulled herself loose.

"Take it easy," said Dag. "Can't people in this country take a joke anymore? Oh, forgive me, little cleaner, did I offend you? That's how people always feel these days, isn't it? Offended."

"Stop it," Peter hissed. His eyes sought out Gina's, but she just rubbed her arm and avoided looking at either of them.

Dag looked at Peter, and Peter could see nothing but contempt in his eyes, knew that was how he was seen at work, as someone who could just be ignored.

Dag shook his head.

"You can't tell me what to do," he said.

"Peter, it's okay," said Gina.

But it wasn't okay, not for him. How often did she have to put up with stuff like this? Every week? Every day?

"You don't talk to her like that. Never again. I don't give a damn what you think of me. But if you so much as look at her again, I'll . . ."

"You'll what, you fucking loser? What are you going to do?"

Dag had taken a step closer and entered Peter's personal space. This was the moment typically Peter would have backed down, given up. But instead he took a step forward and saw a flash of uncertainty in the other man's eyes.

"Get out of here. Don't take your coffee, don't take your fucking cell. Don't say another word. Just leave."

Dag didn't move. Peter stepped even closer, his forehead virtually touching the other man's. He knew he couldn't back down now, knew that he'd rather let himself be carried out. Dag must have seen his determination, because he hesitated and then moved back, casting down his eyes.

And then he left.

The door swung shut.

Gina was motionless. She bit her lip. But she didn't look as scared as she had, and that was all that mattered.

Peter stood in the middle of the kitchen floor, taking unsteady breaths, still unsure of what had just happened. He'd never won a man-on-man fight before, never dared stand up to anyone on his own. He had only ever dared fight in groups, against someone weaker than him. It had always been his biggest source of shame, something he knew about himself but had never thought he could change. He'd always been told he was weak. Always *been* weak. Scared. Repressed.

But now.

He sat down. Could feel himself shaking. But not necessarily in a bad way.

Gina sat down opposite him. Took her napkin and laid it in her lap.

Peter took one more shaky breath. He had felt ice cool when he was arguing with Dag, but now he felt some kind of reaction coming. He placed his hands on the table.

Gina looked at him. Long lashes, black eyes.

"Thanks," she said.

"I'm sorry I didn't interrupt him earlier."

She shrugged one shoulder.

"Dag's a jerk. He's hit on me before."

"Promise you'll tell me if he ever does it again."

She tore off a piece of bread, cut the brie, put the cheese on the bread, and then popped both into her mouth. She chewed, her eyes fixed on him.

"I promise," she said.

Chapter 38

After a night sleeping like a log in a cheap hotel in Paris, Isobel headed out to Charles de Gaulle Airport. She boarded the plane, slumped into her window seat, and watched as they taxied out. Once they were up in the air, she closed her eyes and tried to empty her mind. It would be good to get home after all. Before she'd checked out that morning, Leila had told her that things had calmed down at the pediatric hospital. The fighting had ended as quickly as it started, and things were back to normal. The patients were out of danger, and both the staff and the local population had started to return.

For a while Isobel had thought about asking to go back; she didn't like how abruptly she'd left. But she didn't even have time to open her mouth before Leila said:

"Don't even think about it. You're coming home."

The plane landed at Arlanda Airport at exactly four-thirty in the afternoon, and she managed to pick up her bags, pass though security, and go out into the arrivals hall in under twenty minutes. It was full of people waiting: relatives, families, and the occasional chauffeur watching for passengers from Paris, London, New York, and Pakistan. Isobel got stuck behind a family with a huge number of bags and suitcases. She squeezed past them and was wondering whether to take the Arlanda Express train or forget about the environment and the cost just this once and take a cab into town when she heard a familiar voice.

"Isobel!"

She scanned the crowd. Could it really be true? And then she saw him, as though a spotlight had burst to life in the dim, tired arrivals hall. Alexander—tall and blond, his sunglasses on his head and dressed in a thin leather jacket. She felt herself break into a smile that never wanted to end.

He pushed his way over, and then she was in his arms and couldn't seem to let go. She buried her face in his T-shirt, drank in the scent of sun and leather and detergent. No one had ever come to meet her at the airport.

"What are you doing here?" she asked, rubbing her nose against his chest.

"What kind of question is that?" he asked, and pushed a strand of hair from her face.

Kiss me.

She didn't say it aloud, but he must have seen it on her face. Their eyes locked and the air between them buzzed.

"Isobel," he murmured. She put an arm around his neck and pulled him close; he clasped her nape, his palm covering it, and then they were at each other's mouth, kissing passionately. He held her so tightly that she almost lost her breath.

She laid a hand on his chest, felt the warmth of his skin through his shirt, brushed her thumb over his piercing, and looked him in the eye, feeling desire setting her aflame. *I want you.*

He tilted his head, as though he could hear her. "I rented a car," he said hoarsely, his eyes seemingly almost an electrical blue. He took her bag and put an arm around her.

"Come on, before we start a scandal."

"Are you coming back to my place?"

"God, yes," he said ferociously.

She let him in to her apartment. The air was stuffy, but at least she had cleaned before she left.

"I . . ." she started, but he interrupted her by taking her face in his hands and drawing her in for a kiss, kissing her until she was clinging to him.

"I need to take a shower," she said, nodding toward the living room. "Will you wait?"

"Should I do anything?" he asked, his eyes fierce. "Are you hungry?"

Isobel shook her head. She just wanted to have sex. It was everything she had been through, she thought as she let the hot water wash away her journey and her tiredness. She dried herself and brushed her teeth with short, jerky movements. She wished she owned a sexy silk robe she could put on, but she pulled on some panties and a cami, added a thin cardigan on top, and then padded out, the steam from the bathroom in her wake.

Alexander heard her come out and stood up to meet her. She had on a white cardigan so thin he could see her skin through it, white panties, and a pale pink cami. He could make out her red curls beneath the fabric of her panties; pale nipples through her cami. Her hair was loose around her face, wet at the tips. She had lost weight since he saw her last. He would fatten her up, he decided as he moved toward her. He took her face in his hands, lifted it up toward his own, and kissed her with all his experience and tenderness, his lust, longing, and relief. The kiss became a bite, and then a kiss again. Her tongue found his, grazed it gently, and sucked. It was a kiss that caused Alexander's blood to rush south. He kissed her neck, breathed into her skin. She tasted newly washed and clean, salty from the sweat that had started to gather on her neck. Isobel was soon clinging to him again. He placed a hand on her breast and groaned; or maybe both of them did. He bent his head and tenderly kissed a nipple through her cami, felt her shiver.

"Come on," she said, and took his hand. "Let's go to the bedroom."

Isobel's bedroom was just like her: clean and fragrant, stripped of anything unnecessary. Pale bed linen on a neatly made bed. No plants in the home of a field doctor, but plenty of stones and trinkets from various corners of the world on the window ledge.

Though they were alone, she pushed the door closed behind them, laid her hands on his chest, spread out her fingers, and ran her index finger back and forward over his piercing.

"I want to see it again. If you knew how much I'd fantasized about it."

Alexander peeled off his T-shirt, took her hand, and placed it back on his chest, his heart galloping beneath his ribs. Isobel played with the golden ring.

"It's so damn sexy," she mumbled. She leaned forward and caught it carefully between her teeth, pulled slightly.

The slight tug made lust roar through him. Out to both nipples and groin, made his balls tighten. He unbuttoned his pants. Isobel ran her cool palm over his stomach and then slowly pushed her hand inside. She looked at him intently as she cupped him, moved her hand up and down over his most sensitive skin.

"Did I tell you I love how big you are?" she asked, her voice sultry and husky. A droplet glistened on the tip, and she brushed it with her index finger and then brought it up to her mouth. She sucked her finger, her eyes fixed on him.

My god.

They helped one another take off the rest of their clothes. He pushed the cardigan down, off her shoulders and arms. When it tumbled to the floor around her feet, he cupped his hand against her panties, pressing against her soft mound. She closed her eyes.

"I don't want to wait," she said.

He pushed her back. She fell onto the bed and he followed closely behind. He was on his knees between her legs, stroking the inside of them with his hands. He pulled her panties to one side and pushed a finger inside her—not too deep, just to feel her heat, her softness.

She was breathing deeply, her creamy pale skin glowing, her eyes burning.

"Alex," she mumbled. "I have to ask . . ."

He got up, grabbed the box he'd bought, tore open a packet, and had probably never put on protection so quickly in his life.

"Thanks."

He ran his thumb over her panties, and she shuddered. She was so wet the material had started to turn transparent. She liked it when he touched her like that.

"That feels so good. But I need you inside me," she said.

"No more foreplay? Should I just take you?"

She nodded.

"Say it," he said, as he continued to run his thumb back and forth over the thin material. She had spread her beautiful legs even farther, and she started to shake. He ran three fingers the length of the material, pressing it against her.

"Fuck me," she said, her voice hoarser than he'd ever heard it before, almost desperate.

He leaned forward over her. With one hand, he took hold of her wrist and pushed it up above her head. He took her other wrist and did the same, until he could hold both wrists with one hand. Her eyes glittered.

"Yes," she whispered, arching her back, pushing her breasts toward him.

He tugged at her cami, pushed it up and uncovered her breasts, felt her squirm but just continued with feverish movements. Pulled down the soft, white cotton panties, pushed them to one side, and entered her. He moved roughly, almost brutally, without letting go of her wrists even once.

"Jesus," she panted as she rocked her hips, bucking under him, taking the length of him.

He plowed into her as he held her tight, feeling the warmth and slickness surrounding him, noticing how she closed her eyes, looking the way she had the last time they made love, as though she was disappearing into another place. He tightened the grip on her wrists, pushed her legs even wider apart, and then he just took her. Their hips thudded into one another. Her eyes were tightly closed, her mouth half-open, and she gasped each time he pumped deeper and deeper into her. He felt her tighten, her whole body shaking violently, and as he intently watched her face he saw her climax. He tried to hold out, but his body was rocked with a violent shudder, and then he came too, with a roar.

He let go of her hands, breathing hard against her damp neck, and closed his eyes, fighting the low blood pressure that made his vision go dark. Five minutes, max, that was all. From taking hold of her wrists so hard he was worried he would leave marks until he came in a completely fucking crazy orgasm.

"Wow," he said, collapsing next to her on the bed. They hadn't even made it beneath the covers. He rested an arm above his head.

"Are you okay?" He was barely coherent.

She nodded next to him, pulled loose some strands of hair that had gotten trapped beneath him.

He turned his head. "Sure?"

She nodded again and pulled her cami down over her breasts and stomach, straightened her panties, which she was still wearing.

"Isobel? It was pretty rough, but I got the feeling you liked it. You've gotta tell me if I went too far."

Worry shot through him. Had he misread her?

It had been intense, almost aggressive, and she was unusually quiet.

After a while she said, "I liked it. A lot."

"I was worried I'd hurt you."

"No."

She rested her cheek on his chest, and he pulled her close.

"It *was* nice," she said. Her hand moved to his chest, and he placed his own on top of hers. This physical attraction between them, he had never felt anything even remotely like it. It had felt so insanely good for him, much more than just super-hot sex. More of everything. With her.

He continued to stroke her hand, her arm, couldn't seem to get enough of the fragrant, lush woman in his arms. He placed a kiss on her hair.

She was silent.

There was something in the air between them. He caressed her shoulder, wondering if he was imagining it.

He glanced around her little bedroom. She had a framed picture of a French landscape and another of a woman sewing.

"Who is that?" he asked.

"A Danish artist. Her name is Anna Ancher."

"Your grandmother was also an artist, wasn't she?"

"Yes. She did that." She pointed to an elegant white figurine. "That's the only thing she made that I have left."

Alexander studied its lean lines; it was almost ethereal. "It's beautiful."

"I grew up with her, you know. My grandma."

"You did? Not with your parents?"

She shook her head. "My parents were married, but they didn't live together. They lived separate lives, often in different countries. My maternal grandmother was the one who took care of me. I lived with her until she died when I was ten."

"How was it?"

She shrugged. "Mom and my grandmother didn't get on. They

were so different. My grandfather had left her. Mom adored him and thought that my grandmother was weak. But it was good. She was a kind soul, a true artist, and I loved her very much."

And then she had died. "So you weren't unhappy? It sounds quite lonely," he asked, pulling her closer, feeling her cuddle up to him.

"Unhappy is such a relative word. I was fed, had a roof over my head. But I used to pretend I was a poor, undernourished kid and that Mom needed to come home to take care of me."

She fell silent and he held her even tighter, draped his legs over hers, kissed her forehead. He sensed that the conversation was making her sad. He didn't want her to be sad.

"So, how does it feel to be home again?"

"Well, I mean, the welcome committee was fantastic." He could hear the smile in her voice. "But otherwise, I have mixed feelings. I was scared, but you're always a bit scared when you're out there." She placed a kiss on his rib cage, followed an invisible line first with her index finger and then with her thumb. Alexander closed his eyes, let the sensation of her fingers on his flesh sweep over him.

"My grandfather died in Chad," she murmured.

"He did?" he asked, surprised. "How?"

She said nothing at first, just made small, circular movements with her fingertips. She had the most beautiful hands he had ever seen. Long, slender. Competent and sensitive. He took her hand and kissed her fingertips, one after another, light kisses, pulled her palm to his mouth and nose, breathed her in, inhaled her.

"He was murdered," she said quietly.

He paused. He hadn't had any idea. How could he have missed that?

"Jesus, you're not kidding, are you?"

"He was kidnapped, tortured, and then murdered."

"That's horrendous. Who did it?"

"It was a long time ago. Before I was born. Some local group. My mother has refused to go there ever since."

But she had no problem sending her daughter there, he thought. Did Isobel even realize how that sounded? Probably not.

"Mom had his body brought home. He's buried in Paris. I'm happy about that."

He lay on one side, his head in his hand. She did the same, and he reached out, couldn't stop himself from tracing the curve of her breast with a finger. She had fewer freckles there—the skin was paler. She trembled.

"Are you cold?" he asked, moving her closer to him.

"You asked me before whether it was too rough for me," she said quietly.

"Yeah, I'm sorry, I don't know what came over me." She had just come back from a terrible trip, one that must've wrenched up memories of what had happened to her grandfather, and he had been so rough with her, almost like an animal, when what she probably needed more than anything was tenderness and closeness.

"No, I didn't mean it like that. The opposite."

Her eyes seemed enormous in her pale face, big and gray, with the thickest eyelashes he'd ever seen. She didn't look like someone who had just spent two weeks in Africa; she looked like an elven queen, someone who spent her nights dancing in the moonlight, ruling her kingdom.

She seemed to urge herself on. "I think, no, I *know* that I need more than normal sex to really get off. It doesn't have anything to do with anyone, it's just me. So when you were so . . . I don't know what to say . . . when you were rough with me, I get so turned on by that."

"I'm not sure I really follow what you're saying," he said, unsure whether he had understood her. What was "ordinary sex," exactly?

She took a deep breath and her eyes flared before she glanced down. She didn't look at him as she spoke, as though it was hard enough to talk without having to meet his eyes.

"It's hard to explain. . . . Something happens when I . . . When you . . ."

With a frustrated motion, she pushed back her hair and sat up, legs crossed. She reached for a blanket and wrapped it around her shoulders. Alexander held back a disappointed protest. She shouldn't sit up with a blanket around her, she should be naked in his arms; everything else was a waste of time. But he was interested in what she was struggling so hard to say. She interlocked her fingers, sighed loudly.

"I can barely explain. But when someone else takes over, when you hold me like that, when it's like I . . ."

She ran her hands through her hair until it was like a tangled halo.

"I don't think I can talk about it. Can we just forget I said any-thing?"

Forget that she didn't get turned on by ordinary sex? No way.

"When I hold you . . ." he prompted.

She sighed. "I liked the feeling when you held my wrists, okay? So damn much. I get turned on just thinking about it now. I'm ashamed, but that's how it is. It *wasn't* too rough for me."

"I was worried about hurting you."

"And I came when I realized I might get bruises from your fingers. So, now I've said it. I know. It's totally messed up. I'm a mess."

"So you're saying that you like *more* than what we did?"

She was silent. Played with the blanket. Pulled at a loose thread. "Yes. More."

He had played sex games with women before, of course. Some pink handcuffs here, a bit of dirty talk there. But it didn't sound like Isobel meant something a *little* adventurous.

"It's the only time I can really switch off," she continued. "It's like my head goes quiet for once. And I'm just living in the here and now, completely present. Not caught up in whatever happened before. Or what will happen. Just here. I don't know what it's like for other peo-ple when they have sex—you don't really talk about that kind of thing, especially if you're a woman. I just know that's how it is for me. But I don't talk about it. I only did it once before."

"When was that?" he asked. Of all the thoughts rushing around in his head, that was the only question he could manage. Honestly, he was a bit dazed right now.

"Ten years ago. Eleven, maybe. I was twenty."

"What happened?"

"I was still so immature, especially when it came to men. I hadn't had any boyfriends or rebellious teenage years. Sexually, I was em-barrassingly ignorant. Maybe because I never recognized myself in the way other girls talked about boys and sex and what they liked. And then I started my medical studies and met him, with a capital H. He was older. And I didn't know what were just fantasies and what were real desires. I was inexperienced and unsure and so very much in love. The kind of love you feel when it's the first time. It felt like I wanted to do everything with him. And so I told him. That I had dark fantasies. He was so into it, he wanted to try it out straight away. He said that all men dream about dominating women, that it's natural, that he'd give me what I wanted. But I couldn't really manage to keep up, I think. It wasn't like I'd imagined at all. I panicked, cried. He thought I was playing along, so he just kept going, hurting me, until I was completely hysterical. Afterward he yelled at me, berated me, and said I'd overreacted. That it was my own fault. That I was stupid."

She shrugged as though it was nothing, but Alexander heard her voice break.

"I was so scared after that, I decided to ignore those fantasies. I mean, what kind of woman likes stuff like that? During my medical studies, those deviations were talked about as some kind of sick depravity. A psychiatrist told us it was a defect, a reaction to something the patient experienced as a child, a trauma."

"Did anything like that happen to you?"

She shook her head. "I'm pretty sure I was born this way."

"Who was he?" asked Alexander. What she had described was practically abuse. But he realized the answer the very moment he asked the question.

"You met him. Sebastien," she confirmed. "We broke up afterward, and I was completely crushed."

What a fucking asshole.

"I decided that it was the wrong way for me to go. That I'd rather have normal vanilla sex than go through that again. I've never talked about it, not since Sebastien."

And you've had an unsatisfactory sex life ever since. Worked your ass off to save the world.

"It actually feels pretty good to talk about it," she said.

"Thank you for sharing this with me," he said quietly.

When she looked at him he saw vulnerability in every muscle and movement. He sat up, studied her beautiful face closely, noticing a tiny freckle right beneath one eye. He kissed her softly, gently, as though she were the first woman he'd ever kissed, as though she were the last woman he planned to kiss, as though he wanted to take all the time in the world. It started as a tender kiss, but her response was passionate, and it quickly became something else, something wilder and more primitive.

Isobel squirmed beneath him, twisted her body so that it grazed against his in a thousand places simultaneously, setting off a dark pulse beneath his skin. He pulled off her thin panties, threw them to the floor, admired the red curls against the pale flesh before he started to caress her, to kiss her, noticing that the rougher he was, the more she whimpered. Something dark and ferocious awoke in him, something new and barely controllable. When he pressed her down into the bed, her eyes shone with a fierce light. This wasn't the lighthearted, playful kink he had engaged in on some occasions. This was something completely different. This was dark and dangerous. And then he saw it happen. Saw the control, the one thing that defined Isobel more than anything else, starting to slip away. Something else appeared in its place, a more compliant Isobel with softer eyes and a body eager to please. God, was it very bad that it turned him on? But it was so fucking sexy, the way she suddenly subordinated herself to him. All the strength within her was replaced by submissive pliancy.

"Turn over, onto your stomach," he commanded, his voice rough with tension.

Without a word, she obeyed, presenting her lush ass and luscious curves, shivering but yielding. He tore open a condom packet and rolled it on, and then he took hold of her hands, pressed her wrists down against the curve of her back and kept them there, firmly. He pushed her legs apart with his knees, spreading her before him.

"Yes," she panted into the bed.

He almost groaned. It was incredibly erotic, as if something was taking him over, making him more animal than man. She was still tight and warm after her orgasm, but he pushed into her, so hard that it would have been almost ruthless if he hadn't been able to hear her breathing heavily into the bedclothes. He pulled on her wrists and continued, dangerously close to losing control; pumped away even harder, forced her body to take the length of him, pushed until she was full. He was wild, insatiable.

He shoved a hand beneath her and spread her even wider so he could inch in even farther.

"Oh, God," she groaned.

"Touch yourself," he told her as he let go of one hand. She couldn't quite reach, so he pulled her up, roughly, and then pushed her onto her knees.

"Pet yourself, Isobel," he ordered hoarsely.

She moved her fingers between her legs and started to touch herself. Alexander laid a hand on her neck, the hand not holding her wrist in an iron grip, and held her like that, tightly. He felt her thighs tremble, felt her body shake and start to tighten around him. She was whimpering, her hips were moving, her plump ass was quivering as he thrust himself hard into her, and then she came powerfully.

"Isobel" was all he could manage as her body shook beneath him, trembled around him. He laid both hands on her hips, took hold of her, and thrust into her in a way that was bordering on brutal. And then he exploded. He came and came and came until Isobel collapsed beneath him, and he fell down on top of her.

Jesus fucking Christ.

With the last of his strength, Alexander rolled off of her, lay down next to her.

They were side by side, panting, covered with sweat and with sex. He put an arm over his face, needed to shut the world out for a moment while he pulled himself together.

"Hey, is everything okay?"

He jumped, turned to her voice, and opened his eyes. Isobel had that relaxed expression that only an intense orgasm could produce. Her face was easy, no sign of any tension. She gave him a lingering smile.

"All good. You?" His voice sounded strange to his own ears, as if it belonged to someone else.

"Very good. You looked so serious."

"Nah. Stay there, I'll get something to drink," he said, hoping he'd managed to disguise the strange feeling that had rushed over him.

Alexander got up, found his way to the kitchen, and opened the refrigerator. It was empty, of course. He poured a glass of water but then paused. He went back to her, held out the glass.

"I'm going to run down to the store," he said.

She drank her water and looked at him without saying anything.

He avoided her gaze, pulled on his clothes, and went down to the 7-Eleven on the ground floor of her building. He bought coffee, butter, and cheese. Picked up a chocolate bar and some juice, grabbed some bread and a box of cookies. He waited while the cashier packed his things and handed him the bag, fought the urge to just go back to his own place, forced himself to return to her apartment.

When he'd unpacked the groceries in her kitchen and returned to the bedroom, Isobel looked utterly exhausted. She had spent ten days in the field, been evacuated, had kinky sex, and shared her deepest secrets. The odds of her being completely drained were pretty good.

She had crawled under the covers and was on her side, her hand beneath her chin and her hair like a halo around her.

"Are you sure nothing is wrong?" she asked quietly, her gray eyes serious.

"Absolutely," he lied, and crawled in next to her, still fully dressed.

"Aren't you going to get undressed?"

"Soon," he said absently.

"Alex?" she asked.

"I'm fine. I bought bread. Coffee. Want something?"

She shook her head. "Not now, I'm so tired." She yawned.

"Go to sleep, I'll go unpack everything," he said, though it was already done.

She closed her eyes, laid her cheek on his chest.

He waited until he could hear her regular breathing. Waited a little longer, until he was sure she was sleeping deeply, before he carefully got up, out of bed. He paused and looked at her, but she didn't move, just slept on.

He showered, dressed, picked up his sunglasses, his cell, and paused in the hallway. Undecided. It was a shitty thing to do, to leave her.

But he had never felt like this and it was scaring the hell out of him. The rush when they made love, no, *fucked*. It was like being high on something. His body had been completely intoxicated, his brain had shifted to another, unknown gear. It was like he'd temporarily been in a parallel world with Isobel, a world where the things he normally believed in no longer mattered. But then the high had passed almost as quickly, and left behind . . . something else. Whatever he was feeling now was, for want of other words, a crash.

What he had done to her . . .

It went against everything he believed in.

It wasn't him. It was someone else. A man he didn't like, a man he couldn't be.

Because if she had asked him to stop, he didn't think he could have. What he had done was *wrong*.

And Alexander knew two things now.

Tonight, he and Isobel had barely scraped the surface of what she wanted from a man. What she needed. She wanted more, needed more.

And he would never be able to give it to her.

Chapter 39

I shouldn't have said anything.
The words found their way into Isobel's sleep, into her dreams, awakening her.

She was alone. The bed was empty next to her, and when she padded out into the kitchen, she found a note:

> *Thanks for yesterday.*
> *Loads to think about.*
> *I'll be in touch, okay?*
> *A*

Isobel closed her eyes and tiredly rubbed her face. She really shouldn't have said anything. She had seen it in Alexander, suspected it last night. That she'd shocked him. It wasn't so strange—she was a little shocked herself. She had blurted out the one thing she'd *promised* herself never to tell anyone again. She should have known it would be too much for him. Jesus, it was too much for *her*. Of course it scared him. How could she be so dumb?

Though Isobel knew the answer. She had been knocked off balance by all the stress. The danger, the increased tensions, and the panicked evacuation out of Chad had lowered her defenses. And the feeling of having escaped death had set powerful compensatory behaviors into motion. She saw it often enough. People who had been on the verge of death were thankful to be alive, they wanted to *live*. They wanted physical intimacy, and that invariably led to sex. How could she have given in to such basic urges?

Her sexual preferences didn't define her as a person; she had made that decision a long time ago and she had stuck to it. A few days' recovery and she would've been herself again. She had made do with normal, boring sex for most of her adult life, so why had she been so stupid? And with Alex, of all people? Because he'd given her some of the best orgasms of her life? But an orgasm lasted a few seconds. It wasn't worth this.

The shame.

I really shouldn't have said anything.

There was a new packet of coffee on the kitchen table, next to a bag of freshly baked rolls, a pack of Maryland cookies, and a chocolate bar. When she opened the refrigerator she saw butter, cheese, and expensive orange juice.

She leaned her head against the refrigerator door. She didn't know what to think. Or feel. Everything was a mess.

She drank her coffee, then cut thick slices of cheese, which she rolled up and ate before she moved on to the biscuits. She kept an eye on her cell phone.

But Saturday passed without word from Alexander. And when Sunday evening came and went and he still hadn't been in touch, Isobel shuffled down to the store, bought ice cream and chocolate sauce, and ate it on the couch in front of the TV.

I'll be in touch. Right, sure.

There was something seriously wrong with her. Wrong, wrong, wrong. And now she'd scared off Alexander for good. Great work, Doctor Sørensen.

On Monday morning, Leila called and woke her up.

"You're free, I'm coming to get you and we're going for lunch."

Isobel groaned. Her first impulse was to say no. She didn't have the energy to take a shower, to talk.

"I'll pick you up at eleven-thirty," Leila said, and hung up.

And since the idea of calling Leila to explain that she didn't want to see her felt even harder, Isobel was down on Vasagatan at eleven thirty on the dot. A black sports car, roof down, with the famous jaguar on the hood, swept in and braked abruptly in the middle of the bus stop outside Isobel's door.

"What do you think?" Leila grinned.

Isobel opened the car door. "Don't tell me this is where all Medpax's money has gone?"

Leila snorted. "I borrowed it from Eugene. My Medpax wage barely covers proper shoes."

Isobel hopped in and Leila tore off just as the bus driver behind them blasted the horn. Leila did a sweeping illegal U-turn and the Jaguar flew off away from the center of town.

"You've lost weight," Leila said, with a quick glance at Isobel before she changed gear and swung in ahead of a truck which flashed its headlights at them.

Isobel gripped the door handle. "It's an optical illusion. I've eaten cookies and ice cream for almost three days."

"Real Persian food is what you need. Persian women have perfect bodies and that's because of the food we eat."

"It's not one of those restaurants where you sit on the floor, is it?"

Isobel didn't really want to drive to a far away place to have lunch; she wanted to lie on the couch at home and eat ice cream. A late-night 7-Eleven and a comfortable couch were all a woman really needed. Plus, she didn't want to be in a car with Leila. Who would have thought that the woman drove like a car thief on crack?

"No. You can sit at a table. Why so grumpy?"

"I've got a natural aversion to dying. I've been to some of the most dangerous countries in the world and never been in a car crash yet. Please don't kill me on the way to the suburbs."

She pulled at the seatbelt to check it was fastened properly, while Leila took a curve well above the speed limit.

"We're almost there," said Leila. "As soon as we're on the freeway, I'll really get this beauty going."

Isobel squeezed her eyes shut. If she survived this, she would become a better person, she promised.

"Do you want to talk about how it was?" Leila asked once they sat down. The restaurant was brightly colored, the chairs were red, and the scent coming from the kitchen made Isobel's mouth water. Maybe it wasn't the worst idea in the world to eat something other than sugar and trans fats.

"It was like always, really."

She scooped up some eggplant purée with freshly baked bread

and put it into her mouth. Leila had ordered a table full of small en-
trées, and Isobel suddenly felt famished.

"Other than the fact that war broke out and you were evacuated,"
Leila pointed out. She flashed her patented psychologist look at Isobel over the table.

"You know it's not the first time. I've been through worse things."

Leila gave her another long look, and Isobel avoided making eye
contact.

"How does it feel to be home, then? I know it can be tough."

People often assumed it was nothing but nice to come home.
That it was a relief to return to a functioning society. But the truth
was much more complicated. You left home with so many ideas about
making a difference. Come back and feel like you'd barely scraped
the surface. True, she hadn't been away from Sweden for so long this
time. Still, it took a while to find your feet. To get used to the fact that
the children you saw on the street were healthy, clean, and safe and
that people counted shopping and spending money as a pleasant
hobby. That people wouldn't hesitate to pay fifty kronor for a paper
cup of coffee, an amount that could mean the difference between life
and death in another part of our shared world. That people moaned
about the weather and other meaningless things on social media
while children died because no one had time to care.

"I'm trying to take care of myself," she said, though she wished
she was better at it. Doctors who didn't became cynical and blunt.
That was her nightmare, becoming a fieldwork cliché who'd lost her
belief in the possibility of changing things, even in a small way, for
the better.

"Alexander was worried about you. Did you talk?"

"Mmm." Isobel reached for a bowl of yogurt, scrupulously avoiding Leila's sharp look.

We talked. And other things.

"Isobel? What is it? You know you can tell me if something happened."

Leila's voice was so confidence-inspiring that Isobel could feel
herself falter. Would it be so bad to ask? To get advice about how to
escape the turmoil bubbling away inside her? She didn't believe in
talking about her feelings. Or rather: She believed in it when it came
to other people, people who were normal. She didn't talk about her

feelings, because she was a freak. She'd known that since she was a teen. It had been like a growing insight, that she had fantasies and thoughts the other girls didn't seem to share. But she was a *highly functioning* freak. She didn't burden anyone else. She saved lives and did no one any harm. As long as she didn't say or do anything wrong, it made no difference what she was like on the inside.

"How are things at the hospital?" she asked instead, although she had spoken to Idris that morning. He had a horrible cold but everything else was under control.

"It's stable. You know it's my responsibility to keep an eye on how you're doing?"

That was the downside to brilliant psychologists—they weren't easy to throw off.

"I'm fine, you don't need to worry."

Leila took off her glasses, breathed onto them, and wiped them with a napkin.

"But it's my job to worry."

Did she never blink, or was that just Isobel's imagination? Surely everyone blinked. Fifteen times a minute, on average, if she remembered correctly.

"I know you have trouble trusting people," Leila continued once their main meal had arrived. Bowls and plates of steaming food and cool side dishes.

"That's not true," Isobel said as she filled her plate with saffron rice, spinach stew, chickpeas, and garlic-scented yogurt sauce. "I trust people all the time. It's not my fault most people are so unreliable."

"I only want the best for you. You know that, right?"

Isobel nodded.

"And I promise, you can't shock me, not even if you try. There's nothing you can say that'll make me think less of you."

"Not even if I turn out to be a bad person?"

"But you're not a bad person."

Isobel shook her head. She hated declarations like that. They didn't mean anything.

"We've known each other for only two years. There's plenty you don't know about me."

"I probably know more than you think. But why do we have to be good or bad, kind or evil? People are complex. Most of us are both. It's impossible to be just one of them."

"I don't agree. There's a line between being good and bad, and there's always a choice."

Leila smiled. "Now you're talking about how things *should* be, not how things *are*. Do you think you're a bad person? Really?"

"You just said everyone was good and bad."

"Why do you think you're bad?"

Leila's jet-black eyes were fixed on her.

Isobel stuffed more food into her mouth. Leila waited. Isobel swallowed, wiped her mouth.

"You're right, I don't like to expose myself," she said reluctantly.

"That's an interesting choice of words."

"If you tell people things, they can use them against you. Don't you want more?"

"I eat until I'm seventy-five percent full. How does it feel when I question what you say? When I say that people don't automatically want to use your secrets and weaknesses against you?"

"Like you've taken a course in how to deal with difficult doctors."

"Yeah, it was pretty useful." Leila smiled. "What are you worried might happen?"

People might realize how bad I actually am.

The thought came to her automatically. She was a woman who fantasized about things no woman should like. What normal, modern woman got turned on by that kind of thing? Not playful kink, but real pain and submission. No, there was something wrong with her, and if Leila knew she would agree. Maybe not openly—she was much too professional for that—but quietly, to herself. And then Isobel would be left. Exposed. Defenseless. Ashamed.

"I'm not afraid, Leila. And I don't want to talk about this anymore. Is dessert included? If I die on the way back, I at least want some sugar and caffeine in me."

When Leila dropped her off outside her door, Isobel paused with the key in her hand. The conversation had woken her from some kind of trance. She was an independent woman, a competent doctor, and a reliable coworker. She was all that. But she was also a walking cliché. A good girl with a sense of self based on performance. A grown woman who, at the age of almost thirty-one, still thought she was good enough only when her mother gave her confirmation.

Which she never did.

Isobel looked around. All about her, early summer was in full swing. Stockholm was in glorious bloom, and the first tourists were already arriving. Streets and sidewalk cafés were full of people late into the evening. Enough with the self-pity now. She had made up her mind. She would go out tonight. Not wallow at home. So what if Alexander had dumped her? Again. Life in the field had taught her to appreciate people who kept their promises. Kindness, loyalty, and stability were the best things she knew. *Not* men who ran away when things got complicated. Screw him. And the horse he rode in on. She would get dressed up, drink alcohol, and meet men, loads of men. If her body wanted to live, well then it was time she lived a little. She opened the door and ran lightly up the stairs.

A damn good plan if she said so herself.

Chapter 40

Alexander had done plenty of things in his life he wasn't proud of. Far too many. But he had *never* hurt a woman physically.

He was not a man who hurt women.

Didn't *want* to be.

Only the worst of the worst went for women. And he had never been one to intimidate. Never been turned on by being aggressive or dominant. Never.

Right?

He swung his feet up onto the desk in his newly furnished office. Stared at the empty walls. A memory of what had happened between him and Isobel flashed by. It wasn't that he hadn't liked what they had done. He remembered how he had pounded into her soft, yielding body, selfish and oblivious to anything else.

It was that he *had*. Had been turned on by her whimpering, by his own power.

What the hell did that say about him?

He'd pushed her down against the bed, taken her like an animal. Had the best sex of his life.

He tipped the chair back and stared up at the ceiling.

The whole thing was so fucking . . . confusing? Scary?

His phone rang. Romeo. He had been dwelling on this for almost three days. Maybe it was time for someone else to have a say.

"You disappeared from New York," Romeo greeted him. "Where are you?"

Alexander hadn't told him about the latest troubles in Chad, had just acted on impulse and taken off without saying a word.

"Stockholm. Sorry I disappeared. How are you?"

"I spent the weekend with the family, so I'm a little worn out."

Romeo was the youngest of five brothers. His parents were devout Catholics, his brothers burly, heterosexual firemen. Romeo usually came back from family gatherings with a haunted look on his face, his shoulders stooped.

"Oh, man."

"Yeah. Did you know there's a special circle of hell for sodomites?"

"If religious people spent a little more time being tolerant, they'd have less time to obsess about other people's private lives."

"I get to talk shit about my family, but you don't, *capisce?*

"Sorry. I need to brainstorm something, alright?"

"Shoot, I have a little time before Satan comes to collect my soul."

"Did you ever have kinky sex with any of your partners?"

"Define kinky."

"Anything that isn't vanilla."

"You are aware I sleep with men, right? Nothing about that's vanilla."

"I'll take your word for it."

"Are we talking whips and bondage?"

"Maybe. Yeah, I guess so."

"Why are you asking me? Haven't you? No offense, but you're the sluttiest person I ever met."

"Yeah, don't hold back."

"I'm just surprised. I thought you'd done everything."

"It's never come up. Or maybe I wasn't receptive. But most women aren't as interested in being whipped or tied up when they have sex as you seem to think."

"If you say so. I mean, I've never slept with a woman, so I have no idea."

Alexander hadn't had any idea either. So he had done what he always did when he wanted to understand something. He had studied the subject. All weekend he had read, all kinds of stuff, browsed chat rooms, read articles, followed discussion threads.

"So what exactly do you want to know? Because I'm guessing it's not a theoretical discussion you're after. We're talking about your Isobel, aren't we? The doctor?"

"She's not *my* Isobel."

Romeo was silent, as though he was thinking.

"This isn't like you," he eventually said. "You sound different. Worried. But that can't be right. You're never insecure when it comes to women. What happened?"

"She told me things. What she likes. In bed. And I freaked out."

"How?"

"We had sex last weekend. Rough sex. And then I panicked and left."

"Left?"

"Went home."

"Aha. And what did she think about that?"

"We haven't spoken since."

"I don't get it. Don't you like this woman?"

"Yeah."

"So it probably would've been better if you hadn't run off."

"Sounds about right. Fuck, man, I don't know if I can deal with this."

"It would be simpler if it was just sex?"

"Yeah."

"But it isn't?"

"No."

He liked Isobel. More than liked. He had *feelings* for her. The air in his apartment was cool, but Alexander suddenly began to sweat.

"You straight guys, you always have to make things complicated." The amusement in Romeo's voice held a touch of schadenfreude.

"I'm pretty sure it's not just straight people who make things complicated."

"Maybe not, but listen, Alessandro, I've waited ten years for you to fall for someone. You can be a bit of a jerk when you talk about other people's lives like it's some kind of entertainment. If you like Isobel, I'm sure you'll find a way to give her what she wants. Or are you opposed to kinkiness? If that's the case, I'm gonna have to sit down. I can't take any more surprises today."

He wanted to believe Romeo. That it was nothing strange. But still . . .

"But doing something like that to a woman . . ."

"Yeah, it's gotta be complicated, feelings-wise. But do you mean you'd do it against her will?"

"Are you crazy? Never."

"So that's what I mean. This is something she *wants*. That's what you've gotta sort out in your head."

If Alexander was really honest with himself, there was a dark part of him that was turned on by the thought of a submissive Isobel who let him do what he wanted with her. But what if he made a mistake—went too far and hurt her? What if he lost control? The fear was almost paralyzing.

"I don't know if I can do this."

"You can trust your intuition. And your . . . let's say wide experience of women. Alex, you're one of the best guys I've ever met. You know that, right?"

Alexander laughed. "Yeah, right."

"Don't laugh it off. I've met plenty of bad people. You aren't one of them. If there was anyone I'd trust with my life, it's you."

He wasn't sure he wanted anyone's life in his hands.

"But Alex?"

"Yeah?"

"You can't get kinky with me. To me you've gotta be nice."

"Go to hell."

By dinner, Alexander had made up his mind. With one hand wrapped around a cup of coffee, he sent a text to Isobel.

Hey, sorry I disappeared. Be great to hear from you. Busy?

He waited.

And waited.

Not his greatest skill.

He drummed his fingers. Sent another message.

Are you okay?

Two in a row was fine. More than that was pathetic.

Right? He'd never wondered about stuff like that before. He normally just initiated contact, and either got a reply or didn't. For the most part, he got the response he wanted. Sometimes he didn't. Then he just moved on. Without giving it a second thought.

But now . . .

He waited.

And waited.

Shit.

He had deserted Isobel after she'd told him her deepest secret. He had slept with her right after she came home from a war zone. He hadn't said a word afterward, just disappeared as if she were some kind of meaningless trophy.

She must be furious. And justifiably so. He was an ass, a . . .

His cell phone buzzed.

Message from her. He held his breath. Read.

All vital signs normal. You?

He breathed out, a long sigh of relief that could stretch all the way to her, wherever she was. If she was willing to communicate with him, maybe she didn't hate him. Even though she'd replied using cool clinical medical jargon. He quickly replied:

Be great to see you.

God, he was longing for her.

No reply.

Silence.

He paced restlessly around the apartment. Was just about to let his dignity go to hell and give her a call when her answer arrived with a bleep.

Want to see you too.

He had never sweated so much waiting for a message. He would need to take a shower after this. He asked:

Tonight?

Her answer was immediate this time.

Sorry. Going out.

What the hell? He wanted to see her *now*. And he didn't want her to go out. Who was she going out with anyway? Why hadn't he stayed with her? But even though this whole jealousy thing was new to Alexander, he wasn't so stupid that he didn't know he had absolutely nothing to do with where Isobel went, or with whom. He wrote:

Okay, talk tomorrow?

She sent a thumbs-up in reply. That was all. Still, an emoji was more than he deserved.

He looked at the screen. Scrolled through their old messages. Hoped, against his better judgment, that she would text something more. When his phone buzzed, the noise went through him like a shock, but it was just a picture from Åsa. She and Michel were on their honeymoon in Mauritius, looking annoyingly happy. He closed the picture and opened his computer instead. He buried himself in his work for a while, read through a couple of business plans his accountant in New York had sent over, wrote down his response in an e-mail, and then moved on to the darker side of the Internet. For those who wanted to delve into the world of kink, the Internet was a cornucopia.

At ten, his phone buzzed again. He finished the article on ten beginner's tips for tying up your partner before he glanced at the screen.

We're at the Beefeater Inn. Götgatsbacken. Can you come?

Alexander read the message from Isobel again, worried that he'd misunderstood her. As if he could. There was nothing he wanted more than to go to her. Wherever she was. And whatever the hell the Beefeater Inn was.

He pulled on a jacket, texted her he was on his way, and climbed into a cab within five minutes.

He glanced around the bar. It was a typical street corner dive, not one he'd been to before, not one he would've chosen.

The place smelled of stale beer and fries. Dusty plastic plants in the corners and green faux leather on the wall-mounted benches.

"Over here," Isobel called. She waved from a corner table deeper inside the bar.

When he got to the table, she smiled broadly.

Her eyes seemed a little unfocused The table was covered in glasses and bottles and bowls of nuts. Isobel was sitting with four men. Three of them bearded and sturdy looking.

The fourth was Sebastien Pascal.

Isobel flashed him the same blinding smile again, but this time Alexander caught sight of something else behind it, as if she was holding up a façade. She introduced them.

"Sven and Christian are MSF doctors. We've worked together over the years. Øystein, here, is one of our logisticians, one of the best. We were in Liberia together." She paused, a heartbeat. "And you've already met Sebastien."

Her voice was neutral, but the unspoken words between them thundered in his ears.

Alexander shook hands with the men, one after another. Sebastien last. He took Sebastien's hand firmly, much harder than he had when they'd first met in Skåne. If something broke, there were plenty of doctors here to look at it.

Alexander sat down in the only empty seat. He was opposite Isobel. Sebastien to his right. The other men were spread out, with Isobel in the center. Alexander had a hard time looking away from her—she was positively *glowing*. This was no dumped woman; she was a queen with her court. Three knights and a snake.

"Sebastien dropped in," she said, apropos of nothing.

So. He was here as backup. That was fine with him.

A waitress came over to take more orders. Alexander asked for a bottle of lager, leaned back in his chair, and took it all in. Isobel pulled out her phone, tapped away at it, and he received a message.

He's Christian's friend. I had no idea he'd be here.

He looked at her across the table, happy that he got to be her knight in shining armor.

She hiccupped.

Are you drunk? he mouthed.

"Very," she replied, and gave him a tipsy smile.

"Alexander, how do you know Isobel?" It was one of the bearded superheroes who spoke.

Alexander had forgotten their names; Isobel was all that mattered.

"He's an international jet-setter. That's how we met," said Isobel.

No one seemed to notice how illogical her answer was. But when Alexander saw the number of bottles on the table, he wasn't surprised. They all seemed acutely intoxicated.

"You know she's a legend, right?"

Alexander's eyes lingered on Isobel's beautiful, laughing face. She was at ease no matter where she was, even here, on a Monday evening, in a dive bar.

"That doesn't surprise me," he said, his gaze fixed on her gray eyes. "She's one of the most impressive people I know."

Their eyes met over the table, and he knew that she knew he was trying to ask for forgiveness.

"Tell me," he said. "Tell me about the legend of Doctor Sørensen."

"They're exaggerating," she said, waving her beer in the air.

"Come on, tell him about the time you bought all the medicine in Port-au-Prince."

She shook her head.

"I'd love to hear."

"Okay, okay, okay. It was after the earthquake. We were getting patients who'd been poisoned by something. It turned out they'd gotten drugs from a fly-by-night medical center. My coworker and I headed over there and realized they were prescribing cancer meds to everyone no matter what ailed them. We tried to buy it all, but they refused; I guess they realized they could get more for it elsewhere. So eventually I told them I knew Zlatan Ibrahimović and that I'd get his signature for them if they'd let me buy all the medicine."

"They knew who Zlatan was?" Alexander asked with a smile. He loved how she looked—happy, carefree, mischievous. "I never realized he's so famous."

"Everyone knows who Zlatan is, no matter where you go. At least everyone outside of North America. He is the greatest soccer player, after all—every child in every third world country dreams of becoming Zlatan. In many countries he's bigger than ABBA, Björn Borg, and Ikea combined. Anyway, we bought all the medicine they had, and then we spent a whole day breaking the vials."

"Tell him what happened with Zlatan," the logistician said, slapping his hand on the table and laughing.

"I managed to get in touch with his manager. He sent me two signed photos and I sent them on to Haiti."

The bearded men hooted with laughter and toasted, their beer spilling onto the table.

"So this is what MSF doctors do when they go out? Tell tall tales?"

"Yeah. There was a doctor, when we were in the field, who got kidney stones. Do you know how painful they are?"

Alexander shook his head.

"They say it's one of the most painful things you can experience, one hundred on a scale from one to a hundred. It hurts so much you literally can't keep still. We had to take the doctor to the hospital, and they wanted to keep her in. But she refused to stay, didn't want to take away space from other patients. And she also refused to stop work and head home, like any normal person would have done. So we got some painkillers, and everyone went to bed. She had instructions to wake us up when she needed the next injection. But instead she let everyone sleep, injected herself—which is pretty fucking hard-core—and then assisted with something like ten operations the next day."

"Shit."

"And that's not all. A couple of days later, she got a serious infection in a cut, self-treated it with antibiotics and stitched herself up. And *then* she got pneumonia. She still refused to go home. This was in Iraq. A refugee camp. She worked around the clock. I think she was coughing more than her patients at the end. Eventually, she stepped on a used needle. When that happens, it's standard practice to take HIV medicine—it's a preventative measure. But that treatment can make you very sick, and it did, of course. She had so many side effects she couldn't even stand up."

"What happened?"

"I had to go home," Isobel muttered. "Under protest."

They burst out laughing.

He looked at them.

"You're all insane. That was *you?*"

"It was my first trip with MSF. I was terrified they'd think I was useless."

"I told you, she's a legend."

"Isobel does everything better than anyone," Sebastien said, and his mouth curled slightly. "Like a little machine. *Oui?*"

"She's better than a machine, Sebastien," one of the bearded men said, laughing, and Isobel smiled. But Alexander could see that Sebastien's words had hurt her. Isobel, with her constant struggle to be good, always doing her best. And that asshole sat there and mocked her for it.

Alexander gave Sebastien a long look, came up with a thousand ways to strangle him.

Sebastien snorted and got to his feet.

"I'm going to see if they have any decent wine," he said, and headed for the bar.

Alexander's eyes followed the Frenchman. Watched him position himself at the bar. Alexander hesitated. Heard the others start to talk about yet another trip. Made up his mind. He got up and strolled nonchalantly over to the bar. He pushed his way through to where Sebastien was standing.

The Frenchman looked surprised, and Alexander gave him his best polite, harmless face, as though he was only there to order another beer and exchange a few manly, everyday platitudes. It was a basic poker tactic. Hide your intentions from your opponent while you looked for weaknesses, analyzed what kind of player was in front of you. Alexander had grown up with bullies and could spot one in an instant. The Frenchman was a classic specimen, a hyena who preyed only on the weak. Alexander could handle someone like him with one arm tied.

"So," he said as jovially as he could.

"So?"

Alexander flashed his teeth, made himself tall and wide. He pressed Sebastien against the bar, as though the people behind had pushed him. He smiled. "You and Isobel were together?"

Watchfulness in Sebastien's eyes. Not an experienced player, or not when he faced an equal anyway. "I don't know what she said."

"No?"

"I had an adult relationship with Isobel. That's all."

"She was your student."

"She was over eighteen, and I was the course leader, hardly anything to cry about. She got no special treatment. Plus, she was the one who threw herself at me."

Alexander took another step forward. Dropped the poker analogies and changed tack. He puffed out his chest, pushed against Sebastien, stared.

Sebastien's eyes began to wander. "Look, I don't know what lies she told you, but I don't appreciate you threatening me like this."

"I don't give a damn what you appreciate. And I'm not threatening you."

"Then what do you want from me?"

"I'm going to put this as plainly as I possibly can. So there's no misunderstanding between us. What with the language barrier and all that, you know. If you so much as think anything that Isobel might not like, if you get to her, if you say a single fucking word that I interpret as insulting to her, I'm going to put a hand on your neck, and I'll squeeze and squeeze until your eyes pop out." He raised a hand and Sebastien jerked back. Alexander smirked. He put a hand on the Frenchman's shoulder and patted him lightly. "See the difference? *That* was a threat."

Alexander got his beer and took it back to the table. He gave Isobel a wide grin.

"What were you guys talking about?" she asked suspiciously.

"Don't remember. Anatomy, maybe."

Corny? Sure. Pointless? Probably. But what was he meant to do? After all, he was there as Isobel's knight. And a knight had to stand up for his queen.

He sat back down. Looked at the two bearded men. They were cocky and arrogant, but if anyone had the right to think of themselves as cool, it was MSF doctors.

"The next round's on me," he said. "Now, tell me more about the legendary things you've done."

Chapter 41

Isobel knew something had happened at the bar, because Sebastien looked like he'd been punched in the gut, whereas Alexander simply sat down in his chair with an innocent look on his face. But Alexander was *never* innocent. Sebastien left the bar and approached the table with furious steps, and she assumed that whatever it was, it was about to escalate.

She had panicked when Sebastien turned up, and she sent a message to Alexander without thinking it through. But it felt unexpectedly good now, as though Sebastien really was as unimportant to her as she wanted him to be. A difficult and manipulative bastard, absolutely. But not the least bit important.

Isobel was so lost in her thoughts that she missed what was said between the two men. She heard terse phrases and then saw Sebastien place a heavy hand on Alexander's shoulder.

Oops, that was probably a mistake.

Alexander had frozen in his seat, and it was like watching a golden panther prepare to strike. Sebastien said something in an angry, low voice, and Alexander leaped up. It all happened so quickly that she would've missed it if she'd blinked. Alexander's fist shot out and Sebastien staggered backward. French phrases she didn't often hear began to stream from Sebastien's mouth. Alexander ignored him completely and grinned at her instead, as though he wanted praise. She shouldn't appreciate the fact that he was fighting, but you had to give Alexander credit—he only went for men who really had it coming.

"Isobel, I . . ." he started, but an enormous security guard turned up behind him and put a huge arm around his neck.

"Out," he bellowed.

Alexander rolled his eyes. "Sorry," he mimed over his shoulder, though he didn't look especially apologetic. It actually sounded like he was whistling. She stifled a laugh when she recognized the tune: "La Marseillaise," the French national anthem.

"That was interesting," Sven said slowly once Alexander had been escorted out.

"You okay, Sebastien?" Christian asked as he picked up the chair that had been knocked over when Alexander leaped up.

"He's a psychopath," said Sebastien. He pushed his hair back and rubbed his jaw.

Isobel's eyes moved between them. She got slowly to her feet, and then she did something she'd never done before. Something she had only ever seen in films. She took her beer, a full glass, and emptied it over Sebastien.

"*Va te faire voir, s'il te plaît,*" she said, sweeping her hair from her face. She ignored Sebastien's spluttering and hissing. "Night," she said to the others, who were staring open-mouthed at her, and left the restaurant.

Outside, she breathed in the cool night air.

"Hi, babe," she heard, and when she looked to one side, she saw Alexander standing with his hands in his pockets. He was looking at her.

"You get thrown out too?" he asked.

"Nah, but I guess it was just a matter of time," she said with a smile.

"What did you say to him?"

"Go to hell, please."

Alexander burst into laughter.

She grinned. She really was drunk. It skewed her judgment, and for now she liked the feeling. She'd certainly regret it tomorrow, but the whole point was that she didn't care about tomorrow. She opened her purse, took out her lip gloss, and touched up her makeup.

"What do you want to do now?" he asked, his eyes caressing her lips.

"Don't know. My plan for tonight was to sleep with them. But I'll have to reassess the situation."

"Is that so? All of them, or just a couple?"

"All of them. Apart from Sven. He's married. Actually, Christian's married too, now that I think about it. And I've already slept with Øystein."

Alexander raised an eyebrow.

"Not recently," she explained.

"I'm glad, I have to say."

"It wasn't the best plan, I realize that," she said as they started walking down Götgatan, toward Slussen and the Old Town. She giggled. He took her hand as they walked, held on tight.

"Øystein enjoyed stuff like feather sex."

His grip tightened. "Feather sex?"

"Yeah, you know. You lie there and touch each other with a feather for hours, to get close to the other person."

Alexander shook his head and his eyes watered with repressed laughter. He got such nice lines around his eyes when he laughed. It made him look more like a human and less like a perfect Grecian statue.

"I fell asleep in the middle of it. We broke up not long after that."

"I can kind of understand that. And Sebastien? What did you have planned for him?"

His voice sounded breezy, but Isobel knew it was an important question, not least for herself.

"I don't want anything to do with him. Nothing at all."

"Was that why you sent me a message?"

"I knew you'd come."

"How?"

Isobel stopped.

"Because just before I went out, I found out that the Medpax hospital in Chad had gotten a brand-new oxygen machine. A man who finds, buys, and manages to ship an oxygen machine to a pediatric hospital in Chad is someone you can rely on."

"I can be nice sometimes," he agreed.

"Yes, you can."

He pulled her close.

"But I can also be an ass. Sorry I left you the other night. It was just too much to think about. That's a crappy explanation, but I want to apologize anyway."

"I regretted saying anything. I've missed you these past few days."

"Not as much as I missed you."

He laid a hand on her cheek and kissed her. She leaned in to him and breathed him in. "I could even put up with some feather sex with you," she mumbled against his mouth.

He started to shake with laughter. "Shoot me if I ever suggest it. Should we go in here?"

They were outside the restaurant Gyldene Freden, a pale yellow building that had housed the same establishment for almost three hundred years. She nodded.

They got a table and Alexander ordered a bottle of champagne which Isobel suspected cost roughly a week's pay. She decided she didn't care.

"I want some cheese, too. Alcohol makes me hungry."

"Cheese," Alexander agreed.

In a dim corner of her mind, Isobel knew there were things she had done and would do tonight that she would regret tomorrow. Not least the fact she had drunk so much, she thought, as a waiter uncorked the bottle and poured the wine into tall glasses for them. But for now, it was still today, and today it was great to be giggly from champagne, to sit in a luxurious restaurant in the Old Town, to let herself be drawn to him again.

He reached for her hand over the table. "I thought a lot about what you said."

"That I'm messed up?"

"Messed-up people are the best kind."

"I see why you and Leila get on so well. She likes people who are messed up too."

He stroked her palm, ran his thumb along the lines, raised it to his mouth, kissed it. "What we did. I want another chance with you. Can I?"

She blinked.

"Okay," she said, wondering if this was one of the things she would regret tomorrow. That she had just said yes to more sex with Alexander.

Much later, they strolled home through the night. They walked through the whole of the Old Town, sauntered through the center and eventually made it down to Vasagatan. They stopped every ten meters or so to kiss, like teenagers without anywhere to go.

"Want to come up?" she asked outside her door.

But to her surprise he shook his head. "I'll call you tomorrow. And see you the next day."

"No," she protested unhappily. "I want to see you tomorrow."

"Mmm. Maybe you feel that way now. Can I ask—how is your tolerance to alcohol?"

"Pretty bad," she admitted.

"I thought so. I'm so attracted to you, and I want to do things right this time. I've been drinking. And so have you, a lot."

"I'm not sure I like this honorable side of you," she complained.

"I'm not sure I do either."

"So, speak tomorrow?"

"Absolutely. I'll call you." He looked at his watch. "In ten hours."

"And then we'll meet?"

He leaned forward, one arm on the wall above her, towering over her, and grabbed her waist and kissed her. She kissed him back until he groaned into her mouth. He drew in a ragged breath.

"*Then,* honey, we're going shopping, you and I. If we're doing this, we're going to do it right." He tilted his head and gave her a smoldering look. "Now get through that door before I forget I'm an honorable person."

Chapter 42

"My dad wants to meet you," Gina said, nervously biting the inside of her cheek. She was so unsure of how Peter would react to the request that she'd taken an eternity to say anything. But now they were almost there, and she had finally managed to spit out those difficult words. She had avoided all the questions at home for as long as she could, but that couldn't go on forever. This was tricky. She was a grown woman. Could a Swede understand how important her father's opinion was to her? They had such different customs, the Swedes; they identified first and foremost as individuals. In many respects, she was, of course, Swedish. But not in all. To her, family came first, and being an individual would always be subordinate to that.

"I guess he wants to see the man who's driving his daughter home," Peter said.

"I told him we were friends," Gina said. She gave him a quick look.

He nodded. "Okay."

What would her dad say if they met? Peter was much older than she. And her father hadn't looked happy when she'd told him about the man at work—one of her bosses—who drove her home.

She played with her purse. She had few, no, *zero* Swedish friends. She barely knew how to spend time with one, beyond the commonplace: work, studies, student bars.

If they stepped out of the car together, if Peter followed her up, into her world, everything would change.

She had never brought anyone home, not a friend, definitely not a boyfriend. Not that Peter was a boyfriend, she reminded herself, embarrassed. But what was their relationship, exactly? Could they even be friends? People always talked about differences being good, but no matter where Gina looked, she saw conformity. White people spent time with other white people, and the middle and upper class socialized with one another, enjoying cultural discussion and fine wines. And in Tensta, her home, you saw nothing but immigrants. Was there anywhere outside Peter's luxury car that their relationship could work? Was it wise to burst the bubble? What would happen when the world around them started to pay attention?

Peter pulled up in a parking lot, not outside her door.

"I'll come up with you," he said.

"Alright," she replied, her mouth immediately dry. She pulled at the safety belt. It wouldn't come loose. "I'm stuck," she said.

"Let me see." He leaned over her, his head grazing her breasts, and she froze, overwhelmed by a feeling she couldn't identify.

"There." He undid the belt. They looked at each other.

"Thanks," she said. *We should get out of the car,* she thought. Should stop staring at one another. She blinked slowly.

"Gina . . ." he began uncertainly.

She touched his cheek, felt his rough stubble and his warmth. He took a deep breath, unmoving, as though he had frozen. He didn't look happy, more uncertain.

He looked away.

"We should . . ." he said, and moved so her hand fell down. "You shouldn't . . ."

She swallowed. Didn't know what had come over her.

"Sorry," she said.

"Nothing to apologize for," he said as he opened his door and hurried out of the car. He came round to open her door. Gina stepped out, made a big deal of straightening her clothes, checking that her purse was closed. She hadn't meant anything, it was as if her hand had just moved by itself. She knew that if she raised her hand to her nose, the smell of his aftershave would be there.

"Are you coming up?" she eventually said, still embarrassed by his reaction. He must have thought it was totally improper.

Peter looked up at the tower block.

"Yeah," he said curtly.

*   *   *

Peter was silent in the worn elevator that carried them upward in the gray apartment building. His gaze wandered; he looked down at the tips of his shoes, ridiculously well polished and shining in the flickering strip light. He glanced up, could sense Gina's body warmth in the small space, but didn't dare look straight at her. The numbers on some of the buttons had rubbed off, and someone had sprayed paint over the mirror. What did it say about him as a person, that he'd never set foot in an elevator like this before?

He didn't know what to think about what had happened in the car. He ran a hand through his hair, sweating, wishing he was wearing anything other than a tailor-made suit.

He was going to meet her father, a man for whom Gina had a huge amount of respect. A man he desperately wanted to approve of him, even though he didn't quite know why.

"Gina . . ." he started, wanting to leave, to . . .

The elevator stopped, and the window of escape was gone.

"We're here," she said.

He waited behind her as she opened the door. She stepped to the side. He paused, but then went into the dark hallway. What was he doing? Why was he here, in this hallway, full of unfamiliar smells and other people's private lives?

"Dad?" Gina called. She sounded nervous and his own nervousness skyrocketed. "We have a visitor."

A well-built, slightly stooped man came toward them down the dark hallway.

"Dad?" Gina's nervous voice again. "This is Peter. From work, you know? He gave me a ride home. He does sometimes, like I told you. He wanted to come up and say hi."

Peter had never heard her babble like this. Nervous, slightly shrill. And she wasn't quite telling the truth. He wasn't the one who had wanted to come up. He would've been happy simply to drive away. Not starting to get complicated feelings, to be drawn into her family life. He fought a wave of panic and then found strength in the upbringing that had been drummed into him, more or less literally, since he was a child. He held out a hand and said, calmly and assertively, as though he was talking to a customer or an employee: "Good to meet you. Peter De la Grip."

Her father flicked a switch and the hall grew marginally brighter.

Peter could see posters and photographs on the walls. Mail and shoes and jackets in compartments and on hooks. A few closed doors and a kitchen at the far end of the hallway. That was all: It was a small apartment, would practically fit into his living room.

Dark, apprehensive eyes looked at him, steadily. Gina's father had a severe face. Gray hair. Slippers and a cardigan, but a presence filled with quiet strength. Just when Peter started to feel like an idiot, standing there with his hand outstretched, Gina's father reached out and took it.

"Ismail Adan," he said.

Peter managed not to jump, managed to hold back a grimace of pain, but the man's grip was like a stone crusher. This was a man who had fled war and terror, survived hardships Peter could never imagine. A man who had taken his two young children, left his homeland, and somehow made it here in one piece, to Sweden, a country that probably didn't always treat him too decently.

"Thank you for driving my daughter home so many times," he said, eventually letting go. He spoke with an accent, but grammatically his Swedish was perfect. Gina had talked about how hard he'd studied to learn the new language as an adult.

His dark eyes didn't leave Peter for a second, and Peter could feel himself being evaluated and judged; he had never felt so out of place in all of his life. Gina didn't know her father's age, but Peter guessed the man in front of him was younger than fifty in any case. That meant Peter was closer in age to Gina's father than he was to Gina. As though he needed more reasons to feel like a creep. Christ, what did this man think of him? He stood up straight, tried to look reliable, not like an older white man with dubious intentions.

"How is Amir?" Gina asked, breaking the deadlock.

"It's late," said her father. "Your brother needs help with his homework. There's food in the kitchen. Eat," he added before he left them by opening a door and disappearing into what seemed to be a small living room.

Gina bit her lip and gave Peter a slight smile. "He likes you," she said.

Peter almost burst out laughing, it was such a blatant lie.

"I noticed," he said, managing to not wipe sweat from his fore-head.

But he had done it. He had met Gina's father and survived.

"I'll go down with you," she said.

They were standing in front of the elevator when she said quietly, "Can I ask you something?"

Peter nodded and held the elevator door open for her.

"You can say if you don't want to talk about it."

"Ask whatever you like."

"What you did last summer. To your family. To your business? Why did you vote against your father at the shareholders' meeting? It felt like you sabotaged your life completely. You could have taken over after him if your family still held control, couldn't you? I'm sorry, but I just don't understand."

He was silent. Had had a feeling the question might come up, felt dread.

"It had to do with something that happened when I was young," he eventually said.

She was dressed in a thin, striped cardigan, and pulled it tight around her against the cold wind. "What?"

"Do you ever feel afraid of me?" he asked quietly. "When it's just the two of us, I mean."

She shook her head. "No, not at all."

"Maybe you should."

An uncertain expression passed over her face. "It can't be that bad, can it?"

It could. And it was.

"I raped a girl when I was young," he said, bracing himself.

Gina put a hand to her mouth.

That's it, it's over now, he thought with the deepest sense of re-gret he'd ever felt.

She stared at him from behind her hand, and he hated the fear he could see deep in her eyes. It seemed as though she had taken a step back, but maybe it was his imagination.

"What I did last summer, it was a way of putting things right." How much should he explain? That he had sunk the family business through his vote as a way to atone for things his father had done. Things *he* had done. Horrible things. Unspeakable things.

"And did it?" she asked. "Put things right?"

"I thought so, for a while. The girl I hurt . . . she forgave me. We don't have any direct contact, but we do bump into one another from time to time."

Gina didn't say a thing. He continued.

"And what I'm telling you now, it needs to stay between us."

Her breathing was shallow. He could see she was fighting shock, and he was waiting for her to turn on her heel and run.

"Alright," she eventually said.

"It was David Hammar's little sister."

She frowned as if to try to make sense of it. "Carolina?"

"It was a long time ago, when we were young. It was at school. I went to a boarding school." It was a good school. Famous for fostering leaders and educating the elite. And also infamous for its hazing. He wished he could say he had taken no part. But he had. First he had been bullied. Then he had become the bully. David Hammar had been at the school. On a scholarship. A poor and working-class boy. With a single mom. And a young sister. Peter ran a hand across his face. Christ, this was hard.

"Carolina was fifteen. Some friends and I went to her house. The night ended with her being raped and badly abused. By us. By me. My father hushed it all up. I thought that she'd died, and I lived with that guilt for years, more than half my life, until I found out she wasn't dead at all." His entire life summed up in a few sentences.

"I don't know what to say," she whispered. He didn't blame her.

"I raped a young girl. But there is more."

"More?"

"Yes. David, her brother, tried to bring charges. We beat him, threatened him. It was all hushed up, too. Also by my father. I'm not trying to share the blame. I take full responsibility for what I did. But it explains why I voted against my dad and for David. I wanted to do something to atone for my deeds."

"But why did you do it?"

"The rape? I really wish I had a good answer. I've never been a strong person, I guess. I was weak. And angry—at my dad. At everyone that seemed happy. That's not an excuse, because there is no excuse for it, but when I try to understand what happened, those are the two things that come up. But I don't expect you to understand. Because it is beyond understanding." Beyond forgiveness.

"How old were you?"

He thought back to that fall. His memories of that evening were vague, with only occasional clear moments. "I wish I could say I was a kid, but I'd just turned eighteen." Carolina was just a small, young girl. Brutalized by a group of teenage boys. He still couldn't think about it without wanting to die.

"That's awful."

"Beyond awful. So, anyway, that's why I voted for Hammar Capital and their takeover last summer. Because it gave me a chance to somehow, in some small way, atone for what I did to Carolina and her family. My father has refused to speak to me since, but I still think it was the right decision." He had lost his wife, his position, his mansion. He had often wished there were more he could do or lose, because somehow it just wasn't enough. Well, it looked like his prayers were going to be answered, because now he would lose Gina.

Gina looked at him as though he were a stranger, and he thought to himself that this was just the price he had to pay, over and over again, for what he'd done. He knew he deserved it, but it hurt so much that he suddenly started to have trouble continuing the conversation. He almost wished Gina would run away so that he could go home and just give up for good.

"How is she? Carolina?"

"She's actually really well. She's engaged. You can't ever get over something like that, I know that. But she really seems to have left it behind her." In the midst of so much that was unbearable, that was a comfort. That Carolina Hammar seemed genuinely happy.

"Unlike you?"

"I guess."

He wished he hadn't stayed, hadn't gone up with her. Then the question might not have come up just yet. Family was so important to Gina, it was natural for her to wonder about the relationships in his life. He just wished it hadn't happened yet.

"Gina, I can see that you're shocked. You can ask me whatever you want. How do you feel about what I said? I understand if you . . ."

He fell silent, couldn't bear to say the words. That he knew she wouldn't want anything more to do with him.

She frowned and worried her lower lip. She dragged the toe of her shoe on the asphalt.

"Rape is a terrible thing. I feel shocked, of course, like you said." She fell silent. She still avoided looking at him. "And I'm so sorry. It's a dreadful story. Poor, poor Carolina." More silence. Peter's hands were sweating, the lump in his throat almost impossible to swallow.

"You know, in my country . . . things you could barely imagine here in Sweden happen," she continued, finally looking up to meet his gaze. Her eyes were impossible to read. But she didn't look as shocked anymore, just endlessly sad. "So many women's lives are ruined. By rape. Abuse. Mutilation."

"Yes," he said, swallowing and swallowing. He had ruined Carolina's life. He knew that.

"But Peter, I also know that you can get over it, just like you can get over any other violent crime. Do you know if Carolina got help?"

"She saw a therapist. She said she was well. That she's left it all behind her. And her brother does everything he can for her. He dotes on her."

"I've met David Hammar. He's, uh . . . impressive."

Despite the mood, Peter cracked a laugh. Understatement of the century.

"I wish I could go back and undo it all," he said.

"But you can't. No one can."

"No."

"Sorry I brought it up. It must be hard to talk about."

"I assume there'll be consequences."

"For what?"

"Us."

"Yeah, I guess so. I probably need to do some thinking."

"I understand," he said, his hope crumbling. He understood her.

She pulled her cardigan more tightly around her. "I have to go."

"Of course."

"Good night."

He wanted to reach out, say something to stop whatever it was they had from falling apart. But there was nothing, so he made do with a quiet, "Good night, Gina."

Chapter 43

"What are you doing?" Alexander asked.

"Not much," Isobel replied. She wiggled her toes on the couch. She had worked a few hours that morning, on the follow-up paperwork from her trip. Then she had surfed the Internet, waiting for him to call.

"Do you feel better today?"

"Much. I'm never drinking again." Her hangover yesterday had been epic.

He laughed. "What are you wearing?"

She looked down at her favorite comfortable clothes. Gray and shapeless. "I'm naked," she lied.

"Get dressed. I'll pick you up in an hour. We're going shopping."

Alexander was already outside when she went down exactly an hour later. He looked self-confident and almost radiant. Isobel felt herself being drawn into his wicked eyes. Never again would she think that blue eyes were sweet and innocent; his were thrilling like a bottomless ocean or an infinite space.

"Where are we going?" she asked, thankful for how cool and sophisticated she managed to sound.

"What kind of a question is that?" he said as he took her hand, sending a thrill through her arm, and they headed off toward the city center. "To a sex store, of course."

They took a shortcut across Norra Bantorget, found Drottninggatan, and when they got to the store, Isobel's heart was pounding so hard she had trouble concentrating. She squeezed Alexander's hand. She had been to some of the most dangerous places on earth, seen people die, saved lives; but going into a store that sold sex toys scared the life out of her. Alexander, on the other hand, seemed completely at ease. She peered around the place; it was bright and almost fluffy. Pink, white, and feminine. She studied a shelf full of feathers of varying kinds and gave Alexander an accusing look.

He winked.

"We'd like to look at some whips, stuff like that," he said nonchalantly to the sales assistant.

Isobel looked down at her feet and understood, for the first time in her life, the appeal of being swallowed up by the earth.

They followed the sales assistant, Isobel with her eyes fixed on the floor. *Oh. My. God.* Kill me now.

"You can look up now," Alexander said, sounding amused. "She's gone. What do you think?"

Isobel peered up. They were alone, she noticed, relieved. They were halfway down a staircase, and in this part of the shop the colors were darker. She saw rows of whips, ropes, and blindfolds. Shelf after shelf of dildos, in all colors and sizes. Leather corsets on hangers and expensive underwear made from silk, patent leather, and lace. Boxes and packages of things she didn't even recognize. Equal parts excitement and fear pulsed through her. "I don't know if I . . ."

"Want to leave?"

She rubbed her ear. Her eyes flitted over a set of white handcuffs. Thick, white leather. Matt gold clasps. They looked more like wide leather bracelets than handcuffs.

She shook her head, feeling as if she were baring her soul.

"You like these?" He picked up the cuffs. Oh, but she *loved* them. "What about these?" Alexander held up what looked like small, silver clothes pegs. Aha, nipple clamps. She firmly shook her head. She had sensitive nipples.

Alexander put them down and picked up a small purple dildo. Butt plug, she read on the packaging. She shook her head. Not yet, anyway, she thought. Probably never.

Once she managed to overcome her nerves, they started to work their way through the more decadent shelves. Alexander was curious and calm, and she found herself relaxing. Most of the things in this section made her own inclinations seem utterly tame, she reflected, as she studied a dog collar and matching leash.

Eventually, they had a basket full of things that made Isobel's pulse run quicker. She had said no to the long riding whips but nodded an embarrassed yes to a soft nine-tailed whip made of the same white leather as the cuffs, plus a white paddle. Alexander paid, refused to even talk about sharing the cost, and when she saw the price tag on the crystal-covered vibrator in a luxuriously lined box, she gave in.

"Are you nervous?" he asked when they stepped out of the taxi and headed into his apartment.

"A little." Or a lot.

"I need to fix a few things," he said. "Why don't you get something to drink in the kitchen? I'll meet you in the living room in a minute."

She did as he said, went into the luxurious kitchen and poured a glass of water, and then took it with her into the living room, where it stood untouched on a side table as she waited on the couch.

He came back, sat down next to her, and kissed her on the neck. She took an uncertain breath, had trouble relaxing. It was still afternoon, and light poured into the apartment. Shouldn't they go to the bedroom? Or at least close the drapes?

"Isobel? What is it?"

"I don't know what I've started."

"What are you afraid of?"

"Being disappointed, I guess," she said. So many times, the sex had been good to start with but ended with her lying uncomfortably, her toes freezing, worrying more about her partner's enjoyment than her own.

"I'm going to ask you to trust me now. Okay?"

She nodded.

"Thanks. The first thing you're going to do is tell me what you expect from this."

Come on. *Talking* about it was even worse. "I don't know if I can do this."

"Talk? Sure you can."

"I think it's just a fun, one-time thing for you." She tried to be as honest as she could. "It'll start well but end like it always does. I'll have to choose between faking it or disappointing you."

"So it's not just your own disappointment? You're worried I'll be disappointed?"

"Well, yeah."

"Are my feelings your responsibility?"

She shook her head.

"You're so used to taking responsibility for everyone and everything," he said quietly. "I'm a grown man, Isobel. I'm responsible for myself. The only thing you need to do is tell me if anything feels wrong."

Was Alexander right? Did she try to control everyone and everything?

"Now I want you to tell me what to do."

She frowned, annoyed. The whole point was that she wouldn't have to take charge of things. Didn't he get that?

"I want you to decide," she said, frustrated.

Alexander put a hand on her leg. She practically jumped. His hand moved to the inside of her thigh, and he caressed her, pulled up her dress and pushed her legs apart. Not roughly, but definitely firmly. She held her breath.

"I know. But you have to take part and decide where we're headed. What do you want? Should I tie you up?" He pushed her legs farther apart.

She panted.

"Isobel?"

"Yeah?" she replied, stifled.

"Is this hard for you?"

"A little."

His hand worked its way in, beneath her short dress, and she automatically spread her legs farther. His thumb gently grazed her panties.

"You're wet," he said.

She was breathing heavily now. How could she ever have thought Alexander was boyish? This was a man commanding her body. But he didn't frighten her. Not in the slightest.

He took her hand.

"Get up."

She had always had a weakness for dominant men with self-confident voices. She just hadn't realized how powerful Alexander's was, how he could turn her on with nothing but his words.

"Close your eyes," he commanded.

She complied, held his hand tightly, and allowed herself to be led out of the living room, down the hall. She heard a door open.

"You can look now," he said quietly. She opened her eyes, blinked, waited for them to adjust.

They were in the doorway to his room. But what had been a modern bedroom with a cosmopolitan, hotel feel to it had been transformed into something more like an erotic fantasy. He had switched out the bed. Before, he'd had one of those modern headboards, fabric-covered and soft. In its place today was an enormous iron bed. No covers, just the sheets and pillows on the bed, and more pillows on the floor. At the end of it was a chest. On it were displayed all of the things they had bought. The white leather cuffs. The paddle. The dildo, bottles of oil, ropes, and a silk ribbon.

She looked at him, swallowed hard.

He gently pushed her into the room.

"Take off your dress," he said, calmly but with authority.

She paused at first, but then unbuttoned it and let it fall to the floor. She made an attempt to step out of it, but he shook his head. His eyes moved slowly over her.

"No. Stay there, but take off your bra."

He watched as she unclasped it and dropped it to the floor.

"Now, get onto your knees. Your hands behind your back."

She blinked quickly, glancing at his face. *Are you serious?*

He looked back, calm, confident in himself and his order. He nodded encouragingly toward the floor. "Down."

She sank to her knees, not entirely gracefully. But the rug was soft as lambswool against her knees, as though he'd laid it there just for her. She found her balance, couldn't help but suck in her stomach. Light poured into the room, and she squinted toward it.

"Hands."

Obediently she put her hands behind her back. It should feel wrong, but it didn't.

Alexander crossed the room. Closed the drapes. They were thick and heavy, and blocked out the light, throwing the room into forgiving half-darkness. He lit a match and started to light the candles, lots of them, all different sizes. She was still on her knees on the soft rug, her hands interlocked behind her back, peering at the different things he had laid out. In the store, both the nine-tailed whip and the little paddle had seemed harmless. But now they suddenly seemed much more serious. He came over to her, pushed a strand of hair from her face. "Are you comfortable?" he asked in a low voice.

She nodded into his hand. He ran a finger over her cheek. She swallowed, turned her face toward his palm, closed her eyes, and breathed him in. He smelled clean, was freshly shaven, and she loved that he had done that for her.

Alexander started to unbuckle his belt, pulled it out of the loops on his pants. It was a new leather belt, still glossy, and from her kneeling position Isobel followed the movement with a wary eye. He took it in one hand, wrapped it around the other. She held her breath, felt an unwelcome wave of fear.

"*Shhh,*" he said, as he moved round her. She heard him bend down, felt him wrap the belt around her wrists, several loops. He breathed onto her back and kissed her shoulder blades as he pulled on the belt, firmly but not painfully tight.

"I'm going to give you a safe word. Do you know what that is?"

A word that would make him stop if it all got too much for her.

"If you say *Paris,* I'll stop immediately, no matter what I'm doing. Okay?"

She looked up at him. His eyes were warm, and there was no uncertainty in them. She couldn't believe she had ever worried he wouldn't be able to take command of her. He was a natural. He had taken complete control.

"It suits you, standing there like that."

His index finger ran over her lower lip. With a thumb on her chin, he opened her mouth. She panted.

"You're pretty on your knees, Isobel. Will you do what I tell you?"

She nodded.

He undressed and stood naked in front of her, a gorgeous male specimen. His erection, thick and hard, strained toward his flat stomach. He wrapped his fist around it and moved toward her. She opened her mouth again, and took him in, had time to taste the tiny, salty droplet on the tip of him before he began to move, slowly. She had always liked this kind of sex. It was an intimate act, and maybe it spoke to this side of her, she thought, as she closed her eyes, let him make love to her mouth, sucked him. Alexander stroked her hair to one side, pulled out, stopped her movements. She gave him a questioning look.

"I want you to look up at me as you suck."

His voice was hoarse but firm.

"But . . ." she protested, not liking this command. It was difficult enough with her hands tied behind her back. Plus, it would break her concentration. She liked being bound, having his dick in her mouth; but gazing into his eyes . . . It made her feel awkward. And maybe a little vulnerable, off balance.

"Isobel . . ." he commanded, gathering her hair in one fist, pulling her head back, not hard, but with enough force to remind her of her role in the game they were playing. Their eyes met; his were kind but very determined. Reluctantly she nodded, feeling some odd excitement building inside her. He gripped his erection, guided it toward her again. Compliantly she opened her mouth, almost as by reflex, and took him again, reveling in the salty, warm taste of him. He was a big man and he wasn't too gentle, and it was difficult at first. She had never understood the point of looking each other deep in the eyes during sex. But his eyes never left hers; they were hooded and his chest was heaving. She heard herself panting, could only imagine what she must look like, on her knees, tied, her nipples hardening almost painfully, her juices trickling down her inner thighs, her hair mussed from his hands. She sucked him harder, took him as deep as she could, and after a while it was as if they had connected somehow, as though they were communicating wordlessly.

"That's right," he said, his voice tight, guiding her with his hand in her hair, alternating between being rough and gentle. It was incredibly exciting, adding a whole new layer to sex. With Sebastien she had freaked out, he had scared her. But being manhandled and mastered by Alexander whom she trusted—it was insanely arousing.

He pulled out of her mouth. Let his finger trail her lips. "Sexy Isobel," he murmured, tucking her hair behind her ear. She shouldn't get so excited by this, by standing on her knees, horny and helpless, but she was—more excited than she'd ever been.

"Get up now," he said gently, and put a hand on her upper arm to help her up. He carefully loosened the belt, took her hands, and kissed her fingertips one after one. A wave of disappointment rushed over her. She had hoped for more.

She heard him chuckle behind her, as if he had read her mind, and then he pushed her toward the bed. "Lie down," he said. "On your stomach. Your hands by the headboard."

She got up onto the bed on all fours, pulse racing again.

"Wait," he said. "Stop there, I want to watch." She obeyed and paused on all fours while he moved around the bed. She heard him moving things around but didn't dare look. On one hand she felt incredibly conscious of herself, of her body. On the other hand, she loved being a little degraded like this, ordered around by him. She felt his forefinger sliding in under the fabric of her panties, tracing the seam of her damp lips, and couldn't hold back a moan.

"I love how you get wet for me," he said. "I want you to fuck my finger."

She swallowed hard, but then she started to move against his finger, feeling an almost painful sensation of excitement, feeling the orgasm build up. She moved faster.

"Good girl," he said, and his finger withdrew. "You can lie down now."

She let out her breath, frustrated, she had been so near. But she did as she was told. The sheet was cool and smelled clean. She stretched out her arms and lay still while he picked up the white leather cuffs. He fastened her wrists to the metal railings. They had a snug fit. Her arms were outstretched, leaving her helpless and exposed.

"Comfortable?" he asked. She could hear him move around the room.

"Yes," she replied, knowing she trusted him.

"I'm going to begin by giving you ten raps. Can you cope with ten?"

She blinked into the sheet. *How the hell should I know?*

"Isobel?"

"Yes," she replied.

And then she felt his hands on her body. He kissed her back, her buttocks, and then, before she had started to buck under his administrations, he pulled off her panties with a quick, fluid motion. His hand moved between her legs, and she gasped, eagerly spreading her thighs for him. It was as though something happened in her brain whenever he took control like this; she wanted to be commanded, to be made to please, to serve.

His hands left her body and she almost whimpered, wanting them on her, inside her. "I'm behind you now," he said.

She wasn't afraid. Or maybe just a little. She had been very afraid with Sebastien, but it had been a bad kind of fear. This was a good one. One she knew she had control over.

"Ready?" He asked, dragging the whip over her skin. A shiver ran through her. This was really about to happen. Was she actually letting him do this?

The whip traced her skin. And then it disappeared.

"I'm going to whip you now." She pulled at her restraints, and then the whip struck right over her ass. She didn't know what she had expected. Maybe that he would be careful, play with the whip a little, but still be gentle. But the lash was hard. She heard the crack, and she gasped with pain, but then the next came, and now it really hurt. *Mon Dieu.*

"Breathe, Isobel," he told her.

She took a deep breath. Exhaled. The next lash was even harder, and she pulled on the cuffs.

Crack!

This time, it was slightly gentler, and she let out a shaky breath. Maybe the worst was over after all.

Smack! She yelled.

He was still behind her, and she knew he was waiting for her to ask him to stop. But she didn't want to, so she held her tongue. Breathed in and out, felt the excitement flooding her, could picture herself bound, exposed, being whipped, and panting at the fantasy. The next time was harder again. It still hurt like hell, but now another sensation was approaching, a warmth spreading through her, not just over her ass but through her hips, thighs, to her stomach. She squirmed against the sheet, pressed down into it, wanted to touch herself, wanted to come . . . she couldn't think.

"No," he said, and his voice was commanding. "Lie still."

She groaned in protest but obeyed. Waited.

He gave her another three lashes. They hurt too, but now the pain had definitely crossed over to enjoyment, endorphins taking over, making the pain morph into an excitement beyond anything she'd experienced before, a dark, carnal pleasure sending her nearer and nearer to an orgasm.

She started to shake.

Crack.

She *couldn't* lie still. It felt as if she were about to melt, to come apart. She pulled on the cuffs and felt the last blow. It was hard, much harder than the others, but she could take it, could transform the pain into something she had no words for. This was what she had fantasized about, *this* . . . And then Alexander was next to her. Roughly he pushed a hand between her and the bed, rubbed frantically, and she came so quickly that she barely had time to keep up, just bucked against his hand, came until her vision blurred. The pleasure was so intense, the breath caught in her throat. She panted into the mattress, couldn't speak, couldn't think. He was on top of her now, his weight on strong arms to either side of her, and he shoved her thighs apart and entered her with hard, deep thrusts as she lay there, still tied up on his bed.

He pushed a hand in, beneath her again.

"Please, no more," she begged hoarsely.

But he kept going, touched her gently as he continued to move inside her. He bit her neck, nibbled at the nape of it, and she shook from head to toe. Her arms were numb, and her hair was in sweaty wisps around her face when Alexander slipped out of her and finally loosened the cuffs. Relieved, she pulled her arms in as he flipped her onto her back. She watched him pull off the condom and wrap it in tissue before he pushed her hair from her face and looked at her.

"Are you okay?" he asked.

"Yeah. But I don't think I can talk."

"You're so goddamn sexy." He kissed her breast. "I mean, I've thought you were sexy since the first time I saw you," he mumbled between kisses. "But seriously, this was the most erotic experience of my life. You're perfect; the softest, sexiest woman I've ever known."

He rested on one arm and took a nipple in his mouth, dragged his tongue over it. She pressed into him. "It was completely incredible," he continued, running his fingers along the inside of her thighs. He moved up, closed her mouth in a ravenous kiss.

His hand moved between her legs once more.

"You're going to come again, Isobel," he said.

She wanted to protest, tell him it had never happened before, that it was her medical opinion that multiple orgasms were a myth, but then he did something with those fantastic fingers of his, whispered what he planned to do to her, and his hands, his voice, and the feeling of him as he moved inside her was electric, intoxicating. His fingers were firm, his tongue hot, and she bucked against him, felt another orgasm exploding in mindless waves. As she shook and whimpered beneath him, her body tightening in delicious spasms, he twisted his fist in her hair, pumped himself, and came too, hard and jerky, and a satisfied sound rumbled from his chest before he collapsed. They lay there in a panting, sweaty heap. She ran her hands over his back, enjoyed the feeling of his muscles beneath her fingers, the sound of him breathing against her neck, the feeling of his powerfully pumping heart slowing down.

Eventually, he rolled off her and onto the mattress.

"How do you do that?" she asked as she watched him pull off yet another condom. "I never see you put it on."

He didn't reply, simply stretched out an arm and pulled her close to him.

"How are you?" he asked after a moment. Always this concern for her. She needed to be careful with her heart; this was a man who would have no trouble ripping it in two. When had anyone shown such consideration for her? Strong, smart Isobel, she'll be fine. You can always rely on Isobel. Isobel will figure everything out. She hadn't realized just how much she longed to be taken care of, to be able to rely on someone else being there for her.

"Good," she replied.

He propped himself up on one elbow and studied her face. Took her wrist, turned it over. "You have marks. Was it too hard? Why didn't you say anything?"

Embarrassed, she pulled her hand away from him. There had been such a difference with Alexander. With Sebastien, she had been scared. But with Alexander . . . She *wanted* what he did to leave marks. Wanted to be branded by his fingers and whipping, knowing it was crazy but wanting it still. "I liked it."

"Wait here, I'll be back in a minute," he said, and got up from the bed. When he came back, Isobel felt something soft on top of her, a blanket that was as light as a cloud, as soft as sunshine.

"Here," he said. "Drink."

She drank the water, cold and bubbly, and let him tuck her in, stroke her hair. She crept into his arms. Allowed him to stroke her back and her shoulders. To kiss and hug and rock her.

That was the last thing Isobel remembered before she dropped off to sleep.

Chapter 44

Alexander lay awake, listening to the sound of Isobel's breathing. It was a little past eight in the evening, so he doubted she had gone to sleep for the night. Outside, it was light, the blackbirds still singing. He twisted a lock of her hair around his index finger. Kissed her forehead, smelled her skin. She stretched, exhaled, a long, satisfied sigh, and he smiled. Out in the real world, she was one of the most competent, self-assured, and driven women he'd ever met. And here, in his bed, she was still all of that. But she was also a woman who enjoyed playing the submissive and who dared do it with him. Maybe he shouldn't feel like a king, but he did. That was just how things were when you had the best sex of your life. He heard her breathing change, felt her shift. She had woken up. Her stomach growled.

"Hungry?" he whispered.

"Starving." She yawned.

"Are you sore?"

She turned her head to him and gave him a slow smile. "Yes. And I love it. I'm good."

"Sure?" He couldn't shake the feeling that he'd crossed some kind of line, that he'd done something wrong.

"One hundred ten percent. But I like that you're so nice."

"I'm not so nice."

"To me you are."

"Didn't I just tie you up and whip you?"

"Yeah, and I hope you'll do it again." She sat up, her weight on one elbow, and stroked his forehead, a finger tracing his eyebrow.

"Did you know that there's no objective pain? That pain is always subjective?"

"You know the most interesting things." He took her finger and kissed the tip. Had a woman ever tasted or smelled so good?

"How did it feel?" she asked. "You said it was complicated for you."

"There are so many things you shouldn't feel, shouldn't like. I liked what we did, so damn much. It was kind of scary, to realize that about myself."

But he had enjoyed it. A dark and primitive side of himself that he'd never been aware of.

"It's the same for me," Isobel said with a frown. "I don't know how many times I've heard or read that it's wrong, that it's a deviation, a disturbance, a childhood trauma. In the end, you start to believe it. That there's something wrong with you, that you are fundamentally *bad*."

"So you're right up there with pedophiles, murderers, and rapists, is that what you're saying?"

"Maybe not when you put it like that. But as a woman, you're *meant* to like certain things and stay away from others. It's hard to exist outside those lines. You feel so vulnerable when you deviate. And ashamed."

"You're ashamed of what we did?"

"No. I've made up my mind not to be. It has nothing to do with anyone except you and me." She fell silent. "But, Alexander?"

"Yeah?"

"Can I please have some food before I pass out?"

Alexander nodded, stole a kiss, took a quick shower, pulled on some clothes, and sent Isobel into the bathroom while he got to work in the kitchen.

"There are towels, and I put a robe in there," he shouted as he started to take pots and pans from the cupboards.

When Isobel came back out into the kitchen, her hair was damp. She tied the belt in a huge bow around her man's silk robe. She was a tall, curvy woman, but still, she was drowning in it. He peeled a carrot and handed it to her.

"So you don't starve to death."

"This is like some film cliché," she said, satisfied, as she crunched on the carrot and peered around the kitchen. She leaned back against the counter. "Hot guy nonchalantly cooking food in a super-stylish kitchen."

"Doesn't that normally end with the pretty girl being pushed up against the kitchen island and getting spanked?"

"Not often enough, if you ask me."

He laughed. He loved this playful side of her. This was Isobel Sørensen when she felt safe. Giggly and a little goofy. And pretty goddamn sexy.

He put down the pan, went over to her, grabbed her neck, and kissed her until, with a whimper, she wrapped her legs around him. He put a hand on her thigh. She wasn't one of those women obsessed with working out, and he liked the softness there.

"Did you know you have the world's softest skin?" he mumbled into her neck.

He could just see it, how he would turn her around, lean her forward over the island, pull up her robe, and push himself into her welcoming warmth. Could already imagine her faint panting as he filled her when he suddenly heard a sound from the stove that made him turn around. The water for the pasta was bubbling violently.

"Food first," he said.

He rinsed some small tomatoes in a colander, took out a tub of pale yellow mozzarella, grabbed some fresh basil, and began to hunt for honey and garlic.

"That really does smell amazing," she said, sniffing the air.

Alexander filled two bowls with pasta, sauce, and a generous amount of parmesan, and Isobel poured an Italian wine into simple, everyday glasses. They toasted and started in on the pasta.

"You weren't kidding, you really can cook. Is there anything you can't do?"

He twisted the pasta around his fork. "I can't save lives. I can't run a hospital in the middle of nowhere. Don't make me into something I'm not, Isobel."

"You're pretty okay in the bedroom, too," she said lightly.

"I'll have to work harder then. The way you sounded, I'd hoped you would think I was more than okay."

"I'm a complete freak, so maybe I'm not the best person to judge it. But I think you're phenomenal."

"You're not a freak, far from it." He topped up her wineglass.

"If you knew how often I've been told there's something wrong with me because I can't come like"—she gestured in the air, making quotation marks with her fingers—"'normal women.'"

"You're a doctor. Surely you took an anatomy class? Has it never occurred to you that women are not built all the same? You aren't the one with the problem, you've just been with idiots. Insecure men. Lucky you met me so we could get it right."

"It still feels weird that I like it," she said as she sipped her wine. "That it's such a turn-on to be submissive."

"You're missing the point."

"Which is?"

"That I *like* your weirdness. Christ, I've never had such amazing sex in my life."

"Me neither." She stretched out her legs in front of her—long legs, pale skin, freckles, perfect feet. He would tie those legs wide apart, he promised himself. Lick her.

"How did you learn to make pasta like this?" she asked.

"My best friend is an Italian chef, you know. It's his recipe."

"I guess I'm not the first woman you've seduced with your food," she said with a laugh.

He didn't reply, didn't want to think about how right she was.

"When are you going back to New York?" she asked, starting to eat again. "I mean, you live there, don't you?"

"I don't know. My real home is there, and most of my friends." He shook his head. "I need to think a little."

Alexander played with his glass, wanted to explain that he had never, ever thought of settling down anywhere, with anyone, and that this had all moved so fast, he didn't know what he felt.

"Alex, don't worry." Isobel's voice was unfazed. He saw no disappointment in her eyes, and that should have been a relief. They could have unbelievably incredible sex without immediately having to talk about the future.

Fuck.

He stood up abruptly.

"Want any more?" he asked, eyeing her near-empty bowl.

She shook her head. "No, thanks. But it was really great."

"Thanks," he said. He felt like the world's biggest idiot for ruining the mood, didn't know what had come over him.

Isobel gave him an uncertain look and then glanced up at the clock. "God, it's late. Maybe I should go."

He put the bowls in the sink. Dried his hands and went back over to her. He crouched down, his hands on her legs. "Sorry I was so awkward. I suck at this kind of thing. And I don't know what I want in the future. This . . . it all happened so quickly and it's been pretty confusing."

"Yes," she said, tenderly running an index finger along his nose.

"I want you to stay. Don't go, please?"

She leaned forward and kissed the corner of his mouth. "You're right, it's sexy when someone is on their knees in front of you. I'd love to stay. Can we just ignore all the pressure and see what happens, how things play out?"

Her words were like an echo of the things Alexander himself had said, countless times to countless women. He just hadn't realized how uncomfortable it was to be on the receiving end of that cliché.

But he was an expert at ignoring complicated feelings, and so he smiled, ran his hands up her thighs, and asked, "Couch?"

"But if your dad was Danish and your mom is French, how did they meet?"

Alexander studied Isobel. She was curled up on his couch, her wineglass clasped in both hands. He had switched to water, and the atmosphere between them was easygoing again. They had talked, given one another long looks, touched one another. He wanted her again. And again. And again. But there was no rush. He loved to watch her as she talked, to catch a glimpse of a voluptuous breast whenever the smooth silk slipped open, to watch her push her hair from her face when it fell down for the twelfth time, to watch her slender fingers move in the air when she explained something.

"At a cocktail party in Casablanca. Have you been there?"

He nodded. He had dated a TV anchorwoman there. Learned to speak Arabic and improved his French. Among other things. Not that he planned on telling Isobel any of that. "Did they travel a lot, your parents?" he asked instead, remembering the photos of beautiful Blanche and her somber military husband in different countries and continents. Cocktail parties. Mingling with ambassadors. Premieres. Preoccupied with their own lives.

"I lived with my grandmother from a really young age. She chose to stay home with me so Mom could focus on building up Medpax in Paris. I was in Sweden, and Mom came back whenever she could. Dad turned up too, sometimes." She fell silent.

So much to read between the lines. "No surprise you like to be dominated, then," he said breezily.

She snorted. "What do you mean?"

"You know, all these impossible expectations you've had to live up to. World saviors as parents. Heroism. Even *you* need an outlet somewhere, otherwise you'd be unbearably virtuous."

"I'm not virtuous," she protested.

"I *know*. I still can't believe the best sex I ever had was with a kinky idealist. It goes against everything I've ever believed in."

"Does it bother you?"

"Nope, apparently I like kink."

She gave him a gentle slap on the arm. "Not that, idiot. That I'm an idealist."

"It doesn't bother me, but I don't understand it."

She rested her chin in her hand. "Didn't you have expectations on you? Your family must have plenty of traditions. How was it, growing up?"

"Yeah, well, I guess I chose the opposite path," he said. "I've spent my entire life provoking my parents."

"So we're both ultimately ruled by what our parents think of us?"

"I wish it wasn't true," he said, but he knew she was right. Maybe it was time to grow up and stop making decisions based on what would annoy his father most? Start to think about what *he* wanted from life?

She smiled and twirled the glass in her hand. "Maybe that's why you like to spank women," she said.

"Not women. You."

He received yet another smile in reply, and he knew he would never be able to top this. From now on, he would always be looking to re-create what he'd had with Isobel. And he would fail.

He studied her, saw her eyes glitter. But those worries belonged to the future. Right now she was his, and he planned on exploring and satisfying every need she had.

He took the glass from her hand and put it on the coffee table. "Lie down."

She ran a finger across her mouth; he could see her natural pride battling her desire.

He made a commanding gesture toward the couch.

"On your back."

Her desire won out, just as he'd known it would. Isobel sank down.

"Open your robe."

She obeyed. He leaned forward and ran his thumb over her red curls, traced the slit. She shuddered beneath his touch.

"Put your arms above your head."

She obeyed him again. He placed a hand on one of her ankles. He liked this, pushing and spurring her to go further and further. Slowly, he pulled her long legs apart. The couch was one of the widest models from Svenskt Tenn, the famous interior design company, and she had plenty of room. He put a hand on each leg and kissed his way up them before he looked up at the moist, pink folds so enticingly exposed. Her skin was warm, her breathing shallow, catching in her throat in small pants. He leaned forward and parted her with his fingers, started to lick her. She gasped and sighed beneath his mouth and tongue. But he knew, from the intuition he had developed when it came to Isobel, that this wasn't enough for her. And so he stood up, moved her arms so they were parallel to her body, straddled her, and put his knees on either side of her, trapping her arms by her sides. He looked around, going on a feeling. He really wanted to tie her up, but there was nothing in his living room but upholstered, modern furniture; there was nothing he could use. Jesus, he hadn't realized how complicated this kind of thing could be.

"Stay there like that," he said, and got up.

He fetched the rope they had bought, smooth red nylon, and tied her legs wide apart; he bound one ankle first, and then looped the rope around the base of the couch to repeat the procedure with the other. And then he was on top of her again. Her breathing was much heavier now. He raised the little whip he had also brought back with him, white with a short, ribbed handle at one end and several thin leather strips at the other. He cracked it in the air. She followed the movement with wide eyes, and he saw the way both the sound and the sight of it affected her. When he bent down between her legs to taste her again, she came quickly. He smiled at how much control he had over her.

Her eyes were bright when, after having pulled on another condom, he moved on top of her, lifted her up with one hand beneath her back, and entered her. Her legs were still bound wide apart, and it was sexy, for a while anyway. But it wasn't anywhere near as easy as it looked, to make love to a woman in that position. And so Alexander quickly loosened her legs and dragged her into the kitchen instead. Once there, he simply pushed her forward so that she was leaning over the kitchen counter, put a hand on the curve of her back, and plunged into her again.

"Oh, God," she mumbled huskily. He made her come again, this time first with the help of the paddle, then whip, and then the crystal-covered vibrator, before he thrusted into her, holding her hips, plunging and pumping. As she twisted and bucked beneath him, he pulled out, tore off the condom, and came on her ass and back, marking his territory primitively. He put his hands on her hips, breathing hard, waiting for his heart to calm down, his brain to start to work again. She said nothing, and they stood like that until he grabbed some soft tissues and carefully dried her off. When he was done, she was almost limp, and so he picked her up and she laid her face against his chest. He could feel her eyelashes on his skin, felt the tickle when she blinked.

"If you drop me, I'm going to die of embarrassment," she muttered.

He laughed and sank down onto the couch with her in his arms. It had been oddly intense, as though they had been someplace else and had only just started to return. Isobel shuddered, and Alexander knew she was coming down. Their game was like being high on sex and endorphins, but it also meant that you had to land afterward, and now she was hurtling back to earth. He already knew the signs. The shivering. The silence. The vulnerability. He shifted her gently in his embrace, rocked her slowly, held her to him, listened to her breathing. He reached out and found a blanket, which he pulled up over her. He stroked her hair softly, allowed himself to just *be,* here with Isobel in his arms.

"I need to go to the bathroom," she mumbled after a while.

They untangled themselves and he let her go, saw that she was steady on her legs. While she was gone, Alexander went into the kitchen and grabbed bowls, spoons, and glasses.

When she came back, he had laid out cushions on the floor and lit candles, which flickered in the breeze from the open fireplace.

"So nice," she said. She blinked and then smiled, and Alexander thought to himself that there was almost nothing he wouldn't do to see that smile of hers.

"Come here," he said, and she sat down next to him, like a princess in a Bedouin camp.

He passed her some pillows. Held out a spoon and a little bowl.

"What is it?"

"Chocolate mousse. Romeo's recipe again."

She ate it all. When she was done, he gave her the last of his. She wolfed that down too.

"You're staying over, right?" He wanted it more than anything.

She nodded, licked chocolate from the corner of her mouth.

"Want to go to bed?"

She shook her head. "I don't have the energy, I'm so sleepy. I think every last bit of tension I've ever had has gone."

"Should I carry you again?"

"Let's not tempt fate."

And so he built a bed for Isobel on his living room floor instead. Soft cushions, big, luxurious feather pillows and blankets. She lay down, and he brushed her hair with his fingers, one lock at a time, until it was spread out around her like a flame-red sunset.

They lay tightly together, nose to nose, forehead to forehead, and looked one another in the eyes without saying a word. She put a hand on his cheek. He covered it with his own hand and watched her fall asleep, lay like that until she turned away from him. Only then did he close his own eyes.

He woke long before she did. Watched her, curled up beneath his sheets. Her freckled skin, her even breathing.

He had always loved the beginning, the chase, he thought. But as much as he had sought excitement and exploration, he also disliked the morning after.

But things were different with Isobel. Everything was different, so why not that?

"Good morning," he said when she finally woke.

"Good morning."

"I'm so glad you stayed over," he said.

"Me too."

"Do you have to go anywhere today?"

"No. Do you?"

Alexander shook his head. "I just want to be with you. Want that?"

"Hmm. Are you going to make me breakfast?"

He propped himself up, on top of her, resting on his arms, and looked down into her laughing face. "Didn't you know? I'll give you everything you need."

"Everything?"

"Even more."

"I'll stay then."

It felt more right than anything in Alexander's life ever had.

Chapter 45

Gina was at the kitchen table at home, studying. Her father was in the living room playing chess with a friend, as he did every Saturday. Amir was in his room, door closed. Gina could hear the sound of some kind of video game. She couldn't see the point of playing such games, thought it was a waste of time, but Amir liked them; he could sit there for hours. She brushed aside her worries about her brother, the fact he was always sitting, never leaving his computer, that he had no friends. She had the last exam of the semester next week, a big exam, but she was prepared; she was just going over her notes.

It was a beautiful, crisp Swedish early summer's day, far removed from her childhood memories, full of burnt tones and damp heat. She had been eleven when her family came to Sweden, but her memories of her childhood were blurry and incoherent. She had always wondered if there might be something wrong with her, because she remembered so little, but then they read about it during a psychiatry class. The way children who experience terrible things repress them. Had her childhood been terrible? Vaguely she could remember smells and sensations. Could sometimes remember the sounds of animals and women's voices, but nothing else. Except the fear and pain that day. She would never forget *that*. She listened through the open window. Tensta was like a miniature UN. If she listened closely enough, she could almost make out the dialects of the women laughing down in the yard. She didn't remember any laughter in her childhood. Had they never laughed, or had she just forgotten it?

She looked at the text she had underlined. She knew it practically by heart already, but she wanted to go over it once more. She always aced her exams, and she considered anything below 100 percent a failure. Her classmates were going out over the weekend; she had heard them talk about it all week. One of them had asked her too—they were always nice like that—but she usually said no. She couldn't afford it. Neither in terms of time or money. Spending money on things that weren't absolutely necessary went against her beliefs. Besides, she could use the time to study. That would lead to the future she had made up her mind to achieve, so it wasn't a sacrifice, not by a long shot.

But sometimes, on days like today, there was a small part of her that just wanted to let loose a little.

"Is it going well?"

Her father had stuck his head through the doorway.

Gina nodded, simultaneously moving her notepad so he wouldn't see her doodles. She had replayed her conversation with Peter over and over again. He had looked so pained, and she was truly shocked by what he told her. She hadn't been cleaning while she studied for her finals, so she hadn't seen him in a few days. She wondered how he was holding up.

Her dad took a jug of juice from the refrigerator. "You should go out for a while," he said, kissing her head and going back to his chess.

He is right, she thought, as she squinted out at the sunshine. If for no other reason than to get a little vitamin D. Her mind drifted. She didn't normally have any trouble with her focus, never daydreamed. When others complained that they spent too much time online, in front of the TV, or on their cell phones, she just couldn't understand it. In her world, there was no room for shortsighted laziness. You made up your mind and there was nothing more to it. She flicked through the old exam she was using to practice, fixed her eyes on it. Ten seconds later her thoughts had drifted again.

She got up and went restlessly over to the window.

"Gina?"

Dad again. She turned around.

"Yes?"

"You got a call." He held out her cell. She took it with a frown.

"Who is it?" she asked. No one called her, and especially not on the weekend.

But he simply handed her the phone, looked like he wanted to say something, and then shook his head and left the kitchen.

"Hello?" she said cautiously. It was strange how many thoughts managed to rush through her head. Was it someone who was out to harass them? They kept a low profile, and her father was respected out here. But still . . . This was Tensta. On the other hand, maybe it just was someone who needed last-minute waiting or cleaning staff? Most student receptions were over, but you never knew.

"Hi, Gina. This is Peter."

"Peter?" She recognized his voice immediately, even though they'd never talked on the phone. "Has something happened?" Strangely enough, her first thought was that it was a weekday and that she'd forgotten to go to work. But why would Peter call her? She didn't even know he had her number. She had a prepaid phone card, wasn't registered anywhere.

"Happened?" he said. "Like what?"

"At the office, I mean." It was an idiotic conclusion, she realized. "I don't know what I mean. I was just surprised."

"Is this your number?" he asked. He sounded ill at ease. "Your father answered. . . ."

Gina smiled.

"It's my cell phone, but Dad was closest so he answered." She still didn't know *why* Peter had called. They never spoke on the phone. Did he need her to clean for him? There was such a long silence, she wondered whether he had gone. Maybe he had dialed the wrong number. If that was even possible.

"How did you get my number?" she asked.

"From my sister, Natalia."

Of course.

Extended silence again.

"Where are you?" Gina asked, as Peter said:

"It's such nice weather out."

"Yes," she answered, as he said:

"In the car."

More silence. But now she could hear the low hum of the Mercedes in the background.

"Are you sure nothing happened?" she asked.

"Gina, I really do understand if you can't. Or don't want to. Your father sounded really stern. Plus, I know you want to be with your family. You probably don't have time. And maybe you hate me after what I told you. You know."

"I don't hate you."

She waited. Her heart had started to beat a little faster.

"Do you want to take a walk with me?" he finally asked.

Although it was the question she had started to hope for, it was so monumental when it finally came that she was silent.

She could explain their previous car journeys as Peter just being kind. Maybe even their late-night meals at the office.

But not this. This was another step. In a new direction. If she answered yes, it meant she was taking a risk. And she hated risks just as much as she hated disappointment.

But then Gina looked out the window again. Saw summer outside. She was focused, knew what she wanted from life, was structured and smart. But she was also a young woman. And she liked Peter. And they needed to talk.

About what he had said. About things.

"Yes," she said, and she knew that with a single word, they had changed course. But for the first time since Gina had fled her homeland with her father and brother as a petrified child, and then promised herself not only to survive but to never depend on another human being again, regardless of whether they were people smugglers or Swedish immigration authorities, she wanted to do something spontaneous and impulsive and for her own sake. She would do the thing everyone always talked about but she had never tried. She would live in the present.

"Yes, I'd like that. Are you coming to pick me up?"

While Peter had waited for Gina's reply, he'd hugged the receiver so tightly he had to wipe the sweat from the screen before he could switch it off. He took the headset from his ear and put it down on the passenger seat along with the phone. He breathed a sigh of relief. He had finally dared to call her and she had said yes. He didn't bother with the AC, just rolled down the window and let the early summer breeze blow in his face. He smiled. Gina had said yes, she didn't hate him, and they were going to meet. If anyone needed a mountain moved, he felt up to the task right now.

When he pulled up outside her door and stepped out of the car, he saw her walking toward him, saw her through the worn re-inforced glass in the door, and was struck by a momentary panic. How should they greet one another? He wished he was brave, but he didn't dare hug that perfect human.

Gina came out, smiling. Peter shoved his hands into his pockets.

"Is Djurgården okay?"

"Sure."

Thirty minutes later they parked by the bridge to Djurgården Is-land and walked along the canal. There were lots of people out, and Peter inevitably bumped into people he knew. Djurgården was, after all, where the upper classes went for a walk. He said hello to a cou-ple. They stopped to talk, shook hands with Gina, gave her curious looks, and walked away, whispering. The same thing was repeated. Over and over and over again. With each time, Gina grew more silent.

"Is something wrong?" he eventually asked.

She shook her head, but her brow was furrowed, concerned.

"Gina?"

She crossed her arms and looked away, toward the treetops. "I've lived in Stockholm for over ten years, but this is the first time I've been to Djurgården. It's beautiful, so beautiful."

"But?"

"I feel *wrong*. And your friends. I'm sure they're very nice, but don't you see the way they look at me? You know, I've waited at par-ties where they were guests. And now they don't recognize me. I ac-tually think I just want to go home."

Despair welled up within him. And shame, when he saw her inse-curity. He was the one who had exposed her to this. He had wanted to give her a nice day out, but he had failed. She was right, and he was an idiot.

"Sorry," he said. "I didn't realize it might be like this. I'm so sorry, Gina." Peter ran a hand through his hair, felt a tightness in his throat. No matter what he did, it went wrong. He should have foreseen this. Should have protected her, put himself in her shoes.

"It's not your fault," she said.

"Please, Gina. Don't go home." He was practically begging.

She bit her lip. "Maybe we could go somewhere else?" she suggested hesitantly.

He was so relieved his voice almost shook: "Where do you want to go?"

"If we go back to my place, you'll feel like just as much of an outsider. What about the other side of the city? To Södermalm?"

"I've never been there," he confessed.

She gave him an amused look. "Then what about a walk in Tanto, the park by the water?"

Peter managed to find Södermalm by following signs and GPS. He parked on a street he had never heard of, and thought that he, in his made-to-measure jacket and neat chinos, would probably feel just as out of place here in Södermalm, with its trendy cafés and carefully styled hipsters, as he would in Gina's suburb. But the sun was out, none of the Södermalm inhabitants seemed to stare at him, and Gina no longer looked uncomfortable. He felt his mood improving. As they walked down toward the glittering water, and her slender arm brushed against his, he took off his jacket, rolled up his shirtsleeves, and decided to enjoy what was becoming the best Saturday of his life.

"Are you looking forward to your placement?" he asked. In the car, they had talked about the next semester, when Gina would get to work in the hospital.

"They say you feel more like a doctor afterward, so I'm looking forward to that. But I know it's gonna be really tough."

He smiled, knowing that she loved a challenge.

"Are you doing anything nice over the summer?" he asked.

Summer had arrived so quickly, he hadn't planned any vacations, and the thought of not seeing her for months made him ache. And come fall, Gina would be busy with a whole new, intensely focused life.

She shook her head. "I'll just be at home. I have a little work to do, and I want to save as much money as I can. You know."

He knew. And though it was deeply selfish of him, he was happy she wouldn't be disappearing from his life quite yet.

They bought ice-cream cones. She took a long time deciding between flavors, so he chose one of the ones she had been debating, and said jokingly, "If you don't let me pay, I can't be responsible for my actions."

She nodded, regally, that it was fine, this one time, and they sat down on a rock by the water's edge. Ate their ice creams in silence. Peter never spoke with his mouth full, and Gina sat, straight-backed, her eyes fixed on the water. He was happy, more than happy, just to study her beautiful profile.

"Was yours good?" she asked. He gave her the last of the green ice cream he had chosen for her sake. She ate it with slow, small movements, and he wondered how often she bought ice cream or anything else for herself.

"How's your brother?" he asked. "Is he doing anything over the summer?"

"No."

"Do you think the water's cold?" he asked, quickly changing the subject. He knew there were people for whom summer didn't mean vacations and relaxation, but he hadn't ever spent time with someone who genuinely couldn't afford to do anything over the summer. That wasn't something he was proud of.

Small children paddled in the water a little way away from them, and a dog swam with a ball in its mouth, but it couldn't be very warm.

"I don't know," she said as she wiped her mouth with a paper napkin. "I never swim."

"Not even when you were at school?" he asked, astounded. "Over the summer?"

His own summers had been spent on sailing boats in the archipelago and in the Mediterranean. A couple of times, he'd been to the West Indies with friends, spent long weekends in archipelago cottages with his and Louise's friends. But it was free, wasn't it, to swim in Sweden? Jesus, suddenly he had no idea.

"I took lessons," she said quietly. "I couldn't swim when we got here. Dad was really keen for me and Amir to learn, because he'd read that children drown in Sweden. But I've never swum outdoors. In the ocean or lakes or anything like that." She wrinkled her little nose and said skeptically, "It looks pretty cold. What are you doing?"

"I'm going to go wading," he said firmly as he took off his shoes and socks and put them down beside the sun-warmed rock. He rolled up his trousers and padded the short distance to the water. He put one foot in. It was ice-cold. Couldn't be more than about fifty degrees.

"You Swedes and your obsession with water," Gina said.

"Don't you want to try? It's nice after a minute."

"People always say that. It's my opinion that people are wrong."

"Come on. Or are you scared?" he teased, knowing that Gina would never let anyone believe there was anything she wouldn't dare do.

After a moment's hesitation, she took off her shoes and bared her delicate feet and painted toenails. She was always so properly dressed, in a monotone skirt and a blouse or, like today, a light dress and canvas shoes, that her pale purple nails seemed like the height of decadence. Peter didn't want to stare, but she had really nice feet. Dainty and elegant, with slightly paler soles and the most slender ankles he'd ever seen.

He looked away. The rocky ledge they were on wasn't steep, but he still held a hand out for her as she carefully slid down. Her dress rode up, and she pulled it sharply back down and then took his hand. He held her steady as she tested the water with one foot, felt a pulsing joy from the point where their hands met.

Her grip tightened. "It's freezing," she shrieked.

"Come on," he said with a gesture toward a little pool a short distance away from them. "We're going over there."

They ended up with the clear water up to their ankles. Small fish darted around their feet, and he saw her pleased smile.

"I'm used to it now," she said after a while. "Or maybe I just went numb."

"I'll take you swimming sometime," he said, hoping it was true. Maybe he could invite her entire family. He could borrow a boat. Christ, he could *buy* a boat and take them into the archipelago.

"I think I'd rather skip that experience," she muttered. "Can we get out now?"

Peter spread out his jacket on the threadbare grass, which was dotted with picnickers. She sat down close to him, on his jacket, and they let their feet dry in the sunshine. He wished he dared take her hand again, but there was no reason to, so he resisted.

She wiggled her toes. "It's nicest after," she said.

"Yeah," he agreed.

They sat in silence and let the sun dry and warm them.

"What you said last time. About Carolina," she said quietly as she played with a blade of grass.

Oh, God, here it comes.

"Yes?"

"Is that why you constantly punish yourself?"

"I . . ." he began, but then stopped, because he had no idea what he was going to say. Was it true? Did he punish himself? And if he did, wasn't it a legitimate punishment? "I ruined her life," he said.

Gina gave him a stern look. "But did you, really? Her *entire* life? Because I've met Carolina. And I've gotten to know you. Of the two of you, it's not Carolina who acts like the living dead."

"It doesn't feel like I have the right to move on."

"No. But just because it *feels* that way doesn't mean it's *true*."

"How old did you say you were?"

She smiled.

"I should probably go home. I promised to make dinner."

They got to their feet, gathered their belongings, and started to head back.

They walked along the narrow path next to the water, making small talk.

"Wait," said Gina. She stopped by a tree, placed one hand on the trunk, and raised her foot to fish a piece of gravel from her shoe. Without thinking, without having planned it, Peter held out a hand to her. He gently grazed her cheek with his knuckles. As light as a sea breeze, fully ready for Gina to let fly at him for doing something he had no right to do. But she didn't. She lowered her foot, stood up straight, and just gazed at him. Peter took a step toward her, toward the sweet-smelling, straight-backed being who occupied his thoughts so much she was rarely *not* on his mind, and put one hand on the tree trunk above her head. She was between him and the tree, and her chest was practically touching his when he laid his hand on the gnarled bark. Peter waited, gave her plenty of time to duck out from beneath him if she didn't want it. But Gina stood still. He leaned in toward her, slowly, and brushed his mouth against hers, light, questioning. She closed her eyes, completely still, her back against the tree and her chin slightly raised. Peter took a chance. He kissed her again, for slightly longer this time. And then again. This time, he lingered against her smooth lips.

I'm kissing Gina.

He parted his lips and moved the tip of his tongue over the seam of her mouth, careful, tentative. She was still completely motionless, her hands at her sides. He deepened the kiss slightly. He heard a sigh come from her lips, and he moved his hand from the tree to her shoulders, gently pulled her toward him. Felt her breasts and mouth push against him. He couldn't help it, he breathed out and it sounded like a groan, and then she finally kissed him back, a soft, cautious tongue that shyly brushed against his. It was a mutual kiss, the most beautiful, intimate kiss he had ever had. As though kissing Gina meant starting over.

When she pulled away, he let go of her immediately. His heart pounded in his chest, as though he had just sprinted up a steep slope.

"Sorry," he said.

She touched her mouth with her long, slender fingers, as if she was trying to get a sense of what had just happened.

"Why are you apologizing?"

"I shouldn't . . . Do you know how old I am? And your father."

He was saying all the wrong things, he could hear it himself. But he hadn't been with a woman since the divorce, and even then, he hadn't "been" with a woman all that much. Louise had never taken the initiative, and he wasn't someone who dared to have opinions on whether they would have sex or not. He had carried the absence of physical closeness with him as a punishment he deserved a hundred times over. And now he didn't know what to do, what he *could* do.

"I know how old you are," she said. "You point it out practically every time we meet. But I'm not a kid. It was a really nice kiss."

He didn't dare say any more, was afraid he would extinguish that smile, that look. He gripped his jacket in his hand and held out the other toward her. When she took it, they walked hand in hand alongside the glittering water, and Peter felt something he hadn't felt in many years.

He felt as though even he had a right to be happy.

Chapter 46

When Isobel finished work Monday evening, Alexander was waiting outside her office. Blond and smiling, he stood in the sunshine on the sidewalk on Valhallavägen. Passersby glanced at him, but Alexander only had eyes for her. As they met, he pulled her into his arms, crushed her to him, and kissed her until she was clinging onto him. People continued to pass, some openly staring, but Isobel didn't care; she allowed herself to be swept up into what was maybe just some kind of clinical insanity.

"How was work?"

She had been dazed. Hadn't heard what her colleagues were saying. Had hid in a room and gazed dreamily through the window.

"What are you doing here?" she asked.

"I'm taking you to dinner," he said, covering her nape with his palm, kissing her ravenously. This was madness. All she could think about was how, over and over, she had lain in Alexander's bed, or across his armchair, or against his kitchen counter, being dominated and forced to come in orgasm after orgasm. The physician in her could rationally explain how pain released endorphins, and that these then took over to create enjoyment. But the psychology of it was more difficult. Why was what Alexander did to her, with her body, so good?

Though *good* was, of course, a laughably insufficient word. It was so much more than that. It was like she could be herself, sexually, for the first time. Be with someone who didn't judge her. Feel safe, dare to trust.

"Eat out or at my place?" he asked as his hands moved over her, seeking out her cheek, down over her back, the back of his fingers tracing her spine.

She couldn't think, her body was shouting *take me, take me, take me,* and that was why she said, as firmly as she could, "Out." That way she would have time to formulate some rational thoughts before she was on her back or her stomach in his bed, with nothing but sex and orgasms on her mind. She had never been so irresponsible before, so young and crazy. Deep down, beneath doctor-Isobel, aid worker–Isobel, and ultracompetent-Isobel, the one you could always rely on, there had always been a woman who *hungered* after a raison d'être, to stop hiding away like some dirty little secret. She had repressed that side of herself for so long, but it had always been there. And now this. She would never have believed it if she hadn't experienced it herself. That you could let go with another person in the way she had. And with Alexander, at that. It was incredible.

She had always looked down on people who let themselves be guided by passion, thinking it was a bit pathetic. Well, just look at her now.

Alexander took her to the Mathias Dahlgren, one of the most luxurious restaurants in Europe; spoke quietly with the waiter; and arranged a table in the same self-confident way he organized everything.

They ordered the vegetarian tasting menu and champagne. Expensive, luxurious, outrageous. He took her hand, caressed her wrist.

"This is insane," she mumbled. Alexander had set something free in her, and he was so terrifyingly skillful. As if it was a hidden talent that had just been lying in wait for the right time to be put to use.

The truth was that everything with Alexander was simply the best she had ever experienced.

"Yes, completely insane," he agreed.

He kissed her palm, and she was forced to close her eyes. She pulled her hand away.

"What is it?" he asked.

"I don't know," she said. "I can't think straight." She couldn't evaluate herself and this game they were playing anymore. Was it unequal? Had she entered into an unhealthy relationship? Should she be worried she had given up her independence?

"Is something wrong?"

"This, what we're doing . . ."

"Yes."

"It's so . . ."

He smiled. "Yeah, it is."

She leaned back in her chair and studied his handsome, self-confident face.

"Would you let me do it?" she asked quietly. "What you do to me? Switch roles?"

She had thought about it, how it would feel, what he would say.

Silence.

"Alex?"

"Is it something you'd like?" he asked, holding her gaze. She couldn't read his face. His eyes were pure blue, not a single deviant shade. Blue was the rarest color in nature, she remembered from her biology classes.

"Maybe."

She hadn't thought it through, but the moment she said it, the words sounded right. "Yeah, I'd like to try," she concluded.

"Why?"

She had said it to test him, to try to find some kind of balance in the madness she'd been drawn into.

"I want to know what it feels like for you. And I want you to know how it feels for me."

She held her breath. Was it an absurd request? And how would she feel if Alexander said no, if he only wanted to be the dominant one?

"I guess it's a way for me to experience what it's like for you," he said after a moment. He took her hand again, brought it to his mouth, kissed a finger, bit it gently. "Tell me, Isobel," he said against her skin, his voice low and almost purring. "What would you do if you were in charge?"

It was as though all her blood had been redistributed in her body. That sultry look, that rumbling voice . . .

"I probably wouldn't do anything different from what you did," she answered, barely able to get the words out. She really hadn't thought this through.

"But if you're going to take control," he said, kissing the next finger, "then I need to tell you what I fantasize about."

"Okay," she said, trying to sound brazen and sassy.

Her heart was pounding. It was one thing to cockily suggest dominating Alexander but something completely different to realize that it meant trying to control a man who weighed somewhere over two hundred twenty pounds. It was mostly about mental strength, she knew that, but still. Jesus. Would she be able to pull it off?

"Beautiful, sexy, addictive Isobel. D'you know what I want?" His eyes were half-closed, and his dark lashes cast shadows on his golden skin and angular features. He breathed out, and the warm air from his breath made her shudder.

"I want you to do to me what you want me to do to you later."

"What do you mean?"

He took yet another finger, kissed it lightly. "That there are things you want from me, things you don't dare ask for. That you still think you have to guard your secrets."

"I've never told anyone as much as I've told you," she said honestly.

"One night when you can do whatever you want to me . . . I'm looking forward to it."

"Don't you think I can do it?"

He smiled. "*Au contraire, ma chérie.*"

How many times had she ended up in discussions where men wanted to put her in her place? It was often so subtle that she didn't even realize it until long afterward. That the strange feeling clinging to her was from the small pinpricks she had been dealt, and that started to sting only once she got home. It wasn't that she couldn't cope with being contradicted. Having a discussion and being forced to refine your arguments were par for the course when you worked in the aid community. But there were many men whose sole aim in such discussions was to flatten her.

Alexander, who already talked about aid, fieldwork, and humanitarian efforts in the third world as if he had studied the subject his entire life, had never tried to show off at her cost.

The violent attraction she felt to him was about just that. The combination of arrogance and respect. Yes, she wanted to dominate him. Wanted to force him down onto his knees as he had done with her.

His eyes, so fixed on hers that it felt as if he could hear every word she thought, darkened. Maybe it was the lighting. The candles were lit; the sky was azure blue outside, the way it was only a few days every year; and she felt that they were communicating wordlessly. This game, the one between them, it had set something going. Earlier today she had thought of it like a door she had opened and entered.

But it wasn't a door.

It was more like an opening, ten thousand feet up, that had suddenly appeared and sucked her up.

There would be a battle between them. She loved it when Alexander dominated her, probably more than she dared admit to herself. But she planned on taking this opportunity to create some kind of equality in their relationship.

"If that's going to work, you'll have to tell me things," she said.

"Whatever you want, baby."

No.

She shook her head.

"Not about sex. Personal things."

A cautious look flew over his improbably handsome features. Ah. So he wasn't as comfortable with this as he made out. Excellent.

She leaned back. Watched him, searched for a way in. Remembered how often she had thought that this was a man who had experienced things he would rather hide.

"What's the toughest thing you've ever been through?"

He laughed. Stretched out his legs.

"I don't have any particular traumas. I'm much too busy living in the here and now."

"No. That's not how it works. You can't demand total honesty from me and then give me bullshit in return."

His eyes flashed, and his face changed, went through nuances of feeling. Isobel could see his caution. His arousal. A small, small amount of anger. And fear.

Sweet Alexander. What is it you're hiding from me?

"I saw it last summer. You definitely have your demons."

"Doesn't everyone?"

"Actually, no," she replied. "I've met people who haven't experienced anything particularly difficult. But on the other hand, they're all unbearably boring. So tell me now. I really want to know."

Alexander leaned back. Didn't move his eyes from her, not even when he reached for his glass and took a sip of champagne.

"It's nothing much," he started. "I wish I could say there was some trauma, but . . ."

Mmm, right?

"School?"

He shrugged. Traced a finger around the edge of his glass.

"What happened in school?"

"It was tough, but it's not something I think about today. I got completely frozen out for a while. I stood up for a classmate who got bullied. So they punished me by leaving me out of everything. No one talked to me."

"Did you tell anyone?"

"No. In my family, you don't show your weakness. It wouldn't have helped. So I kept quiet. Got used to it."

"Was this in elementary school?"

He nodded.

"You went to boarding school?"

"Yeah. It was okay. Apart from the usual stuff. Bullying and so on."

"Did the girls like you?"

He smiled slowly. "Yes, Isobel," he said, and his eyes glistened. "The girls liked me. And I liked them. I have women to thank for a lot."

She knew exactly what he was doing now. He was deeply uncomfortable with how close she'd gotten and he was trying to take back control. But she had no desire to hear his many, many, *many* stories about women.

"Tell me about your parents," she said instead, sure there was plenty she hadn't found out yet.

He gave her a blank look. Silence.

But she had seen Leila do this. Wait people out. And so she waited.

"My mother isn't a warm person," he eventually said. His tone of voice was brusque, reluctant. "But I was always her favorite."

"How did that feel?"

He stared at her.

"How do you think?" he eventually asked, smoothly.

"I think it must've been complicated," she answered. "To be loved by someone who probably put her own needs first." She knew how it felt, after all.

"I clung to my siblings. To Peter first. But he couldn't stand me. He's six years older, but my father always made us compete for his attention. I could never understand why Peter didn't see that our parents played us off against each other. As I got older, I gave up trying to reach out to him. Now we have as little contact as possible."

There was something else with this brother; she would dig deeper later, but she wanted to move on.

"Tell me about your father."

Alexander pulled a face and scratched his chin. "He's a racist. A homophobic, chauvinist pig. A cliché."

"What's your relationship like?"

"We *have* no relationship. When I was young, I was what he called sensitive. A deadly sin in his eyes. I had to be toughened up."

"How?"

"Through beating."

"He hit you?"

"Like crazy. Me and Peter. And then I had to spend time doing *manly* things. Hunting. Sport."

"You like hunting?"

"No, I hate it. My dad knew that. To me, it's just innocent animals being killed by idiotic humans."

"That's why I'm a vegetarian. I've seen the way animals are killed, and I won't support that in any way. I understand how you feel."

They fell silent. Studied one another. He bit his lip, and she remembered her initial impression of Alexander. That he seemed lost, without hope. She pictured him as that young boy who'd been abused by his own father, the very person who should have protected him from the hurts of the world. And she finally managed to grasp the fragment of a thought that had been flickering on the edge of her mind for so long. Marius. He looked like Marius when he talked about his family. She saw the same abandonment in his eyes. The same cautious, hunted look.

"There's nothing wrong with being sensitive. You're an intelligent person, so you know that already. But I just want to say it anyway."

"It's all behind me now. My father doesn't give a damn about me, and I don't give a damn about him."

"So what is it, Alexander? What aren't you telling me?"

He sighed. "I guess you're going to keep nagging until I tell you?"

"Absolutely."

He waved to the waiter.

"If I'm going to talk about this, I'll need something stronger than champagne."

Chapter 47

Alexander's fingers toyed with the polished knife by his plate. Suddenly and unexpectedly, the air in the restaurant was difficult to breathe.

Ridiculous.

He reached for the vodka on the rocks, which had just been brought to the table. All his instincts told him to charm his way out of this, not to let Isobel in. But new needs had arisen. He wanted to be honest with Isobel. And not just using those same empty words he'd used on what had to be hundreds of women.

I want to be honest with you.

I'm not playing any games, not with you.

Stupid clichés he had uttered countless times. Phrases that meant nothing other than that he wanted to get laid and afterward move on without being accused of breaking any promises.

No. He wanted to be honest for real, and no one was more surprised than he.

But that didn't mean it was easy. On the contrary. Christ, it was hard. Almost so hard he wished he'd stayed in New York and gone on with his empty, semi-alcoholic, basically uncomplicated life.

"I don't know where to start," he said, trying for breezy but sounding suspiciously choked up to his own ears. "It's really nothing in comparison with what you've seen. No torture. No hardship."

He fell silent. How had this happened? It was just meant to be about sex, this whole thing with Isobel Sørensen, conscience of the world. When did it stop being "just" anything? Though in truth, he did know. Isobel wasn't simply another face in a long line of women. No, he was actually starting to envisage she was *the* woman. And the ironic thing was that he would never deserve her, not in the long run, and not if he told her everything.

"Tell me anyway. And start from the beginning."

He nodded, suspecting that whatever Isobel asked of him, he would do. Even if it meant that he would share secrets he had sworn to keep buried forever. "You have to understand that I know I've won all of life's lotteries," he began. "White, Western male; rich, born in a safe, wealthy, secure country. I *know* I've won one of the biggest prizes possible, by pure luck. I knew that before you and I started . . . before we started to hang out."

He fell silent, didn't even know what he should call whatever he and Isobel were doing. Were they dating? Were they a couple? Did she even want him for anything other than sex? "Though obviously I've become more and more aware of it. Of how lucky I've been."

"But?"

"My childhood was strange. The more I think back to it, the weirder I think it was."

"In what way?"

Alexander ran his finger along the edge of the vodka glass. He hadn't really articulated this aloud before. "The contrast between the material excess and the emotional distance, for example," he said thoughtfully. "Our father was hardly ever home. I think he only wanted a family so he had something to show off. He was never interested in us kids as people. Not in Mom, either. So when he was home, the atmosphere was pretty repressive. Everyone would be on tiptoes around him, and there were constant undercurrents in the air." He stopped. Did she really want to hear this?

But she nodded. Encouragingly. "What kind of currents?"

"A lot of anger. Disappointment, resentment, and disapproval. And a load of other stuff I didn't understand back then, but that I realize now must've been partly linked to my mother's constant infidelity." He stared down at the clear liquid in his glass. Being home had been almost unbearable at times. Gustaf De la Grip was a harsh man. Publicly he was respected and praised; privately he was used to getting his way, demanding and dictatorial. He never tolerated contradiction. His word was the law, both in boardrooms and at the dinner table. You never knew when his fist would lash out, when you would get hit over the head or sent away without food.

Peter had been beaten and ridiculed the most. It was as if his oldest son irritated Gustaf to no end, and there were times during their childhood when Peter had looked like a scared stray dog, always cowering from kicks and blows. But Alexander had gotten his share of beatings too. Being slapped, pinched, pulled, and hit hurt and was horribly humiliating. But the worst had been watching his brother take a beating. He still remembered how he stood there, tears steaming as Peter cried while trying not to, their father, cold, merciless, telling them to shut up, not to be disgusting babies. Peter's frightened eyes. The humiliation they shared but never ever talked about, too ashamed.

To this day he couldn't even begin to fathom how a grown man could hurt a child. His own flesh and blood. How could you beat someone so much smaller, someone so totally dependent on you? Someone you should protect. Alexander realized he'd been quiet for a long time. He tried to shake off the stifling mood. Isobel was watching him with sympathetic gray eyes, and he continued.

"Peter and Natalia, my brother and sister, did everything they could to get our dad to acknowledge them. But in my entire life I've never heard him say a kind word to any of us. I never even tried to win his approval."

At least his father hadn't beaten Natalia. If he had, Alexander probably would have killed him.

"You didn't?"

"No. I just wanted him *not* to see me."

"You mentioned your mother being unfaithful?"

Jesus. He had just blurted that out. He had never talked about it with Natalia and Peter, not with anyone. No one even knew what he'd seen, the things he'd heard. Ebba had an enormous need for male confirmation. She was a vain woman and maybe—maybe—he shouldn't blame her so much. Being married to Gustaf had to be a trial.

But how many whispered calls had he overheard as a child? How many times had she disappeared, leaving him all alone? *"Mommy is going out for a while. Be a good boy, Alexander. Don't cry. Don't tell anyone."*

"She was a typical upper-class housewife. I sometimes think it would have been better for her if she had something to *do*. Her mood was so volatile. She could be loving and happy one minute and then suddenly lash out, furious. Or turn ice-cold. You never knew when it would happen or what you'd done."

Today he realized it must have had at least something to do with her love affairs. Her mood must have been affected by whether she was being satisfyingly courted or had just been rejected. But when he was younger, he had been convinced it was his fault that Mommy was unhappy. That he somehow was bad, that he was lacking.

"But you and Natalia were close. Could you at least rely on one another?"

He smiled. "Yeah, we made a club. She took care of me."

Their entire childhood Natalia had been there for him, stable and strong. Had he been there for her? Or did he simply take her for granted?

"The messed-up thing is that Dad detested how close I was to Natalia. He used to mock me for it, said I shouldn't spend all my time with girls. Once, when I was five or six, I think, it was just the two of us and him. It was the weekend, I don't remember where Mom and Peter were, but Nat and I were alone with Dad. He got mad with me for some reason, and he punished me by taking her out and leaving me at home. I think they went to Skansen Zoo. Natalia always loved animals, and she was so happy he wanted to spend time with her. But I was alone all day and evening. I never said anything, I didn't want to ruin things for her." Alexander took an unsteady breath. It sounded so stupid when he articulated it, but he'd been so afraid, he could still feel that awful fear. He hadn't known when—*if*—they would come home.

Isobel reached out and took his hand. "That sounds cruel."

Well, that was his father in one word. Cruel.

Alexander withdrew his hand and waved to the waiter for yet another drink. "Natalia isn't his biological daughter, did you know that?"

She nodded. "I read it in the paper last year."

Yeah. It had been quite a scandal when the truth came out.

"I still love her just as much, though."

"And what about Peter, how did he take it?"

"As much as it pains me to say anything good about him, his attitude toward her hasn't changed at all."

From out of nowhere, he felt a wave of gratitude toward Peter. Alexander had been sure Peter would abandon Natalia when the sordid truth came out, but as far as he knew, his big brother had stood by her. Not that it even slightly atoned for everything else Peter had done.

His second vodka arrived, but he let it stand on the table.

"But there is more?" Isobel said.

"Yes."

"Tell me."

He scratched his chin, knew he was stalling. But how did you even begin to explain? "I have always liked girls," he started. "Not just in a sexual way, at least not always. I was small and shy as a child, and I liked playing with them, but my father hated it. That was why he dragged me out into the woods to murder animals. To be more manly, get some guy friends. But as I got older, girls started to like me in a different way. And that's not a boast, Isobel, just a fact."

"I believe you," she said with a warm smile.

"It was confusing for me, in the beginning. The way they suddenly looked at me, whispered, tittered, said things I didn't understand."

"How old were you?"

"Eleven, twelve, maybe."

"Still a child."

"I guess. Natalia's friends came to our house, made a point of saying hello, giggling, blushing. I get it now, it was hormones, but back then it was pretty confusing." He could still remember the odd feeling. Being ogled and subjected to scrutiny and not understanding it. "And then, the spring I turned thirteen, Åsa Bjelke moved in with us because her family was killed in a car crash. Her mother and my mom were best friends, and she is my sister's best friend."

"She is older than you?"

"Åsa's six years older than me."

"Already a woman then?"

"Yeah."

He remembered that summer as if someone had etched it onto

the inside of his skull. The strange thing was that he never actively thought back to it. Aside from when he saw his family, when they were all together. Then it all came back, and powerfully.

"No one could claim it wasn't a dream situation for any teenage boy. One of the most beautiful women in the world had just moved in with us. But things got . . . *complicated*."

"Did she seduce you?"

He shook his head. "No, she's always been more like a big sister. I think we're too alike. We flirted, sometimes a bit too much, nothing else. But with her friends, it was different. One of them was my first. She seduced me one evening. Not that it was difficult. She was nineteen, experienced, and beautiful. I think I lasted about ten seconds. She just laughed at me, like it was a fun game." He glanced at Isobel. This version of how he'd lost his virginity was something he had kept to himself. The acute shame he'd felt that summer. The confusion and mixed feelings.

"Was it, for you? Fun?"

He lifted a shoulder, shrugged. "I can't lie. It was exciting, to begin with. She said she would teach me things. And she did. She and her friends."

"So there were more than just one?"

He hesitated before he said, "Yes. I was their pet project. I think I slept with ten girls that summer. They passed me among themselves. Talked about me, often in front of me. While we were doing it, it felt as if it was the only thing I wanted. And it *was* incredibly exciting. But afterward . . . I can't explain it. They weren't mean, not really, even though they teased me and bossed me about."

"How?"

He shrugged.

"Tell me," she urged.

"They called me their plaything, their sex doll. And they laughed at me, made fun of me when I didn't understand what they were asking of me, that kind of thing. Not mean, really."

She was frowning. "If you say so." Her voice lacked conviction.

"And they taught me to be really good at sex, to think about their enjoyment, which obviously was a very useful education. But they decided everything, commanded and did as they pleased as if I were some kind of toy. And they punished me if I did something wrong," he added.

"They did?"

"Yeah. The oldest made me drink alcohol, much more than a few sips, made me smoke her cigarettes, and then they called me a bad boy. As I said. It was a strange summer."

He looked down. He rarely thought about it. Other than when he moved in those women's circle. Whenever he spent too much time with them, it affected him. Threw him off balance. Made him feel . . . dirty. Could Isobel understand? Could anyone? He didn't even understand it himself. On one hand, it had been a boy's wet dream. But on the other hand, he had felt . . . used.

Isobel's voice was kind when it cut through his thoughts. "You were so young, Alex. Did anyone know what was going on?"

"I don't even think Åsa knew. I've never been much of a believer in talking about things."

"You haven't had anyone to listen. People always say that you should have said something. They think it's shame that stops people from talking. But the fact is that people often don't talk because the people around them are bad listeners."

How he had wished that someone had seen what was going on. Stopped it. Told him he was too young, that there were too many of them, that he had the right to say no. That he wasn't a sex toy to pass around. Christ.

"I see those women sometimes. Some of them are married now. A few have kids. But I've never talked about it with any one of them." He could feel their looks, though, when they met, could imagine them laughing at him. "You're the first to ever hear about it."

"I thought I saw something last summer. You looked so haunted. Like you'd just visited hell."

"I never thought of it like that. But that's what it's like when I see them all. Some kind of limbo. Last summer—it was just too much. I went straight back to New York and drank for a week."

Isobel didn't seem shocked, but then again she wasn't someone who was easily shocked. "How does it feel now?" she asked, her voice steady and warm. God, he could get addicted to that voice.

"Like I said, I don't usually think about it, even though I know it must have affected me."

"Maybe even more than you think?"

"The thing I struggle most with, it's my feeling that . . ." He fell silent, didn't know if he could even express this.

"Go on."

"That women are only ever with me for what I have to offer them physically and financially."

He waited for her to argue, to smooth it over. But nothing came. And so Alexander continued, for the first time putting into words the things that had plagued him for so long, had affected all his relationships with women. "They like the good bits, the fun parts. They like the sex. The surface. But no one is interested in the inside."

In me as a person.

He almost expected Isobel to laugh, to disagree, to joke it away, but of course she didn't. He hadn't realized he had been carrying this raw pain, that it ran so deep. Had never realized how it hollowed him out. How he had *longed* to be seen. How afraid he'd been that he was his mother's son to the core. That he would exist only if he slept with someone. He wiped his brow, noticed his hand was shaking.

Isobel leaned toward him. The candlelight danced in her gray eyes, making them look like diamonds and stars. She rested her hand on his, and Alexander felt, ridiculously enough, his throat tighten.

"Thanks for telling me," she said quietly.

They sat in silence. All around them they could hear the clink of porcelain. Smell the aromas of food. Hear hushed conversations. Their food arrived, but he wasn't hungry, and she didn't touch hers, either.

He gave her a wry smile. If Isobel wasn't hungry, she must have been shocked after all.

"I'm so sorry, Alex. What you described, it's sexual abuse."

"No," he denied. "Nothing so serious as that."

She cocked her head. "So you're telling me that you were abandoned by your parents, left alone and scared, physically and sexually abused, but it wasn't serious?"

"Not in comparison to what other people endure."

"You can't compare it. Oh, Alex, I wish I'd known before I started to talk about swapping roles. I'm sorry. I shouldn't have suggested it. It must be hard for you; I really understand if you don't want to do it."

He studied her. A strange euphoria was taking hold of him, as if he were a balloon eager to soar. As though the things he hadn't realized were weighing him down had suddenly disappeared. Like a pressure, a constant, unwelcome feeling, had just gone up in smoke. And something else had taken its place. Mostly relief. But also happiness. Confidence. And trust. He felt a wide grin breaking free. He felt like a king. A person—a *man* who could do and choose whatever he wanted to.

"No, I want to try it," he said, confidently.

"But after what you said . . ."

"No. As of today I've left that behind." He had. And besides, he trusted Isobel. Completely. It was an incredible feeling.

"You have to promise me that you'll say something if it feels wrong. It should only feel good. Can you promise me that?"

"Absolutely."

"What if I go too far? I'm not experienced." She smiled wryly. "And I'm rather strong."

Alexander laughed and found himself again, left behind the confused teenager he'd been, and stepped back into the adult man he'd become.

He took Isobel's hand and held it across the table. "You could never go too far with me, babe," he said.

She raised an eyebrow.

"Okay, fine," he said with a stifled laugh. "If I can ask for one thing, it's that I'd rather not have a vibrator shoved anywhere."

She nodded graciously, and Alexander thought it was probably just as well he'd given her at least that limitation. A new kind of excitement coursed through him. Had he really just agreed to it? For real?

He caught her gaze. Something had happened here tonight. A new closeness he had not experienced before. He raised her palm to his mouth, pressed his lips to her skin, breathing her in.

"So, how should we do this?" he asked quietly.

"Tomorrow," she said. Her eyes glittered.

He kissed her hand again, murmured his words between kisses on her warm palm: "Do you want to come to my apartment?" He loved having her there; just the thought made him hot as hell.

"No, no. I'll call and tell you where to go."

He smiled at this bossy side of her. It was sexy.

"Fine," he said.

"Now let's eat."

So they ate, talking about food and wine and films they had seen, not about sex. Alexander's good mood had returned in full force. He was so happy to be here, with Isobel. To eat and laugh with her, flirt with her. To crave her. There was nothing hidden between them; she knew everything about him now. And he knew more about her than anyone else ever had. Tomorrow he was hers to do whatever she liked with.

It electrified his entire being.

He could hardly wait.

Chapter 48

Gina stared out the subway train window. Rock walls and platforms sped by. People stepped on and off. Played with their cell phones or looked straight ahead. She liked to take the subway, liked how it linked the city to all its constituent parts. You could take the train from Tensta to Central Station, change, and take another to Östermalm and, by doing so, step on in one world and climb off in another.

It had been a terrible mistake to get mixed up with Peter. She was someone who never did anything without thinking, planning, and analyzing, but this time it all got away from her. She had told herself she had control over her feelings. Had thought the fact they were so different in all respects would protect her from starting to feel something. Completely wrong, apparently, because he had kissed her and she'd been in turmoil ever since.

She played with her leather satchel. She was on her way home from the exam. It was a rare luxury, being able to go home in the middle of the day. Her bag was full of nonfiction texts and the blue A4 block she'd brought from the institute, covered in tightly written notes. She had bought the bag with her own money, been so proud of it and what it symbolized. But now she saw it with completely different eyes. Saw how simple it was, how worn and cheap.

She *hated* that.

Peter had kissed her. A real kiss. She still had trouble believing it. Without thinking, she brought her fingertips to her mouth, let them linger there. She wished she hadn't enjoyed it so much. That she hadn't been affected.

When she went through the exam afterward, she had gone cold with shock. She had missed a subquestion. She wouldn't get full marks. She couldn't explain the fear she felt at the thought. She had gotten the maximum number of marks on every test they'd taken. On every assignment and every question she'd ever been given in her medical studies, she had gotten perfect results. Now she'd lost at least one point. Because she wasn't focused. Because she had been out, wasting time, instead of concentrating. It was unbearable.

Gina got off at Tensta, wandered through the run-down underpass, took the steps up to the center, and walked toward home in the heat of the sun. She had to stop this. Everything. Her cleaning job was temporary; she would work her final shift there soon. Then whatever had happened between her and Peter would be gone, as if it had never occurred.

It wouldn't even be difficult, she told herself. She had survived so much. This was nothing.

"Hello? I'm home!" she called as she came into the apartment.

She heard voices from the kitchen. Her father and Amir. At first she thought they were having an argument, their voices were so loud. But then she heard them laugh. Did they really laugh so infrequently at home that she almost didn't recognize the sound?

And then another low voice, one she recognized immediately.

Peter.

She hurried into the kitchen, her body tense. This wasn't right. She saw her brother first. Amir's face glowed in a way she had never seen before, or not in a long time, anyway. He was talking loudly, gesticulating with his long teenage arms, laughing.

"What's going on?" She felt Peter's eyes on her, but she avoided looking at him.

What is this?

"We have a visitor," her father said.

"I can see that," she said, finally looking at Peter. Suntanned. Big in their little kitchen. "When did you get here?"

"I wanted to surprise you." He grinned. His hair was slightly ruffled, and he had rolled up his shirtsleeves. His jacket hung over the back of a chair. There was a sports bag on the kitchen floor, and she could see water bottles and training clothes in it.

"He brought soccer cleats! For me! And goals, can you believe it? Actual goals! He's just gonna change and then we're gonna play!"

Amir was practically yelling with excitement. He had on slender soccer boots and sports clothes, and they were so bright and new that it hurt her eyes.

Her father laughed as Peter lifted up a net bag full of bright new balls and orange cones to show them to her.

Gina's eyes flitted between them: Peter, her dad, her brother. Three against one, she thought. Was she the only one who saw the danger here?

Peter disappeared. Gina filled a glass with water, drank, studied her father and brother without uttering a word, and waited until Peter came back, now in his sportswear.

"Want to come?" he asked with yet another of his wide smiles.

Gina shook her head. Peter left with Amir, who was happily chatting away. The front door closed behind them.

Her dad said nothing, just picked up his newspapers and went out into the living room and sat down in an armchair.

Very deliberately, Gina seated herself at the kitchen table. Waited with drumming fingers. Inside, she was simmering away.

When they came back, Amir's cheeks were rosy. He was sweaty. Peter laughed and talked loudly about penalty kicks and offensive techniques.

Amir disappeared to take a shower. Peter stood there, smiling, his hip against the kitchen counter. His hair was even messier than before, and his skin had color. He looked satisfied as he took a drink from a blue plastic bottle.

A white man, the center of everyone's attention.

Gina played with her glass of water. Irritation washed over her in waves.

"What are you doing here, Peter?"

"Playing soccer," he said, wiping his forehead. "We had fun. You should've come."

She frowned. Either he was pretending not to notice she was angry, or else he really couldn't see it.

"I guess you thought you could just sweep on down to the suburbs and hand out a bit of charity," she said coolly. "Get some attention. Maybe relieve your guilty upper-class conscience a little?"

"No, no, it was an impulse," he said. "I remembered you said you wanted Amir to get out more. Didn't you see how happy he was? I thought you'd be happy too." He scrutinized her. "Are you mad?"

His amazed tone didn't make things any better.

"So what happens afterward? When you get bored? How do you think things will be then? When we can't afford to buy new shoes, when he grows out of everything?"

Peter frowned. "I didn't think . . ." he started.

"Right," she interrupted him, her irritation reaching new levels. "You didn't think because you don't *need* to think. Life's easy for you. You do whatever you want without having to think. Give the cleaner a ride home in your expensive car. Buy toys for a lonely boy. Like some kind of fucking Santa Claus."

"But . . ."

"This is you going too far. You should have checked with me first. How do you think this is going to end? You can see how we live. You sweep in with your expensive clothes and your ridiculous gifts. They probably cost more than we spend on food in a month. How do you think that feels? Or do you think we have no pride?"

"I really didn't mean to . . ."

They heard Amir shout for a towel, and Peter fell silent. They waited as Gina's father spoke in a low tone. The mumbling died out.

Peter lowered his voice.

"I didn't realize you would be so angry. I still don't really understand what I've done wrong. The only thing I wanted was to do something for someone."

"But why, Peter? Why do you feel like you have to do something for someone in my family? Why do you think you have the right? Did I give you the right?"

"No."

The expression on his face was closed. It was just as well, because this could never lead to anything good. Life wasn't a fairy tale. They had fled all the way to Sweden. A country she had never even heard of. Left behind her mother's grave, everything they owned but the clothes on their backs and their bags, and spent weeks on the move. She had lived in asylum centers. Seen her family broken down, heard her father cry at night, seen her brother change, lose hope, lose interest in the world around him. She had helped build them up again, knowing they needed her strength and determination, that they relied on her. Nothing good came from hoping for things, believing that anyone else, society or people who came from another world, could be trusted. Hard work, realistic expectations, and her own intelligence, they were the only way forward.

"You have a low opinion of me," Peter said. He had put down his water bottle and shoved his hands into the pockets on his shiny, new track pants.

"Do I? Tell me, what am I to you? Us out here? Did you think I would be grateful that you bought us things we could never afford ourselves? That what we need most of all is some new stuff?"

His brows lowered "Now you're being unfair."

"But don't you know that? *Life* is unfair. That's what you don't understand."

She hadn't realized she was so angry at him. It all came pouring out. She knew she was ruining things now, that she sounded completely unreasonable and that she was probably overreacting. But it was as though another part of her had barged in and taken over. It hurt, being in an inferior position. To be reminded of their differences as she sat in her own kitchen. For a few moments last weekend, she had forgotten. Peter had made her lose focus, made her think about him instead of herself and the future she needed to secure for her family.

"There can never be anything more between us," she said, feeling she had made up her mind. When she forced herself to look at it objectively, and she needed to be objective, not see things through some kind of fantasy filter, Peter De la Grip was just one white man among many. They might as well be from different planets, their expectations of life were so different. With Peter, she could feel herself being reduced to something she didn't want to be. She wanted to be strong. Independent. She knew what it was like to be dependent. Had experienced enough fear and powerlessness for a lifetime, and then some. She couldn't end up there again.

"I had no ulterior motive," he said quietly.

She sneered. "Really? No ulterior motive? You know, I find that hard to believe. Are you telling me you didn't want to sleep with me? That it's not sex you're after when you come here, spreading your joy? I have trouble believing I've misunderstood things that badly."

She had gone too far. Gina could hear it herself, and she saw it in him.

Peter held out his hands. There was no laughter in his face.

"What do you want me to say? That I misunderstood our relationship? Clearly I have."

"A black girl, what were you thinking? Have a little fun in the suburbs between two blond wives?"

He went pale, looking like she had hit him. Gina almost hoped he would do something rash now, something to prove she was right, that he was a bad person.

She watched him struggle with his words. He really wasn't someone who had them on his side.

"I can't apologize for who I am," he eventually said. "I came here to give your brother something he hasn't had in a long time, and I did it because I thought it would make you happy. That was my only motive. Amir laughed the entire time, and he met another boy his age. They're going to hang out tomorrow. That was all."

"But you have no idea about our world. How can you fail to see the enormous differences between us?"

"Of course I see them."

"So why can't you see the difficulties?"

"But now you're the one creating differences between people. Not me."

She rolled her eyes. "That's so naïve you should be ashamed. Are you really telling me you don't make distinctions? Between people from your class and mine?"

"I try," he answered. "Isn't that obvious?"

"Nothing you do makes any difference. I wish none of this had happened."

Peter's face was empty; he looked tired. "What do you want me to say? Do?"

"Nothing. You're just going to go back to your normal life."

"So now I should disappear? Were you just playing a game this whole time? I don't get it."

She knew he was thinking about their kiss. That goddamn kiss.

"Go, Peter," she said.

He opened his mouth to speak, but closed it again. It was just as well.

"Gina . . ." he eventually said, pleadingly.

She shook her head. Her pride had won out. It was for the best.

And so he left. Passed her by. Took his bag. Forgot the water bottle. Closed the door behind him.

She blinked. She had been horrible. Said unforgivable things. He hadn't raised his voice once. Hadn't slammed the door. Just left, silently. Maybe he was relieved she had done the thing they both knew needed to happen.

Gina took an unsteady breath. She looked up. Her father and Amir were on the threshold, looking at her.

"What happened?"

"I won't be seeing him anymore," she said firmly. She looked at Amir. "And you won't either."

Her brother simply turned on his heel, went to his room, and slammed the door.

"You know I did the right thing."

"He's a good man, Gina."

"And what is that assessment based on?"

"Don't be like that with me. He was polite and respectful. He was kind to your brother. He talks to me like an equal. He was really trying."

"It's possible to try too hard."

"You know that I trust you and your judgment." Her father shook his head. "But this time, I think you've made a mistake." He walked away from her.

Chapter 49

"*Bonjour, Maman.*"

Isobel kissed her mother's smooth, powdered cheek.

"You're sweaty," said Blanche.

"Sorry," Isobel meekly murmured before they walked in through the wide entrance to Nordiska Kompaniet together. They moved through the luxurious department store, between well-kept Östermalm youths, upper-class men and women weighed down with bags, and affluent tourists, toward Café Entré on the street level.

"Blanche, wait!"

A man around Blanche's age stopped them. Isobel recognized him from the tabloids as a count and friend of the king. Blanche's face lit up. They launched into a conversation in French, and Isobel waited impatiently. Blanche Sørensen was still a well-known face, and people often wanted to get her attention to talk. Sometimes Isobel wondered whether it was her mother's way of keeping her anxieties about growing old at bay—allowing herself to be admired by men. Blanche held out her hand and the gray-haired aristocrat kissed it elegantly before he dipped his head to Isobel and disappeared.

"He called on me when your father died. Now he's married to a woman thirty years younger than he." Blanche shook her head. "Men."

Isobel laid her jacket over the back of her chair.

"What would you like, *Maman?*"

She had thought about canceling their coffee date at the last minute, but she hadn't dared. What did that say about her? A grown woman who didn't dare say no to her mother.

"Just a coffee," said Blanche. "I'm not hungry, though I haven't eaten since breakfast. But I'm not much of one for food, as you know."

Ordinarily, Isobel would have pointed out that her mother needed to eat, following which Blanche would say something about how little and seldom she ate, how uninterested she was in food, before she went ahead and ordered a sandwich that she would then devour. But Isobel didn't have all the time in the world today, so she simply fetched coffee for both of them. She cast a glance at the clock behind the counter. She was meeting Alexander in three hours, and she had one last thing to pick up. Had she ever felt more expectant or terrified? Felt more alive and reckless, like an exciting, sexy, attractive woman? Stupid question, of course. She knew the answer was no, no, and no. She set down the coffee cups on the table. She didn't really need any caffeine, if she was honest; her body was jittery enough already.

"It's been a while. What's so important that you don't even have time to see your mother for days?"

"I called," Isobel pointed out.

"If you think that's enough, then . . ."

Isobel weighed her words as she studied Blanche's pale green dress. An item of clothing like that probably cost enough to pay many of Medpax's bills. "I was at your dinner," she reminded her. "And since that, I've barely been at home. I don't know if you heard about Chad, but it was tough. I ended up in the middle. . . ."

"This coffee is cold," Blanche interrupted her, putting down the spoon. "I like my coffee scalding hot, you know that. Can't they even manage to make a decent coffee anymore? What's wrong with people?"

"I'll get another."

Isobel got up, fetched a new cup, and sat back down. She cast another glance at the clock.

"Can't you make it five minutes without looking at the clock? Do you do this with everyone, or is it just me? It's very impolite."

"Sorry. Is the coffee better?"

But now she had managed to annoy her mother.

"I don't know why it always has to be so difficult to spend any time with you. All of my friends have such fun with their daughters. Anne af Scheele goes on vacation with her daughter. Nina Bengtzén's daughter is so kind and considerate. Why do I have to have a daughter who can't even sit still and drink a cup of coffee?"

"*Maman*, I . . ."

"And what have you done with your hair? Aren't you too old for that hairstyle? It's nicer when you have it up, more classic. It's all over the place now. Considering your big bone structure, you should think about things like this."

She refused to get into a discussion about her appearance. She loved her curls, loved wearing them loose and free.

"Please, *Maman*. Could we talk about something else? We never agree on these things anyway." She smiled as accommodatingly as she could. "I've just been in Chad. Don't you want to hear about the hospital?"

"Sorry, I didn't realize this conversation was only going to be about you."

Isobel blinked. Even for her mom, that was unusually spiteful. But she couldn't win, because Blanche was never consistent in her criticism. If she went to Chad, it was the wrong thing to do. If she traveled with Doctors Without Borders, it wasn't right either. The whole point of most of their conversations was that she could never make her mother happy.

"Your dinner was really nice," she said quickly.

Please, God, if we don't start to argue, I'll never ask for anything ever again.

"I suppose so. It wasn't anything special."

Blanche sipped her coffee.

"I met a man I think you know a while ago," said Isobel, well aware that men were the topic of conversation Blanche loved most after talking about herself. "Eugene Tolstoy. He knew Grandmother, he said. Do you know him?"

"I think we met. I know who he is. Ebba De la Grip's brother, *n'est-ce pas?* That woman is something of a goose, but Eugene is handsome, if I remember correctly."

"I know his nephew, Alexander De la Grip," she said quietly, holding her breath, and regretting the words almost instantly. But she had to say something about Alexander before she burst.

"The playboy? Why on earth?"

"We get on rather well actually."

Blanche furrowed her smooth brow. "But I don't understand. Why does he want to spend time with you?"

And here I thought it would be a bad idea to tell Mom about Alexander. Hah!

"Isobel, I'm only saying this for your own good. Don't be stupid and think a man like him is interested in you. Men can't be trusted, and certainly not that one."

"What makes you so sure of that?"

Way to go, Isobel.

"He only wants one thing, you know that, don't you? Men aren't like us women—they do what they want. Just be careful."

Keep quiet now. Just. Be. Quiet.

"Things aren't always black and white," she said. Apparently she was entirely incapable of keeping her mouth shut today.

"You're naïve if you believe that. And you'll get hurt. Unfortunately, I can promise you that."

"Don't you think there are men you can trust?"

"No. Say what you like, but life has taught me that."

Isobel knew that in some way that barb was aimed at her. Because Blanche had been careless enough to get pregnant with Isobel. Because Blanche, as a Catholic, hadn't been able to have an abortion and married Isobel's father instead. There was only one picture from the ceremony; Isobel had found it at her grandmother's house and kept it. A stiff-looking Hans Sørensen and a three-months-pregnant Blanche. Unhappy faces, unhappy marriage. And a daughter who would be dumped with her grandmother as soon as possible. A child who would always long for her mother, the beautiful creature who swept in every now and then, with French expressions and exciting scents, and for her father, who barely turned up at all. She had heard them fight about it once, her mom and her grandmother. About whose responsibility Isobel was.

"You don't need to care about what I say," *Maman* continued, and Isobel shook off her old sorrows, brushed them away like dust from her shoulder. They were old wounds, and they didn't actually hurt as much as they used to. "But I know what I'm talking about. I've been around longer than you, and you've never understood men, not like I do."

Isobel looked down at her cup. She had to leave soon, otherwise she would end up saying something she really regretted.

"I know I said I could stay, but I have to go," she said quickly. "I have a meeting. With a seamstress."

"I should do that too. Once, I only needed to enter a room and all the men would look at me. You can't understand how that felt. How difficult it is to grow old."

"Everyone grows old, *Maman*," said Isobel. "And you're still beautiful," she pointed out, because despite everything, it was true. "There isn't a man in here who hasn't looked over this way at you."

"It's hard to have had something and then lose it. I wonder if it won't be easier for you. I'm your mother, and in my eyes you'll always be beautiful. But you know what I mean."

Isobel had to stand up. If she didn't leave right now, her mother would manage to destroy all of her self-confidence.

"I'm sorry, but I really need to go."

"Go on, then. It's not my place to have opinions on that."

"Maybe we can do something next week?"

"Call me. I'll just be at home," Blanche said, as she always did, though it wasn't at all true. Her mother had a packed social schedule. If Isobel had been in a more quarrelsome mood, she would have pointed that out, but she had faced enough criticism and digs for today. Surely she couldn't be expected to tolerate more than this per meeting?

"Are you going to stay here?" she asked.

Her mother adjusted her scarf, touched her earrings. They were her grandmother's, Isobel realized, the diamond ones, antique and glittering—the ones her grandmother had promised her.

"I'm staying. A friend is coming by, if you're leaving anyway."

So, she had arranged to meet someone else. Isobel never learned, always got sucked into her mother's guilt trips. Isobel leaned down and kissed her on the cheek. "Bye, I'll call you."

She left the café. When she turned around to wave one last time, her mother had already been joined by the gray-haired count. She didn't look up.

Isobel rushed down the steps and out of the store. She paused to take a few deep breaths outside. She had survived. She hailed a cab and used the short car journey from Hamngatan to calm herself down. She closed her eyes and thankfully felt some kind of equilibrium start to return. Her anticipation about what she and Alexander were about to do was, despite everything, stronger than the pain of a bruised ego. She stepped out of the car. Lollo opened the door and let her in with a wide smile.

She looked at the garment Lollo held out.

"It's perfect," she breathed.

"Do you plan on telling me what it's for?" Lollo asked as she carefully zipped up the protective cover and handed Isobel the hanger.

Isobel shook her head. She raised her arm so the hem wouldn't drag on the ground. She would take another cab and change when she got there.

"My God, I'd kill to know what you're up to," Lollo said, envy in her voice.

Isobel said good-bye. Maybe her mother was right, she thought as she waited on the sidewalk.

Maybe she was naïve and reading more into her relationship with Alexander than she ought to. And maybe all men were unreliable. But that wasn't something she planned on worrying about right now. Maybe later, but definitely not now.

She smiled as she climbed into the taxi. Soon she would be playing with Alexander. And there was no room for any doubts.

It would be a memorable fight for dominance.

She planned to enjoy the battle. And she had every intention to win.

Chapter 50

Alexander had received directions from Isobel to get into a cab and wait for her to send the address, so here he was in the car, driving around aimlessly. Stockholm passed by outside, but he had a hard time dealing with the uncertainty of not knowing what was about to happen. On the surface, it might look like he moved through life taking things as they came, but until now he had never understood just how much control he exerted over his own life, how accustomed he was to controlling his world.

His cell phone beeped.

Bastugatan 16.

Alexander gave the driver the rather posh Södermalm address, leaned back in his seat, and ran his hands down his thighs. He had dressed completely in black, as she had told him to. Narrow black chinos, black T-shirt. Black socks, black shoes. No underwear. Not as sexy a feeling as you might think, but Isobel was in charge, and he obeyed. On one side of him was a bag full of the toys they had bought, on the other a bouquet wrapped in cellophane.

The cab pulled up outside a red building from the late nineteenth century.

Alexander walked through the doorway, waiting for his eyes to adjust to the darkness. The place smelled faintly of cigarette smoke.

"Alexander De la Grip?" he heard, and an elderly woman with a furrowed face and a checked apron appeared. She looked like a concierge from an old film, and it suddenly felt as if he had stepped back in time.

"Please," she said.

She opened the door to an elevator covered with ornate iron dragons and red, velvet-clad walls. From the ceiling of the elevator, a golden lamp shone faintly. She pressed a button, closed the barrier, and shut him in. The elevator rattled upward.

When it stopped, he stepped out.

Isobel was standing in the doorway to an apartment, and Alexander's heart almost stopped.

"Hi," she said quietly, and a shiver coursed through his entire body. In her white dress, she looked like a goddess, momentarily come down from Olympus to amuse herself, unconcerned by whether her pleasures would be too much for an ordinary mortal partner to handle. She had one hand on her hip.

"Come in."

"Where are we?" he asked when he stepped into the apartment. He put down the bag and glanced around. "Whose place is this?"

The décor was extravagant, all dark colors, full of gold and oriental patterns. So far from what he would have expected of her.

"Does it matter?"

"Isobel . . ."

"No, I don't have to explain anything to you."

She raised an eyebrow and asked: "Are those for me?"

He held out the bouquet. It was the first time he had given her flowers, and he had spent a long time in the store before he caught sight of the orchids. Wild, exotic, luxurious flowers in a vibrant lime green color. She took the bouquet and let her eyes move over him. She nodded approvingly, went away, and returned with a heavy vase. She placed the orchids in it and then set it down on a table in what had to be one of the most overcrowded rooms he had ever seen. Golden frames and mirrors, dark furniture, masses of paintings and other little trinkets. Heavy velvet framing the windows. Stunning views out toward the glittering water of Lake Mälaren, the inlets of Kungsholmen and Norrmalm—the entire city, actually. The place looked familiar somehow. He knew he had never been here before, yet he recognized the style. He took a step toward her but she shook her head so he stopped.

"Take off your shirt," she ordered.

Without a word, he did so, dropped it to the floor and stood still, letting her eyes have their fill. He had good genes, was strong and toned from boxing, and he had nothing against the avid way Isobel was staring at him. As he started to unbutton his pants, she gave him a quick shake of the head.

"No. I'll tell you when. I want to talk first." Her voice was steady, but he could see the change in the color of her face, see the blood making her cheeks flush, clearly make out her pert nipples through the silky material. She was naked beneath her thin, billowing dress—there wasn't a sign of panties or a bra.

"There's champagne," she said with a gesture toward a silver bucket. "Pour half a glass for me. And a whole one for you. Drink it and then pour another."

"Are you planning to get me drunk?" he asked, amused.

"No. But I plan to lower your inhibitions."

"Babe, I have no inhibitions," he said. But he did as she said—pulled off the foil, unwound the metal wire, twisted the cork free, and poured one glass for her, one for himself. Raised the glass to her, looked her in the eyes, and sipped the ice-cold liquid.

"Drink," she ordered.

He emptied the glass and poured another.

She smiled. "Good boy."

But there were limits, even for him. He did not like to be called a boy. He took a step toward her, an automatic attempt to restore the balance between them and regain the control he hadn't realized he would miss so much.

"No," she said, and he paused again. "Sit there." Isobel pointed to a leather-clad chair with a high back and no armrests.

Alexander reluctantly obeyed. He put down the glass and sat, leaned back against the ornate leather backrest.

Isobel came toward him. As her dress billowed around her body, he caught a glimpse of pale curves through a slit in it, and then she was in front of him. Alexander's hands went up. He wrapped them around her waist, spread his legs, and pulled her toward him. He buried his face against her stomach, inhaled the intoxicating smell of her. Isobel placed a hand on his head. At first she caressed him, but then she grabbed a fistful of his hair. She pulled his head back, looking him directly in the eyes.

"From now on, you don't do anything I haven't told you to. Not with your hands, not with your legs, nothing."

He squared his shoulders.

"I'm going to give you a safe word," she said.

"I don't need one."

She pulled slightly, and he resisted the temptation to move away from her.

"I'm going to give you one," she repeated calmly. "Your safety is my responsibility, and you have no idea what's going to happen today. So if you say *gold,* I'll stop. Okay?"

"Okay then," he said.

"Are you going to obey me? No matter what I say?"

He met her gaze, had trouble bringing himself to answer. Define obey, he wanted to say.

"Say: Yes, Isobel," she urged him, pulling slightly at his hair.

"Yes." Shit, he really hadn't thought it would be this hard.

Her grip tightened.

"Yes, Isobel," he said quickly.

She smiled—a slow, satisfied grin—and let go. "Good boy."

"For God's sake, Isobel," he snapped, and he ran a hand through the hair she had been holding in an iron grip. He really hated that phrase.

She cocked her head. "Who's in charge?"

He ground his teeth. Part of him wanted to get up and leave, tell her to go to hell. He wasn't here to be degraded, hadn't realized what it would take to subordinate himself. What she would demand of him.

"Alex?"

"You're in charge," he said under his breath.

She handed him the glass. "Drink."

He did as he was told. Emptied the glass. He had come here on an empty stomach, and the alcohol went straight to his head.

She was in front of him again. Her dress moved provocatively around her body, and he was on the verge of reaching for her again. It was automatic.

"Put your hands behind the back of the chair," she ordered.

He hesitated, but then reluctantly complied.

She rewarded him with a smile that went straight to his cock. Then she pulled her dress up over her thighs, spread her beautiful legs, and straddled his knee. She placed her sweet-smelling hands on his face and kissed him deeply. He squirmed beneath her, and she pressed herself against his naked chest. She broke off the kiss, took hold of his head, and pressed his face against the deep neckline of her dress. He greedily kissed and licked her skin, wanted to use his hands but held them obediently behind the chair.

When Isobel got up from his knee, he was breathing so hard he felt giddy. Alcohol, testosterone, and carbon dioxide were a heady cocktail in his bloodstream.

"God, Isobel, let me . . ."

"Not yet," she said. The thin material of her dress was damp where he had kissed her. She ran a hand over one of her magnificent breasts, smoothed out the material so that it strained against her generous curves and the hard, pouty nipple. He stared, feeling he would do and agree to anything to get her back on his knee.

"What would you like to do right now?" she asked gently.

"Get up, throw you onto that table, and fuck you. Hard," he said through clenched teeth, not remembering ever being so horny.

She smiled sweetly and gave him a long look, as though she was weighing up a number of different options.

"Yes, maybe we'll finish up with that," she eventually said. She leaned against a black table that looked at least a hundred years old. Stable, steady, overloaded with bowls, pots, and other trinkets. Her dress parted, revealing her thighs again. God, he loved her soft thighs. She started to touch herself. Almost distractedly, her index finger disappeared among her red locks, moving, petting, teasing.

Alexander didn't blink, his gaze firmly set on the enticing scene. She then came over to him and pushed the same finger into his mouth. He sucked. She inserted another, and then a third, moved them in and out, used his mouth the way he wanted to use her body. It felt as if flames were licking his body now, hissing, crackling flames of lust.

"I never understood the point of masturbating in front of someone else," she said quietly, and pulled her fingers from his mouth. He wanted to leap up, take her back, but it was as if he were rooted in his chair. Her finger moved among her red locks again.

"But people can change," she said, and she started to finger herself more purposefully. She put her other hand on Alexander's shoulder, steadied herself against him while she moved her fingers increasingly quickly. Her breaths were like a hot wind against his cheek, and his entire body howled at him to take over.

"If you touch me now, that's it for this evening," she said in warning. "I want to come without you laying a finger on me. You only get to look, understood?"

He couldn't nod, couldn't answer, could only stare.

The scent of her. The warmth vibrating between their bodies. The wet sound of her fingers moving. The slight pain when she dug her fingernails into his shoulder—all of this made his head pound, his blood roar. She came silently, powerfully, and then stood panting in front of him. The smell of sex and of Isobel reached him, and he wanted to eat it up, drink it in, wrap himself up in it. He had practically come too. Isobel looked at him with hazy eyes. She grazed his lip with her index finger and he caught it in his mouth, sucked it as if it were the only thing that stood between him and everything worthwhile in the world.

"Please, Isobel, please, I want to be inside you," he said huskily, feeling that he would go along with anything.

"Soon," she said.

She took her champagne glass and sat down on a low, plush couch opposite him, sank down into the dark velvet.

Alexander licked his lips, following every movement she made. She sipped from her glass, crossed her legs, pushed her hair from her face.

"This is Eugene Tolstoy's apartment," she said. "He let me borrow it."

That explained the brothel-like elegance. Alexander hadn't known his uncle had an apartment in Stockholm, but Eugene had always been rather secretive, so . . .

"Did he know what you planned on using it for?"

She bit her lip. Her cheeks were rosy, and she looked exactly like what she was. A sex goddess. *His* sex goddess.

"What do you think?"

"I probably don't want to know. Can I come over and sit next to you?"

She nodded, and he quickly moved over to her.

"Are your trousers tight?"

"So goddamn tight."

He was so aroused it hurt.

She looked down at his erection, leaned forward, and moved her hand up and down, up and down over his pants, until he couldn't sit still any longer.

"Isobel," he warned her, and took hold of her wrist.

"Let go of me," she said.

"I don't want to come in my pants," he pleaded.

Her eyes narrowed. Their gazes locked.

"Shit," he swore, and let go of her hand. He didn't want to come like this. In his pants. Like some horny teenager. She caressed him. He gave up and let himself go, moved toward her hand. He panted, it throbbed, his body began to contract, and he closed his eyes. But just as he thought he was about to come, she stopped.

"Get up."

He opened his eyes, couldn't really think; his heart pounded, and he had practically no blood left in his head. But he did what she said.

Isobel stayed on the couch.

"Take them off."

He unbuttoned his pants with some effort. He carefully pulled them down, stepped out, and then stood naked and erect in front of her.

She leaned forward, brushed against him, and he shook, actually *shook* at her touch.

She looked up. "You want to fuck me now, right?" she said.

He nodded eagerly, could already see himself taking her, harder than ever, taking sweet revenge for the torment she had subjected him to.

Isobel raised her chin. "But I'm not ready."

She got up from the couch, brushed against him with her shoulder, and he shuddered. She opened the bag he had brought with him and took out the white whip. When they'd bought it, Alexander had thought it almost looked like a toy. In her hands, it definitely looked real.

"See the ottoman?" she asked.

He turned around, spotted the piece of furniture—a big, heavy divan or footstool, without a backrest, square, bulky, covered in dark velvet fabric. Golden lion's paws as feet. Typically Eugene. Probably smuggled Russian goods from some old royal palace.

"Lie over it. On your stomach. I'm not going to tie you up." She smiled demonically. "Yet."

So far, he had been sure he would be able to cope with whatever she suggested. But now . . . Would he really do this?

Reluctantly, he got down on his knees. He steeled himself and lay down, over the ottoman, as she'd told him to, then adjusted his position. Isobel came over to him. As she got on her knees, he heard the rustle of her dress, saw the white material from the corner of his eye. She put a hand at the base of his spine, stroked his back. He shivered, was about to explode, just from her cool touch.

"If I do this, I'm going to do it properly. If you don't want it, then say so. Otherwise, say: Yes, Isobel."

Alexander stared at the floor and was struck by the surreal sensation of being naked, on his stomach, on top of an ottoman, in one of the most decadent apartments he had ever seen, trying to decide whether he was going to let a red-haired goddess spank him or not. He studied the oriental rugs. If he wanted to back out, now was the time to do it.

But he didn't. Couldn't deny that he was more turned on by this game than he'd thought was possible.

"Yes, Isobel," he said, his voice sounding forced to his ears.

"Good boy," she murmured.

She reached between him and the ottoman and took hold of him. He couldn't help but groan when he felt her longed-for touch, but he forced himself to be passive, to be jerked off by her long, strong fingers. He had never realized how vulnerable he would feel, how the slight sensation of uncertainty could increase his arousal, how frustrating and stimulating it was to have no control over what was happening.

He closed his eyes, felt his balls tighten, the blood rush to his cock. She let go. Stood up. Left him again, just as he was about to come. He had to bite his lip hard to stop himself from swearing, to stop himself from begging her to continue.

"Lie still," she said.

He forced himself to relax, to empty his mind.

Felt a breeze when she raised her hand.

Heard the sound of the whip whistle through the air.

Chapter 51

Isobel saw Alexander's body tense as she flicked the whip in the air. Would she really be able to go through with it? She had based this all on her own likes and dislikes. Gathered her fantasies and experiences, and then simply decided she was going to dominate him, force him to be submissive. She had expected it to be tough. What she hadn't expected was to be *so* turned on by it, almost high from the experience.

Satisfying herself in front of Alexander had been a decision born in the heat of the moment. She had come more quickly than ever before, and when Alexander begged to take her, she had been seconds from saying yes, from letting him make love to her on the floor, against the wall, wherever.

She cracked the whip in the air again and saw his muscles tense in preparation. His body was like poetry: tanned, muscular, and glistening with sweat. She was glad she had stopped herself from surrendering too fast, that he had followed her lead, that she had kept control. She knew it was a one-off, that this wasn't a role she wanted in the future.

But now.

She dragged the whip tails along his back, saw him shudder.

Now she wanted to take all she could.

She raised the whip and brought it down on his buttocks. He jerked but didn't say a word. Even though it must have hurt.

"Relax," she ordered. "Breathe."

Alexander inhaled sharply. She raised the whip and brought it down again, making sure to hit only muscle and fleshy areas. His entire body shook. She paused. He said nothing, just breathed. Was she being too hard? She crouched down, reached a hand beneath him. Ah. He was so big, she couldn't get her hand all the way around him, warm and wonderfully hard. She leaned over him, bit his ear. He groaned, moved eagerly beneath her, toward her palm. She let go, and he made a growling sound of protest.

She raised the whip again, let it fall. Again. And again, even harder. Still, he said nothing. She wiped her brow.

She couldn't keep it up much longer. Who would have imagined it was so damn exhausting to whip someone?

She hit him twice more, one on each buttock, really getting into it. She heard a stifled sound.

She stood still, allowed her breathing to calm down, making him wonder. This was what she found hardest herself. Not knowing what would happen. She wanted him to feel it.

"You can get up now," she said. "Stand up. And kiss me."

He lay still for a second, as though he was gathering himself.

And then he rose to his full height. Naked and sweaty, his eyes wild, he grabbed her, kissed her hungrily, almost vehemently, pushed a leg between her thighs, made her ride him as he wrapped an arm around her like steel.

"Wait," she panted, her hands on his chest.

He was about to take over, but this was still *her* night.

"Isobel," he groaned against her mouth. His expert fingers caressed her, his talented mouth kissed her, and she yielded. It felt so good, she loved this madness. Being desired, coveted.

"Baby," he said huskily.

Her eyes narrowed at the arrogant word.

Alexander respected her, she knew that without a doubt. But this was about the balance of power, and she wasn't prepared to hand it over to him yet. She pushed him away. Gestured toward one of the bedrooms with her head.

"There's a bed in there. Lie down on your back. One hand by each bedpost. Wait for me."

He looked about to protest, so she just turned on her heel and left him, went into the bathroom and closed the door behind her. Jesus, this was intense. It was like trying to keep your balance on a tidal wave. She splashed water onto her face, checked her makeup and hair. She stared at her reflection. Her eyes were enormous, her skin practically glowing. This was a woman she had never met before.

She went out again. Would Alexander have done as she said?

When she pushed open the door to the bedroom, he was actually lying down. Naked and outstretched on the enormous antique bed. His face a mix of frustration, arousal, and uncertainty, and his gaze never left her. But he lay still, as she had told him, completely at her mercy.

"One hand by each post," she reminded him.

He obeyed, an intent look on his face.

She unbuttoned her dress and let it fall to the floor. If you faked being comfortable with your nakedness, it practically became true, she thought. And the way he stared at her, it was hard to feel anything but flattered.

She climbed up onto the bed and straddled him, positioned herself with her knees below his hips, studied his handsome face, his muscular chest.

She leaned forward, took the silk ribbon she had already tied around the bedposts and looped it around his wrists, one at a time, until he was tied fast. Silk was good in that respect, strong and durable but still easy to loosen. She tied the silk in bows and smiled at how it looked. Alexander sought out her gaze, and she stroked his beautiful, angry face.

"This is difficult for you, I know," she said soothingly. "But you can do it. Trust me."

"Let me inside you," he whispered. "It'll be so good. I know you want to. You know how much you like it. Come on, Isobel."

"Yes, I want it," she said quietly, almost giving in to the fervor in his voice. "But first, I want to do something else. You aren't in charge here."

He looked like he was about to explode. His body quivered beneath her, like an animal. "Christ, Isobel. I can't bear this much longer. Let me *do* something."

She clambered from the bed and went to fetch the ice bucket.

"What are you going to do with that?"

She leaned forward and gripped his erection, moved her hand up and down a few times before she let go. He was so close to coming now, she could practically see his orgasm rising up through his body.

"Not yet." She smiled. She filled a glass with champagne. It was so cold the glass was immediately damp with condensation, but she took some ice cubes from the bucket and dropped them into the glass anyway.

"Ready?" she asked.

His eyes widened. "No," he bellowed.

She poured the champagne over his stomach and crotch. He swore. She straddled his legs again and licked him, lapped up the liquid, licked his thighs, his stomach, the skin around his trembling erection. She moved her fingers over him until he shook. She caressed him, carefully, so lightly and gently and tantalizingly that he started to pull at his bonds out of frustration. He was angry now, she saw; there was fire in his eyes, fury in his limited movements.

She picked up the whip again. Dragged the soft tails over his erection, saw real fear pass across his gorgeous features. She wouldn't admit it, but it was arousing to see his fear, to have him in her power.

He was breathing hard, his eyes not leaving the whip, his muscular legs tense.

But of course she hadn't planned to use it on him like that. Instead she lay down comfortably next to him, her head at the foot end of the bed and her feet by his hips so that he could see all of her. She spread her legs, could see his smoldering gaze fixed on her. She wasn't even sure she had seen him blink. His arms were stretched, the veins and tendons raised beneath his tanned skin. She laid one of her legs over his, spread herself, half closed her eyes, and began to touch herself.

She sighed gently, moved her hips.

"Isobel."

Alexander's voice was pained, the sweat glistened on his chest. His cock trembled against his stomach, mesmerizing, enthralling. It had shrunk with the ice-cold champagne, but now it was big and hard again. She slowly pushed the handle of the whip inside herself. The short grip was hard and ribbed, and actually really arousing. She played with the whip, pushed it in and out, as she touched herself with her other hand. She did this until Alexander pulled so hard against his bonds that the bed shook beneath them.

Isobel came, panting and violently. She pulled out the handle, stood up, filled her champagne glass, and held it to his mouth.

"Drink," she said.

He craned his head forward and drank, desperate gulps, spilling most of it.

"Good boy," she said, and leaned forward to kiss his mouth. She bit his lip, licked his neck.

"Untie me now. I'm going crazy."

Alexander wasn't a naturally submissive man. Dominating him was a bit like trying to tame an angry bull or a wild horse. It was hard, but it was exciting. Reading the feelings on his face and trying to anticipate his reactions. Seeing his resistance, pushing him to accept her demands. But he had earned what he wanted now. And besides, she was longing for him.

She reached for the colorful packages she had laid out on the nightstand, took a brown one and ripped the foil open. The faint smell of cocoa hit her. She rolled the condom onto him with a steady hand. She would rather have done it with her mouth, had studied YouTube videos of women rolling condoms onto dildos using their mouths, and she had tried it herself. That was why she had bought the flavored kind. But it was difficult, they were so sticky, and she hadn't felt the least bit sexy, so she made do with her hands. She had tested the flavors and liked the strawberry, hated the mint, and eventually settled on chocolate. The things you did to broaden your mind, she thought, straddling him, gripping his cock and pulling him toward her. His hips strained toward her so hard she almost lost her balance on the bed. She gave him a stern look.

"Lie still."

"I can't," he hissed.

"And stop pulling on the ribbons," she said sharply. "You'll hurt yourself. If you can't do what I say, then . . ."

She started to move away.

"I will, I will. Come back. Christ, come back, please."

She kissed his chest, gently bit his gold ring. He lay still. But he was sweaty, his jaw tight, and she realized she had pushed him as far as she could.

"I'm going to undo the ropes now," she said. "But you can't move your hands until I say so, okay?"

He nodded.

She untied one. Then the other. She held his gaze. His eyes were almost black, but he lay still just like she told him. She moved over him, adjusted her body. He closed his eyes.

"You're so close, aren't you?" she murmured. "Do you want to come?"

"God, yes."

"Not yet."

She rode him slowly, knew he would want to move more roughly, quickly, knew he was using all of his strength to obey her, to restrain himself.

She paused.

He made a growling sound. But he didn't move his arms. She put her hands on his shoulders and began to slowly ride him again.

"Now," was all she said.

She felt the balance of power shift in the blink of an eye, it was like standing on an unsteady block of ice before it swayed and sent her plunging straight down to the bottomless depths. Alexander's hands moved so quickly she didn't even see it. One second she was in control, the next he had grabbed her hips, lifted her up slightly, and then brought her back down as he thrust upward so hard that she panted. Ah, but she loved this, when he took over, when all his strength was unleashed.

She allowed herself to be overpowered by his newly liberated energy, just held on as he threw her down onto the bed, rolled on top of her, pushed her hands up above her head, and held her wrists as she wrapped her legs around his waist. He pushed into her and thrust away hard, so deliciously, masterfully hard. He came with a roar, and as the edges of her vision began to dim she came too, as though it was the easiest thing in the world to have yet another orgasm.

He collapsed onto the bed next to her, breathing heavily, groaning into the sheets. He was shaking.

"Are you good?" she asked hesitantly, had never seen him like this.

He answered by violently turning toward her, burying his face into her chest, wrapping his arms around her, and continuing to shake. She stroked his hair gently and waited it out. After a while, he moved a little, wiped his face with the back of his hand. She touched his hair again, felt her heart swell.

"Sorry," he said, his voice muffled.

"Don't apologize," she said. "I know how it feels. It's very powerful."

He breathed, she could feel his heart pounding away, and they lay in silence. The apartment was high up, so there were no sounds from outside.

"My God," he eventually said. She could hear from his voice that he had gathered himself together. "I don't know what to say. That was . . . intense. Way beyond anything I've ever experienced." He looked at her. "And you were like a fucking wet dream."

"You seemed a little angry for a while," she said, studying his face for any sign of regret. But he looked peaceful.

"I probably was. But not really. Never angry. Sorry, my head's a complete mess."

"I hadn't realized how hard it is to be so dominant," Isobel said, her fingers playing with his hair. "Sometimes I had no idea what to do."

"It seemed like you were totally in control of everything."

His voice was steady, and he lay on his back next to her. She lay down on the arm he had stretched out.

"I understand so much more now," he said after a moment. "It was much harder being in the submissive role than I thought." He moved and groaned.

"Does it hurt?"

"You're right, you're strong," he said with a laugh. "It hurts even more now."

"That's because the endorphins are going. Their function is to mask pain. When they leave the body, that's when you really feel the pain." Isobel blushed a little, didn't know why.

Alexander looked at her, kissed her on the forehead. "How are *you?* Tell me how it was for you. Was it tough? Fun? And do you know how sexy you were?"

"It felt good. A little strange. Like I exposed myself."

"Still? Oh, babe, when exactly are you going to start trusting me?"

She didn't answer. Because Alexander had it all backward. She trusted him, a lot, at least when it came to sex. More than she'd ever trusted anyone else. It felt safe with him. And that was a terrifying feeling. She snuggled closer to him.

He stroked her arm, kissed her gently, mumbled nonsensical phrases about how soft she was, how smooth and sexy and perfect, everything she needed to hear. This tenderness . . . He was a fantastic lover, she had never doubted that. But he was also a good person, on so many levels. It was getting harder and harder to remember how different they were, and what wildly different things they believed in.

She closed her eyes, just wanted to be here and now, ignore complicated feelings.

It was his turn to smooth her hair.

"That's so nice," she mumbled.

"Yeah, you like it when I play with your hair. Tell me something about yourself that I don't know. That no one else knows."

She felt his fingers in her hair, deft, tender, and the words came from nowhere: "Sometimes, I'm so tired of fieldwork I just want to curl up and die." She fell silent, amazed. She hadn't even realized she felt that way. The words had just come out; she hadn't consciously thought them.

"Do you mean that?" He sounded curious. "I thought you were practically made for it. And everyone I talk to uses the word *legendary* at least once whenever they talk about you. Why do you feel that way?"

She had them sometimes, if she was being super honest, second thoughts she normally batted back.

There might be something else for me.

All her life she had adapted to other people's needs. She had no family of her own, nothing to keep her at home, not even a fixed job. She had placed a value on that, on always being able to leave, had always thought she *wanted* things that way. But had she really done it for her own sake? She barely dared consider the thought.

"I got taken prisoner once," she said quietly, touching the golden ring in his nipple, sniffing at his skin. Was it possible to be addicted to the smell of someone? The taste? And what happened if you got addicted and then had to stop? Would life lose color and meaning? Or would the longing pass?

She could feel Alexander stare at her, knew he was shocked. "You never told me. When? Where?"

"Last fall. When I was in Liberia."

"Jesus. So recently. What happened?"

"It was so quick," she said slowly, didn't want to remember how terrified she had been, completely at the kidnappers' mercy. "I panicked, did everything wrong. They tied me and I was so scared. I was completely terrified—I'd never thought it would happen to me. They took me at a roadblock and drove off."

"But were you . . . ?"

Alexander fell silent, but she knew what he wanted to know. The thing people always wondered.

"Raped? No. They let me go as soon as they realized I was a doctor. They weren't interested in me. It was chaos down there, so many different warring groups. It was a mistake."

But during those hours she had spent with an automatic weapon pointed at her, she hadn't been particularly strong. She shuddered involuntarily. One of the men had eaten oranges or tangerines and she still couldn't smell that scent without being reminded of the kidnapping. Alexander's arm around her tightened, and she curled up to him, reveling in the protective, almost possessive gesture.

"But why didn't you tell me? It must have affected you."

"I never talk about it. Only Leila knows. That was why she wanted to send me on the safety course. The strange thing was that when I had to be evacuated from Chad, lots of the fear came back. I don't know, maybe I'm not cut out for this in the long run."

"Maybe you want more from life?"

She closed her eyes again. God, she couldn't talk to him about what she wanted from life. Not yet, not now.

She wanted a family. Children. Was that selfish? Wanting things for herself when she could be out there, making a difference to the world?

"I guess so," she said. "Did I tell you about Marius?" Children like Marius were one of the many reasons she kept going. Because if she didn't, then who?

"Yeah, you mentioned him."

"He lives on the streets. He is only seven or eight, a small child, but he's homeless, an orphan. Moves from place to place. He disappears sometimes. Other times he comes to the hospital. I met him when I was there last fall. There are plenty of kids I've been fond of, but then had to leave without knowing what happened to them. You never get used to it, but you learn to switch off. But for some reason, Marius is special."

She had given him blood when she was there that fall. They weren't allowed to do things like that, of course; there were rules. But he had been so ill, so wretched. There were no blood banks—you just asked the relatives if they had considered being donors. But since he was all alone in the world, no one could or would give blood to Marius, and when she realized that she and the boy had the same blood type, the decision had been easy. She had given him hers, and he had gotten better. Her blood literally ran through his veins now.

"He's named after a Chadian soccer player. When I think of him, I know I have to keep working."

"I don't plan to argue with you, not now," he said, and gave her a tender kiss. "You're a complicated woman, Doctor Sørensen, and someone should have a serious talk with you. But not now. I've never felt as good as I do tonight. Anyway. The future has a way of working itself out."

Isobel had no desire to end up in a discussion that couldn't possibly end well either. Because, in contrast to Alexander, she knew that the future didn't have a tendency to work itself out at all. Just the opposite, actually. Her experience was that after the good times, bad times invariably followed. And it was probably time for that all too soon, because things had been good for so long now.

"Is there anything to eat in this sex nest?"

Isobel nodded. They got up, drank tea and ate sandwiches in the kitchen. Talked about art, about films, and about travel. Then they made love again, calmly and tranquilly this time. In bed, beneath the covers. Deep kisses, soft movements. Cozy and intimate, completely free of kink. Afterward they just lay for a long time, gazing into each other's eyes, and it didn't feel even slightly corny. Alexander fell asleep before her, and she lay there awhile, just watching him. He looked different when he slept. Awake, he was always in motion, had such tremendous energy, but now he looked so peaceful. His dark eyebrows and lashes gave character to his golden face. She brushed his forehead with gentle fingers.

She was falling in love with this man. Really falling.

She knew it was stupid, that it was the last thing she had planned to do. But Alexander had a depth and a sensitivity that was impossible to resist. Developing serious feelings for a man notorious for his sexcapades was a quick route to heartache, she knew that, of course; she wasn't stupid. But she could stop her feelings about as easily as she could stop a particularly virulent virus. Nature wasn't kind. It was unrelenting and utterly lacking in compassion. You had to let things take their course, when it came to both viruses and love. If you were strong, you would survive without too much damage. Isobel pulled the covers up over them, moved closer to him, and closed her eyes. God, she hoped she was really strong. Because this had the potential to crush her.

Chapter 52

"I'm meeting Natalia and my mother for lunch today," Alexander reluctantly said the next morning.

Isobel sat opposite him, her hands wrapped around a cup of coffee. "I'm behind on a whole load of paperwork," she said, giving him a languid smile. Her face was relaxed, and he wasn't sure it would be humanly possible to drag himself away from her. He watched her as she absentmindedly studied the headlines on a leaflet. She had on a simple T-shirt today. The makeup was gone, the sexy dress packed away. He liked her even better this way. The things he had experienced in this apartment . . . What they'd shared . . . It was a completely unique experience.

He had done things with this woman that he'd never done before. Strange how closely linked to her he felt now.

He got up, rinsed his mug, and poured her more coffee from the machine.

"I'll call you later," he said, bending down to kiss her. She wrapped her arms around his nape, and he pulled her tightly to him. God, he didn't want to go, wanted to stay here and kiss Isobel, make love, ignore other people's expectations. But he had promised Natalia.

He walked down to Fotografiska, the Swedish Museum of Photography; arrived early, grabbed a table in their fancy restaurant, and immediately lapsed into thoughts of sex and Isobel.

"God, you look serious," Natalia greeted him.

Alexander looked up. He had been so deep in thought that he hadn't even noticed his sister arriving.

He stood up, gave her a hug, and then pulled out a chair for her. "Mom is just parking the car. She'll be here soon."

"Parking? I didn't even know she could drive."

"I told you, she's changing. Please, Alex could you try? Just a little? To not be so mad at her?"

He groaned. "Can we please talk about something else?"

"Sure." Natalia smiled innocently. "How are things with Isobel?"

Christ, he should have known she would move on to that topic.

"Why are you asking?"

She surveyed him carefully. "You were down in Skåne together. And you seemed pretty affectionate at the wedding. I wasn't the only one who noticed. Quit stalling and tell me, are you together or not?"

Were they together, he and Isobel? Truthfully, Alexander had no idea, only knew that what he felt for her was starting to resemble an obsession. But he didn't want to talk about Isobel, not with his nosy big sister. It was too private. Natalia would just sink her teeth in and start to rave about how he had to dare and a load of other carpe diem crap he didn't want to hear.

And then she surprised him by gently saying:

"You're so smart, Alexander. Don't you want more than empty-headed bimbos and constant partying from life? For your own sake?"

He had never told Natalia that he worked in New York. Why? It was getting harder and harder to see the logic in that decision. But he had started to create distance between them at some point, and it had been easier to just continue that way. It was long past time to talk to her. Tell her what he had built up back in New York. It was deeply selfish to keep her in the dark. So what if she felt proud and told Mom, and everyone found out and he had nothing to hide behind anymore? He would just have to cope without his reputation as a playboy and a player. Was it so dangerous? Wasn't he strong enough to carry a few expectations on his shoulders? He forced back a wave of panic when words like *responsibility* and *adult* began to dance in front of his eyes.

Were things moving too fast? Was he about to get tangled up in something far too complicated? And what did Isobel want from him? Could a woman like that ever take a man like him seriously? In the long run? Was he good for anything other than crazy-good sex?

"Here's Mom," Natalia said as she raised her hand in a wave.

Alexander sighed but adopted as polite a face as he could. He suspected this lunch was part of Natalia's plan to bring him and Ebba closer together, so he would try to keep the hostilities to a minimum.

Their mother came toward them, swaying elegantly between chairs, pastel colored, slim and smooth. When Alexander was a boy, he'd thought she was the most beautiful woman on earth. Today, he could see the coldness and self-centeredness that her beauty didn't quite manage to hide. And he was glad she was no longer an important-enough person in his life to be able to hurt him.

That was what people didn't understand when they talked about closeness and intimacy as something desirable. Only if you cared about someone could you get hurt. Only if you loved someone could being abandoned crush you completely.

He stood up, gave his mother a brief nod, and then pulled out a chair for her, without offering a hug or a kiss on the cheek, even a shake of the hand. He could make an effort for Nat, but there were still limits.

"Thank you."

Ebba sat down without a word about his lack of warmth, as though she was eager to keep him in a good mood. Well, that was at least a welcome change.

"I don't think I've been here before," she said.

"No, it's on the wrong side of town. I guess you don't normally come over here," he drawled.

Natalia gave him a warning look. Ebba simply smiled and placed her napkin on her lap. She must have done something to her face. It was smoother than normal, not a wrinkle in sight though she was nearing sixty.

"I'm not quite as uneducated as you think," she said amicably.

"But Mom, even I've been here before."

"Anyway, I'm happy Natalia suggested it. It's good to try new things—that's what I've always thought."

That statement was so out of character that Alexander wasn't sure he had heard her correctly.

"And I'm happy the three of us could meet," she added.

"Peter couldn't come," Natalia added hastily.

Thank God for that small mercy at least. Alexander wasn't sure he could make it through lunch with his mother *and* his brother without exploding. Was Peter even in touch with Ebba, or was that just wishful thinking on Natalia's part? He glanced at his mother and sister, talking in low tones about what they would order. He had to admit that it felt a little strange that Peter was frozen out of the entire family. It was one thing that *he* couldn't stand his brother, but the idea of their mother freezing him out felt heartless, even for her.

"I hear you've been spending time with Blanche Sørensen's daughter," Ebba said as they were brought bread and water.

Alexander glared at his sister.

But Natalia shook her head, mouthed a firm *I haven't said a word*.

"We've met a few times."

"Is she nice?"

"Lay off, Mom," he said sharply.

"I'm just making conversation. Isn't that allowed?"

"Not about things that have nothing to do with you."

Ebba blinked rapidly, and he saw her eyes turning shiny. "I don't understand why you're always so mad at me," she whispered, her voice trembling, and Alexander knew she really meant it. Ebba really didn't *understand*. The anger he felt was so goddamn pointless. She was who she was. Maybe it was too late. Maybe it had always been.

"Please," Natalia said, giving him another pleading look.

He bit his tongue, drummed his fingers, and looked away. He knew he was about to ruin this lunch for her. But didn't Nat know that was what he did? He hadn't asked her to have these expectations of him. If she had them and was disappointed, she only had herself to blame.

Or was he only justifying his own bad habits?

He nodded that he understood.

He couldn't love his mother, but for Natalia's sake maybe he could stop hating her.

Maybe.

"Shall we order?" Ebba looked at him. The pale face he had once loved studied him with an appealing look. She wasn't smooth at all, he could see that now. Wrinkles around her eyes and mouth betrayed her age after all. She had abandoned him, over and over again. Manipulated him, lied to him, always put herself first, to the detriment of him and his siblings—her own children. But all the same, she was only human.

He gave her a light pat on the hand.

"We'll order, Mom."

He smiled at Natalia, who blinked violently several times.

Thanks, she mimed.

And it did actually feel as if another weight had lifted from him.

Chapter 53

Leisurely Isobel went around and cleaned up after them in Eugene's opulent apartment. She drifted from room to room, straightening tablecloths, remembering things they had done, blushing a bit before moving on. Every now and then, her cell phone would buzz and she would read yet another message from Alexander, pausing and grinning.

It was probably a good thing he'd had to leave, that they both had a moment to catch their breath. Not that it stopped her from *aching* for the next time they would meet. With a quick glance she made sure nothing embarrassing had been left behind in the bedroom or under the couches.

In the kitchen she put the last glass back in the cabinet, checked she had packed all of the . . . ehrm . . . *equipment* in the bag, wrapped the flowers in their cellophane, and went down to the cab she had called.

At home she searched for the biggest vase she owned—an heirloom from her grandmother—and put the orchids on the kitchen table. As she admired the exquisite bouquet she tried to remember the last time a man, a *lover,* had given her flowers, but had to give up.

She had only just changed into her sweatpants when Alexander sent another one of his messages. Just a red heart this time, and she felt her own heart swell. Ah, but this was too ridiculous. It was like being sixteen and head over heels in love. Aside from the fact that she'd never had such strong feelings for anyone when she was sixteen. Or ever.

She sat down at the computer. She was behind with everything, needed to get into some kind of serious working mind-set.

Isobel managed to work effectively for a few hours before she began to yawn. She brewed some coffee, took a quick shower, and sat back down at the computer.

Another text, the twentieth or so of the day, asking: *How soon can I see you?*

It probably wasn't a very smart idea to let Alexander take up so much of her working time. But God, she longed for him.

Need to work. Later, okay?

Sipping her coffee, she opened a medical site to look for a particular study, clicked on a link to a newspaper article, clicked on another interesting link, and suddenly found herself on the couch, surfing the net for anything related to Alexander De la Grip. Out of self-preservation she avoided things she had already read about him—didn't want to read old gossip—and found an article about Romeo Rozzi's career instead, which she read with great interest. Then she moved on to another Web site and saw pictures of one of Romeo's restaurants, activated another link, ended up on a famous rooftop terrace in New York, studying the beautiful people's faces, and caught sight of . . .

She frowned and then couldn't help it. She knew the wise thing was to leave the page, but instead she looked closer, against all better judgment.

Yup, it was Alexander, looking very drunk. With two young women in his lap. An arm around one of them, a hand on the other's thigh. She read the caption. "Playboy billionaire plays fast and loose with gorgeous blondes." There wasn't much difference between this picture and every other she'd seen. Aside from one thing. She had to check her calendar just to be sure. Double-check against her Skype account.

Yeah.

This was taken on Alexander's latest New York trip. The same day they'd started to Skype, as a matter of fact, when he had *sworn* to her that he hadn't slept with that girl with the strange name or with anyone else. She had believed him then and she still believed him. This stupid photo didn't have to mean a thing. But still. It did. A little anyway. She clicked down the site but now she just couldn't stop herself, so she started Googling him seriously, reading everything that popped up. Years and years of escapades came on her screen. Pictures of Alexander and famous women. Notorious women. Actresses, pop stars, and heiresses. Parties, premieres, and one scandal after the other. And everywhere Alexander—grinning, drinking, partying, actually looking quite happy, in a sort of debauched way. Occasionally she thought she spotted an almost desolate look on his face, but maybe it was just her imagination.

It wasn't that she was jealous, not too much anyway. She knew this was who he was, had no illusions about his past. As a matter of fact, she wasn't so concerned with the pictures online as she'd thought she would be; they didn't tell her anything she didn't already know. But another thing had been nagging her, in a dark corner of her mind. Something that had been lying there, in wait. Something she hadn't allowed herself to examine too closely. But now it came to the surface. All the stuff he'd told her, the revelations about his mother's infidelity and the abuse he'd suffered as a young teenager; how much damage had it caused? Everything she knew about the human psyche, everything she'd read and experienced told her it would be difficult for someone with that kind of background to really have a deep, emotional relationship with a woman. But that didn't matter, right? Because she didn't want a relationship with Alexander.

Or did she?

She got up from the computer. Washed her face. Walked around restlessly. Was she overanalyzing this? Probably. But it didn't change the fact that she had some serious decisions to make. Oh, she could just go with the flow, enjoy the ride, and all the other bullshit people said when they were trying to fool themselves into making stupid decisions. But that wasn't her. She wanted, no *needed,* someone stable. Dependable. She was old enough to know herself. Could Alexander be all that? Because she didn't believe in trying to change people. In her opinion people pretty much were who they were, period. And Alex was a player. It didn't diminish her feelings for him. She had fallen for an amoral billionaire playboy. That was a fact. But she had to stay sober about this. Had to rely on smart Isobel, not sex-crazed Isobel. It would be a scary prospect to start committing to Alexander.

She had to be brutally honest and ask herself if she was anything more to him than another victory in a long line of conquests. She mulled it over. Yes, she really did think she was more, if her instincts were to be trusted.

Her cell phone buzzed. It was him. Her silly heart started to flutter. Oh, but she had totally fallen.

Want to meet tonight? I'll make dinner. Satisfy all your appetites.

Isobel read the message. And then again. Could hear his deep voice in the words, feel his touch, sense his laughter. Even through a short text she was drawn into his remarkable force field, remembering their wild lovemaking but also the closeness she felt to him. Damn, this was so dangerous.

And then something else struck her, made her freeze. Had she really talked with him about not going into the field anymore? That was madness. How could she even think about that, much less say it aloud? People like her, doctors like her, *professionals* like her, simply didn't do that. She was a person who, more than anything else, wanted to help others. She needed to be of use to the world, had felt like that as long as she could remember. That meant she simply couldn't indulge in every shallow whim that happened to strike her. Definitely couldn't let sex and infatuation guide her actions. Surely she was more sensible than that.

She spent a long time looking at the display, reading the letters.

Be logical, Isobel. Be smart.

Slowly she tapped in her reply: *Maybe not today*.

Stared at it for a long time, wondering whether she should add anything else before sending it.

But what else was there to add, really? This had gone much too far already, was leading her astray, making her choose the wrong path. Hurriedly she pressed send, then switched the phone to silent and returned to her work.

When everything came crashing down around her, she always had her work. Though, right now, at this moment, she was uncertain whether it felt more like a blessing or a taunt. But she didn't pick up the cell phone the entire evening. It had gone on long enough. She had to be wise. Even if it hurt like hell.

Chapter 54

Two days after the fiasco at Gina's house, everything was grayer than ever in Peter's life.

He hadn't heard from her since the catastrophe.

It was over.

If he was so inclined, he might have drunk himself stupid, he thought as he studied the people streaming past him on Norrmalmstorg. It was five p.m. and everyone was headed home. To their families, friends, to pick up the kids from day care, he assumed. Bankers passed by, then a couple of well-known venture capitalists, and a bank manager hurried across the cobblestones. He saw a newly appointed press spokeswoman and two speech writers. They were all half-running, seemed to be in a rush somewhere. Things moved so quickly in this world. Young, hungry talents were always snapping at the heels of the elite. In a few years half these people would be gone, and the other half would have climbed even higher up the ladder.

He knew he should get up from the bench and go home, but he couldn't bring himself to do it. Just the thought of standing and then walking back to his empty apartment felt impossible. He was a shell. A dead, self-pitying shell. And he only had himself to blame.

It had been a stupid impulse to buy Amir those soccer things.

He rubbed his face, ashamed.

Alexander was the drunk in the family. Natalia the sensitive financial genius. He was the dutiful one. The one who did nothing rash, the one who followed the rules. Those few times he hadn't, it had ended in disaster. Just as it had Tuesday. He had left the office early, filled the car with new things, and then driven out to Tensta with a feeling of joy buzzing through his entire body.

And it had all gone so well at first.

Until Gina came home.

He really did understand what had upset her, he thought with shame. It had been rash and badly thought through. He should have checked with her first, listened to what she thought Amir needed. But he had never been good with words, and he knew how much Amir meant to her. So he had done it for Gina's sake. To try to show his feelings.

Christ, how could he have been so stupid?

It had backfired and now he had lost her, the person he cared so much about.

He looked away from the sun. It was getting warmer, people were dressed in short sleeves, but he was frozen beneath his skin, in his bones. He knew he didn't just "care about" Gina. It was much more than that.

Peter looked up and allowed his gaze to sweep aimlessly over the bustling square. Five more minutes and then he would have to pull himself together, he decided wearily. He continued to watch people, and when the crowd suddenly dispersed, he caught sight of Alexander walking toward him over Hamngatan. Peter peered at Alexander, his carefree, popular, brilliant little brother: tall, square-shouldered, and well-dressed among taxi cabs, buses, and harried big city dwellers. Alexander always looked as if he had just stepped out of a luxury aftershave ad. Peter felt a perverse satisfaction at not being seen, at being able to study his brother in secret, but of course it didn't last. Alexander caught sight of him just as he was about to pass by. His step shortened, and he seemed to hesitate, as though he would rather pretend he hadn't seen Peter, but then he turned and headed for the bench.

"Why're you sitting here looking so gloomy?" he greeted him.

"I'm not gloomy. What are *you* doing here?"

Alexander nodded toward Smålandsgatan. "My foundation is over there. I'm headed there. I came from home," he added.

Right, Alexander had an apartment in Stockholm these days.

Alexander studied him more closely. "How are things? You look awful."

"Well, thank you."

Alexander sat down on the bench next to him.

Peter sighed. Company was the last thing he wanted.

They said nothing. Watched the passersby.

Alexander swung a foot up onto his knee. "Natalia is worried about you. God knows why, but she is. Could you call her?"

Peter gave a humorless laugh. "You're hardly the one to give relationship advice."

"It wasn't advice. It was a request. You can be civil and call her, can't you?"

"I know you don't give a damn about me. You don't have to pretend you do."

"I'm not pretending. Respectfully, I don't give a damn about you. But Natalia does, and I happen to like Natalia. So call her."

They sat in silence again.

"I saw Mom yesterday," Alexander continued.

"Lunch? I couldn't make it." He hadn't been able to bring himself to meet them. He had barely managed to drag himself from bed.

"Why? Did something happen?"

"I thought you said you didn't care?"

Alexander ran his hand through his perfectly ruffled hair before he spread an arm along the backrest. During the few minutes Alexander had been there, at least five women had turned around to stare at him.

"Doesn't it get old?"

Peter remembered all the times Alexander, with his devastatingly good looks, his smile, and his force-of-nature charm, had swept in and helped himself. How many girls had he been interested in, only for them to fall for Alexander? No one could compete with his brother, not least him, a depressed, divorced loser.

"What?"

"Oh, nothing."

"What's the deal with you and Gina, by the way?"

"Why are you asking that?" he snapped, the pain of hearing her name almost too much.

"Just a question. I saw you talking to her at the christening and then at the wedding."

"There's nothing going on." Not anymore.

"You aren't bothering her, are you?"

He froze. "Bothering?"

"You know what I mean."

"No, I don't," he said, though he knew exactly what Alexander meant. "Maybe you'd care to explain?"

"Christ, Peter. I just don't get how you could do it. How can you live with yourself?"

Peter closed his eyes. So, it was time. He and Alexander hadn't talked about the rape of Carolina Hammar, not once. Of all the things that had happened since last summer, that was one of the things that tormented him the most. The fact that Alexander knew, that he hated him as a result, but that he had never said anything.

"I don't get it either. Maybe I can explain it somehow, but I can never excuse it. I regret it in a way I can hardly describe. There's nothing you can say to me that I haven't already said myself. Nothing you can accuse me of that I haven't already accused myself of a thousand times."

"But how? Why? You just don't do that."

"No," he agreed. How could he explain it to Alexander when he still couldn't understand it himself? He had liked Caro. They had talked, often. She had been kind to him and he was attracted to her, in a relatively innocent way. But things had gone wrong that night. There had been a huge amount of peer pressure, and he had given in. "I'm not placing the blame anywhere else. My friends and I had been drinking, and we got each other excited. One thing led to another, and then when it was done it was too late to undo it." He had been drawn in, been too weak to refuse. He didn't excuse himself, didn't place the blame anywhere else, but he was trying to comprehend the incomprehensible.

"It was eighteen years ago. Carolina and I have talked. She's forgiven me, moved on. I voted against Dad and for her brother. I don't know what else I can do. When do you think I'll have atoned?"

"I don't know."

Peter knew he had changed since last summer, that he was someone else now. And yet people still saw him as the person he had been. It was a paralyzing feeling. To know you had improved, had tried, but were still seen as who you had been before. Scum.

"I get that you feel . . . betrayed?"

Alexander just shook his head. "Betrayed. Shocked. Repulsed. Take your pick. And the fact that Mom and Dad knew all along. It's too much. Don't you realize how it's affected our family all these years?"

"Yeah. But you know I thought Carolina was dead. I've lived half my life in the belief that I killed a woman. I'm not saying I've atoned for what I did, but I wouldn't wish that feeling on my worst enemy."

Alexander smiled ironically. "Not even me, you mean?"

"You aren't my enemy, Alex. You're my brother. I let you down, I know that. But . . ." His last words were stifled. He wanted to say he loved Alex, but such words were never spoken in their family. No one had ever said it to him, and he had never said it himself, not even to his ex-wife.

Alexander's jaw clenched.

"Do you still speak to Dad?" he eventually asked.

Peter shook his head. "He doesn't talk to me anymore. I don't give a damn."

"And Mom?"

"We speak occasionally. I mean, she's so loyal to Dad, but I think she's actually a little tired of him. She's getting old, maybe she's re-assessed her priorities."

"She's good with Molly," said Alexander.

Peter smiled. "Yeah, who would have thought that?"

"I thought you liked Mom."

"Believe it or not, I do like her. I can see that she has lots of faults. But she's my mother, and I don't have the right to judge her."

"Do you ever hear from Louise?"

Peter shook his head.

"Do you miss her?"

Peter thought about it. "Not even a little bit. That's terrible, isn't it?"

"Nah, Louise wasn't a good person. Even you didn't deserve to be married to her."

"Thanks, I think."

This must be the longest conversation they'd had in many, many years. He had been so jealous of Alexander for so long—his entire life, actually. It was a terrible feeling, jealousy; it completely devoured you. And it was shameful. But that was gone now, Peter saw. He had gotten over it when he met Gina.

"Jesus, I still can't believe you raped a girl. I feel like I should hit you."

"*I* feel like I should hit myself, so I understand. Want to? Would it feel better?"

Alexander sighed. "No."

He took out his cell, looked at it with a concerned expression, as though he was waiting for something that never came.

"Everything okay?"

"Yeah, why?"

"You've been checking your cell constantly."

"Sorry. I just thought I'd get a message. It's nothing."

"Alexander?"

"Yeah?"

Peter wanted to say that he would never hurt a woman again. That he would rather die than raise a hand to anyone, but he was interrupted by: "Peter?"

And his entire world stopped.

Gina.

"Hi," she said, and the hair all over Peter's body stood on end. He got up, his eyes not leaving her for a millisecond.

Gina Gina Gina.

"Hi there," Alexander said with a smile, also getting to his feet. "How are you? What are you doing here?"

"I work here," she replied, nodding her head toward Peter's office, without looking at Alexander. She looked only at Peter. "Or did. It was temporary. I'm here to pick up my things." Her voice was breathless, as if she had trouble concentrating on her words.

Peter looked at her.

She looked at Peter.

Alexander said something else, but Peter didn't hear what. He just continued to look at Gina, trying to drink in her features. Would this be the last time he saw her? Did she hate him? Was there anything he could do?

"Are you going to the office?" she asked quietly.

"No. I was headed home. I just ended up sitting here."

"Don't you have the car today?"

He shook his head. Hadn't even bothered to pretend he had anywhere else to go after work.

"Are you okay?" she asked.

"No, I don't think so," he said.

"He really does look pretty lousy," said Alexander.

"Though I feel better now that you're here," Peter said, ignoring Alexander. His heart was pounding so hard he could hardly breathe.

Gina bit her lip. She cast a glance at Alexander.

Peter did the same.

Alexander looked at them both, suspicious.

"Why do I get the feeling you want me to leave?"

"You were on your way to the foundation, weren't you?" said Peter. *Go,* he urged silently.

Alexander shook his head. "Would that be fine with you, Gina?"

"What?" she asked, as her eyes flitted across Peter's face. Dark, worried, darling eyes.

"That I leave?"

Gina nodded so eagerly that Peter almost laughed. Never before had a woman wanted Alexander to leave and Peter to stay.

Alexander gave Peter another look, rolled his eyes, and put on his sunglasses. And then he held out his hand.

"Good luck."

Peter looked at it before he took it and shook it, long and hard.

"Thanks," he said, serious.

"Bye," said Alexander, and he loped away.

And Gina, God bless her, she didn't watch him go.

"We need to talk," she said.

Chapter 55

Gina walked quietly next to him. Peter didn't speak either, and the silence between them grew and grew.

"Where do you want to go?" he eventually asked.

"Where can we talk?"

"A café?" He pointed toward Stureplan.

"No. Do you live nearby?"

He nodded.

"Let's go there, then."

They said nothing else during the short walk to his street.

"You live here?" Gina asked, looking up at the gray building with wide eyes.

"Yeah," he replied, embarrassed. The property was undeniably grand. He punched in the door code and held the door open for her.

"There's no elevator," he explained. "I live on the fourth floor."

They went up the wide, marble Östermalm stairs in silence. Gina glanced at the letter boxes; exclusive prefixes like *von* and *af* were in the majority here, signs of the noble lineage of the occupants, but she didn't comment.

Peter unlocked the door, stepped to one side, and let her in.

He took her jacket and hung it up. "Let's go into the living room," he said. "If you sit down, I'll make some tea."

When he came back with two mugs, Gina was on the sofa with a pillow on her lap.

Peter sat slightly away from her, not wanting to intrude. She twisted the corner of the pillow between her thumb and forefinger.

"I wanted to apologize," she finally began.

He almost tripped over the words in his rushed reply. "You don't have anything to apologize for. I'm the one who should apologize. I should have talked to you first."

"I know I can be hypersensitive. Suspicious. It's something I need to work on."

"You've been through a lot. You've had reason to distrust people. I'm sure it's saved you plenty of times. But believe me, you have nothing to apologize for as far as I'm concerned."

"I was just a kid when we left Somalia. Dad was married, did I tell you that? To a younger woman. My mom died when Amir was born. Dad got remarried so we'd have a mother. But she was from a tiny village, and she had different ideas from ours, and a huge clan behind her. You've met my dad. He's a good man. His new wife wanted me to get married to a cousin of hers. I was eleven."

Peter said nothing. As an eleven-year-old, he'd had all the material comforts there were. Had gone to school. Played soccer with his friends.

"Amir was so small, but Dad's new wife wanted nothing to do with him; she pushed him away. It was horrible to watch. Dad tried to talk to her, but they just argued. And then he ended up fighting with some of the guerillas. Things got dangerous. So he took us, and we left." Her voice sank. "He left everything for us."

"I understand," he said. "What happened to his wife?"

"She was a woman who always looked out for her own interests," said Gina. "She was probably just relieved to get rid of us. Since then, it's been the three of us."

She quickly wiped her cheek.

Peter got up and fetched a pack of tissues, handed her one, and sat down next to her. Gina blew her nose.

"I overreacted," she said. "When you came over. But I was scared. I know you meant well."

"It's okay, Gina. My sister always talks about how white men with power need to be more sensitive to other people's needs. I used to think she was a pain, but lots has changed. I'm just at the beginning. You can be mad at me. There are so many times I haven't spoken up, pretended not to hear. I've got a lot to make up for."

"I'm not mad at you."

She reached out and touched his wrist.

Peter's heart practically stopped in his chest. Gina leaned forward, put a hand on his shoulder, and kissed him on the lips. At first, he didn't dare move, but then he kissed her back, tenderly, reverently.

She pulled away. Gave him a serious look.

"In my country, young girls are subjected to female genital mutilation, Peter. Do you remember we talked about it?"

He had trouble breathing. "Yes," he said quietly. He swallowed. Couldn't get another word past his lips. *No, God.*

"My mother had been against it, but Dad's new wife was worried no one would want to marry me, and she said people would call me a whore. She decided to have it done to me when Dad was away. I know some people call that custom a cultural expression, but it's not. It's a horrible mutilation of a young girl's sexual parts. Cruelty and repression. It leaves scars for life, painful ones. Destroys a woman's chances of being able to enjoy married life. Of having children without complications. It's *not* religion." Her gaze was steady.

His mouth was completely dry. "I'm so sorry," he said helplessly, cautiously taking her hand. It was slender and light in his. She wore a simple silver ring around her thumb, and he wanted to cry at the thought of what she had told him.

"Peter?"

"Yes?"

"There were so many of them. They forced me down on a rug. Four or maybe five women. They were going to use a razor blade. I was so scared. But Dad came home, just in time and he snatched me away, saved me from them, simply refused to allow it," she said. "Refused. He saved me—many girls don't survive—and then we fled. He gave up so much for my sake. And he's never put any demands on me. He trusts me. But *I* have demands of myself. Do you follow?"

Peter nodded, though he didn't quite understand. This was so far removed from his everyday life.

"I promised myself I would wait for a good man. A kind man. I really haven't been so good at trusting. I've seen too much. But now it feels like I've found him."

She squeezed his hand, linked her slender fingers through his. The contrast was so damn beautiful his throat burned. Peter cleared his throat.

"But you know I'm not a good person? I told you what I did. Of all the men you've met, I'm not the best, I can promise you that." His voice broke. If he could just go back in time, start over, atone for his sins. "You know what happened, I . . ."

"Idiot," she said, and she kissed him again.

Peter wasn't quite sure what was happening. But Gina was on his couch, kissing him, and so he decided not to analyze the situation too much.

He pulled her to him, gently. She put an arm around his neck, and their kiss deepened. Without thinking, he raised a hand to her breast.

She froze, and he pulled his hand back.

"Sorry," he quickly said.

"Idiot," she mumbled into his mouth.

"Gina, I can't . . ." he choked. He hadn't been with a woman in so long. He would embarrass himself. She was so beautiful, deserved the best.

"Don't you want to?" she asked quietly.

He laughed at the question. It was so far from the truth. "Yeah, so much it hurts," he said honestly. "But Gina . . ."

"But what?" She gave him a serious look. Dark eyes, skin like silk.

"I don't understand," he said, frustrated. "*You* want to? With me? Why?"

She slapped him, square on the face. It was so completely unexpected that he could only stare. She had small, slim hands, but she was strong, and her palm made his cheek sting.

"What are—?"

She hit him again. Hard. His cheek burned. Peter got up from the couch and she did the same, stood in front of him breathing heavily.

"Gina," he said helplessly. What had he done?

She positioned herself. He saw her hand approaching, and she hit him again, even harder this time. The sound echoed through the room. She didn't wait, and raised her hand again. Peter tensed.

She lowered it; her hand fell to her side.

"*Why?*" she asked, breathlessly. "Because. Because you're a *good* person. Because you think you're bad, that you have to stay away from women, and because you think you're some kind of monster.

But I've met monsters, Peter. Real monsters. *You* aren't one of them. You don't hit back, not even when I hit you like that, completely unprovoked, like some madwoman. You're a gentleman. You're kind, you're considerate."

"But what I did to Carolina . . ."

"Everyone has the potential for both good and evil. Everyone can cause pain. But you're not the person now you might have been when you were at school."

"I don't think I could do something like that again. God, I hope not." He had made a promise to himself that he would rather kill himself than do anything like that again. Not because he was a good person but because he wouldn't be able to live with any more guilt. "I regret it so much."

"You gave my brother the one thing he wanted most. You gave your time. You listen. You're thoughtful and you care. That's why. Idiot," she added.

"But—"

"No." She sharply cut him off. "No buts. I want to sleep with you. If you don't want to, fine. But if you do, you have to stop going on about being a bad person."

"I want to," he said quietly.

She stuck out her chin, and defiantly said, "If you don't want to, it's okay."

"I do. More than anything. Not to sleep with you, but to make love to you."

She bit her lip. "Well, then."

They kissed again, standing, embracing. An adult, awesome, magnificent kiss.

She pulled away, and her eyes fell to his chest.

"There's just one thing you should know."

"What?" He stroked her upper arm, thought that he could be happy with a world in which he got to caress Gina's smooth skin.

"It's not a big deal," she said, though she still avoided his gaze. She chewed her lip. "But I should probably tell you."

"What?"

"Don't freak out, or give it any importance. But technically, I'm . . ." She swallowed, looked up, and met his eye. "I'm a virgin."

"Are you kidding me?"

"Yeah, right? No. I've never slept with a man. And you're the only one I've kissed."

He had no idea how she had made it through life un-kissed, but he was apparently smart enough not to say anything more. He already had performance anxiety at the thought of being with this beautiful, young woman. He had to make it perfect for her. Offer her something other than tea to drink. Some food, maybe. Court her.

"Peter?"

"I need to sit down."

"We don't have to do anything."

He took her hand and pulled her down onto the couch, touched a hand to her cheek, and kissed her. "I don't think there's anything I want more in the world right now."

He didn't say it, but he thought the words.

I love you.

Over and over again.

I love you, Gina.

The relief made Gina want to giggle. But she wasn't sure she had ever giggled, so she smiled and allowed herself to be kissed by Peter again. She had told him, and he had taken the news splendidly.

She hadn't planned on being a virgin at the age of twenty-two. That was just how things had panned out. She wasn't one of those girls who'd had a boyfriend in high school. The years went by and she never met anyone she liked, and suddenly she was so old it was starting to get embarrassing. Logically she knew she couldn't be the only adult virgin in the world, but she had been waiting for the right person, and he had never turned up. Until now. In the shape of a divorced, white financier. Someone up there must really have a sense of humor.

Peter took her hand. They ended up in the bathroom. It was about the same size as Gina's family's living room.

"Wow," she said, reluctantly impressed.

"I know," he said, as he took out some soft hand towels and put them down on a bench. "The real estate agent waxed lyrical when I bought this place. I thought it was ridiculously big, but now I'm pleased. Now that you're here. I thought we could take a shower to-gether?"

Gina nodded. She took another step into the room, and it was like entering a spa. Not that she'd ever been in one, but it smelled so clean and aromatic. The lighting consisted of tiny bulbs, like stars in the ceiling. Everything was subdued, calm, soft.

Peter took off his shirt, and she glanced at his chest. He was in good shape. Not super muscular, but still pretty solid. Narrow hips, a dark blond line of hair that disappeared into the waistband of his pants. She should feel shy, but it was as though they'd passed that stage. Instead she put a hand on his chest and spread her fingers over his muscles. Her hand was dark, almost black against his faint tan. He put a hand on top of hers, kissed her, and she thought that it had probably been worth it, waiting for these kisses.

They helped one another undress. Peter was so unbelievably gen-tle with her, with featherlight fingers and soft kisses, that she felt like a princess. The bathroom was big enough for a group of armchairs. Peter sat her down in one of them and squatted in front of her. Slipped off her canvas shoes and put them carefully to one side. Ran his hands over her calves and up, over her hips. Helped her take her panties off, folded them up. He was so tender, so calm, that Gina al-lowed herself to be swept along. He kissed her knees, her stomach, and her collarbone before they went into the shower together.

Gina had studied medicine for almost two semesters. She knew her anatomy. They had taken classes in chemistry, biology, and the physiology of the body. But that said, she had no idea how a man's penis would feel in her hand, how warm and hard and intimate it would feel in her palm. Had never realized how different someone else's fingers would feel as they wandered over her skin.

He lathered her up, carefully, gently, almost humbly. The shower rained down on them and they kissed. He rinsed her off, dried her in an enormous towel. Crouched down, dried her feet, her calves, her thighs.

"You're so beautiful," he whispered.

And Gina felt beautiful. Not just exotic and young. But like a de-sirable grown woman.

They made love in his bed. He took his time with her, kissed and touched her until she was more than ready. He was careful when he entered her, and it felt so good that Gina thought to herself that it had been really smart of her to wait for him.

She stroked his hair, felt him move inside her. It was better than she had expected. Different, but better. More serious. He was so chivalrous and attentive to her every need, so good and protective.

Afterward, they lay and talked. Touched one another, got close, adjusted to their newfound intimacy.

"Are you okay?" he asked for maybe the fifteenth time as he gently caressed her nose, her forehead, her mouth. Kissed her, doted on her.

"I think this has been one of the best days of my life."

"I *know* it's the best day of mine," he said. "Did it hurt?"

"Not a bit, actually. My poor body must have been so shocked to be having sex that it forgot to protest."

"If it's alright for me to say so, I love your body."

He fell silent, and the word *love* hung in the air.

Gina smiled and put a hand on his face. She had strong feelings for him, otherwise she wouldn't have done what she had. But she was in no rush. And she knew Peter wouldn't put any pressure on her.

He moved closer to her, on top, and Gina giggled. Again. She rolled her eyes and then laughed out loud.

And then they made love again.

Chapter 56

Alexander put his cutlery to one side. He was having trouble concentrating on lunch, even though he was the one who had suggested it. It was two days since he had last seen Isobel. Twenty-four hours since she had last replied to one of his messages.

What the fuck had happened?

He didn't want to press too hard. But it wasn't his imagination, was it? That she'd withdrawn from him? Did she need to think? Had something happened? What could it be?

"Are you planning to tell me why we're here, or do you want me to keep guessing?" Leila Dibah asked as their coffee arrived. She studied him with her dark, all-seeing eyes, and he wouldn't have been the least bit surprised if she could actually look into him, read his thoughts, and was amusing herself by listing all of his many shortcomings.

"I want to talk finance," he said as he wondered whether Leila knew anything about what was going on with Isobel.

"I'm listening." Leila stirred her jet-black coffee.

"How much would you need to get Medpax back on its feet?"

Her face didn't move; she didn't even blink.

"A ballpark figure?"

"Yes."

"A million. Maybe less. We just passed an audit, so there can't be any ambiguity around any donations. There has to be complete transparency."

"Of course. I'll talk to the foundation."

He had the money, after all. He wouldn't worm his way in to Medpax, try to take control or anything like that, but he couldn't let Isobel's organization go under. The hospital needed more oxygen machines and staff, otherwise children would die. He might just as well give money for humanitarian aid as for anything else. Plus, he knew it would have a direct impact. Medpax didn't pay high wages, had no inflated administration costs, and definitely didn't have any field-workers sunning themselves poolside. And he wanted to support Isobel's organization, *do* something.

"Can I ask, why is it you decided this?"

"I thought I should try to do something for the world for a change." And I want to prove I'm worthy to a woman I care a lot about.

Leila looked skeptical.

"So this has nothing to do with Isobel?"

"Why? Has she said anything about me?"

Why didn't she reply to his calls and texts anymore? What could have changed during the short time since they last saw each other? They had parted as though . . . well, as though they meant something to each other, but now: nothing. Had he misjudged her that badly?

Leila raised an eyebrow. "*Said* anything? Like you were in high school, you mean?"

"I just wondered."

She stirred her coffee. "When you're a psychologist, people always expect you to encourage them to *talk* about things."

"I tried to talk. She's avoiding me."

Leila smiled. She definitely had a mean streak, he thought. But he was dying to talk about Isobel, so he could tolerate some nastiness in return.

"That's not what I meant. You should know, it's my professional opinion that people are useless at talking to one another. And whenever they do, it mostly ends in misunderstandings."

"Mmm," he agreed. He had always thought that talking too much and too deeply was a mistake. But that also meant he had no idea what he should do now. "What do you think I should do?"

Leila held out a hand and studied her shiny, black nails. "The thing is, Isobel is someone I care a lot about. She was in Liberia last fall, did you know that?"

"Yes. I care about her too. I hope you realize that."

Leila made a deprecatory gesture.

"What she probably didn't tell you is that when all the other field-workers stayed four weeks—because they can't cope for any longer than that—Isobel stayed eight. You can't even imagine what she went through. That woman is tougher than anyone I've ever met."

"I know that already," he clipped, wondering what Leila was getting at.

"I don't understand you. If there comes a point where I have to choose between Isobel's well-being and your money, I'll choose Isobel in a blink of a second. She's never had anyone to fight in her corner. She's a tough doctor but a complex person. The truth is that since you came on the scene, she's changed."

"Changed how?"

"She looks like a calf that's been put out to pasture for the first time in its life, and doesn't quite believe it's real. And I feel slightly responsible for that, because I encouraged this, back in the beginning."

Alexander didn't know what to say to that.

Leila leaned forward over the table. Gave him a stern look. "If you're just having a bit of fun with her, I suggest you think carefully about whatever it is you're doing."

"I can't see that is any of your business."

She smiled, that evil smile again. "Then we're on the same page. So don't ask me whether Isobel has said anything. Talk to her."

Alexander nodded coolly. The check arrived, and he paid in silence. They got up, and he helped her with her jacket before they went out to the street. Leila took out her cigarillos, lit one, and breathed in the smoke.

"I'll be in touch about the money," he said.

She blew out the smoke. "Thanks for lunch."

Idris looked so worn out, Isobel thought worriedly.

"How's the cold?" she asked over Skype.

"It's not bad," he answered, as she'd known he would. There wasn't a doctor on earth who would admit they were sick unless they were dying. But he looked really sick.

The Skype image flickered, and Isobel waited as weather, satellites, or maybe just Murphy's Law did its thing.

"How are you?" he asked once the sound and picture were working again.

"Just a little jet-lagged," she lied.

She knew she looked worn out, too. But she couldn't sleep, and since she didn't want to be one of those doctors who wrote out a prescription for sleeping tablets the minute things got a little tough, she lay awake instead. Brooded. Cried.

"How is Marius?" she asked.

Idris shook his head. "I didn't want to say anything. I don't know where he is. But you know how things are, he disappears sometimes." She nodded, bleakly, knew how the boy tried to get along. Maybe he was in N'Djamena, the capital. Maybe he was dead. She felt a stab of almost unbearable pain.

"It'll be better when the new doctor arrives. He is sharing some kind of visa trouble."

"You're probably right. Take care," she said, hoping that at least Idris would get a good night's sleep. And that Marius was safe somewhere.

They said good-bye, and the feeling of guilt threatened to overwhelm her.

What was she doing? How could she dream about a life with a playboy like Alexander when there was so much else that was more important than being someone's exciting sexual conquest? She should be ashamed. And she was.

Her cell rang, and she picked it up.

"Hey, it's Leila," she heard in her ear.

Isobel frowned, tried to remember what day it was. Friday. "Did I miss a meeting?"

"No. I just wanted to check if you were okay."

"Why shouldn't I be?"

"I saw Alexander De la Grip today. We had lunch."

Shit, even hearing his name hurt.

"What did he want?" she asked, trying to find the exact right carefree tone, but she had a terrible feeling she failed miserably.

"He wants to give Medpax more money. I wanted to check you were okay with that."

"I guess so. Why wouldn't I be?"

"Because there's something going on between you. And because it's a lot of money."

"How much?"

"A million."

"I see."

She heard Leila sigh deeply on the other end of the line. Yes, well, there was plenty to sigh about today.

"Isobel, I know I told you to have fun. I'm sorry if it was bad advice."

She almost smiled. It couldn't be easy for Leila to admit something like that. "Nothing happened. Or, it's over now. He's not the man for me. And I have no problem if he wants to give money to Medpax. Or does he expect something in return?"

"No."

Isobel wanted to ask more. Whether they'd talked about her. How Alexander was doing. Whether he was as miserable as she was. But, of course, she said nothing. There were limits to how pathetic she wished to appear.

"Thanks for calling," she said.

As soon as she hung up, the phone rang again.

Like some damn call center.

She looked down at the caller ID, didn't want to admit even to herself that her heart beat that little bit harder at the thought that Alexander still hadn't given up.

Mom.

Yippee.

"Hi, Mom," she said, and stretched out on the couch. She looked at the vase of orchids he had given her, still fresh and vibrant.

"How are you?"

Blanche launched into a monologue about people who annoyed her, articles she would write, and things she needed help with as soon as possible. Isobel closed her eyes.

"Mom, I don't think I'll be able to come over this weekend." She could barely get up off the couch.

"What kind of nonsense is this? Are you sick?"

"No, but . . ."

"Being idle does no one any good. Have you found a better job yet? You know I think you should continue your studies, pursue your doctorate. When I was your age . . ."

"Mom, please. I'm feeling a little down. I just . . ."

"Down? What do you have to be down about? You're young and

healthy. I don't know what's wrong with you. And you came home early from Chad. Honestly, I'm a little disappointed in you. If you're going to keep sneaking off like this, you won't amount to anything."

Isobel put an arm over her eyes and stopped herself from groaning loudly. "I didn't sneak off. I was almost caught in the middle of a clan war."

"Surely you're exaggerating."

She couldn't, she just couldn't. "I'm your daughter. Why do you always have to be so horrible?"

Long, hurt silence.

"So I'm the villain now, as usual. Just for loving you. No one will love you like your mother. But I'll just have to accept it, like everything else. Sorry for bothering you."

"I just don't understand why you have to criticize everything I do," tried Isobel.

"There's no talking to you when you're in a mood like this."

"So hang up then." She didn't even know where the rebellious words had come from.

"Isobel! What's with you?"

"There's nothing wrong with me. You're the one who moans about me all the time. You don't know what it was like in Chad. You just call to complain and talk about yourself."

"Well, sorry for having an opinion, for breathing. I don't know how you got so easily offended. Talking to you isn't pleasant at all today."

Silence. She was gathering herself for an attack, Isobel could *hear* it.

"It's no wonder you don't have a man in your life."

Isobel blinked violently, stared at her toes, felt the familiar powerlessness inside. It made no difference what she said or did. She was never good enough. Her entire life, she had striven to keep her mother in a good mood, and normally, she would have apologized by now, steered the conversation to safer ground, repressed any urge to stand up for herself. But instead, something that had never happened before happened.

She snapped

It was enough.

"You know what, Mom, you can go to hell," she said, and hung up.

Shame she couldn't slam down the receiver. She put the phone down, took a pillow, pressed it to her face, and screamed herself hoarse, yelled straight into the fabric and stuffing. She shouted until it hurt, until she ran out of breath, took away the pillow, inhaled, and got ready to scream some more.

When she heard a knock at the door, she paused, the cushion in the air. Sat up.

No one ever knocked on her door.

No one even knew the door code.

No one but Alexander.

"Open the door, Isobel. I can hear you shouting in there."

"Go away."

"Open this door. I'm worried."

She hesitated, then reluctantly got up from the couch as he continued to pound the door.

"Isobel!"

"Yeah, yeah, I'm coming," she muttered. She passed the mirror in the hallway, saw that she looked puffy, pale, and awful, but decided it made no difference. She unlocked the door, unhooked the chain, and pulled it open.

"Can I come in?"

Oh, *mon dieu,* he was so handsome it was blinding. She shook her head but moved to one side and let him in anyway.

"You didn't reply to my messages," he said once she closed the door. "Don't I deserve an explanation? What happened?"

Alexander looked Isobel over. He was deeply relieved that she seemed okay. When he first knocked, he hadn't heard anything, and thought maybe she wasn't home. But then he heard a stifled scream, and when she didn't open the door, he had seriously started to wonder whether he should kick it down. But she looked like usual. A little pale, her hair an untamed mass around her face and shoulders, but otherwise the same as ever. Her apartment was also as he remembered it. Neat and clean on the surface, just like its owner, but full of hidden secrets.

Isobel stood with her arms folded, radiating all kinds of distance. Her eyes were dark. Dark gray, like a gloomy November afternoon.

He just wanted to pull her into his arms, take in the scent of her hair and neck, and tell her everything was okay, that he could fix whatever was wrong if she would just tell him what the hell it was.

"I don't understand what happened," he said, following her into the living room.

Everything had been good when he'd left her in Eugene's apartment. Jesus, how could that already be two days ago?

"Nothing happened. But we can't go on like this." They were still on their feet in the middle of the room.

"But why? What did I do?" He searched her face for a clue, battling a mix of anger, worry, relief, and dread. He shouldn't have left her. She was fine when he did. And now this. "I don't understand," he added, frustrated, not knowing if he ought to shake some sense into her or crush her to him and never let her go.

She shook her head, took a step away from him, was practically speaking to herself. "I saw a picture of you and two girls in a club in New York. The same day we Skyped." She frowned.

Alexander breathed out. At least he knew what she was talking about now. He could fix this. He hadn't done anything; surely she would understand.

"I was out and I was drunk, but I didn't sleep with either of them. We didn't do anything. I would never do that. You have to believe me."

"I do believe you. Like I did with that other girl. But don't you see, it makes no difference—there'll always be some other woman with you. I don't think I can cope with the uncertainty. Always worrying. Never knowing for sure."

He couldn't fight down the anger that rose within. She was being incredibly unfair. "So you believe me when I say I wasn't unfaithful, that I would never be unfaithful, to anyone, but you still can't trust me? Because I am who I am?"

"I'm sorry. I thought I could manage a relationship like this. . . ."

He felt the anger keep building inside him. So that was what this was about. He should have known. "Like this? Can't you at least be honest?"

"I *am* honest."

"No," he insisted. "You're not honest at all. Tell me, what do you think our relationship is about? How do you see us?"

Her breathing was heavy but she didn't back down. "There is no us. What we have is just about sex. I thought I could handle it, but I can't. I'm sorry."

"I care about you, Isobel. A lot."

The words stuck in his throat. This was excruciating.

"I care too. Far too much. Things shouldn't have gotten so far."

"But this is just a misunderstanding. We can straighten it out."

"I heard you want to give more money to Medpax," she said, moving away from him again.

"You surely can't have any objections to *that?*"

"But I do. For you, this Medpax thing is just a bit of fun until it's over, in what, two weeks? But for me, it's never going to be over—it's the most important thing in my life. We're playing in totally different leagues."

"I really don't understand," he said, and he had the terrible feeling that their conversation was about to slip out of his hands. Though wasn't that how things always ended up? When it really mattered, he was replaceable, not someone whose feelings mattered.

"You have good sides, Alexander, I know that. But you think your money gives you the right to do whatever you want. This is real for me. I can't just do a bit of work with people having a tough time, tell everyone how good I am, and then head off to some paradise island to unwind. This is about my values. And they're completely different from yours. In every respect."

"So this has nothing to do with you being worried about what people might think? That's not what's really going on here?"

"What the hell do you mean by that?"

Alexander took a step toward her.

"That you're so afraid someone might see behind your perfect façade. Or find out that saintly Doctor Sørensen is actually a completely normal person. You've got faults and shortcomings just like everyone else. Don't try to make this all about me. You're worried what people will think if we're really together. Afraid that your holier-than-thou doctor friends would judge you if they found out you actually like a playboy. Because in your world, it's being perfect that counts—people can't have bad sides. But you don't have to be perfect."

"That'd suit you, wouldn't it?" she snapped.

"And what the fuck is that supposed to mean?"

"That it's the excuse you give yourself to keep acting like a kid. Do you know how many times I've heard you say something is just for fun? I'll be sick if I have to hear it one more time. Things are important to me. You don't take anything seriously. I can't have that in my life."

"And you take everything too seriously," he snarled. The conversation was filling him with a rage he hadn't felt for years. By this point in his life, he should be used to disappointing people he cared about. But he hadn't quite realized how important Isobel's opinion was to him, hadn't anticipated this attack. "Not least yourself, or am I wrong? And I think you use other people's suffering as a means of making yourself feel good." It was an awful thing to say, he knew that, but God, he was hurt.

"Well, we can't all spend our lives navel-gazing in our luxury Manhattan apartments."

They stared at one another. Maybe it was just as well things had ended up like this, he thought. It was clear he would never be able to live up to her idea of what a man should be. He cast a quick glance to the bedroom. The door was closed, and it felt like it was two different people who had made love in there.

"Well, good luck saving the world," he said. "Since you're clearly the only one who can do it. And good luck making your mother proud, by the way—that's what you live for, isn't it? It's gone so well this far."

Those last words had just come out. Isobel's eyes shone, but her voice was steady when she replied: "It's not that I'm not grateful. Your money will do a lot of good."

"My money is fine, but not me, is that it?" He hadn't realized she could hurt him so badly, thought he was immune. He had told himself that the only thing he wanted was an uncomplicated summer romance with Isobel. When had it turned into *this?* He had to fix this somehow. But how? Clearly nothing he did was good enough for Isobel. He bought oxygen machines, drank less, saved Medpax. And he was faithful—he had assumed that was understood—but apparently there were no limits to how low Isobel's opinion of him could sink.

"I thought you got that I hate infidelity," he continued.

"I don't know what to think. Please. We'll just say things we regret if we keep going."

He was on the verge of losing it. Nothing helped. He almost started to laugh. He didn't even eat meat anymore, for Christ's sake. But it was impossible to measure up. It was like fucking déjà vu—the suspicion, the hopelessness of it all.

"Isobel, please," he said, painfully aware that he was close to begging.

"It's better if you go," she said quietly.

He looked at her, taking in her slender shoulders, the smooth lines of her body, the eyes that met his, full of pain and resolution. Maybe she was right after all. She was a good person, someone who deserved more than he could give. And he'd had enough anyway, couldn't stomach feeling this worthless any longer.

"Maybe you're right. If you want me to go, I'll go."

She nodded.

He stood there for a moment, looking at her. Waited for her to change her mind.

But she didn't, and so eventually Alexander turned and left. Out into the hallway. Opened the door, went out, and closed it on her and the life he had always known he could never have.

Chapter 57

After the front door closed, Isobel stood for a long time, just staring straight ahead.

This might be the biggest mistake you've ever made.

But it was done, and just as well, and if she told herself that over and over again, maybe it would become true.

She spent the rest of Friday eating all the sugar and fat she could find in the kitchen. As she sucked a spoon of egg toddy, everything Alexander had said replayed over and over in her head. Like some terrible film with an unsympathetic heroine and crappy ending. She could just hear Leila's voice over it all, as an accusing soundtrack.

You're so judgmental, Isobel. You think you're better than other people.

She fell asleep with the uncomfortable feeling that Alexander was right in all respects, and she was wrong.

Saturday offered gray weather. The idea of going out was just too overwhelming, so she tidied instead. She liked to tidy. To wipe, vacuum, and polish. To throw away paper, create order, and regain a sense of control. On Saturday evening, she went down to the 7-Eleven, ignoring all of the laughing, happy, party-going people, and bought candy and coffee for extortionate prices, and then slouched back up to her couch to obsess over Alexander and how alive he made her feel. She hadn't thought there was a stronger sensation than how you felt going out into the field. The feeling of being 100 percent alive. But she had found it with Alexander, and now she had ruined it. Again.

She chewed on banana-flavored candy, enjoying the artificial taste she knew she ought to find repulsive but secretly loved. If she was honest with herself, and maybe it was about time, it had been so liberating to let someone in. And Alexander had really *seen* her. It couldn't be her imagination. And despite the words she so rashly had spat at him, she had long since known that he wasn't a bad person. Just the opposite.

He's all you've ever wanted, Isobel, the persistent voice in her head kept repeating.

But she had pushed him away. Because she was afraid. Afraid of what it would mean to like, maybe even love, a man like Alexander. Afraid of what it said about her. She remained on the sofa, chewing, crying until she fell asleep.

Sunday morning began with her phone buzzing so violently on the coffee table that it was practically jumping up and down.

Isobel, used to springing into action from one moment to the next, was immediately wide-awake, knew that no one called at six on a Sunday morning unless it was an emergency. Leila, she read on the screen. Her pulse picked up, and her brain kicked into gear.

What is it this time?

"Isobel Sørensen."

"It's not good." Leila's voice was curt, professional. The voice people used in their field of work when all other options had been exhausted.

"Tell me. What happened?"

"Idris is sick. Really sick. They don't have a doctor now."

"What does he have?"

Isobel ticked off the symptoms in her head and worked it out before Leila answered, "Meningitis."

God, Idris, if you die now . . .

Isobel was already getting to her feet. "I have to go," she said.

"Can you?"

"Yes."

"I was hoping you'd say that. There's a plane tomorrow. We got the last cheap seat. Are you sure? I need to let them know right away—they won't reserve it otherwise."

She wanted to go, desperately. But she knew she was also fleeing—again. She needed time to think. Should she talk to Alexander? Explain herself and try to fix everything. Was it even possible? But her own needs were, of course, petty in comparison to the needs of the pediatric hospital.

"I'm sure," she replied, on her way toward the chest of drawers in her bedroom.

Passport. Ziplock bags full of toiletries. Vaccination record. She went through the necessities she needed to take with her. Malaria tablets, duct tape, water purification tablets. Brushed everything else aside. It would have to wait.

"I'll call the airline," Leila said, hanging up.

The Arlanda Express train was full, and Isobel had to stand all the way to the airport the next morning. She was first to get off, grabbed her worn, old rucksack and headed for the check-in counters.

Alexander hadn't called, of course. She had been awful, had more or less thrown him out. Maybe she had said things he wouldn't or couldn't forgive this time. She irresolutely played with her cell phone but chose the easy way out and boarded the plane without calling or sending a message.

She took a wrong turn during her stopover in Atatürk Airport in Istanbul, Turkey, and was close to missing her connecting flight, and when they finally landed in N'Djamena, several hours late, it was well past midnight. The sky was dark when she stepped off the plane, the constellations different from back home, and the sensations the same as ever: warm, dusty, and loud, despite the late hour.

She found her bag and went through security, past armed men. She was surprised when no one came to meet her outside. She paused, knew it could be dangerous to venture out alone. But it was equally dangerous to wait around, so she hailed a cab and made her way to the hotel Leila had managed to book, without any trouble. She checked in with the yawning receptionist and went up to the room, where she managed to take off her shoes, fix a hole in the mosquito net with the duct tape, and shake the bedclothes for insects before crawling into bed.

"*Bonjour, madame,*" a girl said politely when Isobel came down the next morning. The girl looked about five, but she was probably at least nine. No adults turned up; the girl seemed to be the only person working in the entire hotel. Isobel paid, and the child carefully folded the notes and then placed them in an ancient cash register. Isobel hesitated, but when no one else appeared, she took her backpack and stepped out into the dust, the heat, and the deafening traffic of N'Djamena. It seemed to be market day—carriages, animals, and carts with merchandise crowded the streets. She caught sight of a man who was watching her, feeling a prickling sensation when she recognized him as Muhammed, the father of baby Ahmed. He just stared at her, his bird's feet tattoos making his face ominous. And then he was gone, swallowed by the crowd in the streets. She let out a sigh of relief. Maybe she had just imagined it. She still had two of the bottles of water she'd bought in Istanbul, plus an energy bar, so she decided not to waste any time looking for breakfast and to head straight to the hospital instead. She put on her rucksack, then glanced at her cell phone. Her heart stopped. Alexander had called while she was checking out. And now, a message arrived.

Everything went so wrong. Sorry.

With that, life suddenly felt bright and colorful again. Alexander didn't hate her. She had been rash and mean, but he would give her another chance, even if she didn't deserve it.

She quickly replied: *So sorry. Was stupid. Landed. Will call tonight.*

A car came toward her, its horn blaring. She looked up. A man leaned out of the wound-down window.

"Bonjour, Docteur," the driver said. "To the hospital?"

Cautiously Isobel nodded at the man, whose name she remembered was Yannick. He was occasionally hired by some of the other humanitarian organizations to drive people around, but he had never done work for Medpax before.

"Wasn't Hugo meant to pick me up?" she asked, not quite comfortable traveling the long distance to the hospital with a man she didn't know. No one answered when she called the hospital, and Leila hadn't had any more information to give her.

Yannick shrugged, a gesture that could mean anything: Hugo is sick. Hugo is away. Hugo is dead. And then she once more caught sight of Muhammed. He was much closer this time, and it was not her imagination. It was him, with a serious, angry expression on his tattooed face.

"Can you drive me?" Isobel asked hastily, her mind made up. She didn't want to stay in N'Djamena, was eager to get on the way. "Five dollars?"

He shook his head. "*Non, madame.* Twenty."

She held up ten, used to this kind of haggling. "That is all," she said, and he went along with it with a satisfied grin. He leaned over the passenger seat and opened the door for her.

Isobel looked for Muhammed, but once again he had disappeared in the chaotic streets. Hurriedly she walked around the car, put her bag inside, and jumped in. The signal on her cell came and went, and she realized that her answer to Alexander's text hadn't been sent, so she pressed send again just as Yannick put his foot on the gas pedal. As the rattling car sent goats and hens scattering to the sides of the road, she saw the message was delivered.

Through the window she took in the swarms of overloaded cars, animals, and people passing by. Aid workers, Chinese guest laborers, and military men. Children everywhere. Lone beggars at crossroads. And then the red landscape, women with baskets and bundles, and more children. It was already so hot that the sweat was pouring down her. She switched between drinking her water and clutching her cell, glad she had left the city. Yet another text arrived, and she read it with a smile. It was crazy, really, that they could keep in touch despite the fact they were on different sides of the equator.

Landed?? Where are you?

For some reason, she had assumed Leila would have told Alexander, but as she was about to reply, the car shook so much she couldn't press the right buttons. Isobel steadied herself with her hand on the roof and decided to reply when she arrived at the hospital instead. The car careened down the bumpy road. Yannick slowed down and pointed to something in the road ahead of them.

"Checkpoint," he said.

She saw. It hadn't been there before. In itself, that meant nothing. Roadblocks had their own unpredictable life cycles, but they were never a welcome hindrance.

Isobel wiped her sweaty palms on her pants. Most of her money was hidden in her bag, but she also had some dollars in a special robbery wallet that she could give them.

Please let it be okay. Just let me get to the hospital.

The two men who strolled up to them were young and armed with automatic weapons. Scarves around their heads, wearing khaki pants and gym shoes. When they peered into the car, she tried to evaluate whether they were high, but then hastily averted her gaze. Don't provoke them.

"Where are you going?" one of them barked. He was dressed in a red T-shirt and had a long scar running down one cheek. It disappeared beneath his scarf. A machete scar.

"The hospital," Yannick answered. He nodded at Isobel. *"Docteur."*

Isobel could feel their eyes on her, but she continued to look down, to make herself as meek as she could while her heart pounded in her chest, as if she'd run for miles. Her mouth was dry as gravel. A bird shrieked as one of the men reached into the car, and she forced herself not to jerk back. He took her bottle of water. Backed up. Said something to Yannick she didn't hear and then waved them through.

They passed. When Isobel looked in the rearview mirror, she saw the man who'd taken her water standing with a phone to his ear. She wiped her hands on her pants again, saw them shake.

Yannick sped up, and the roadblock and soldiers disappeared behind them. Isobel leaned back against the seat, exhaled, and forced herself to relax. She watched the flat, red landscape rush by again. The car jumped and shook, but they'd made it.

She smiled weakly at Yannick, still feeling an aftereffect of fear. Yannick simply stared straight ahead, focused on his driving, she assumed. His face was completely empty as he drove. The car slowed down again.

"What's happening now?" she asked in French, but she saw rocks, sticks, and tires covering the road. The road was narrow here, and there was no way they could drive around it. She wondered how the rubble had ended up there. The car came to a halt. Her impatience to make it to the hospital grew. She wanted to know what was going on, to be rid of this debilitating worry and uncertainty, to get to work. And then she saw a car coming toward them, on the other side of the rubble. It approached rapidly.

"Do you know who they are?" she asked as the other car screeched to a halt and its doors flew open. Several men, she counted six, ran toward them.

"We need to turn around!" she shouted, but Yannick did nothing. He just raised his hands as the men, shouting, circled the car.

It happened so quickly that Isobel had no time to do anything but swear before the doors were torn open. She held up her hands in the air to show she was unarmed. Tall men with angry faces yelled in a local dialect she couldn't quite understand. How close were they to the hospital? An hour? Fifteen minutes? It made no difference. Suddenly Isobel's upper arm was in an iron grip, and a man pulled her from the car so violently that she hit her head. Without thinking it through or planning ahead, she pulled her arm toward her as she pushed him away as hard as she could with her free hand. She almost got free, was mentally ready to make a run for it, but a blow hit her on the chest, and it hurt so much that she remained in his painful grip, panting for air.

A hood was placed over her head, and then she had fibers and hair in her mouth. There was no air under the thick, dirty fabric, and panic welled up inside her. Yet another hand took hold of her, this time on her other arm, and she was dragged to her feet. More hands appeared, moving over her, roaming over her body and pulling at her clothes, and she couldn't help but hysterically fight back. The men continued with their rough manhandling, but then they stopped, and she knew they had been looking for her cell, that they didn't plan to rip off her clothes and rape her. She heard shouts and yells, muffled and difficult to make out because of the hood, and then she was dragged over the rubble. She stubbed her toe on something and was then thrown into what she assumed was the backseat of the soldiers' car. Her mouth and nose were pressed down. She hit her head on a hard surface, had something heavy on her back, and then the car started with a roar.

Fragments of the hostage course darted through her mind.

You need to try to work out where they take you. It can mean the difference between life and death.

And then everything went dark.

Chapter 58

A few of us are headed to the West Indies. Want to come?
Alexander read the message that arrived right after Isobel's. There had been a time when he would have said yes immediately, and already been on the way to new thrills. But now it just felt stupidly uninteresting. The only conclusion was that he had changed, re-markably, quickly, and completely against his will. Because this wasn't something he had wanted. Nothing he'd chosen. He was still unsure whether he liked the change—so far, it had caused pain more than anything. He was used to his lifestyle, had told himself he enjoyed no-strings-attached sex and expensive pleasures, that they were more than enough for him, that he didn't need anything else. And at some point during his childhood, he had stopped believing that love was for him. Maybe not consciously, but it was true all the same.

At first he hadn't realized what had happened. What was wrong with him? Like some creeping illness.

But it was love. He loved Isobel. He was laughably unfamiliar with the sensation. Unfamiliar with feeling so much. Joy, confusion. Anger. Alternating between them.

He wanted to talk to Romeo about it. Ask for advice. But Romeo had met someone, was newly infatuated and quite insufferable at the moment.

Alexander rubbed his face. He hadn't gotten any more messages from Isobel. Where had she gone? And where the hell had she landed?

He scrolled through their messages. Saw their relationship grow. Should have smiled, but instead felt a weight on his chest. He brought up her number. Wanted to hear her voice, not sit and wait for a text. Almost hoped that she did want things to end. Could barely cope with all these feelings.

Her phone rang. No one answered.

He called again.

He kept trying all day.

But no one answered. And no more messages arrived.

After a night of tossing and turning, Alexander called Leila. It had struck him, sometime around midnight, that she might know where Isobel was. As the phone rang, he started to pull on his jacket, search for his keys and wallet. He was going crazy indoors, needed to get out.

"Leila here," she answered, her voice tense.

"Where's Isobel?" he asked, not bothering to say hello.

"She should be in Massakory now."

Alexander stopped, his keys midair.

"Chad? She was just there. You pulled her out because it was too dangerous."

"Things have cooled down. And this was an emergency. Idris is sick, so they had no doctor, and she chose to go. She knows what she's doing, and I never would have sent her if it was dangerous. Chad is relatively stable."

He ignored the fact that Isobel obviously had been eager to go. "Have you been in touch? Did you hear from her?"

Leila sighed. "No, not yet."

Alexander heard her tapping away at a keyboard and she practically disappeared, the way people tended to do when they lost their focus and became preoccupied by the screen in front of them.

"What's this about, Alexander? I have a lot to do," she said, sounding faraway.

"Who might know more?" Alexander asked, irritated. He really didn't give a rat's ass about how much she had to do.

"About what?" she asked, but he could hear that her thoughts were elsewhere.

Alexander paused. Then he spoke crisply into the receiver, using the voice he had been born with, and taught to use—his upper-class voice, the one that made people snap to attention.

"Listen to me, Leila. Who can I talk to that might have a fucking clue about where Isobel is? Now?"

Ten minutes later Alexander had the man from the security company on the line.

They instantaneously ended up at each other's throats. No, the security guy couldn't give him any information. No, there were no reports of conflict in N'Djamena or Massakory. No, he wasn't interested in hearing his opinions, and no, he wouldn't get back to Alexander with more information.

Alexander heard a click on the other end of the line.

As he headed toward the center of town, he called Leila again.

"I hear you called the security company," she said frostily. "They weren't happy. You should really stop annoying them."

"They're idiots. There has to be someone I can talk to."

"Alexander, I say this with the greatest respect, but lay off. Nothing has happened. She's in Chad. She's working." Leila was silent for a moment. Tap, tap on the keyboard. "Did you consider the possibility that maybe Isobel doesn't want to talk to you? She told me things were over between you."

"Maybe not," he said, and hung up. He didn't want to waste time talking to Leila.

Was the psychologist right? Was he wrong? He could be, of course. He couldn't think clearly when it came to Isobel.

What the hell should he do?

He had ended up by Stureplan, stopped dead, and people had to swerve to avoid running into him.

He sat down on a bench and scrolled through his contact list. How could one person have so many useless contacts? Models, bloggers, nightclub kings, chefs. Financiers, actresses, and . . .

Financiers.

He scrolled back to the number. Waited impatiently.

"David Hammar," his brother-in-law answered, his voice curt and effective.

"It's Alexander De la Grip. I need help. Where are you?"

"The office."

He got up. "I'm coming over; I'll explain on the way."

Hurriedly Alexander walked to Nybroplan, past the inlet and on to

Blasieholmen, where Hammar Capital was based in a white building that looked out over the waters of Saltsjön Bay. By the time he was buzzed in, David already knew everything.

Not that there was much to know.

"I sent a message to Tom Lexington as we spoke," David greeted him. "He's on the way."

Aha, the huge security guy. Couldn't hurt, anyway.

"Jesus, I don't know if it's just my imagination," Alexander said, giving voice to his doubts as he shook his head at the offer of coffee. "Maybe she simply doesn't want to talk to me."

David looked at him. "That's the best-case scenario."

"I guess so."

David's gaze was assessing and deadly serious.

"If it was Natalia we were talking about, I'd do exactly the same. If that's any comfort."

"You said you argued?" Tom Lexington asked a quarter of an hour later.

Alexander met his dark eyes. Could he see suspicion in them, or was it his imagination? It was like being on a gangplank; nothing was stable.

"Yes. But then we both apologized. By text. And she said she would call."

It sounded pretty weak, even to his own ears.

"When?"

"She was meant to call last night."

He felt like an idiot. David was by the window, his arms crossed, watching them without saying a word, without showing an emotion.

"Is she the kind of person who keeps her promises?" Tom's voice sounded like rumbling war and brutal violence, and for some reason that was reassuring.

"Yes."

"It could be you're having a communication problem?"

Alexander nodded reluctantly. Maybe he was overreacting after all.

"It's probably nothing," said Tom.

"I get that. But if it is something, what could it be?"

"Most often in this kind of situation, it turns out the missing person has been in a car accident. That's the biggest risk in those countries. She could be in the hospital with no way to get in touch."

Alexander clenched his jaw. That sounded bad enough to his ears.

"At this point, I need to know exactly what it is you are after," Tom said. He exchanged a look Alexander couldn't interpret with David.

"I want to know what's happened, of course," Alexander replied bluntly. Wasn't that obvious? He wondered if the enormous man wasn't a little dumb.

"My question is about what you want to pay for, nothing else," said Tom.

Alexander shook his head, didn't need to think, knew they were just wasting time. "I want to know where she is," he said coolly. "If something's happened to her. I'll pay whatever it costs. Money is no problem."

"Give me half an hour."

Tom disappeared into an adjoining room, was gone for fifteen minutes, and then returned.

"I just spoke with a guy in the vicinity. He's going to go to N'Djamena and ask around a little." He wrote down an account number and a figure, then passed the note to Alexander. "Get a Western Union account. Transfer the money here. Let's start like this. My man will start to check the hospitals and clinics as soon as he gets there. Stretchers and rooms—health care isn't exactly modern in those parts. Do you know for sure she's in N'Djamena?"

Alexander tried to forget the image of an injured Isobel, unconscious on some filthy stretcher. Dirty needles and local medicine men.

"No. She just said she'd landed. She had a stopover in Istanbul, according to Medpax."

Was he wrong? Had she disappeared in Istanbul? Would that be better? Worse?

"Okay," said Tom. "Now we wait."

"For what?"

"To see if she gets in touch first. That's still the most likely outcome. It's Africa, so her silence could mean anything—a stolen cell, a dead battery, bad coverage. If we haven't heard from her by tomorrow morning, we'll see what my guy has found out."

"Tomorrow? But what if she's been kidnapped? Shouldn't we do something?"

He surely didn't need an expert just to sit still and wait. Alexander couldn't help but glance at David. Did Tom really know what he was doing?

"If—and I mean *if*—she's being held captive, we won't hear anything for days," Tom said gravely. "If that's the case, the wait will be part of the kidnappers' tactics."

"What? Why?"

"Because it's the worst thing possible," said Tom, and if Alexander hadn't known that Tom most likely lacked all normal, human feelings, he might have thought he could see compassion deep in his dark eyes. "To break the victim's friends and family with the wait."

David took a step toward them and spoke.

"Tom knows what he's talking about," he said quietly.

Alexander nodded. It was becoming obvious that Tom was an expert in this.

"Can you get me a photo of her? Preferably black-and-white."

"Yes."

Alexander rubbed his face. Arrange a photo and transfer money. It felt so goddamn insufficient.

Alexander still hadn't heard a word by the next morning. It was less than twenty-four hours since he had started to be seriously worried, but Alexander was already exhausted. Breaking the friends and family by making them wait. How the hell were you meant to survive this?

He called Leila again. "Did you hear anything?"

"No. She should be at the hospital by now. But it's chaotic there now that Idris is sick; it's hard to get hold of anyone at all, and there is no Wi-Fi to speak of. I can't get hold of our man Hugo, either. He was meant to pick her up from the airport. But maybe she missed the plane in Istanbul, or the plane might've been delayed, or Hugo might've forgotten. Things happen, but Isobel is used to it. She's trained to cope with all kinds of unforeseen events."

"But don't you think she would have been in touch?"

Leila hesitated. "We have routines for this kind of thing. We'll have to wait and see awhile longer," she eventually said.

Alexander ended the call. If another person told him to wait and see, he would break something.

"My guy, Lutz, has arrived in N'Djamena. He was in the vicinity."

Alexander stirred the coffee they had ordered and wondered what someone was doing in the "vicinity" of N'Djamena, but he refrained from asking.

Tom Lexington sat with his back to the wall, watching the other people in the café. He looked like the kind of man who knew people in the worst places on earth and who was just waiting to be hired to find missing field doctors in Africa.

"He did some asking around. No injured white woman anywhere. And he went out to the pediatric hospital. The locals say she never turned up. He can't find anyone who saw her at the hotel. But someone who could be her did check in."

Tom held up a cell phone photo of a signature. Alexander nodded; he recognized Isobel's writing. So she *had* arrived in N'Djamena. A part of him had hoped she was still in Stockholm, that she was just ignoring his calls. But she had been in N'Djamena, written her signature on a slip, and now she had vanished.

"A local fixer, Hugo, was meant to be her chauffeur and to pick her up," Tom continued. "He's their contact down there, but he got sick and went to the medicine man, and he took something that knocked him out for a couple days. So, to summarize: She made it from the airport to the hotel, but after that there's no sign of her. We're going to try to follow the signal from her cell. Do you have her number?"

Alexander gave it to him.

"Lutz will go to the phone company and try to get some information. He'll have to bribe them."

"How much?"

"Send a thousand. Dollars." Tom got up. "I'll call as soon as I hear anything else."

"Thanks."

As Tom left, Alexander immediately transferred the money using his cell phone. Enter some digits, send money halfway across the world. Wait, wait, wait. His inaction was making him crazy.

Tom called again that evening. "Her cell pinged out in the desert," he said without bothering with greetings.

"What does that mean?"

"Unfortunately I think we need to assume something's happened to her."

"What?"

"I can only speculate. Either someone stole her cell, or she's been captured. The cell phone is in the desert; we don't know much more than that. But it's a long way from the pediatric hospital. Far from the capital. Far from everything."

Alexander stared out the window. It was a perfectly ordinary Swedish summer evening. People were walking along the waterfront. Holding hands, eating ice cream. What was he expected to say to this?

"I have time," Tom said on the other end of the line. "If you wanted, I could head down there. Continue the search."

"Yes," Alexander immediately replied. More than anything, he wanted Tom Lexington to go to Chad and find Isobel. "I have money," he continued. "I mean, I really have money. Buy a plane and head down there. Now."

"I always fly coach. There's a plane tomorrow."

Alexander looked at his watch. It wasn't even six p.m. "Tomorrow? Can't we go now?"

Tom snorted. "*We* aren't going anywhere. And *I* need to pack."

"Tom," Alexander said coolly, "if you think I'm going to stay in Stockholm while my woman has been kidnapped by some desert people in fucking Africa, you're damned wrong. I'm coming. *I'll* book the tickets. *I'll* get the money. *You* can send a list of what I should pack. I'm coming, understood?"

Tom was silent, and Alexander held his breath.

"Well ain't that fucking fantastic," Tom said, and hung up.

When they landed in Istanbul late the next day, Tom and Alexander had exchanged fewer than ten words.

At the airport in N'Djamena, they were met by a crop-haired, tanned man who introduced himself, with a thick South African accent, as Lutz. There was something violent about him, as if death were close on his heels. He might as well have had *mercenary* tattooed on his forehead.

N'Djamena was like nowhere Alexander had been before. He had been to Africa, of course, but for exciting desert trips, reckless surfing, and parties on the most luxurious yachts in the world. Drinks, staff, and beautiful women in rich, lush, and blooming countries.

N'Djamena in contrast consisted of old asphalt, glaring men, and completely insane traffic. Jeeps and rattling pickups, undernourished children, and white plaster buildings with Arabic lettering on the signs.

They followed Lutz, went to a café, and drank sweet tea. Alexander looked at his watch. He had started a timer on his phone, and it kept track of the amount of time Isobel had been missing. The seconds flew by, running away like sand in a digital hourglass.

Lutz spread out a map. All three men leaned in over it.

"Her phone is somewhere in this area," Tom said, drawing a circle with his finger over blurred lines and numbers. "Until further notice we'll assume she's there too. She *might* have been taken because she's a doctor. It might be that some clan needs her help. If that's the case, they'll treat her relatively well."

Lutz bared his teeth.

"If she's been kidnapped, it'll probably be brutal. They don't like white people here," he said with a growl. "They think all Westerners have money, and they want to lay their dirty paws on the gold. Fucking vermin."

Alexander met Lutz's pale blue eyes and decided that he hated this South African murderer.

"We can begin to get a team together," Tom explained. "I've started to pull some threads. But if we don't know where she is, there's nothing we can do. Still no witnesses?"

Lutz shook his head. "I've asked around. Nothing yet."

"But you said she was here?" Alexander asked, pointing at the map.

"Yes," said Tom.

"So can't we just go down there and look?"

Lutz gave a scornful laugh, and Alexander wanted to get up and beat him stupid, work out all his anger and frustration.

"That area is as big as southern Sweden," Tom said evenly. "All we can do now is wait."

Alexander's cell phone rang. Leila. He wanted to refuse the call; it was her fault, her fucking fault, but he answered: "Any news?"

"No. I wanted to see if you'd heard anything. I'm starting to wonder."

He hung up and looked at the timer again. Again and again.

Chapter 59

Air, water, sleep, and food. Those are our basic needs. In roughly that order. The physiological needs are the most important, the absolute minimum of things a human needs to survive. But which need came next in the hierarchy? Isobel tried to remember. Was it security? Love? Psychological needs came after the physiological, she was certain of that. But did love even belong there, among psychological necessities, or was it really just a modern construct? Someone had said that to her once. That love was a recent invention. Alexander, wasn't it? She tried to recall his exact words, but it was difficult. It went so fast, being reduced to someone who could think of nothing but quenching her thirst.

She licked her lips, even though she knew it was stupid. How long had it been since they'd torn her from the car, forced her to change clothes, taken her shoes, and thrown her in here? She had really thought that she could keep track of time. But it was so dark. At least two nights had passed—she had been so cold her teeth had chattered twice now. But it was day again. She knew that because it was so hot she couldn't think. So, at least two nights had passed, but she supposed it could be even longer. Could it be as much as a week? She had no idea. They gave her very little to eat, and her skin was looser than it had been, which meant she had been losing weight for a while.

So maybe it was a week after all.

Things shouldn't have ended up like this. She shouldn't be locked in a clay hut with only her own thoughts for company.

Things should have ended happily.

She should have realized what she felt, dared to take a chance on Alexander, and lived happily fucking after.

Now she would probably die.

Alone.

They hadn't even given her a blanket. There was nothing but floor, walls, and ceiling. A tiny window, nailed shut. A bucket. If the cold or the thirst didn't finish her off, there were always the mosquitoes and malaria. Or the abuse.

So many ways to die.

She was ashamed of how afraid she was.

And she was so sad she'd never had the chance to tell Alexander she loved him, because of course she did.

Undoubtedly she ought to be happy and thankful that she had gotten to experience at least a little love. But she was furious—the whole thing was just so goddamn senseless.

She didn't know who the men holding her were, but she suspected they had been tipped off by the chauffeur, Yannick. She shouldn't have gone with a new driver, her instincts had warned her. He'd seen her money. Probably he'd alerted them. And there was something else, nagging at the corner of her mind. Something about a bird. No, feet. Bird's feet. A tattoo. The father of little Ahmed, yes Muhammed. She'd seen him, hadn't she? At the market, staring at her, hatred in his eyes. Was he involved in this? She tried to remember, but there were so many men here, some of them with their faces covered.

Maybe it was fate. Her grandfather had died here, murdered by Chadians. It was arrogant to assume they would treat her any better. She was a foreigner, a stuck-up Westerner with an arrogant savior complex, and they believed they could make money off of her.

They had hit her, but she wasn't seriously injured, not as far as she could tell. She carefully examined her body again. No broken bones, no vital organs in danger, her kidneys were working, her lungs were fine, her heart was still beating. Well, if they were going for a ransom they needed her alive. Not that it stopped them from abusing her.

She heard voices. Oh, God, they were coming.

The door opened. It was so dark in her prison that the light was painful.

Swallowing as they came closer, she blinked rapidly, tried to steel herself. Wasn't that Muhammed? She tried to focus, thought she saw the tattoo at his cheek, but the light was too blinding and she had to avert her eyes. She didn't want to show any weakness. Wanted to be dignified to show that she deserved their respect. That she could be useful to them. That even if they hated her they didn't have to beat her so badly, take out their frustrations on her.

But Isobel was only human, and she cried when they eventually left.

Chapter 60

That evening, Alexander and Tom left the hotel and went out to find something to eat in N'Djamena. Alexander had wanted to stay in the same hotel Isobel had been in when she was last seen, but Tom had clipped out short phrases about security and risks and then dictatorially chosen another hotel, and there were only a certain number of battles Alexander could bring himself to fight, so he'd given in.

Lutz had reported all the information he had to Tom and already moved on. To Iraq or Syria or somewhere equally as hospitable, doubtless.

They sat down and picked up the menus. There were kids everywhere, gaunt children who silently slipped around the tables and watched the guests—wealthy Chadians and foreigners—with cautious eyes. They came up to the diners, begged and offered things as soon as the waitstaff disappeared and the guards looked away.

Fruit, shoe polish. Massages.

A small, scrawny boy approached their table, but he was immediately chased away. He gave Alexander a beseeching look but disappeared under the blows of a waiter.

They ordered. Alexander took what Tom told him to without protest.

"Not a good idea to get sick right now," Tom said curtly, ordering unopened bottles of water instead of a jug. "And avoid the ice."

Alexander's fingers drummed impatiently on the tablecloth. He didn't want to sit in a restaurant and make small talk about the local food. He wanted to *do* something. The scrawny boy snuck up to them again. He was thin, and his clothes hung like rags around him. His gaze didn't move from Alexander.

"*Monsieur?*" he whispered in French.

Tom shook his head warningly as he tore off a bit of bread, put it in his mouth, and chewed it briefly and efficiently.

"Don't give him anything; they won't leave us alone."

Alexander demonstratively took a coin from his pocket and gave it to the boy. Tom rolled his eyes and reached for his beer. "Suit yourself."

The boy took the coin but stayed by the table. He moved his lips. He pulled at Alexander's hand. "*Le docteur,*" he said.

Alexander studied the boy more closely, feeling something prickle at the back of his neck. "What?"

"*Monsieur,*" he repeated, glancing around with a frightened look. The waiter was approaching with heavy steps. "You have been asking questions, yes? You're looking for Doctor Isobel." His head darted back and forth, then his thin throat worked. "I saw her," he whispered almost inaudibly.

Tom took a swig from his beer and glared at the child. The waiter had almost reached them.

The boy stayed put with a defiant expression. Every now and then his eyes flicked to the plates of food at the table. When had he last eaten?

"What's your name?" Alexander asked as he handed the child a piece of the garlic-scented bread they had been served with the stew. Firmly he waved the approaching waiter away.

The boy took the bread and it disappeared into a pocket.

"Marius," he said, almost inaudibly.

Alexander sat up straight. Could it be?

"I know who you are. You're her friend, aren't you?"

The boy nodded. "*Oui,* from the hospital."

"Tom, I know who this boy is," Alexander said. "Isobel talked about him a few times."

Tom turned to Marius with a deeply skeptical look.

"What did you see?" he asked in French, studying the child.

"I saw them take *Docteur* Isobel. Where the road is narrow. In a car. Many men with guns. I was there, on my way to the hospital. She screamed."

Tom gave Alexander a warning look, and Alexander had to use all his might to sit still and keep quiet. No good would come of him showing his anger, his powerlessness. Tom looked at Marius again, still suspicious. The man was born a sceptic.

"Do you know who they are? Which clan they are from?"

"*Oui, monsieur.* I know the village."

"Okay," Tom decided. "Let's take him to the hotel and see if he can point it out on the map."

"So. We have an eyewitness who confirms she was taken," Tom said after Marius showed them where he had seen Isobel. They were talking with low voices. Marius was asleep on the couch in Alexander's locked room; Tom had refused to let the boy go.

"That's if we can trust the kid. We can't dismiss the idea that someone might have sent him to give us false information."

"Is that really likely?"

"No. But we can't take any risks."

"What should we do with him?"

Tom shrugged. "I can't let him go now."

"You mean we are kidnapping him?"

"Call it what you want," he replied without looking up from the map of Chad.

"So. We know where she's *probably* being held, and by whom. What we don't know is why—whether it's money or politics. Or both. What we *should* do now is go home, tell the police a Swedish citizen has been taken, and let them and the authorities take over. But I'm guessing that's not what you want."

Alexander didn't even bother replying. He wasn't leaving Chad without Isobel; it was that simple.

"If we're going to rescue her, there'll be a price to pay," Tom continued. "People and money. And it's still uncertain. We only have a street kid's word for it."

"He seems trustworthy."

"Yeah."

"In concrete terms, what do you need?"

"I need to get eyes on that desert village the kid pointed out. Verify that she's actually there. Put together a rescue team. A scout and a sniper, six men for the actual rescue, eight in total. Weapons. Two or three cars." Tom frowned, concentrating. "A helicopter, I think. For me."

"Can that be arranged down here?"

"Anything can be arranged. It's all about money."

Alexander smiled grimly. "I have money. Do it."

Tom turned his wrist and looked at his watch.

"I'll get the ball rolling. Keep an eye on the kid."

Tom disappeared, and Alexander remained sitting as night fell over N'Djamena and the ridiculously expensive hotel.

"I made a few calls," Tom said when they met for lunch the next day. They could hear the muezzin between the buildings; Alexander hadn't gotten much sleep, but Marius had slept soundly for twelve hours on the couch, eaten all the food he'd been given, and then sat down in front of the TV with the remote control.

"They're on their way, from various parts of Africa. They have weapons and vehicles, and all the other equipment we need."

"Mercenaries?"

Tom shrugged. "They're not nice guys, but they'll do what they need to as long as they get paid. So now you and I need to go and buy some bags. Tomorrow we go to the bank and empty it of dollars and euros."

"What happens next?" Alexander asked when they left the bank the following day. Each carried a black leather bag full of notes. Two of Tom's mercenaries who had arrived the previous day—silent, serious men—kept them company. "It's virtually a death sentence to take out lots of money in this country; we need guards," Tom had explained laconically.

"We get moving," he answered now.

They went quickly to the hotel and put the bags on the table in Tom's room.

"So what do we do now, then?" Alexander asked impatiently as Tom closed the curtains and secured the locks.

Everything was moving so goddamn slowly.

Isobel had been missing for six days now, but they hadn't heard a word from her kidnappers. Was she even alive? Could she have died without his sensing it? He refused to believe it, clung to what Tom had once said: Regardless of who the kidnappers were, she was worth money to them.

But Tom shook his head firmly as he emptied his pockets onto the table. He spread out money, electronics, and pieces of paper, then started to sort through them.

"From now on, there is no *we*. I can't have a civilian getting in the way."

So, that's the way the wind blows.

"Fine," said Alexander. He crossed his arms in front of his chest and leaned one shoulder against the wall as Tom gathered his things, folded maps, and began to pack his equipment into a bag.

"I need to find an FOB. Somewhere we can meet. Test the weapons, practice, plan."

Alexander nodded. A Forward Operations Base. It sounded logical. "Excellent. Out in the desert, maybe?" he said agreeably.

Tom peered suspiciously at him.

"I need to learn the helicopter. There'll be a load of tactical talk. Pretty tough."

"Sounds great."

Tom jerked shut the zipper on his bag.

"It'll be two, maybe three days out in the desert. Worst conditions imaginable. We'll sleep under the cars. Eat sand and drink dirty water. Wait."

"I see."

Tom sighed deeply. He squashed an insect on his neck. "You're going to come, aren't you."

"Yup."

"Damn, you're annoying."

"Not at all. I'm an asset."

"But can you keep your cool? Knowing that she's suffering while we have to train and plan? That they might be torturing her, that it might end with us just finding her dead, raped body? That the only thing you might have to do is to identify what little is left of her?"

Alexander knew that Tom's words were deliberately brutal. He steeled himself. *Don't think about it.*

"I can manage," he said curtly.

"You were a parachute ranger?"

"Squad leader. Damn good."

"You can go with the scouts, then. We'll get you a weapon."

"Fine. What are you going to do with the boy, Marius?"

"He's with us until it's over. Period. I don't trust anyone. That's the only way to survive here. The kid is coming with us, and I'll keep an eye on him until it's too late for him to warn anyone. He can leave then. He's a street kid, so no one is looking for him. I'm going to meet the others. They're at the entrance now. Is her mother alive?"

"Yes."

"What was her maiden name?"

"Blanche Pelletier."

"French?"

"Yes."

"And Alexander?" Tom gave him another of his black looks.

"Yeah?"

"Answer your goddamn phone sometime," he hissed, and pulled the door shut behind him.

Alexander hadn't even heard it ring, but he had missed calls from Leila, David, and Natalia.

He called Leila first, but she knew even less than he did. As soon as he hung up, it rang again. David Hammar.

"Your sister is worried," he said brusquely when Alexander answered, and then Natalia was on the line.

"David is hiding something from me, so I guess it's serious, whatever you're doing. Do you want to know just how little I like being treated like an idiot?"

"Sorry. But it's bad. Isobel is gone."

"Are you really in Africa? With Tom Lexington?"

"Yeah," he answered, and he knew his sister was much too sharp not to see how badly it might end. "Natalia?" He swallowed. "If . . . if it doesn't go well for me, but she's okay . . . will you tell Isobel that . . . you know."

"Alexander, you have to tell her that kind of thing yourself."

"She's been kidnapped, for God's sake."

But Natalia knew him too well, wasn't put off by his outburst. "I heard that. You should write it down or something. You can't just leave and maybe die and not say how you feel in your own words. You know that, right?"

"I don't plan to die."

"Well, no one does."

"You know my friend Romeo Rozzi? If I send you his number, can you call him and tell him?"

"Sure. Peter is here too. Wait."

And before Alexander had time to say he didn't want to speak to Peter, his brother was on the line.

"I just heard. How are you?"

The last thing Alexander expected was for it to feel good to hear Peter's voice. His big brother. He could just see them, his siblings and David, together, worried for his sake.

It might be the most ironic thing he had ever experienced. To realize how much they meant to him only when he was facing the most dangerous thing he'd ever done. He was relatively certain he would survive—it wasn't a case of being worried for his own sake—and he figured that the others knew that.

"Okay," he said.

Aside from the fact I'm headed off to fight in the desert and might have lost the only woman I ever loved.

"Is there anything I can do?"

"We're going to need to fly out as soon as we've got her. A medically equipped plane would be good."

"I'll arrange it. You have my word."

And Alexander knew, without a shadow of a doubt, that if Peter promised something, he would keep his promise. "I'll send a message with all the details I can."

"I'll get it all ready," said Peter, and then there was silence. "I love you," he added. The words were chopped and sounded strange coming from his mouth. "I want you to know. That I do."

Alexander's throat tightened.

If he managed not to mess up too much, Tom and the others would cover his ass. It wasn't fear for his own life that had him at the end of his rope, that made this phone call sound like a farewell. He knew what the photo of Isobel meant, knew why Tom had asked him for a black-and-white image. Simply put, it was easier to identify a dead or tortured body in that way. Easier to see past the beaten tissue and the red, blue, and green swelling using a photo in gray scale.

The risk that they would fail was, in other words, looming.

And if Isobel died down here . . . If he lost her . . .

"I have to go," he said, hanging up. He couldn't bear to listen to his siblings' caring voices any longer. He took a shaky breath. Ran his hand over his face. Felt sweat, sand, and stubble.

If Isobel died . . . then he wouldn't go home, it was that simple.

"Alexander?" He heard Tom's voice on the other side of the door. How long had he been standing there, knocking?

Alexander opened the door and was met by Tom's searching look. He pulled himself together. He wasn't going to die, and he wasn't going to fall apart. He would write a letter to Isobel, send Romeo's number to Natalia, and tell Peter what he needed to know. He had a plan. "I'm okay. What do we do now?"

Tom smiled, that same grimace Alexander assumed was the closest Tom Lexington ever came to a real smile.

"Now we leave for hell."

Chapter 61

They had hit her again today. Not all of them. But a few of her captors were more brutal than the others. It wasn't unusual. Westerners were often hated here. If they wanted to get money for her they wouldn't beat her to death, she supposed. But God, they scared her. They had screamed at her too. Terrible things. Isobel wished she could say she had been brave and that it hadn't affected her, but that simply wasn't true.

Last time she was held captive, in Liberia, it had been for less than twelve hours. How long had she been here now? She had no concept of time and was slowly losing control of herself. They were in charge of her body and her freedom, but she was also starting to lose control of her thoughts. Thirst made her act against her better judgment. When they gave her a mug of cloudy water she drank it, though she knew it might be full of bacteria that could kill her more quickly than any beating or torture ever could.

What was going on out there? Had they made a ransom demand yet? Had they even taken her for money? But yes, she was relatively certain of that, had heard them shout about dollars. If so, they'd keep her alive. Right? If they didn't want to kill her just to make an example. Or by accident.

But maybe no one even knew she was here. Why was it taking so long if they did? Medpax would pay, wouldn't it? Or Alexander? He had money—surely he would offer a loan if they needed it? Or maybe he had left for New York after she'd behaved so badly. Had her lack of reply to his message gotten to him? Maybe he was in some New York club right now, making out with glamorous women, buying them drinks, and he'd stopped thinking about the argumentative, troublesome field doctor with serious trust issues.

Stop. Don't give in to pointless worry.

Stay strong, Isobel. Be dignified. Respectful.

Show them you're valuable.

She sat up and crossed her legs, rubbed her face, and smoothed her hair. Methodically she forced herself to go through old course literature in her mind. Semester 1: The Healthy Human. After that, she would go over everything she'd learned on the hostage course. And then, if it wasn't too painful, she would try to do some kind of physical training. Maybe. Isobel almost smiled. Not even being held captive could motivate her to exercise.

The door opened without warning.

She was forced to turn her head away and close her eyes. The light was too painful. The man who opened the door yelled, but she had trouble understanding his dialect. He came forward, pulled her hair until her eyes watered.

Phrases and pieces of the course danced through her mind. *If your treatment starts to get worse, it's a bad sign; they've decided to get rid of you.* But they had hit her the whole time, threatened and starved her. How could she tell if it had gotten worse?

Try to get them to see you as a person. Hysteria threatened to well up inside her. It was hard to try to be seen as a person when someone tied something over your eyes and another pressed something cold and metal against your temple and yelled something that sounded like "Bitch, you're going to die now."

Chapter 62

Alexander and the sniper, who had arrived with the rest of Tom's team, left the dark green Land Rover at the prearranged spot in the desert. The sniper called himself Kill Bill. He was twenty-two at most, with white-blond hair. Kill Bill didn't say much, but Tom had told Alexander he was one of the top ten shots in the world, so nothing else mattered.

After they left the car, they crept, under the cover of darkness, the last five hundred or so meters to the hillocks from which they would watch the village.

If they spotted Isobel, Tom and the rest of the team would attack within forty-eight hours. That was the minimum amount of time they needed to prepare and coordinate the attack.

Alexander and Kill Bill lay down behind the hill. They pulled the camouflage tent over themselves, took out powerful night-vision binoculars, located the village, and began their wait. As the frostbitten night turned into orange-tinged dawn, Alexander reported the little he had seen to Tom over the radio.

When the sun came up, movement began down in the village. The dogs came to life, smoke started to rise from one of the huts, and people came out. Alexander counted. Again and again. Women. Children. Young men. Old people.

Tom and his team were about thirteen miles away. All the information was relayed to them, and Alexander assumed they were building models in the sand and going through various scenarios as they waited. In that sense, he thought, it was like poker. The more you knew about your opponents, the better.

"But we can't attack a village unless we know for certain she's being held there," Tom said grimly.

Alexander had to agree. Reluctantly.

"How is Marius?"

"The kid? He's no trouble."

Alexander wanted to ask more, but Tom disappeared, so he took the cigarette Kill Bill held out to him instead, lit it, and inhaled the smoke.

The day passed, the sun bore down, and the insects crept over them. They drank warm water, which tasted like chemicals but which rinsed the sand from their teeth at least.

Alexander listened to the conversations going on in his headphones. They were conducted in brief, strongly accented commando English with the occasional French phrase.

Two village soldiers, dressed in khaki and carrying automatic weapons, suddenly appeared in his sights. They went toward the hut farthest away from Alexander's vantage point. He followed them with his binoculars. They opened the door and disappeared into the low mud building. He waited. This was the first time there had been any activity there. The door opened again and the two men came back out. They were carrying or dragging something between them.

"Is it her?" asked Kill Bill. He was looking through his gun sights. Alexander wanted to tell him to put down his weapon, to avoid hitting whoever it might be, but right then he saw her. Red hair. A long kaftan, like the rest of the villagers, indescribably dirty. She hung between them, her feet trailing in the dirt.

"It's her," he confirmed. "Is she alive?" Just then, he saw her cough, get to her feet. One of the men shook her, and then all three disappeared into another hut. Hardly able to hold his voice steady, Alexander reported it over the radio.

"Woman sighted. Likely being kept in the northernmost hut."

Ten minutes later, the men came out again with Isobel between them. They opened the door to the farthest hut, went in, and then came back out without her.

For the rest of the day, Alexander stared at the building in which Isobel was being kept. No one came or went. Did she have food? Water? He had known it would be tough, but this wasn't tough—it was unbearable. Was she dying in there right now?

"You should get a couple hours' sleep," the sniper said, unaffected by the situation.

Alexander nodded.

"Everything good?" He heard Tom's voice over the radio.

"No news," he answered, trying to keep his frustration from his voice. He had to trust Tom, knew they had only one chance and that everything had to go right when they took it. But this waiting was the worst thing he had ever experienced.

"We need another day out here," Tom said. "You've gotta keep it together. Eat. Sleep. When we get going, you and Kill Bill are our eyes up there. We'll go in under darkness. Bill will give us covering fire if we need it. You have to guide us. I need to know you can handle it."

"I can handle it."

He had done it time and time again during his military service. Kept watch for days under the most extreme conditions. Back then it had been an adventure, a chance to feel like he was really good at something. Now it was suddenly life and death.

When Alexander woke, it was dark. The sniper waited until Alexander had his binoculars ready, then pulled his hood over his head and immediately fell asleep.

"We'll go in when it's darkest." Tom's voice on the radio was completely calm, as though he was reading the back of a bottle of dishwashing liquid. "With night vision. Night combat, particularly in inhabited areas, is tricky as hell; we have to assume there'll be civilian injuries. It's not going to be like in a film, no dangling from helicopters, no exploding doors. We go in, open some serious fire, get her out. If it all goes to plan, she's out in under a minute. Then she's into the helicopter and away."

Tom's voice sounded completely clear. Did he ever sleep?

"Does it normally go as planned?"

The radio hissed.

"Never. There's no manual for hostage rescues. But we have backup plans. Two cars waiting. A stretcher ready. Everyone knows what they have to do. This is what we've been training for."

"How will you get into the hut?"

"You haven't seen anything that suggests it's mined, so we'll go in by the door. But we need to know how much she weighs."

Alexander thought about her curvy body. Isobel was tall, for a woman, but she had looked so thin. "One hundred sixty-five, maybe one hundred sixty pounds. Why?"

"We'll prepare an injection. We might have to give her something for the pain, and we don't want to kill her with too much morphine. Tomorrow night's the night. In less than twenty hours."

The radio fell silent. Alexander fumbled for his cell phone. Glanced at the timer, which counted how long she had been gone. It was rushing toward two hundred hours.

Chapter 63

Under cover of the desert night, the six soldiers moved forward. Alexander followed them with his binoculars. Each man was wearing night vision goggles and protective vests, and they were heavily armed with automatic weapons and pistols in holsters at their hips. They moved forward slowly because their goggles made the world green, robbed them of their sense of depth, and forced them to err on the side of caution. Alexander knew they were completely silent, every loose bit of metal taped down. These men were experts at tracking, rescuing, and killing.

"*T minus ten,*" he heard over the radio. Ten more minutes.

The helicopter should be ready at the base, its engine ticking over, ready to lift off. They had already moved the cars, hidden a couple hundred yards from the village.

Alexander and his sniper directed the advancing soldiers quietly over the radio. From their raised position on the hill, they gave their orders: stop, wait, continue.

When the force was one hundred meters from the village, Alexander saw one of the men put down a stretcher. If Isobel was injured, they would carry her out on that.

"*T minus five.*"

He knew the plan inside out, minute by minute. Tom would be cranking the helicopter up now, before lifting off and attacking at the exact same moment the men on the ground opened fire. Tom would fly in from one side while his sniper provided supporting fire.

The men in the attacking force all had fluorescent fabric on their helmets, so those with night vision goggles could see them and avoid shooting them. That was the plan, anyway. The radio crackled.

Seconds now.

And then: "*Showtime.*"

Isobel woke to a sound she didn't recognize. It was like a faint pounding, but she couldn't place it. A storm?

She sat up on the floor. It was so dark she couldn't see her own hand in front of her. She leaned against the wall and wrapped her arms around her knees. Her heart raced. Was it just her imagination?

No. It was getting closer. *Dunk, dunk, dunk.*

And then the world around her exploded. The roar of an engine, shots and shouts, and then the door of her hut flew open and huge men started to yell in English. Behind them she could hear chaos and death.

She quickly raised her hands, showed her palms. She didn't want to be shot by mistake.

"*Identify yourself,*" a man shouted as he shone a flashlight into her face.

She couldn't see a thing. "Isobel Sørensen," she said with a hoarse voice; she had trouble shouting over the noise.

"Your mother's maiden name?"

She blinked, shouted, "Blanche. Blanche Pelletier," and knew that this was the man's way of checking she was who she was meant to be.

Two heavily armed men stepped forward, grabbed her, and pulled her to her feet.

Alexander had been so focused on the soldiers going into Isobel's hut that at first he hadn't noticed what was going on outside.

"My bird's hit." He suddenly heard Tom's voice in his headset. "Fuck."

Alexander peered through his binoculars at the helicopter, saw it lurch.

"Shit. Right in the ass." The helicopter lurched more powerfully. "I've lost control. We're going down."

Helpless, Alexander watched as the helicopter fell, saw its rotor blades hit the ground, the body crumple and then explode in a great column of smoke. Alexander stared; his eyes burned. The helicopter was a huge ball of flames. No one climbed from the wreckage.

He got up. Started to run.

The first thing Isobel saw when they pulled her from the hut was an enormous blazing fire. She had heard the crash. Something big had exploded. A light airplane, or maybe a helicopter.

"Medics," one of the men yelled.

"What's that?" she asked cautiously when a young man covered in weapons, equipment, and wearing a helmet with some kind of binoculars on his forehead came toward her with a needle. She still wasn't sure whether she had been rescued or kidnapped again.

"Painkiller."

"No!" she said, trying to sound as much like a doctor as she could. She didn't want anything to knock her out. "I'm not hurt. No need."

The soldier hesitated as if he had been looking forward to jabbing her. "We have to get out of here," the leader bellowed. She heard fragments of conversation; they were talking into some kind of communication equipment.

"Negative, no sign of them."

"Plan B."

"We've got to get her to the cars."

And then she heard a familiar voice.

"Isobel!"

She blinked violently. It couldn't be?

"Isobel!" He was closer now, no hallucination.

"Alexander!" she shouted back, tried to orientate herself in the darkness, amid the gunfire and chaos. The soldiers had started to drag her behind them, and then she felt a familiar rock-steady arm around her shoulders.

"Isobel!"

"You're insane. What are you doing here?"

"We need to get out of here," he shouted into her ear. "Can you walk a little farther? Are you hurt?"

She just stared. The air was full of smoke and flames, and his face was covered in dirt. She couldn't believe it was Alexander, in combat gear and with an automatic weapon in his arms, binoculars on his helmet, and heavy desert boots.

"What are you doing here?" she repeated as they half ran, half crouched as quickly as they could.

"Two hundred meters to the cars."

She nodded.

He held out his hand, took hers, and then they raced toward the jeeps. Alexander tore the door of one open, she flung herself in, and he leaped in after her. The car started, a reassuringly strong motor roared, and the vehicle took them away at high speed.

"Tom?" Alexander asked as he unscrewed the top of a green water bottle and held it out to her. She drank but forced herself to stop after a couple of gulps. Knew she wouldn't be able to keep it down otherwise.

One of the soldiers shook his head.

"He didn't make it? Are you sure?"

"Positive. He's dead," another of them shouted over the roar of the engine. "He was in the helicopter when it came down. We lost both him and the sniper."

"Shouldn't we get him? His body?"

But when Isobel followed Alexander's gaze back toward the village, she knew it was impossible, that it would be suicide to go back there. Besides, she had seen the fire. No one could have survived that.

"Now," a soldier yelled.

"Who was Tom?" Isobel asked as they rattled on at breakneck speed through the desert.

"He led the operation. David Hammar's friend. You met him, at the wedding."

"Oh, God," she said, her hand going to her mouth.

People had died to save her. Tom and another man in the helicopter. Maybe people in the village. There had been women and children there. Had any of them died? That wasn't an easy thing to bear. She fought against the wave of nausea that had started to well up.

"Lexington was a soldier," the driver said over his shoulder as the car lurched forward. "He knew the score. Our mission was to get you out. It was a success."

Isobel squeezed Alexander's hand, still couldn't believe it was true. So many people had worked together to get her out. And Alexander. Here, in Chad. She leaned against his shoulder, allowed herself to shake along with the car, thought that a little bit of pain medicine wouldn't have hurt, now that the adrenaline had started to leave her body. She coughed. Drank slowly again.

"How did you find me?" she asked after a while. The whole thing still felt surreal. Shock. She was probably in shock.

"Marius, he saw them take you. He found us in N'Djamena."

"What was he doing in N'Djamena? It's so dangerous." Had he walked all the way there from Massakory? It took grown men thirty hours to walk that far. Was he hurt? "Where is he now?"

"He's back at the base. You're not going to like this, but Tom tied him up in one of the cars. They'll let him go soon."

"If he helped you, it's going to be dangerous for him. He has no one to protect him. He'll die."

Alexander squeezed her shoulder, carefully.

"I know," he said heavily.

"Where are we going?" she asked when they came out onto a wider road and picked up speed. She wondered how Idris was, but even she could see that they couldn't go to the hospital right now. She would just be a burden.

"My brother chartered a private plane. They're taking us there. It's medically equipped, and it has its own staff. We'll get on board and get the hell out of here as quickly as possible."

She stared out the window. Made her decision. It was set in stone. "Marius has to come," she said, and fixed Alexander with her gaze. His face was dirty, and she could see days of stress forming taut lines. But he nodded.

"We'll go get him." He gave an order to the soldier driving the car.

They made a sharp U-turn and Isobel relaxed.

Leaned back against the seat. Closed her eyes for a few seconds. She would just have to hold it together awhile longer.

As the car braked in a cloud of desert sand, the sun had just started to rise, painting the dunes in vibrant red and orange tones. Isobel and Alexander hurried out. One of the soldiers followed them, muttering that they didn't have time for this shit. The other one remained in the car, the engine running. When they reached the parked jeep Alexander said with a frown, "He's not here."

"What do you mean?" Isobel asked, worry shooting through her when she saw that the car was empty. "Where is he?" she asked the soldier.

"He was in the car, tied up."

Alexander scratched his dusty stubble. "Well, now he's gone."

"Where can he be?" Isobel looked around but saw nothing but sand, dunes, and a rising sun. No footprints, no trace of a small boy.

"We have to go," the accompanying soldier said, impatience in his voice. "It's too dangerous to stay out here."

"We can't leave without him." Isobel's voice almost broke. She couldn't, just couldn't go home, not knowing he was safe.

Suddenly she heard the soldier rattle his weapon. "Don't move," he snarled and at the same time Isobel saw them. A man with a child at his side. Muhammed. The man whose child she hadn't managed to save. And Marius was beside him, looking small and tired and scared.

"What are you doing with the boy?" Isobel said as fear snaked up her spine. Why had Muhammed taken Marius? "Lay down your weapon," she snapped over her shoulder at the soldier, who ignored her completely and continued to aim straight at Muhammed.

"What are *you* doing with the boy?" Muhammed asked, his eyes intent. The tattoo moved beneath his clenched jaw. A wind made his clothes billow.

Marius looked at her, his eyes huge, his frame shaking. She just couldn't lose him now. She lifted her arms, showed her palms.

"I want to take him with me. Please don't hurt him."

"You left him in the car. Tied."

"I'm so sorry. That was wrong. But no one will harm him, I promise."

Muhammed's grip on Marius's shoulder didn't loosen. God, please, please, don't let Marius get hurt. Please.

"Ma'am. I can take him down."

"Do not shoot, do you hear me? Alex?"

"Nobody shoots," he said, his words those of a commander.

"What are you planning to do with him?" asked Muhammed, drawing Marius closer.

"I want to give him a future."

He gave her an angry look. "Like you did with my son?"

"No. A better future. In my country, where children don't die like that. Please."

Their eyes locked over the Chadian desert. A proud, angry, grieving father and a desperate healer. And then the miracle happened. Muhammed slowly released Marius and the anger seemed to leave him. "Go with her," he said roughly, looking at Isobel as he carefully nudged Marius toward her. "Take care of him."

"I will. Thank you, Muhammed," and then she had Marius in her arms, hugging him tightly, feeling him cling to her. "Thank you," she repeated, tears in her eyes.

"Good-bye, *Docteur*. Go with God."

An hour later, they climbed on board the waiting private plane. Marius held Isobel's hand, tight. Alexander disappeared to talk to the pilot as they taxied out.

They had removed some of the seats and replaced them with a stretcher, and instead of newspapers, soft drinks, and trolleys of duty-free goods, Isobel saw first aid items and painkillers. A nurse offered to help her, but she tended to her injuries herself, and then saw to Marius. He was undernourished and dirty, but his lungs and heart sounded good. She pulled a much-too-big sweater over his head and wrapped a blanket around him. After that, she changed clothes herself—pants, a T-shirt, and a warm sweater—and then they were given soup to eat, served by the silent, efficient staff. She laid Marius down on a row of seats, put a blanket over him, tucked him in, awkwardly and with inexperienced hands, but with an ever-increasing protective instinct.

His eyes drifted shut and she said, "Sleep now. I'm not going anywhere." She nodded to the nurse, who sat down next to the boy to watch over him.

Alexander came back. He had taken off his helmet and protective clothing, and he handed her a bottle. "Drink. It's some kind of nourishment." He waited as she tasted it.

"Isobel?" he said after a moment.

"Yes?" She wiped her mouth.

"I love you, in case you haven't already figured that out."

She gazed up at his dusty face. His blond hair was covered with sand and dirt, making his blue eyes more piercing than ever. No desolation in them, just heat and determination. And so much love. Her heart swelled; it was almost too intense. She simply answered, "I love you too. So much."

His eyes glistened and his throat worked before he said, with a hoarse voice, "I'm glad. And you aren't just saying that because I saved your life, are you?"

She smiled. "I *am* grateful that you saved my life. But I already loved you before that. A lot."

He took her hand and kissed her palm, sending warm rivulets of pleasure through her entire system.

"What do we do with Marius?" She glanced at the sleeping boy, the problems already starting to mount up in her mind. He had no papers, no passport. Could a child seek asylum? Had she done the right thing, tearing him away from everything he knew?

"It'll be okay. We'll refuel in Switzerland, land in Sweden, and then we'll work out all the paperwork when we're back home. I promise, Isobel, that whatever happens, I'll fix it."

He made it sound so easy. He bent down toward her and gave her a dusty, stubbly, heartfelt kiss, and she decided that, for once, she would believe that when someone promised something, they would keep their promise. She pulled his head toward her.

He made a pained sound.

"Shit."

"What?"

"I suppose I should've said something, but I just wanted to get you out of there as fast as I could."

"What happened?"

"We were supposed to get a happy ending—"

He held up a hand and studied it grimly. It was covered in blood. A stain was spreading quickly over his stomach, up toward his chest. His face grew pale. "It must've started bleeding when I took the flak jacket off."

"Are you hurt?" She leaped up from her chair. "Why didn't you say anything?"

"Some dumb macho thing, I guess. Pretty stupid. Sorry," he repeated weakly. And then he collapsed.

Chapter 64

Alexander tried to focus his eyes. Isobel's worried face hovered above him. She was covered in Band-Aids and bruises, but she was alive. He had saved her. That should even up the score despite all his sins. His throat burned, but he had to say it before it was too late. He could hear a roaring noise around him. He had a vague feeling he should be able to identify the sound. Thunder?

"I love you," he croaked. It hurt when he talked. But it hurt when he didn't, too, so he continued. "You know that, right?" Or had he already said it? Everything was so fuzzy in his head.

It was of great importance that Isobel knew. That he loved her. That she was the best thing to ever happen to him.

"Yes, Alexander," she said, her voice sounding oddly amused.

A blessed, cool hand touched his forehead. He wanted to tell her that her hands were the finest, smoothest hands there had ever been. He blinked slowly. Her face floated round, round, round.

"I love you," he mumbled. "I love you."

"You've said that twenty times now. If you don't calm down, I'll have to stop the morphine. And then it's really going to hurt."

"Ah, is that why I feel so good? I thought it was love, but it's morphine." He grinned. "I love morphine."

Isobel's mouth twitched, and Alexander already knew he would do anything in the world for that smile.

"I think I got a little shot up," he said. "Maybe someone should take a peek. If it's not too much trouble."

"You had a serious bullet wound," she said. "I took out the bullet and sewed you back up." She touched his forehead again. He had to find a way to get her to keep doing that, it felt so good.

"I was bleeding like a pig," he mumbled.

"Yes." She nodded.

Her face floated away.

"Did you fix me up?"

Her face came back. A lamp came on behind her and made her look like an angel. His angel.

"Yes," she answered. "Lie still, I need to give you an injection."

He lay still, obedient. Something struck him. "If you sewed me up, I must've been pretty bad back there."

"Yes, Alex, you were."

The lamp disappeared and everything started to shake. "Where are we?"

"The plane's going to land at Arlanda Airport soon. We're home."

"Isobel? Answer me honestly now."

She nodded.

"Will I make it?"

Her eyes glistened. "Yes."

"And you're okay?"

"Yes. Just grazes."

"Nothing else?"

"No, I promise."

"Can I tell you something? That I never told anyone?"

"Whatever could that be?" There was a smile in her voice.

"I love you."

She leaned forward, put her soft lips against his, and whispered, "Yes, I know. And I love you."

"So, what do you say? Should we live happily ever after, then?"

"Yeah, it feels like it's about time."

Alexander closed his eyes. Thought that he should have told her he loved her. But satisfied himself with having plenty of time to do it in the future. The rest of his life.

Chapter 65

"How are you?" Natalia asked as she stepped into the hallway and gave Alexander a hug. He held his dear, elegant, big sister tight for a moment longer. She had called him every day the past six weeks, but she looked happy now that the danger had passed.

"Come in. No pain, but I have an impressive scar. My girlfriend gave it to me. Want to see?"

"No, thanks. Keep your clothes on, please. My interest in scar tissue is pretty much zero. We'll just have to make sure to avoid any more gunshot wounds in the future—you're getting unbearable. Did Mom arrive already? She said she'd be here early."

"She's in there. She picked Eugene up from the station. Now she's helping with the food."

"She is? Helping?"

"Do you think maybe she switched places with an alien?"

"Well, my little brother went to Africa to save his girlfriend from desert rebels, so I pretty much believe anything."

Natalia moved farther into the apartment, toward the murmur in the living room, and David, who had come with her, stepped into the hallway and shook Alexander's hand.

"I'm glad you're well too, and I don't want to see your scar either," he said. He had Molly in his arms. She studied Alexander, her pacifier bobbing up and down in her mouth.

Alexander stroked his niece on the cheek and said, "Thanks. Listen, I know you don't want to talk about it, but I want you to know I'm so sorry Tom can't be here with us."

"Thanks." A shadow passed over David's face. Telling his brother-in-law that Tom had died in the helicopter crash had been one of the hardest things Alexander had ever had to do. He knew Tom's death had really thrown David; the two men had known one another for a long time. They were all shaken by the loss.

Isobel, who'd held it together during the flight, had a tough time after she got back home, when the trauma of the kidnapping caught up with her. Natalia, Peter, and David had taken care of everything those first few days. Filled out papers, made calls, and overcome bureaucratic obstacles. Made sure Isobel met a crisis team. Made sure Alexander was treated rapidly and got back on his feet. And that Marius felt safe. But it was Isobel who had suffered the longest and the most deeply. She still had nightmares and episodes of anxiety, depression, and flashbacks, but they were gradually shorter and she was headed in the right direction. Or, as Leila said, it took more than kidnapping, mercenaries, and explosions to break Dr. Sørensen.

"Tom was a warrior. He knew what he was getting into. It's awful, but I can't really talk about it yet. Sorry."

David's eyes grew shiny. He gave Alexander a pat on the shoulder and followed his wife into the apartment. Alexander watched him put an arm around Natalia's shoulder and press his lips against her dark hair. Natalia's gold bracelet glistened, and she put an arm around his waist, strong and supportive.

Alexander heard another knock at the door and turned to open it again.

"Hi, Gina," he greeted his next guest. "Welcome to my place."

"Thanks," she said. She seemed composed, but he suspected she was nervous.

Peter was behind her, helping her take off her jacket and handing it to Alexander. Alexander hung it up and then let his gaze follow Gina, who was already talking to Natalia farther down the hall. "So, you two are together now?"

"Yeah."

"She's too young for you."

"I know," Peter agreed. "Too young. Too good. Too everything. She's starting her third semester soon. If I'm lucky, she won't get tired of me."

"I hope you're lucky, then," Alexander said honestly.

"Thanks, Alex. Gina is really looking forward to seeing your Isobel. She talked about it the whole way here, how much she admires her. She's clearly something special."

"Yeah, Isobel is special. One of the really good ones. You're not the only one with a woman you don't deserve."

They eyed each other. Peter looked younger somehow, not weighed down as he had been all these years. Not so rigid.

And then Peter pulled him into a hug, and they embraced for what might have been the first time ever. A tight hug that represented reconciliation, goodwill, and a future.

Alexander cleared his throat. Peter quickly wiped his eyes.

"Right," said Peter.

"There are drinks and food back there," said Alexander. "Just help yourself." He wanted to add something else, something about how both he and Natalia would be there for Peter if he needed them, something about how Peter had never looked so happy during all the years he was married to Louise, but the moment came and went too quickly.

Peter nodded and went to join the others. Since all the guests had arrived now, Alexander followed after him. He looked around.

Everyone was here. Or everyone who meant anything on a day like this, anyway. Mom and Eugene. Blanche. Leila. Even Romeo, who had flown in from New York with his new boyfriend and refused to let Alexander serve anything but the food from his restaurant. Åsa and Michel, tanned and in love after their honeymoon. And then the children, of course. Marius and Molly. Truly, everyone who meant anything in his and Isobel's shared life. Which, today, they would make public by officially moving in together.

He caught sight of Marius, standing with his tiny hand in Ebba's. Alexander's mother patted Marius's hand as she smiled warmly at Peter and then gave Gina a quick hug that at least *looked* heartfelt.

The time of miracles was clearly here to stay.

Alexander went over to the little group. He exchanged a glance with Peter and then put a protective arm around Marius's shoulders. The boy was still much too thin, but according to the pediatrician, he was on his way to catching up. He would start school in the fall, and he could already speak some Swedish.

"Thanks, Mom," Alexander said quietly. "Thanks for everything."

"You don't have anything to thank me for. I know you don't believe it, but I really do want to help."

Ebba looked over to Gina and Peter, who stood admiring Molly. "It's all so new, but I'm doing the best I can," she continued. "You're my children—all I want is for you to be happy."

"Even if it means marrying the enemy, adopting African children, and getting together with the help?"

"There's no need to be vulgar, Alexander. But yes. Even if you dismantle everything I thought I stood for." She gave him a meaningful look. "*Even* if Natalia meets her biological father."

"You knew that?" he asked, astounded.

"I just want you to be happy. That's all I ever wanted."

"It hasn't always been obvious."

"No, I know. I hope you can forgive me sometime."

It was the first time she had even come close to admitting she had done anything wrong. Maybe Natalia was right after all: Their mother had changed.

"I probably wasn't a very good mother. My goal is to be a better grandmother."

He put a hand on her arm and squeezed it gently. "Thanks, Mom. That means a lot."

Ebba's eyes shone, and she turned away.

Alexander met Natalia's eyes over his mother's head. She looked moved. Good Lord, this was already turning into a sobfest.

Isobel washed her hands and studied her face in the bathroom mirror. No trace of any bruises. She looked normal. And she had finally started to feel like normal too.

The first few weeks had been terrible. Physically, she had no visible wounds—in contrast to Alexander, who was more than happy to show off his pair of impressive scars. And mentally she was recovering, even if it had been really tough for a while. They had hit her, but nothing else. Threatened, abused, and frightened her, but they hadn't raped her, and she was glad she had survived. And she was feeling better. It was just as everyone said: If you were surrounded by people you loved, you could survive most things. Yes, things had definitely turned around.

She closed the door behind her and smiled at the murmur of the guests.

She and Alexander hadn't left each other's side these past few weeks, but today was their official moving-in day. On the way to the main room, she passed Marius's bedroom, which looked like it could belong to any other seven-year-old: full of colorful fabrics, LEGO bricks, and children's bookcases. She walked past her and Alexander's room, smiled at the secrets the seemingly normal bedroom hid, and pulled the door shut slightly; it felt too private to have it open, even if nothing was visible.

They had taken it easy the past few weeks, reveling in their new-found closeness, but they had agreed on a mix of vanilla and kink in the future. She was still slightly surprised by how uncomplicated Alexander was when it came to all that. Also she was deeply thankful that Marius was a child who slept soundly. And that they had plenty of people nearby to babysit. Natalia, Peter, and both their mothers had offered.

She snuck into the kitchen.

"How's it going?" she asked Romeo, who was busy checking on his staff and the preparations.

"*Ciao, bella,*" he greeted her, slapping at his boyfriend's hand just as he was about to reach for a croustade.

Isobel leaned against one of the kitchen counters and took a couple of deep breaths.

"You alright?"

"I just need to gather my thoughts for a second before I go out."

"Nervous?"

"A little." She still had trouble with lots of people, panicked easily, felt trapped.

Leila came out. She studied the handsome Romeo with great interest before she turned to Isobel.

"There you are. Can we smoke in here?"

Romeo blurted a loud string of Italian profanities, and Leila rolled her eyes.

"Okay, okay, okay." She sighed and put the cigarettes back.

"Is everyone here?"

"Alexander is serving drinks and some kind of snack he claims he made himself. People are talking. It's fine. Everyone seems nice. For now."

"Let's see how long it is before the mothers clash," Isobel said.

"Yes, it's fascinating, the way they manage to hiss insults between compliments. They're incredibly similar, of course, though they don't realize it. And Eugene, that sweetheart, he's taken it on himself to mediate between them. Though he looks pretty drunk already, so there'll probably be blood spilled fairly soon. How are things with you and Blanche?"

Isobel pulled a face. She grabbed a piece of gherkin when Romeo looked away. "If this were a film, I would've told her to take a hike, but you can't do that in real life."

"No," Leila agreed. "Most people just tolerate their parents, no matter how awful they are. That's what being an adult is all about. But you don't *have* to do anything."

"No, I suppose not." Isobel pulled at her earring. Her mother had given Isobel her grandmother's diamonds and a little painting as moving-in gifts. That was the closest Blanche would ever come to an apology, but it was enough. "Did you speak to Idris?"

"He's doing better, working flat out. He says hello, and hopes you and Marius have time to Skype soon."

Things had ended so well, she could hardly believe it. Idris had gotten better and an MSF doctor had arrived at the hospital only a few days after her kidnapping.

"I'm so relieved." Isobel chewed the gherkin. She paused. "Leila, I have to tell you something. Alexander already knows. I've accepted a job at Karolinska Institutet. A research post, in crisis medicine. I've decided to stop working for Medpax. To stop working in the field altogether, actually."

Leila didn't look the least bit surprised. "You'll do more for the world that way, if I know you. I was waiting for this. Sven has offered to go to Chad."

"Really? What about his wife?"

Leila smiled. "She left him for a TV gladiator."

"How sad for him."

"Mmm. Very."

Isobel bit her lip to stop herself from smiling. "I still feel a bit like a quitter."

"But you always do."

"Can't you even fake empathy? I was a hostage for nine days."

"You aren't a quitter. Our feelings aren't always the truth. Should I embroider that for you as a wedding gift?"

"Am I getting married?"

"You aren't going to get engaged?"

"Not as far as I know." Though she had her suspicions that Alexander had something planned for this evening.

He joined them in the kitchen, and once more it was as though the sun had suddenly decided to shine in through the windows. He had cut his hair short. Stopped wearing his ridiculously expensive suits. He had actually matured. Strangely enough, she loved him more with each day; she wouldn't have thought it was possible to feel so much love for another person. She fought back stupid tears, didn't want to ruin her surprisingly perfect makeup. If Alexander planned to propose, she wanted to look good.

"Could you give us a moment, Leila?" he asked.

"Rather not," she muttered, but she left.

Alexander pulled Isobel into his arms. "Marius is talking to my mom."

"How's it going?"

"Would you believe me if I said well?"

"She's been so nice to me."

"No one is more shocked than me. Did you tell Leila your plans?"

"Yeah, she took it really well."

"So. Now it's too late to back out. Now we live together."

"I don't want to back out."

"I'm so afraid I don't deserve you."

"Pah, no you aren't."

Alexander took her hand and they went back to join the others. He gave her a glass, kept an eye on her, didn't leave her side.

Of course Alex deserved her, Isobel thought as she listened to him ask Gina about her studies. More than he could imagine. This man, who served vegetarian food for her sake, who invited his family and friends to prove he was serious about their relationship. Who fought desert rebels and brought Marius home without a moment's hesitation.

They sat down and she looked around. People were talking and laughing. Even her mother looked happy, sitting between Eugene and Peter.

Alexander stood up and clinked his glass.

"I want to thank you all for coming today, to celebrate with Isobel, Marius, and me."

He fell silent and his eyes glistened before he continued.

"Isobel. You're a fantastic doctor. A spokeswoman for those lacking a voice. An inspiration and an example. You're beautiful, funny, and smart, and the most incredible person I ever met. I'm so happy you and Marius want to live with me."

He fell silent once more. Put his hand into his pocket and pulled out a heart-shaped box in black velvet. The women in the room took a collective breath. Marius bounced in his seat, clapping his hands.

Alexander opened the box and went down onto one knee.

Isobel could hardly breathe. It was unbelievably clichéd, she knew that, hadn't even realized people did this in real life, not in Sweden at least. But apparently there was a romantic side of her that loved this grand gesture. Because how else could she explain the tight feeling in her throat?

Her eyes didn't move from Alexander. The room was dead silent.

"Will you be my wife?"

She bit her lip, tried to control herself, but gave up with a rather ignominious sob. Her makeup would be ruined now. She squeezed his hand tightly.

"I'd love to."

He breathed out. "Thank God for that," he said, with such a relieved voice that shouts of joy rang out.

The guests laughed, applauded, and began to hug one another. Champagne corks popped, glasses were filled, and then the women crowded around Isobel to admire the ring. Alexander was drawn into hugs and congratulations, and Isobel caught a glimpse of him in the middle of it all. He pinned her gaze with his; pure happiness on his face, a wide grin tugging at his sensuous mouth. She saw her own joy reflect in his eyes, marveled at the warmth of his kindness.

I love you, she mouthed, and he came to her, reached for her through the laughing guests, drew her to him, and caught her lips in a fierce, demanding, uncompromising kiss that made the breath go out of her.

"I love you," he said while the cheers in the room and the heat in those perfectly blue eyes made her cheeks flush. It was an amazing thing, this feeling that swept her. Thrilling. Promising.

"I thought you didn't believe in love," she teased.

He answered by giving her a wicked grin and kissing her again, his lips softly moving against hers. "You have turned me, Dr. Sørensen," he murmured with a gleam in his eye. "To love. And other things."

Epilogue

Tom Lexington opened his eyes.

He was in pain, which meant he was still alive.

His mouth was so dry he couldn't swallow. If he had the choice, dying of thirst wouldn't be his first preference.

He would rather not die at all, actually. Even if there had been days lately when his certainty about that had started to falter.

He heard voices outside the door before it suddenly flew open, and he was hauled up onto his feet. Roughly. He couldn't hold back a groan of pain. There wasn't a single part of him that didn't hurt.

They dragged him out into the sun and the heat.

People rarely thought of it.

That there were some alternatives worse than death.

They pushed him down onto his knees, and Tom had a grim feeling he would soon get to experience at least a few of them.

Connect with Us

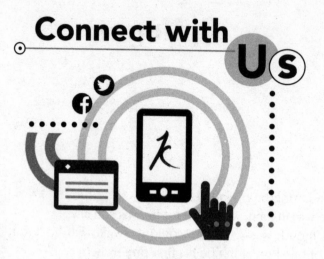

Visit us online at
KensingtonBooks.com
to read more from your favorite authors, see books
by series, view reading group guides, and more.

Join us on social media

for sneak peeks, chances to win books and prize packs,
and to share your thoughts with other readers.

facebook.com/kensingtonpublishing
twitter.com/kensingtonbooks

Tell us what you think!

To share your thoughts, submit a review,
or sign up for our eNewsletters, please visit:
KensingtonBooks.com/TellUs.